DIRTY PROMISES

BOOK 2 - DIRTY TEXAS SERIES

JA LOW

Copyright © 2016 by JA Low

Updated © 2023

All rights reserved. No part of this eBook/paperback may be reproduced or transmitted in any form, including electronic or mechanical, without written permission from the publisher, except in the case of brief quotations embodied in critical articles or reviews.

This is a work of fiction. Names, characters, businesses, places, events, and incidents are either the products of the author's imagination or used in a fictitious manner. Any resemblance to actual persons, living or dead, or actual events is purely coincidental. JA low is in no way affiliated with any brands, songs, musicians, or artists mentioned in this book.

This eBook/paperback is licensed for your personal enjoyment only. This eBook/paperback may not be re-sold or given away to other people. If you would like to share this eBook/paperback with another person, please purchase an additional copy for each person you share it with. If you are reading this eBook/paperback and did not purchase it, or it was not purchased for your use only, then you should return it to the seller and purchase your own copy.

Thank you for respecting the author's work.

Cover Design by Simply Defined Art

Model: Douglas

Photographer: Wander Bookclub Photography

Editor by Swish Design & Editing

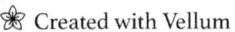 Created with Vellum

VANESSA
PROLOGUE

The clock strikes midnight, and a new year begins. All of Sienna and Evan's wedding guests are watching the spectacular fireworks display over the valley and out toward the ocean. The surrounding beaches are having their own colorful celebrations lighting up the entire coastline. Christian's strong arms wrap around me, and I snuggle into his embrace.

"Vanessa, I love you," he whispers into my ear, his prickly chin resting on my shoulder.

"I love you, too." He pulls his arms tighter around me. It's not uncommon for us, as best friends, to share this sentiment with each other. Christian lets out a heavy sigh, and his breath tickles my skin. Slowly his large hands turn me in his arms so that we're face to face. Golden, whiskey-colored eyes stare into mine. There's an intensity shining from them, which is most unusual, and it's a little unnerving. Typically, his handsome face has a bright smile across it, except for now.

"No, V... I love you." Yeah, I heard him the first time. Rough hands move from my waist to my face, his calloused thumb gently rubs the apple of my cheek. "Not as the best-friends-forever kind of love, more like..." He pauses, mulling over his next words. I watch as a frown falls across his brow. "I love you as in you-are-the-one kind of way."

I let out a nervous laugh thinking he's joking, but he's standing there so still, staring at me. Maybe he's drunk. The bar has been open and free-flowing all night, and he has been enjoying it. Perhaps he's caught up in the night's atmosphere, and that's given him an overwhelming sense of love for me when in reality, he's just horny. I'm sure it's just a bad case of lust or maybe heartburn. "Ness?"

"What?" Pretending I didn't hear what he just said, I'm hoping to forget his little confession.

"You don't have anything to say?" He sounds annoyed with me.

Shaking my head, nope, there's nothing for me to say because I'm trying hard to forget the bombshell my best friend just dropped on me. I'm dreaming, right? I have to be because this can't be happening to me right now. I reach out and pinch Christian. "Ouch," he groans, rubbing his arm.

Shit, I'm not. We both agreed to have fun with each other. He's my best friend for God's sake, my anchor, the one and only man I can depend on. Christian's never developed feelings for a woman before. Why now? Why me? He's the world's biggest player, and he has actual trophies from various award shows calling him *'World's Biggest Player'* proudly displayed in his bar at home.

We live together, we work together, and we party together. We've been in each other's lives twenty-four hours a day for the past five years. I've seen it all, even the groupies doing their walk of shame out of our home. The same way he's seen my random hook-ups traipse the same path. I share everything with him, and he knows all my deepest and darkest secrets. But love, it complicates things. It complicates what's right between us.

"Chris... no!" Pulling myself from his arms. I need some distance to think clearly. My body reacts when it's around him. I need my head clear to deal with all this. I didn't know us hooking up again would lead to a declaration of love. Shit, how naive am I? I thought I'd stumbled upon nirvana when Christian agreed to pursue a friends-with-benefits relationship with me. I thought being older and wiser, we could handle such a relationship—that sex was just sex.

It's not like we've even been exclusive with each other since we agreed to this arrangement. Christian loves going to The Paradise Club, an exclusive celebrity-only sex club, and I don't mind sampling the delights on a night out. But love, as in forever and ever? My heart starts to race, my chest starts tightening up, and I think I'm having a heart attack. I'm too young to have heart palpitations. Is he trying to kill me? Is that his plan to off me by declaring his love for me?

"V, look at me," Christian commands.

I can't. I just can't because I'm scared at what I might see in Christian's eyes. I stare at my feet instead. Wow, my toes look super cute. I like the color Sienna chose for them.

"Ness, stop freaking out and look at me." He knows me so well, and this time he sounds more authoritative with his command. My eyes slowly lift from my pedicure to where his whiskey-colored ones are staring back at me. He takes my hand in his, his thumb rubbing over my palm, soothing me. "No one can compare to you, Ness."

My traitorous heart just skipped a beat at his words. I shake my head at him, I don't want to hear it. I can't listen to it because once those words are out, they are out. You can't stuff them back into Pandora's box. Once that bitch is open, nothing can close it again.

"I tried, I tried so hard to get over you, but you're so far under my skin." I can see the emotion written all over his gorgeous face, and any woman would kill to have Christian Taylor utter these words to them. Honestly, deep down inside of me, hidden under a million layers of crap, there's that girl bouncing up and down with joy, but—

"But... we live together." Such a pathetic excuse, even hearing those words come out of my mouth makes me cringe.

"And yet, that doesn't stop you from crawling into my bed most nights." He arches his brow at me.

I shake my head again. "Don't," I whisper.

"Doesn't stop you from straddling my dick on the couch during a movie or..." I cover his mouth with my hand, muffling the rest of that answer.

"I never hear you say no," I hiss at him, dropping my hand from his lips.

"Why the hell would I, Ness? You're fucking hot, and I love you." His hand lightly runs down my arm, sending shivers across my clammy skin.

I hate how my body reacts to his touch.

I hate how my body yearns for him.

I hate that I want him so much.

"But... you're my best friend." God, why do I sound like a whiney bitch?

"Don't you think that's a great foundation to start a relationship?" Those whiskey-colored eyes challenge me to disagree.

Shaking my head, I reply, "Chris, you weren't supposed to fall for me."

"How could I not, Ness? You're beautiful, sexy, you look after me, and that accent of yours does things to my dick. I trust you, and there aren't many people I trust. You also swear like a biker, drink like a sailor, and fuck like a pro."

Pushing hard on his chest, he takes a step back from me, his eyes searching mine looking confused by my reaction. "Wow, what a glowing reference." Anger boils to the surface, and I don't know why I'm pissed off. I shouldn't be. A hot, tatted-up rock star declares his love for me, and I'm pissing all over it.

"Why the hell would you want to be with someone like that?" I can't make this verbal diarrhea stop. "I don't sound like a woman you want to bring home to your family."

Christian's eyes narrow. "My family loves you, Ness, and you know it." It's the truth. I love Christian's mom. We always hang out together when she's in town, but that's not the point.

"It would ruin everything we have worked so hard to build, and you can't go and change the goalposts now," I mumble, wrapping my arms around myself.

"What?" Christian raises his voice at me. "Haven't you liked being in my bed all these months?" He tilts his head to the side, daring me to deny it.

"Fucking you is different from being with you." Shit. I cover my mouth with my hands, surprised I said it. I didn't mean it. I watch as my words make him flinch. Moments pass as we stare at each other in silence.

"Okay, I get it. I'm good enough to fuck but not good enough to date. I'll only ever be one of your many fuck toys you play with." He sounds furious, and when he puts it like that, it sounds kind of horrible. "I never thought you were like that, Ness. I never thought you saw me like that."

He crosses his muscular arms over his chest, the same ones I've spent night after night curled up against. Now I feel like a bitch because he means more to me than just being my fuck buddy. But that's the thing, I had Christian in a nice little box, and now he's decided to jump out of it and turn it into a giant heart-shaped box instead.

"Christian, you're more than that to me, and you know it," I say on a whisper, trying desperately to say the right words but not finding them.

"Are you sure about that, Ness?" The sarcastic tone filters through the night air.

"I thought it was always going to be you and me, having fun, messing around. I never thought there'd ever be… more." I'm lying here, of course, I thought about it. Every man I date I compare to him, but I'd never tell anyone that. That secret is locked away in the vault, next door to my heart.

"You thought for the rest of our lives we'd just fool around?" The silence stretches out between us as his question hangs in the air.

"I'm sorry that I finally had the guts to say how I feel, Ness, about what you and I have between us. It's once-in-a-lifetime stuff. We're meant to be together, and you know it." His arms unfold from his chest as he pulls me to him. "I want happily ever after with you, and I'm sorry if that makes you feel uncomfortable. These feelings I have for you scare the absolute shit out of me, but I'm willing to give this a try."

He smiles that goddamn smile that melts my stone-cold heart. "Someone needed to be honest with their feelings here. Five years we've been in and out of each other's beds, and yet we haven't become sick of each other. That must mean something."

Pulling myself out of his arms, I put distance between us. "I'm sorry, Chris, but I can't. I can't love you like that. I don't think I can love anyone like that."

"Nothing? You feel nothing for me?" he asks, thumping his chest. Tears surprise me as one falls down my cheek.

"I can't give you what you want, Christian. I'm sorry."

"You're a fucking liar, Ness. Don't forget, I know you. I can tell when you're lying to me, lying to my face. Have you forgotten what it feels like between us?"

Grabbing my face, pulling me closer to him, he presses soft and desperate kisses against my lips, showing me the chemistry that sizzles between us. He sets my whole body on fire. My hands automatically grab hold of his hard body, pulling him closer to me, feeling his warmth against my chest as those luscious lips claim mine. This will probably be the last kiss between us. We can't continue a physical relationship anymore. We have strayed into uncharted territory, and extreme feelings have become involved.

I don't want to hurt Christian, but I can't be the woman he wants me to be. I'm too broken, and he may not see that because it's a side I keep hidden from everyone, even from myself. I'm not worthy of his love. Christian deserves a whole woman, not this shell of a woman, who struggles every day with the scars deep down inside her. He doesn't realize it yet, but this is goodbye. Resting his forehead against mine, our lips are swollen from the intensity of the kiss.

"I felt exactly how much you love me in that kiss, Ness."

"I can't. Why is that so hard for you to understand? I have my job, we live together, our friendship. I'm sorry, I'm not risking all that for some fantasy life you think we can have together." Christian looks stunned by my words.

"I'm not capable of loving you the way you want me to." But I do, I fucking love him so much. What he doesn't know is one of the reasons I crawl into his bed most nights is because he stops the nightmares, the scars that seek me out in the darkness.

I start to walk away. I can't be here anymore looking at his devastated face, knowing I've hurt the one person I promised myself I'd never hurt. I can see his big heart break into a million pieces as I toss his confession in his face.

"I'm sorry, Chris, it's not worth the risk." He stares at me for a long moment, and then something passes over him. He pulls his shoulders back and straightens to his full height.

"Okay, Ness, I hear you loud and clear. I'm not worth the risk. All I am to you is a convenient cock." I hear the hurt in his voice, and he takes a couple of steps toward me. "I'd have made you happy if only you had the guts to take a chance. Don't worry, V, I won't make that mistake again. As I said, I hear you loud and clear." And with that, he turns away from me. I watch as he disappears back into the wedding where all our family and friends are happily enjoying their night.

I think I've just changed the course of my life forever, and I don't think it's for the better.

1

VANESSA

FIVE YEARS EARLIER

"I can't believe you're here!" Camryn squeals, opening the door.

"I know, I've missed you so much, it's been too long." I pull her into a tight hug on the front doorstep of her Venice Beach home. I can't believe I'm now living in LA. The sun is shining, the sky's blue, and I can hear the waves crashing in the distance, reminding me so much of my home in Australia. In the last couple of years, I've been working in dreary old London where it rains regularly, and the weather is usually miserable most days. It's finally great to be back in a place filled with permanent sunshine again.

"I know you just arrived, but I hope you're in the mood to party because tonight we've been invited to some swanky party in the Hills." Her blue eyes shimmer with excitement. I'll probably be suffering from jet lag, so why not spend the night awake at a Hollywood party instead of staring blankly at the ceiling in my bedroom.

"Just like the old days." I smile, high-fiving her. I met Camryn a couple of years ago when she was the event assistant organizing an album launch for some B-list pop star I was managing. We clicked over our mutual hatred for our bosses and our dreams of running our own businesses one day.

Last year, Camryn decided to move to Los Angeles from London and try her luck working here on events. Within a week of arriving, she worked for one of the most exclusive event companies in Hollywood. Through one of her many contacts, she set up an interview with Montgomery Records while I was visiting her on vacation a couple of months ago. And now, here I am in LA, about to start my new job as the record label's public relations executive. I'm so excited and can't wait to start my new life. I need it after the drama I left behind in London.

Hours later, we're pulling up to a large mansion in the Hills where we're greeted at the gates by a huge security guard. Once our names are checked off the list, we're allowed inside the luxurious home filled with beautiful people.

"Welcome to La-La Land, Ness." Camryn laughs as she pulls me toward the backyard. A large bar is set up beside the pool, and a clear Perspex dance floor has been built over the top of the pool—people are dirty dancing to the DJ's music on top of it.

Not five minutes after ordering our drinks, we're being hit on by two older men, and they are kind of gross and aggressive. They are old enough to be our dads. I'm not accustomed to this level of American enthusiasm, and they are creeping me out. Camryn rolls her eyes at what they are saying as she expertly rebuffs the men's advances, pulling me away and back into the safety of the party. "You will find men like them at most Hollywood parties. They are used to getting what they want," Camryn remarks.

"Cammie!" A large, tall, blond-haired man yells, sweeping her up into his arms, twirling her around as she giggles.

"Doug." She smiles as he puts her feet back down on the

ground. His blue eyes look at me. "Who's your beautiful friend?" he asks, winking at me. Thankfully, he isn't giving off creeper vibes.

"This is Vanessa. She's just moved over from London. She is the newest PR person at Montgomery Records."

Doug's face lights up. "Oh, fantastic. Monty, that old bastard, his bark is worse than his bite. If he gives you any problems, you let him know Doug Vincent is a friend, and that will shut the old fucker up." Doug lets out a big hearty chuckle. "Now run along with you two little sex kittens, there are some delicious young men here for you and me." He waves as he makes his way back into the crowd.

"Doug owns West Coast Productions. He's best friends with Monty. They went to school together or something like that," Camryn rambles on, waving her hands in the air as she talks.

The parties in London were so different from this. I feel like I've stepped onto a Hollywood set. All these larger-than-life characters walking around, it doesn't feel real. We head back toward the bar area, and more people have arrived, filling up every nook and crevice of the house which hangs precariously on the edge of a cliff. I say a prayer to the earthquake gods to stay calm for tonight because I don't want to slide down the mountain when the big one hits.

"Camryn!" A giant blond bear calls out behind us.

"Oh my God, Lance Burrows is here. He plays for San Diego," Camryn whispers to me. Not sure if that's supposed to mean something?

"I met him last weekend when I worked at his friend's wedding. He's so hot." The giant bends down, kissing Camryn on the cheek. The kiss makes her giggle. Camryn is a flirt, there isn't anyone she can't get, but she's no slut. She knows how to work what Mother Nature gave her, which was a shitload of hotness—bitch!

"Nice to see you again." His eyes are firmly stuck on her bouncing cleavage.

"This is my friend, Vanessa. She's just arrived from London." I smile at him as his eyes also stick to my chest. *Football players!*

"This is my buddy, Kane. He plays with me at San Diego," he says as he introduces us to another equally huge man. The two of them are so big, I feel like I'm on the set of *Honey, I Shrunk the Kids*—one wrong step, and I could be squished.

Kane has jet black hair, a chiseled jaw, and the greenest eyes I've ever seen. His bulging muscles are encased in a white-collared fitted shirt that, at any minute, the buttons could pop off and go flying in different directions. His tailored black slacks fit tightly around his tree-trunk legs. He kisses my cheeks, and a tiny flutter takes off in my tummy.

As the night progresses, his conversational skills are left lacking, unless it has to do with football, something I'm not particularly interested in talking about. I should make my escape.

"It's been nice talking to you, Kane, but I just flew in from London today, and I'm suffering from jet lag." I try and stifle a fake yawn. Kane looks a little upset, but I kiss him on the cheek to smooth things over. It's the polite thing to do.

"It's been nice meeting you, Vanessa. Do you think I could grab your number?" he asks, smiling at me, which I'm sure works on hundreds of girls, just not this one.

"I'm sure I'll see you around." My eyes drift to where Camryn and Lance are sitting close together. "I start a new job on Monday. My life is about to get crazy," I explain, giving him a broad smile, hoping that will help lessen the sting of rejection.

"Oh yeah, sure, see you around," he calls out as I disappear into the party.

I've been busting to go to the bathroom for ages, but Kane hadn't stopped talking to allow me to go. I make my way through the crowd and wander inside the grand home where I see a small lineup to use the facilities. After waiting a couple of moments for the bathroom, I go inside and take care of business. I check my makeup, fluff up my hair, and step out, right into the chest of one of the older men who were trying to pick us up at the bar earlier.

"We meet again, beautiful. I told you I'd have you in my arms by the end of the night." He chuckles. His beastly dark eyes look me over, making my skin crawl. Giving him a tight smile, I try to move away from him. He's so large, he makes the hallway small, and I find it hard to get around him.

"Where do you think you're going?" he questions while he grabs my wrist painfully hard. I try to get past him.

"I'm going back to my friends." My eyes look down at where his pudgy fingers are holding me. "Please let go of my wrist."

His grip gets tighter, and my heart starts to accelerate. This situation is making me uneasy. I look around, hoping someone is waiting to use the bathroom and can stop him, but the hall's deserted. Panic begins to crawl up my neck. Shit, this isn't good.

"You're so exquisite." His hand touches my cheek, making me wince. "Do you know... I can make you famous," he purrs, his gaze roaming over my body. Cursing myself for choosing this strapless dress, which shows off my ample cleavage, his beady eyes are all over them.

"No thanks, I don't want to be famous." I try and wiggle free from his tight grip.

The man sniggers. "Everyone wants to be famous, beautiful." He grips my wrist tighter. "I'm sure you're going to love getting on your knees. Just like they all do in the end."

"You're hurting me," I whisper.

He laughs a dark, murderous laugh. "You have no idea how much I want to hurt you," he says, pushing me up against the hall wall, his repulsive erection pressing into me. My entire body tenses, and I'm going to be sick.

"Get off me," I shriek while trying to push the old man away, but it's useless. He's still holding my wrist so tightly, he's going to snap it in two. At this point, I don't know if I care if he snaps it as long as it means he lets go of me. He pushes my hand against his hardening dick that's straining through his cheap pants. Panic grips me. He's so much stronger than I am and can easily overpower me. Think, Vanessa, think.

His lips touch my neck, and it makes my skin crawl at its touch. "Get off me. Get the hell away from me," I scream, hoping someone can hear me. When no one comes, the creep laughs. He bends down and licks my neck again.

"Fuck, you taste like peaches. I wonder if your pussy tastes the same. I can't wait to taste it."

"What! No way, fuck you. Get off me." I push him harder this time, hoping some superhuman strength will hit me, and I can get free. My adrenaline is already pumping, but it's like trying to move a fucking mountain. I need to find another way to get away from him. "Please let me go. I won't tell anyone." I try begging, but it just makes him laugh harder at me.

"I'm not worried about you telling anyone, beautiful, and they wouldn't believe you, anyway. Do you have any idea who I am?" I shake my head because I don't. He tries to lick my neck again.

"You're disgusting!" I spit out, making him snarl.

"I'm going to like teaching you a lesson, you fucking bitch."

Oh shit! I made him angrier. He yanks my wrist, pulling me down the hall. I try digging my heels into the hard floor, but it's hopeless. I keep slipping. Think, Ness, think. Managing to get my shoe off, I hit him over the head with it. Thankfully, I have my spiky Louboutin heels on tonight. The shock of the heel against his head makes him let go for a moment. He then starts spewing profanities at me, his face turning a lovely shade of red as he rubs the egg on his head from my shoe.

I try and make a run for it.

"Fucking bitch." I hear him scream.

As I run down the hall, I look behind me, making sure he isn't following. I'm not watching where I am going, and I hit a wall of muscle with such force that we both end up on the floor in a tangled mess of limbs. Dazzling whiskey-colored eyes look up at me, tattooed arms wrap around me, and my breasts are pushed against a hard chest.

"Fuck," the deep, accented voice mumbles, his eyes fall to the cursing beast behind me. His arms tighten around me. "Are you okay, angel?" he whispers. I shake my head as the creep looms over us.

"Get up. We haven't finished what we started." The man tries to grab me, but the tattooed guy pushes me out of the way.

"Don't touch her," he roars. The older man looks at this guy and mumbles.

"Fuck off, she's mine. Give her back. We have unfinished business to attend to." My mystery man pulls me up from the ground, his kind eyes looking at me, trying to work out if he's telling the truth. All I do is shake my head.

"Looks like she doesn't want to go with you." He positions himself in front of me while the creeper looks at me cowering behind my rescuer, weighing up his odds. Seeing that the man has a good twenty years on him and probably double his strength, judging by the bulging muscles on display, he gives up.

"Fine, have the stupid bitch, she's nothing but a cock tease, anyway."

"Fuck you!" I scream. How fucking dare he after what he tried to do to me. Then, without warning, I throw my other shoe at him, the one I had been clinging to fiercely. It hits him in the face.

Wiping his nose as a small trickle of blood falls from it, he yells, "You fucking bitch." He launches himself at me, but my rescuer stops him quickly.

"Move along before I show you how much of a bitch you are when I have you screaming for mercy on the ground," he growls back. The older man's eyes flick to mine, then back to my rescuer, and he walks away, grumbling, holding a hand to his nose.

2

VANESSA

My mystery man turns his attention to me. The full force of his handsome face stuns me for a moment. He rests his palms on my shaking shoulders.

"Are you okay?"

I can't stop staring at this beautiful man with his golden-brown hair pulled back into a messy bun and tanned skin from days spent in the sun. His long, muscular arms are adorned in colorful tattoos, and then there are those eyes like glistening shards of amber, pulling you into him.

I nod, maybe because I'm in shock but also because words seem to fail me in the presence of such a good-looking guy. Then without thinking, and I'm going to blame it on the shock, I launch myself into his arms. I wrap myself around his large frame, trying to keep my tears at bay, giving him the tightest hug I've ever given anyone before. His manly scent tickles my nose as my face buries itself against his firm chest. A deep, timbered laugh vibrates through my body as he holds me tight.

"Wow, maybe I need to rescue beautiful women more often

if this is the response I get." He thinks I'm beautiful. Gingerly I let go of him.

"Sorry about that." I take a step back from this perfect stranger.

"Nothing to be sorry about, darlin'." His smile lights up his entire face. Straight white teeth flash against his weathered skin. I like his accent as well—he sounds like he's just stepped off the rodeo circuit and directly into Hollywood.

"Well, thank you. I don't know what I'd have done if you hadn't appeared." The words hitch in my throat, thinking about that disgusting man and how his grubby hands had touched me.

"You had it under control, angel. Remind me next time never to piss off a woman when she has heels on like that. They could be used as weapons." He makes me laugh. I'll always make sure that I have heels on wherever I go from now on, knowing what they can do. We both stand there for a moment, taking each other in. "Not sure about you, but I could use a drink," he says, breaking the awkward silence.

"I think that sounds like a great idea."

He retrieves my shoes and hands them to me. I slip them on, holding onto his strong arm for balance. Once I have them on, he takes my hand and walks me back through the party and straight toward the bar. The bartenders are busy serving others, so we wait for our turn.

"So, you're not from around here, judging by that accent."

"Originally from Australia, but I just arrived from London today."

"So, you're sticking around in LA, then?"

"Yeah, I will be for a while."

He gives me a panty-melting smile. "Cool."

It's at that moment that a bartender stops in front of us.

"Four tequilas, please." It doesn't take long for the bartender to pour out the shots and hand over some salt and lime slices. "Here." He hands me two shot glasses. "Bottoms up." He smiles, knocking back the shots. I follow suit, the liquid heating a path through my body. The tart taste of lime hits my lips as I try to balance out the tequila.

"Nice, I like a woman who knows her way around a tequila shot." His eyes never leave my lips wrapped around the slice of lime. Is he flirting with me? I sure as hell hope so. He hands me a glass of champagne and grabs a bottle of beer for himself.

"Let's grab a seat." He points to a spare armchair near the pool. Taking my free hand, he pulls me toward the chair. He takes a seat and motions for me to sit on his lap. I raise my eyebrow at him. He laughs.

"Fine, I can be a gentleman and stand." He moves to get up from the chair. I stop him with a hand on his chest.

"I think I can handle sitting on your lap." He sits back down again with a smile on his face. I sit down on his lap. One of his hands rests on my thigh, and the other hangs over the edge of the chair holding his beer.

"So, what brings you to LA besides the weather? Let's face it, London's weather sucks." He laughs.

"Tell me about it. I felt like I was one winter away from turning into a vampire." We both laugh at my joke. "I was offered a job here."

"So, what do you do?" I knew that would be his next question. I don't want to tell him what I do for a living. Usually, when I tell guys I'm a PR executive for a record label, they want to hand me a demo. Men have dated me in the past to get further up the ladder. I don't trust any of them.

"I... I'm an event planner." I've heard Camryn talk about it enough I can bluff my way through. It's not like I'm ever going to see this man again. "What about you?" He stills for a moment and takes a sip of his beer before answering.

"I... um... am a chef." He smiles. He's hot and can cook, but before we can delve further, I hear my name being called from behind.

"Nessa, there you are. I've been looking everywhere for you." Camryn stops and eyes me sitting on some random hot guy's lap. Her eyes widen. "Kane said you had gone home, you were complaining about jet lag or something." The mystery man stiffens at hearing another guy's name.

"Sorry, I sort of told a white lie. I couldn't sit and listen to Kane harp on about football anymore." Camryn nods in understanding.

"So, um… who's this?" she questions my mystery man.

"I was her knight in shining armor." Camryn frowns, not following his train of thought. "Your friend ran into some trouble at the bathroom."

Camryn's face turns to me. "Are you okay, babe?"

Rubbing my wrist where the guy had hurt me, I respond, "Yeah, one of those old creeps from before tried to get handsy with me, but this guy saved me." I tap his thick, tight thigh with my hand.

"Actually, I was just her backup. She had it all under control. Did you know she has lethal skills with heels?" We both laugh at our inside joke. I could laugh about it now. Camryn looks at each of us, and her face falls when she sees the bruise growing on my wrist.

"Ness?" She points to my wrist.

I rub it again. "It's okay."

Camryn doesn't look happy about it. "Lance and I were just leaving," she tells me as the large football player walks up behind her, his arm resting around her shoulder. His eyes drop to me, sitting on this guy's lap. He's probably not happy about it because not long ago, I was flirting with his friend.

"Ready to go, Cam?" His deep voice breaks the silence.

"Um… yeah, sure. Ness, you ready to go?" Camryn looks between the mysterious man and me.

My stomach sinks as I have to leave this man. Cammie is my ride home. Slowly, I slip off his lap. "Thank you for helping me tonight," I say as he stands up.

"Anytime, angel, anytime." We both stand there looking at each other, not knowing what to do.

"I owe you a drink," Camryn says, looking at my rescuer. "I mean, it's not every day someone saves my best friend from some sleazeball." He shoves his hands into his jeans' pockets, looking a little uncomfortable with the attention Camryn's giving him about his heroics.

"Why don't you come back to our place and grab a drink there?" She smiles, fluttering her eyelashes at him. He turns to me, gauging my reaction, and I nod in agreement.

"Okay, sounds like fun," he answers as he entwines our fingers together.

"Welcome to La Casa de dos Perras," Camryn says, laughing as we enter.

"The house of two bitches," says mystery man, raising his eyebrows at Camryn.

"You caught that, hey?" She giggles.

"I'm from Texas. I speak a little Spanish." He grins at her. Oh, that's why he sounds like a cowboy. Texan accent, hot!

"I think I'm going to like this place." His warm breath tickles my skin as we grab drinks from the kitchen. We head up to the top deck of our home where there's a large open terrace. During the day, you can see the ocean in the distance.

The house is beautiful, a three-story, modern home Camryn's renting from a friend. The deck has a couple of large sunbeds, a hammock, and a small table set up. Camryn and Lance snuggle up on one of the sunbeds, leaving my mystery man and me on the other. We both lay back on the sunbed side by side, looking up to the stars in the night sky, which are hard to see because of all the excessive light around us. A warm summer nights' breeze blows against my skin.

"I haven't done this in ages," I confess, looking up into the night sky.

"What? Bring home some strange hot guy?" The mystery man wiggles his eyebrows at me.

"No, that's a common occurrence," I joke, elbowing him in the ribs. "I mean looking up at the stars, like this." Slowly, an arm makes its way around my shoulders. I snuggle into his embrace. We stay silent for a while enjoying each other's company and the free light in the sky. I can hear the flirty giggles of Camryn, then a deep groan from Lance. My body is on high alert with sexual tension swirling around us on the terrace.

"Thanks again for saving me tonight, I just..."

His lips kiss my forehead. "Anytime, sweetheart, anytime."

The faintest touch of his lips against my heated skin sets my body alive, and every nerve is on fire. I let my hand rest on his hard chest, and the tiniest hum passes his lips. Whiskey-colored eyes darken as they move from my face to my lips. I let my hand move over his torso, feeling every bump of pure muscle against my fingertips.

His body stiffens the further my hands explore. I let my fingers run over the colorful tattoos on his arm, tracing the designs. His intense stare is locked on mine as my hand moves from his arm, then over his denim-clad crotch. The mystery man appreciates my roaming hands, judging by the impressive bulge trying to break free from his jeans' confines. Each brush across that area makes his breath hitch, and I like the sounds he makes.

Rolling on top, I surprise him. I let my legs fall either side of his, my aching core pressing against his eager bulge. Looking behind me to see if Camryn and Lance are still here, I'm relieved to see they have moved on downstairs. My fingers start to unbutton his fly slowly until his hand stops me.

"Angel, you don't have to thank me like this." Looking at him, a little shocked, he thinks I'm doing this as some kind of thanks for saving me. Letting my hand wrap around his erection, I give it a hard squeeze, making him groan.

"It's going to be you thanking me in a minute for the way I'm about to blow your mind." I smile as mystery man's eyes widen.

3

CHRISTIAN

"I like a confident woman." It's the truth, especially this divine creature straddling me, undoing my fly. My palms are pawing her bare ass where her dress has ridden up. Who knew faking a toilet stop to get away from groupies would lead me to where I am now? This beautiful goddess is grinding herself against my aching cock.

I remember feeling her firm breasts and heavenly, soft body against me as we tumbled to the floor. Thinking it was some groupie getting creative with her stalking skills until I saw her jade-green eyes staring at me with a panicked look across that beautiful face. It was seconds before I heard a male voice screaming behind us. Her warm body shook as the booming voice came closer. My instinct set in as I tried to protect this angel from some creep spewing profanities at her.

I laughed when she threw her shoe at him, clocking him square in the nose. She probably broke it with the amount of blood gushing out of it. My heart did a tiny little somersault at her feistiness. Now here I am at her home where she's slowly undressing me, her beautiful eyes focused on the task. I like her accent, the Australian twang mixed with that English refinement. It got my dick hard. Who the fuck am I kidding? The whole package got my dick hard.

Looking down at where she's now situated, her caramel hair is spilling around bare shoulders, and those generous tits are pouring out of her low-cut dress like two perfect melons, plump and delicious. I can't wait to taste them later. Our eyes catch for a moment as she licks her pink lips and gives me a mischievous smile.

I realize my dick is pointing sky high. I've been so lost in my thoughts that I hadn't noticed she had pushed my jeans down to my ankles. I watch as her lips wrap around the head of my cock. I swear I see stars, not just the ones hanging above my head in the night sky. I let out a deep groan.

Fuck, and her mouth is perfection. I don't want her to stop. My fingers entwine in her hair, pulling her harder against my dick. Oh fuck, her caresses feel so good. Soft, warm hands start stroking my balls, sending white-hot heat up my spine. Her skilled fingers move from stroking to rolling my aching balls around and around. She's good at giving head. I've been given plenty of blow jobs in my life, but this one, this one is in my top five of all time. I watch as her head bobs up and down in perfect rhythm. If she keeps up this pace, I'll embarrass myself and shoot a mother lode down her throat before I have time to give her an orgasm.

My motto is ladies always first.

Pushing her away slowly, perfect wet, pink lips fall with a pop from my protesting cock. Sitting up as I shuffle back against the lounge, a tiny frown line appears on her forehead. "Don't worry, angel, we're so far from done, it's not even funny."

Grabbing her waist, I pull her on top of my lap. My fingers start on their own path of exploration between her legs, gliding over soft skin until I hit her G-string seam. Such a tiny thing, it's hardly worth wearing it. My knuckle meets her wetness, and she's ready for me. "You really liked sucking my cock?"

Her face lights up in a sultry smile. "It's a very nice cock." My calloused fingers slide back and forth against her slickness as she lets out a heady groan with each movement.

"Like that, angel?" Her top teeth bite into her bottom lip as my fingers sink into her.

"Fuck," she moans. I never tire of hearing a woman moan like that while my fingers or cock are nestled inside her. Curling my fingers, I stroke across the delicate nerves that make every woman go crazy. With each skilled stroke, her warm, little cunt clamps tightly around me as she starts to buck.

"That's it, angel, ride them. Ride them hard." My thumb slides across her blossoming little bud. With each tentative stroke, it makes her push harder against my hand, searching for the perfect mixture of pleasure and rhythm.

I let my eyes roam over this beautiful creature bucking against my fingers, that caramel hair blowing in the summer's night air as her head is tilted back, arching in pleasure. Her fingernails are digging into the flesh of my shoulders. I don't care if she leaves any marks, I'm hoping to add more to the collection tonight. Those fluttery moans are heaving from her chest, perfect feminine squeals of delight. I add a third finger to my repertoire, filling her, the heady gasp that comes from her mouth makes my cock leak. He's so desperate to be inside of her. He is excited at the prospect, and why wouldn't he be?

This woman is divine. A couple more strokes of my thumb over her sensitive clit, and she's shaking, strangling my hand as her orgasm rips through her, making her whole body shake with pleasure. I think the whole of Venice Beach heard her scream. Sparkling green eyes open before me, her cheeks are flushed, and she's breathing hard.

"I want more." She smiles, capturing my mouth with her lips. There's a sense of urgency. She lavished me with her lips, our tongues dueling between each other, all the while my fingers stayed snuggly inside of her. "Please say you have protection?" she questions in a whisper, capturing my earlobe between her teeth, giving it a hard tug.

"Fuck!" I groan as she plays with my earlobe. She couldn't know that's my sweet spot. But fucking hell, she knows now. Warm lips trail down my neck, across my collarbone, up toward my other earlobe. "Yeah, I have protection." I never leave home without it, but at this moment, my mind has left me as she sucks my other lobe into her mouth.

"Good, then let's fucking use it," she whispers into my ear. Fuck, that's hot. I swear all of my blood has left my body and moved south in preparation for what's to come. Using my free hand because there isn't a hope in hell, I was going to remove my fingers from her cunt, I try and grab for my wallet in my jeans' pocket.

"Let me," she says, pulling the condom out, throwing my wallet to the floor. Grabbing the foil, she rips it open and places the condom at the tip of my glistening cock in readiness.

"You're going to have to take your fingers out of me to fuck me."

I love that this chick talks dirty. Honestly, I don't want to take my fingers out of her, but I do want to fuck her, so I have no choice. Achingly slow, she rolls the condom down my shaft, biting her lip as she does so. Begrudgingly, I finally pull my fingers from her. She lets out a curse when I place them in my mouth. Jesus, fuck, she tastes so sweet.

"Don't worry, angel, I'll make sure you're nice and full again." Grabbing her hips, I position her slowly against my cock, but she has other ideas as she suddenly drops down on it vigorously.

"Fuck!" We both groan at the fullness. Her heat engulfs me, and her eyes roll back in her head as her hands hold onto my shoulders, steadying herself. I'm not a small guy, and most women think twice about me. My girth usually gives them pause, but she didn't even bat an eyelid, taking me hard.

Clumsily, I unzip her dress. I need to see her tits bounce as I fuck her. I throw the offending dress to the floor with the rest of our clothes. My eyes zero in on her tits, perfectly round and natural, so fucking natural. The way they bounce is beautiful, and her tight, pink nipples are standing at attention for me. I capture one of them between my teeth.

"Yes," she whimpers. My hand starts massaging one breast while my mouth devours the other. I swap and give equal attention to each of her spectacular tits. With each suck of her delicate nipples, she grinds against me harder. Her head is thrown back in ecstasy as I thrust harder into her.

"That's it, angel. Fuck me, ride me, use me." And she does just that. Handing over control in the bedroom never happens. I always like to be in control, but tonight this woman could ask me to do anything, and I would for her, just to hear her breathless whimpers and heady sighs.

My balls begin to tighten as she continues to ride me like a rodeo queen. She needs another orgasm before I come, and it needs to be quick because I don't think I'll be able to hold out for too much longer. This has to be a record and not the right kind of record. My thumb finds that delicious little bud again. My other hand finds her lush ass cheek and gives it a hard squeeze. Fuck, her cunt nearly squeezes me dry with that move.

I push her harder and harder against my thumb, ensuring she gets the right amount of pressure and friction. Her sobs are like music to my ears, and she's getting closer and closer and tighter and tighter until she explodes around me. I want to hold on longer, but her orgasm is choking me, and I can't hold it, coming not far behind her. She collapses on top of me, exhausted, a satisfied smile on her face, her lips meeting mine in a soft kiss.

"That was fun." She wiggles on top of me. I'm still buried deep inside her, capturing her hips as she makes me hard again.

"The fun's not over yet, angel, and next time I make you come, I want you to scream my name," I say, slapping her ass, making her squeal.

"Yeah, and what's that?" she questions me. We haven't exchanged names yet.

"Chris."

"Well, Chris, I'm Nessa, so next time we come, we both know exactly what to be screaming."

4

CHRISTIAN

"Wow, he's alive," Axel, my twin brother, jokes. I punch him in the arm as we're ushered toward the conference room by the sexy blonde receptionist. My eyes watch as her hips sway with each step.

"Mr. Montgomery will be with you in a moment. Please make yourselves at home," she says with a nervous giggle, her arm pointing to the fully stocked buffet like a game show model. There's also a fully stocked mini-bar, which the blonde points out to us. All our eyes are on her ass as she bends over and hands each of us a drink. When the blonde leaves the room, the boys start at me again about my disappearance all weekend.

"We thought you had finally been taken by a stalker and tied to a bed, being made to be some chick's sex slave," Evan jokes.

"Or, you had been drugged and whisked away to Vegas and made to marry some stalker in a secret ceremony," Finn adds.

"No, no, my favorite was an alien abduction." Oscar laughs.

"You guys are just jealous I got to spend all weekend balls-deep inside one of the most beautiful women I've ever seen." They all flip me the bird.

"Pretty sure we all did okay on the pussy front, little brother," Axel smirks. He's fucking two minutes older than me. It shits me that he calls me little brother, and he knows it.

"And, Evan, if you must know, yeah, I was tied to a bed all weekend, and she most definitely did use me as her sex slave." It was the truth. I let Nessa tie me up a couple of times. It was a first. The whole control thing, I don't give it up ever, but for some reason, when it comes to her, I'm complicit. My bandmates groan at my comment.

"I'm surprised. This girl must have a magic pussy if she's caught your attention, especially all weekend," Finn declares.

"This woman is amazing." My mind was still thinking about all the things we did together. She was most certainly sexually adventurous, her appetite ravenous. I think I met my match with this girl, and it's kind of exciting.

"Fuck, the boy is in love." Evan throws a muffin at my head, bringing me back from my sexual memories.

"Fuck off, man. I don't have time for love." Pegging the muffin back at Evan, I watch as it disintegrates when it hits him.

"But you like her?" Of course, my brother picks up on that shit, and the whole twin thing sucks sometimes.

"Yeah, and not because she knows how to suck cock… but we had fun together. I mean, who knew watching TV with some chick would lead to some of the best sex of my life."

"Stop it, please. It's like someone has body-snatched Christian and brought back some pussy-assed version instead." Oscar chuckles.

"Fuck you, man." I throw my empty soda can at his head.

"Are we going to meet this chick? Because seriously, I want to high-five her for taming my little brother." Axel gives me a shit-eating grin.

"Back off, man, she's mine," I tell him.

Axel raises his hands, pretending to defend himself. "Seriously, bro, are you that hung up on this chick that you don't want to share her with me?" My brother and I have shared girls by doing the whole switching out twin thing in the past. Sometimes they knew, sometimes they didn't. There is no way in hell I'd let him anywhere near Nessa.

"I found her first, and that's it." Calling dibs on a woman is pretty sad and a first for me. Axel laughs.

"Wow, who knew Christian would be the first to fall for some chick," Oscar ribs me.

"I'm not falling for—" The door swings open, and in walks Monty, a larger-than-life man dressed as if he has just stepped off his yacht in St. Bart's in his cream pants, pink polo shirt, and boat shoes.

"Welcome to the family, boys," he says, slapping his hands on the conference table loudly. Last week we officially signed with Montgomery Records, and today we're just here for a photo shoot and some PR stuff for the label.

"I'm so happy you boys are coming on board with us. We're going to have so much fun over the next five years." You can see the dollar signs in his eyes as he looks over all of us. He gave us the most creative licenses with our music compared to what all the other labels had to offer, so it's a pretty sweet deal.

The meeting continues with Monty praising us repeatedly, which is nice, but I don't need my ego stroked. I know Dirty Texas is fucking incredible, and our lives are going to change. We pose for some photos as we sign the contract. Afterward, we sign some promotional material for his kids.

"Great, now the boring stuff is out of the way. I want you to meet with your new PR executive. We pride ourselves on personalized service here at Montgomery Records. You will be given your own dedicated executive to look after your account, so we can grow your profile together."

Sounds good. Wonder if she's hot? There's a tentative knock

at the door. "Come in, sweetheart," Monty calls from his place at the head of the table.

The door opens wider. That's when my entire world stops, and everyone else ceases to exist. Standing before us is Nessa, the woman who asked me to leave her bed first thing this morning to get ready for work. A woman had never asked me to go before, especially after what I thought was a fantastic weekend together. But this morning, she was practically pushing me out the door.

My eyes take her in. She looks so fucking beautiful. Her caramel hair is pulled up into a tight bun, she's wearing a white blouse that's done up a button higher than is needed hiding those gorgeous tits from view, a black blazer, and a knee-length black skirt that's molded to her ass. My eyes drop to her feet, where she has sky-high heels on that look like weapons, reminding me of the weekend. It makes me smile. Her eyes fall to where I'm sitting, and the smile is quickly wiped off her beautiful face, and I don't like it.

5

VANESSA

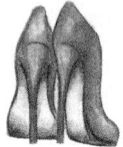

Fuck, fuck, fuck!
    What the hell is Chris doing in the conference room? Today I'm meeting my very first clients, Dirty Texas. I don't understand why he's sitting with the band? Monty introduces the boys to me, and then it clicks, he is Christian Taylor, the goddamn guitarist for the band, and he's also a twin. There are two of those gorgeous fuckers running around. Looking over at his brother, Axel, who looks exactly like him, the main difference I notice is Axel's tattoos are all blue origami style, and Christian's are multicolored.

    Axel gives me a wicked wink, but nothing, not even a tiny butterfly flutter in my stomach, happens. Instead, my body is reacting to Christian's presence, and I hate it. I can feel my nipples tighten and my pussy clench remembering our weekend together. I also hate that he looks so hot sitting there casually in a red T-shirt that's pulled across his muscular chest, the tight shirt showing off his sculptured body, a body that only this morning my tongue was exploring. Ripped denim jeans and Chucks finish off the rock- star outfit. His golden-brown hair hangs over his face in messy waves as if someone's fingers had been running through it.

Oh wait, they had.

Me!

Fuck, fuck, fuck!

Keep it together, Vanessa, you're a professional, and he's a client. Forget about the multiple orgasms he gave you over the weekend. Forget about the way you sat and watched movies in bed binging on popcorn and ice cream. Just forget about his magic tongue and cock and hands and... fuck, I can feel myself turning red. This isn't good. Those whiskey-colored eyes haven't strayed from me since I entered the room. I'm trying to ignore him as Monty speaks about my role with the band. But in all honesty, I've no idea what he said because I'm too busy panicking.

Finally, Monty dismisses me, and I head back to my office, slamming my door shut. I start to bang my head against it. How the fuck could I have been so stupid? How the hell do I not know the band members of Dirty Texas? Picking up my phone, I call Camryn.

"Hey, bitch," she says.

"Fuck, Cam. I've fucked up," I whisper into the phone.

"What do you mean? It's your first day, how the hell can you have already fucked up?" she asks.

"Remember the guy I met at the party?"

"The one you kicked out this morning after spending all weekend with him?"

"Yeah... well, Chris isn't a chef. His name is, in fact, Christian Taylor. He's a fucking rock star and my very first client."

"Shit," Camryn screams down the phone. A knock at my door startles me.

"I have to go."

"Okay, girl, good luck. Cocktails tonight at The California Bros. You have to fill me in on everything."

Putting my phone down, I call out, "Come in."

"Well, this is a surprise." That voice, that damn voice that makes my panties wet. Christian is standing in the doorway of my office as if he doesn't have a care in the world.

"You're telling me. I thought you were a chef."

"And I thought you were an event planner," he states as he prowls toward me. I sit up straight. Now is the time to be professional. Yes, I had a weekend of the most fantastic sex, but now he's my client. "So... Vanessa, what are we going to do about this? Because I sure as hell wouldn't mind a repeat performance of the weekend." He rounds the edge of my desk and stops in front of me, his massive presence looming.

"It was a one-time thing, Christian." Saying his full name feels strange, mainly as I was used to screaming out his other name.

"We both know it was never going to be a one-time thing, not when the chemistry between us is this good." His hand drops and brushes my cheek. "I think I lost count how many times I made you come this weekend."

I don't care how good the sex is between us, it's all null and void now that we work together. Pushing myself up and out of the chair, we're almost chest to chest, face to face.

"We work together. Nothing can happen," I state, looking at Christian directly.

"So, we can't mix business and pleasure?" Large calloused fingers dig into my hip.

"I'm a professional, Christian. No matter how great the weekend was, nothing can happen ever again." I try to even my breaths, but his large presence is all-consuming. Christian puts a hand to his heart as if my words have wounded him.

"You sure, angel? Because I bet if I put my fingers between your legs, your panties would be soaked, wouldn't they?" Ignoring him because it's the fucking truth, they are soaked. I can feel his breath against my skin. His body heat is radiating off of him, and his musky scent is filling my nose, setting my skin on fire. It isn't fair. Why does this man have to be my client?

"I'm going to kiss you now because I fucking can't stand being this close to you and not touching you." Huh, what? No, that's not professional, kissing isn't allowed.

Before I have a chance to register what he's saying, his mouth is on mine. Large palms hold my face as his lips torture mine, my hands fisting his red T-shirt as I melt into his kiss. His body pushes against mine as my bottom hits the desk behind me. These lips, I can't get enough of these lips. His hands leave my face and travel over my body until they end up at my waist. With ease, he lifts me, so my bottom is sitting on the desk. Skilled hands push up the hem of my pencil skirt as he nestles in between my legs. What the hell am I doing?

"Christian, stop," I order, pushing him away from me. Both of us are breathing hard, my eyes flick toward the bulge in his jeans, and I subconsciously lick my lips.

"I know what you want, and it's all yours." I shake my head, trying to make the fuzziness of desire leave my mind.

"We can't. I can't. Things are different now." I jump off my desk and fix up my skirt. I can't believe I let him push me that far. "I need this job, I'm good at my job, and I'm going to be the best PR manager you have ever had, and I can only do that if we..." waving my hands between us, I continue, "... keep our relationship purely professional."

Christian frowns. "Seriously?" He looks confused. I'm sure he isn't used to women saying no to him. I can totally understand why, but today is going to be a first for him. I can feel my body protesting against what I'm saying, but it's for the best. I learned my lesson the hard way with interoffice affairs, and I'll never put myself in that situation again.

"I'm sorry, Christian. We just can't. You do realize we're

going to be working closely with each other for the foreseeable future?"

Raking his hands through his hair, "Yeah, I get it. I just... fuck, Ness, I can't stop thinking about you." I'm a little taken aback by his honesty.

"I'm sure by the end of the week, some new girl will have your attention, and you will have forgotten all about me." Ugh, I hate that thought, it makes my stomach sink. Some other girl is going to get the benefits of his exceptional skills.

"It's not like that. You were the first girl that I've wanted to spend time with and not just to have sex with. This weekend was..." he rubs his face as he starts to pace, "... fuck, Ness... this weekend is one I'll never forget. You were fucking perfect."

My heart begins to race. I can't believe this man is saying these things to me. He could have any woman he wants in the world, and he's telling me he wants more.

"I'm sorry, Christian."

"I know it just sucks." His whiskey-colored eyes meet mine. "Look, I'm not going to deny that when we have meetings, I am so going to be picturing you naked, okay?" This makes me laugh.

"Fine. I'm not going to deny that there might be times that I might picture you naked as well." My comment makes him smile. "But we keep it professional." Christian rolls his eyes. I know I sound like a broken record, but he doesn't understand what it's like to have your life ruined because of some stupid office gossip.

"So, what would be a professional kiss then?" he asks, wiggling his eyebrows at me.

"I'm pretty sure a kiss isn't very professional." Folding my arms in front of me, I try to be serious.

"No? I'm sure it can be. Wanna try?" The smile he gives me makes my knees weak.

"Not really." I try and feign indifference.

"Come on, Vanessa, I'm sure you can handle a professional kiss from me." No, I'm pretty sure any kissing between us I won't be able to handle. He moves toward me, leans in, and kisses each of my cheeks. I can feel my entire body zing from the sparks. "See, totally professional." He smirks at me.

"Fine, point made, that's all the kissing we can have between us in the future." He rolls his eyes at me.

"Fine, Vanessa, you win. Friends, then?" he asks, holding out his hand for me.

Shaking it, I agree. "Friends."

6

VANESSA

I've been organizing Dirty Texas' first gig with Montgomery Records for the past two months. It's a special invite-only gig, and there's a waitlist a mile long to get into it. The buzz the event has generated has been tremendous. The radio stations have been promoting this gig, alongside the release of their first single as the album will launch next month.

This is my first gig with the label, and I want to show everyone that I'm the right person for the job. I pop my head out from behind the black curtain, looking at the hundreds of fans, media, and industry people waiting for the boys to step out onto the stage.

"Wow, what a great atmosphere," Isla comments as she pops her head out as well. She's Oscar's Dirty Texas bass player's younger sister, and also the band's assistant. I wasn't sure if I was going to like Isla at first. She was pretty standoffish as this blonde, Scandinavian, ice princess. When she realized I was more interested in doing my job than banging the band members, she thawed toward me.

"I'm so fucking nervous," I confess.

"You've done so well, Ness. Seriously, I know the boys are happy. They may not show it all the time because they are male, but they can see all the hard work you have put into tonight. They appreciate it," she encourages, squeezing my arm.

I take a deep breath before I reply, "I guess we better get this show on the road. Otherwise, those fans out there are going to riot, and that's going to be a PR nightmare."

We both laugh as we head back toward the dressing rooms where the boys are getting ready. Isla opens the door, and the boys look up from their pre-show rituals. Having the full attention of the Dirty Texas boys still awes me. Five of the most gorgeous men on the planet, according to *Cosmopolitan* magazine, can make the best of us giddy like a schoolgirl.

My eyes automatically land on Christian as we enter the room. They always do. Of course, he looks every inch the hot rock star in his black jeans, Chucks, a gray tee pulled tight across his chest, and a flannel shirt wrapped around his waist. His hair is pulled up in his trademark man bun.

I hate that after all this time, his presence still affects me. I hate how the smallest of touches can still set my body on fire as if my body remembers every single one of his previous touches. I hate that I have to watch him pick up groupies and pretend that it doesn't affect me, all because I told him we should be friends.

I told him we needed to remain professional. It kills me having to keep my distance. When I watch him on stage in his element, he looks like a god, his golden-brown hair dripping with sweat, the satisfied look he gets on his face as the screaming crowd calls out his name. Those strong arms holding his guitar, nimble fingers working their way across the strings so smoothly, remind me of the way they worked me over and over again.

"Ness, Ness." Isla elbows me in the side. Shit, I totally spaced out thinking about Christian again. The bastard gives me a smirk as if he can read my mind. I notice he adjusts himself with his hand like he too was thinking the exact same things. Pull it together, Ness, this is a big night. Don't get distracted by the hot rock star.

"Sorry, so many things on my mind." I try to cover my dirty thoughts. Christian coughs at my statement. I glare at him before I launch into what's happening tonight. I let the boys know who will be here, what will happen after the concert, and give them the after-party details at the club next door.

Before we know it, it's showtime.

"MORNING, PRINCESS." I swear I hear Christian's deep timbered voice as a face nuzzles into me. A wet tongue starts licking a path down my neck, sending goosebumps over my body. It's been a while since I've had someone in my bed, and this dream is the most action I've had in a long time. I picture a body pressed against my naked back, their arousal pressing against my bottom. I push back against it, feeling it slide through my ass cheeks' crack, teasing me. Large arms wrap around my naked body. I picture them with colorful tattoos, just like the ones Christian has. Calloused fingers find my aroused nipples, slowly playing with them, each hard tug awakening my body. That felt so real.

Where the hell am I?

I ignore that question because what he's doing feels too good. I need to come. If the only way I can do that is via a wet dream, then so be it. The same calloused hand moves between my legs, teasing my folds as they slip through my wetness. A tiny whimper falls from my lips.

"Fuck, I love how you're always so ready for me." Christian's Texan accent is like an aphrodisiac. A finger slips inside of me, making me arch my back in pleasure. Then another joins it as they start to pump into me. A large thumb sweeps across my clit, sending goosebumps over my body. Yes, I can feel my body come alive. The tingles start and dance over me. I push harder against the calloused thumb needing that extra pressure against my aching clit. I'm so close, so close, and then the hand disappears.

"No." I hear myself groan.

"Don't worry, angel, you'll be full again soon," the voice whispers as a hard cock nudges me from behind, a hand pulls one of my legs open, so the cock can tease me back and forth through my slickness. Yes, this is what I need.

"Fuck me," I beg. It's my dream, and I can beg if I want to.

"I've missed this so much." I imagine Christian's murmur against my back. It feels so real—his teeth sink into my bare shoulder, the tiny bite of pain mixed in with the intoxicating pleasure of his cock as it enters me, stretching me, filling me.

Yes, yes, yes.

A hand holds my hips as they start to buck, over and over again, fingers twisting my nipple with each hard thrust into me. Yes, dream sex is the best. The fucking best. My whole body is tingling—this will be one hell of an orgasm, I can feel it making its way over my body. Suddenly, I'm rolled onto my stomach, my face planted into the soft bed. A large body is hovering over me, kicking my legs open wider, starting a hard assault into me, over and over again. Each thrust against the bedsheet is rubbing at my aching clit. He pumps into me harder and harder. I can hear his desperate moans as he fucks me.

"Yes, yes, yes," I scream as the friction and the thrusting push me over the edge, and I come—the best orgasm of my life. Thank God, I'm already lying down. Otherwise, I'd have collapsed. My body feels like it's floating on a cloud. He continues to fuck me through my orgasm, and moments later, I feel him come inside of me. I can feel his slickness between my legs. What the ...? That felt real, too real. Hot lips travel down my spine with feather-light kisses.

"Fuck, Ness, you're perfect." Christian's voice floats over the room. I shake my head because I need to get him out of it. "Ness, you okay?" the voice asks. Then reality comes crashing down around me, and I can feel his heaviness against me. This is real. This isn't a dream.

"Get off me," I scream, trying to push him away from me.

Christian rolls off of me. "Ness?" I pull the sheets up around me, and I can feel the wetness between my legs. I can't meet Christian's eyes. I thought this was a dream. "Ness, look at me, dammit," Christian growls. Slowly I open my eyes, and two whiskey-colored ones are staring back at me.

"This shouldn't have happened," I whisper.

"I didn't see you saying no." His face looks serious, and his voice has a slightly angry tone to it.

"That's because I thought I was dreaming," I blurt out. Christian looks stunned.

"So, you didn't want to fuck me?" His tone sounds a little hurt.

"No... I mean, yes... I don't know. I didn't think this was real," is all I can manage to say.

"I thought you wanted me?" he questions, sounding a little vulnerable. I'm silent because there's nothing to say. Of course, I want him. He knows how to give me the most amazing orgasms. But I promised myself that I'd never mix business and pleasure, not after everything that had happened to me in London. I learned my lesson the hard way. A small trickle slides down my leg. Shit!

"You forgot protection," I yell, realizing what it is. I pick up my pillow and throw it at him before jumping off the bed.

"Fuck, Ness," he mutters, while running his hands through his hair. "I just—" The rest of his sentence is cut off as I slam the bathroom door and jump into the shower. Christian bangs on the bathroom door.

"Ness, open up. Please!" he yells. I ignore him as I try and wash him from my skin. "Please, Ness. Open up. You're killing me with your silence." I can hear the anguish in his voice. Grabbing one of the fluffy white towels, I wrap it around myself. Christian almost falls on top of me as I swing open the bathroom door. "Just talk to me," he begs.

"There's nothing to say." I move past him as I look for my clothes from last night to get dressed in. I can't believe I now have to do the walk of shame. The rest of the boys better not be awake. He watches as I get dressed. He's still naked, and my eyes are distracted by his freely swinging cock. It makes me mad all over again. "Please put some clothes on!" I yell at him. Christian freezes for a moment before pulling on some red boxer briefs.

"That better?" Ugh, I hate his face at this moment.

"I have to go." I head toward the hotel door.

"Ness, please, can we talk about this? I'm sorry, I thought after last night that you wanted another round, that the reason you were still in my bed is that you wanted me."

Last night's antics hit me. It was the after-party, Christian had a million and one groupies all over him, and he loved it, and why shouldn't he? They played amazingly. He deserved to bask in his own glory. But I didn't need to watch it, so Isla and I kind of got wasted.

She confessed that she had a big crush on Finn, and seeing him with the groupies all the time messes her up. We found a group of hot guys, and before we knew it, both of us were making out with some of them. I had come back from the bathroom, and Isla had disappeared with one of the guys, and my guy was waiting for me. He asked me if I wanted to get out of there, and I did. He took my hand, and we made our way toward the exit until Christian stopped us.

Things are still fuzzy, but he basically told the guy to fuck off, that he was taking me home, that I had drunk too much. For some reason, I didn't argue. I just followed his lead. It was a silent journey back to the hotel. He ended up carrying me as I stumbled in my heels. Sammy asked if I needed anything, and I just waved his concern away. I started singing Britney Spears' 'Toxic,' which made Sammy laugh. He said his goodbyes and went back to the club to the rest of the guys. Next thing I know, I'm throwing myself at Christian. He was fending me off, telling me I was drunk. But I ignored him and told him how much I wanted him. Then just like that, we were fucking like rabbits. Shit! I can feel my cheeks redden from the memories.

"I'm sorry, Chris, but it was a mistake." I look at him standing there like a fucking god.

"Why, because we work together?" His face is like stone.

"Yes." I distract myself by playing with my phone in my hand.

"Talk to me, Ness," Christian commands.

Letting out a heavy sigh, I respond, "Let me just message Camryn to come to pick me up, then we can talk." He nods in agreement, and I send off a quick message to Cam to come and get me.

Christian is sitting in the living room on the sofa with a water bottle for each of us. Thankfully, he has put on more clothes. He pats the seat next to him as he hands me the water bottle. Our legs touch as I settle on the couch, and I feel it, I feel the spark between us.

"You can't deny the chemistry between us, Ness," Christian whispers.

Looking at the floor because I can't look at him, I whisper, "I know." It's the truth.

"Then tell me why we can't try something. I've never wanted to try something with anyone before you, Ness. It's freaking me out, but for some reason, I want something with you." Hearing his confession makes my heart sink because, in an alternative world, I'd love nothing more than to be with this man, but unfortunately, we just can't.

"There's a reason why I left London and came to LA. This job offer came at the best time for me." I play with the label on my bottle. Camryn and Sienna, my two closest girlfriends, are the only ones who know the reason why I left London, and now, Christian will too. I just hope it doesn't make him change his opinion of me.

"I worked for this indie record label in London. I loved it. It was the best job in the world. The owner was this young, hot guy, and all the girls in the office had a crush on him. Yeah, I thought he was cute, but there were heaps of cute guys in London to hook up with, I didn't need to go after the boss."

I chance a glance at Christian, he smiles and urges me to continue. "We had to work on a project together, and I got to know him better, and long story short, we started seeing each other." My heart is racing, and I think I'm going to be sick. "But what I didn't know was that he was married."

"Oh," Christian comments.

"Yeah, oh. I found out he was married when we were working late one night, and his wife surprised him at work. She caught us screwing on his desk."

"Shit, Ness. I'm sorry."

Shaking my head, I continue, "She screamed at him that she couldn't believe he was still screwing around with all these desperate interns. The month before, she had caught him with someone else in the office. She called me a whore and told me that she was going to ruin me. I was obviously the straw that broke the camel's back." Christian squeezes my hand. "And she kept her word. Apparently, she came from a very wealthy family, and he had used her daddy's money to start up the label. He couldn't lose everything he built, so he let her destroy me. She made a scene in the middle of the office telling everyone, even clients, that the only reason I made it so far was because I was sleeping with people to get ahead."

"Tell me they didn't believe her? You're brilliant at what you do."

"Most of the girls in the office were worried about their jobs because most had apparently slept with him. So, I was the scapegoat. What really did it for me was when I was invited to a meeting late one night for a big client. I arrived, and it was a room full of men and my boss. He told them that a perk of owning his own label was the access to sweet pussy and what women like me would do to further their careers." Christian's hand tightens around mine. "He told me I needed to get on my knees and suck them all off if I wanted to keep my job at the label and if I wanted him to get his wife to back off."

"What the fuck! That fucker, if I find out who he is, I'm going to fucking kill him, you hear me." Looking at how angry Christian looked made me feel good. I just wished I had people like that around me in London.

"He's nothing, forget him. I have."

"But Ness, you're amazing at your job. What you have done for us so far after a couple of months has been more than our old label did for us in years. You are fucking awesome." Christian's praise makes me smile.

"Thank you. That means a lot. And just for the record, I picked up the jug of water on the conference table and dumped it over my old boss' head and told him to shove his job and his pin dick up his ass before I walked out and never looked back. So that's how I ended up in LA."

"Nice."

"Now you understand why I can't do anything with you." Christian's eyes look at the floor.

"Yeah, Ness, I understand. It sucks because I like you, but I understand." He doesn't look at me. My hand reaches for his chin to tip it up so he can look at me, those whiskey-colored eyes sparkling.

"I wish things could be different, Chris, I want you to know that." He smiles at me. I lean forwarded and lightly kiss his lips. "Can we still be friends?" I ask.

"Yeah, Ness. I'd like that. If that's the only way I can have you, then I think I can handle that." My phone buzzes. Camryn is downstairs. Jumping up from the couch, I head toward the door.

"Ness," Christian calls out. I turn around and look at him. "If you ever leave Montgomery Records or are no longer our PR Manager, then I'm coming for you. Just so you know, you've been warned." The look he gives me is heated. Nodding my head, I sneak out the door.

7

CHRISTIAN

THREE YEARS LATER

"Welcome, boys," Nate Lewis greets Axel and me at The Paradise Club.

"We thought you were in Europe?" Axel questions him.

"Yeah, just back and doing a quick run over the clubs. Hopefully, I'll see you two at the opening in Monaco next month."

"Maybe we can arrange a quick trip over there," Axel says with a smile. The Paradise Club is an exclusive sex club for celebrities, the rich and famous, and anyone who's a VIP and can be harmed by the press finding out about their extracurricular activities. Nathaniel Lewis is the king of the domain. He has opened exclusive clubs around the world, and my brother and I always try to make it to an opening, since they're pretty legendary.

"Well, have fun tonight, boys," Nate encourages, clapping us on the back as he walks off into the darkness.

"What are you up for tonight?" Axel asks. My brother has particular tastes when it comes to sex. He's into domination and kink, whereas I'm just down for sex—hot, hot sex with a beautiful woman or two or three.

"Might check out the voyeur room. It's always a good place to warm up." He nods and follows me toward the large glass wall that looks into a room that basically has one large bed. Sometimes it has a couple of people in it, but other times, it can have a full orgy going on. People like to congregate around and watch, sometimes that leads to people fucking up against the window. It's hot.

It looks like tonight there's an orgy going on. The room is full of beautiful women and only a couple of men. Axel and I watch for a couple of moments, my eyes landing on a hot brunette going down on some blonde while a big hairy man pounds her from behind. Nice. Girl-on-girl action always gets my dick twitching.

"Shit. Is that Kane?" Axel nudges me.

Looking at the man who currently has a blonde riding him while eating out a brunette, I shake my head. I must be seeing things, but I swear I see his football tattoo on his arm. I've been looking at that ugly tattoo for the past two years since he started dating Vanessa. He's a grade-A douchebag, but Ness seems happy, so I put up with him.

"No, there's no way in the world that's him, is it?" Shaking my head, Axel and I stare for a little longer, trying to work it out. The brunette moves off his face and toward another man, and that's when I see red.

"Chris, don't." Axel grabs me. My eyes watch as Kane keeps fucking the blonde, his hand playing with some other chick's tits.

"I'm going to fucking kill him," I growl.

"Yeah, and you will get us kicked out of here," he whisper-yells at me.

"I don't fucking care! He's cheating on Ness. Our Ness. Don't you fucking care?" Axel pulls me away from the voyeurs watching as we're definitely ruining their vibe with our fighting. He pulls me out past security, out of the building, and back into the dark alleyway. When he finally lets me go, I kick a trash can over.

"Calm the fuck down!" he yells at me.

"Fuck you! Ness is our friend, and you don't give a shit." Grabbing my brother by his collar, I push him up against the brick wall and get up in his face.

"Of course, I give a shit, but I don't think we should make a scene."

Letting go of his shirt, I pace the dark alley. "I have to tell her, Axe."

"I know, man, but she loves him," my brother reminds me. My stomach sinks at the thought that Vanessa is in love with this fucker. "I don't want to break her heart," he adds. Leaning back against the wall, we both stare into the darkness for a while.

"She needs to know that he isn't the man he says he is. How many times has he done this to her? He doesn't deserve her."

"Do you want to tell her because it's the right thing to do, or do you want to tell her so she's single again, and you might have a chance?"

I stiffen. "Fuck you." I push off the wall and start pacing. "How the fuck could you say that to me?"

"Sorry, I just know you have feelings for her."

"We're friends, I told you that." It didn't take long for Axel to work out who the mystery girl was every time we were around each other.

"Yeah, I know, but I also see the chemistry between the two of you."

"Hey, I make sure I don't flirt with her. She has a boyfriend."

"Chris, I'm not saying you flirt with her. I'm saying that you guys get along really well. It's nice seeing you two together, that's all."

"So, you're saying I shouldn't tell her, let her think this dude is trustworthy?"

Axel shakes his head. "She might not believe you, so..." He trails off.

Shit, what happens if she doesn't believe me? I have no evidence because no phones or cameras are allowed in the club. I just have to trust in our friendship that she does.

"Hey," Vanessa greets me, bouncing through my front door. She has her own key. It's easier as she's always here, anyway. "It sounded serious on the phone. Please don't tell me I'm going to have to do damage control because of last night?" Her green eyes look at me.

"No, no, I was pretty tame last night." I give her a weak smile as I kiss her cheeks.

"Then what's the matter? What's so important that you needed to see me so early on a Sunday?" We sit down on the large couch in my living room that looks out over the pool, down the valley, and over downtown LA. The view is spectacular, but at the moment, it makes me feel sick.

"So, well... um." Fuck, I'm nervous. "Last night, Axel and I went out to this club." Vanessa nods, following the story so far. "It's a special kind of club," I add.

Vanessa frowns. "What, like a night club?" I shake my head before I answer her.

"No, more... um... exclusive and set up for... um... you know..." Why am I embarrassed to tell her about it?

"What, like a sex club?"

"Yeah. It's basically set up for VIPs to have uninhibited fun without the paparazzi finding out or people selling stories to the media."

Vanessa smiles. "Cool. I'm glad you have somewhere you

can go and relax. It sounds like fun. If I were single, I'd totally be there checking it out with you." She giggles at me, and the sound hits my dick, making it twitch to life. Fuck, I had no idea Vanessa would be interested in something like that. "And, I get it, especially after the couple of disasters we have had recently with the paparazzi," she tells me, giving me the 'mom' look.

"Yeah, yeah, I know, that's why this club is great. I can get my rocks off without creating a headache for you."

Vanessa laughs. "I love how considerate you are, Christian."

"But, I saw something last night, and you need to know about it." My stomach sinks now that I've started the conversation.

"Why?" she asks.

"I saw Kane there." I think I'm going to be sick.

"Kane? No, you have to be wrong. He's away on some football thing." I can see the frown lines marring her forehead.

"No, Ness, Axel and I were both sure it was him. I saw his tattoo."

Ness stills for a moment. "What was he doing?"

Shit, I don't want to tell her what he was doing. Fuck, she doesn't need to know that. "He was with a couple of women." I can see the information hit her, and slowly the realization sinks in.

"You're wrong, you have to be wrong." Tears start to flow as she hits me with her hands. Fuck, I hate it when she cries. Pulling her against me, I wrap my arms around her.

"I wouldn't be telling you this, Ness, if I wasn't one hundred percent sure it was him. He cheated on you, and from what I've found out from the club, he has been a member for the past three years and frequents the club a lot."

She lets out a sob, her whole body is shaking with tears, and she cuddles into me. "I'm sorry, Ness. I'm so, so sorry. He doesn't deserve you, that fucker doesn't deserve a beautiful, wonderful, caring, hot, sexy woman like you." I comfort her by stroking her hair. Vanessa is silent for a long time with intermittent sniffling.

"Are you sure, Chris? Like really sure." Her bloodshot eyes stare at me.

"Yeah, babe, I am."

"Fuck, how could I be so fucking stupid?"

"No, he's the stupid one. Who the fuck cheats on someone like you?" Looking down at her, my heart breaks. She looks so lost and fragile, not like the strong, confident, ball-breaking Nessa I know.

"I guess I just wasn't enough for him."

Grabbing her face in my palms, I look into her eyes. "Never. You're more than enough for a real man to handle. He's nothing but a low-life punk who doesn't realize the incredible gift he has in front of him."

Her lips touch mine in the barest of kisses. "Thank you, Christian." My heart is racing because here she is wrapped in my arms, and all my dick can think about is burying itself so deep inside of her, hoping to make sure she forgets about her loser boyfriend. But that's not what I do. Instead, I pull her tighter against me and hold her because that's all I can ever do.

"Can I stay here with you? I just..." She hiccups on her tears.

"Of course, you can, you know I'd do anything for you," I whisper, kissing her forehead. That's where we stay for the rest of the day—sitting on my couch watching movies, eating ice cream, and pigging out on popcorn. Vanessa's phone keeps ringing. It's Kane, and she ignores every one of his calls and a million and one texts, which makes me happy.

"What does he want?" I ask because curiosity is getting the better of me.

"I don't know. Here, you read them." She hands me her phone. There are heaps of messages from him asking where she is and who she's with. He told her he was working hard and even took selfies of himself training. This is bullshit, the fucking lying bastard.

"He wants to visit you tomorrow, seeing as he's passing through town back to San Diego. What do you want me to say?"

"Fine, tell him I'll see him back at my place tomorrow." Vanessa is emotionless as she watches some old black and white movie.

"Want me to come for moral support?" Looking at me, she gives me a weak smile.

"No, I can do this. It will be easier if you're not there. You two don't get along as it is, adding this on top of it will just fuel the fire."

Yeah, Kane and I most definitely aren't friends.

8

CHRISTIAN

"Chill out, man, it's going to be okay," Evan says as we work out in my studio.

"I'm just worried about her," I tell him. The boys see that Vanessa and I get along quite well, they used to rib me for it, but they can see the genuine friendship that's grown between us over the years.

"She'll call if she needs you," Axel reminds me. I just hope Kane doesn't convince her that it's not true or ask her to forgive him. Not sure how I'll react if that's the way she's going to go.

A couple of hours later, we're in the swing of things at my home studio when my phone starts ringing. Jumping up, I answer it.

"Hello."

"Christian." It's Camryn, and she's crying.

"Nessa... is Nessa okay?" My heart is racing. I know something's happened.

"No, she's in the hospital. I found her unconscious on the floor. Kane hurt her. There was so much blood." Camryn bursts out crying again. What the fuck?

"Text me the information, I'm on my way," I yell at her before hanging up.

"I'm going to fucking murder that son of a bitch!" I scream, racing for the door.

"Dude, what happened?" Oscar asks.

Nearly pulling my hair out with stress, I yell, "That fucker, that fucking piece of shit touched Ness. He put his fucking hands on her. Camryn found her unconscious, and she's in the hospital." The rest of the boys jump up from their places in the studio when I say hospital.

"I'll call Isla, get her to organize a car," Finn says, running off to find our assistant.

"That fucker," Axel growls, punching the wall.

It wasn't long before we arrive at the hospital and find Camryn in the waiting room, looking pale. Her blue eyes widening when she sees us, she launches herself off the black plastic chair into my arms.

"I'm sorry I wasn't there, Chris. She told me she needed space. I should've fucking been there." The poor thing is shaking like a leaf as uncontrollable tears run down her face.

"Can I see her?" I ask Camryn because I need to see her.

"Yeah, but she's heavily sedated. She's going to be okay. Thankfully, there was no internal bleeding, just a lot of bruising and swelling."

Camryn holds my hand as she takes me into the hospital room. The loud beeping of the machines fills the room. There Vanessa is lying helpless on the bed, her caramel hair fanned out behind her head, her green eyes that usually sparkle are closed. There's bruising all over her face. Her lush, pink lips have dried blood still on them.

"I'm going to fucking kill him. How the fuck could he do this to her?" My hands are balled into fists, my entire body shaking with anger.

"I introduced them, Chris. I'm the one who brought this

monster into her life." Camryn starts crying again. Pulling her into my arms, I try to comfort her.

"You didn't know."

"I broke up with Lance over this." This is surprising since she has been with him for the past couple of years. She hiccups on a sob. "That bastard stuck up for his friend and told me maybe Vanessa provoked Kane because she's known to be a bitch. That Kane was sick of her nagging and her workaholic nature, she never had time for him, and he needed a woman to satisfy him instead of breaking his balls all the time. That's when I realized Lance probably frequented that club as well with Kane. Then it sunk in that Lance was cheating on me also, which he was."

Fuck, what a bunch of fucktards. Who the hell cheats on these beautiful women? Seriously, I'm ready to give them both an ass whipping. I don't care that they are fucking football players, I can take them on.

"Forget them. Those bastards aren't real men. You deserve better. Vanessa deserves better."

Camryn turns to me, her bright blue eyes glimmering with unshed tears, "She only dated him to get over you."

Huh, I'm confused.

"Don't forget I was there the first night you two met. I also have lived with Ness over the last couple of years. You two have a connection. I know it hurts her seeing you with other women, and I'm sure you don't like seeing her with other men."

I shake my head, I'm not going to deny it.

"She wanted to move on. Obviously, you two can't be together while she's working at the label, and I know she loves her job and wouldn't give it up for anything. It just sucks because I think the two of you together would be amazing."

"It's not our time, Cammie. One day it will be, but we're not ready for it yet. Until then, we just have to be friends." Camryn lets out a big sigh.

"Well, don't wait too long, Chris, because someone else might come along and sweep her off her feet, and you will be left watching from the sideline again."

Kissing me on the cheek, Camryn walks toward Nessa, whispers something to her, then kisses her forehead. She walks out of the room, leaving the two of us alone before the police arrive.

9

VANESSA

I'm trying to open my eyes, but they are heavy, the darkness keeps pulling me under. I am too weak to fight it. Bits and pieces of grainy images filter through the darkness but not enough for me to understand them. Something touches my hand, but I'm paralyzed to move it. Why the hell does my brain not work? I don't know what's happening.

"Why did you do it?" My question hangs in the air.

"I was doing you a favor. You don't have time to fuck me, Ness. You're always too busy with those fucking rock stars to service your boyfriend," Kane spits at me, his face has gone red. I don't understand why he's upset at me, I'm not the one cheating.

"Are you fucking serious? I love my job. I'm damn good at my job. If you wanted a trophy wife, you should've chosen one of those bimbos who are continuously hanging around you. I'm sure they would love nothing more than to stay at home waiting for you to walk through the door ready and willing to suck your dick. I'm not apologizing for my job." My body is shaking with anger.

"You know why those women happily service my dick? Because that's what they are there for, and that is all they are good enough for. They are stress relief. That's why I'm with you. I can't marry any of those sluts," Kane splutters.

"Seriously, they are good enough to suck your dick but not good enough to marry? And I thought rock stars were bad." I shake my head in disbelief. Kane is a fucking pig. How the hell did I fall for him? I must have been drunk or on drugs. Kane stalks toward me, getting right up in my face. My heart is racing because I can feel the aggression pouring off him in waves. He's scaring me.

"I bet you happily suck those rock stars' cocks? That's why you're too tired for me because you spend your days fucking them, don't you?" Poking me hard in my chest, he sends me back into the wall. Fuck, that's going to bruise in the morning.

"Fuck you. I'm a fucking professional," I spit back, Kane's words reminding me of that bitch in London, flashbacks from a time I'd rather forget. Kane grabs me and starts shaking me violently.

"You're a fucking slut, aren't you? I know you've fucked them. Tell me, you stupid bitch." My head is shaken back and forth like a damn rag doll. I can't catch my breath as I'm in shock. I've never seen him like this before. Finally, he stops shaking me, but I don't think he's done yet. His large hand wraps around my throat, squeezing it tight. "Tell me, Vanessa, have you fucked any of them?" I could see the fire in his eyes. His fingers keep squeezing harder, slowly cutting off my air, and the room starts to spin. Then a sharp pain creeps across my face. I blink a couple of times, trying to focus. Fuck, Kane just slapped me across the face, so I wouldn't pass out.

What's he doing?

I thought Kane loved me?

Shit, what the hell is he going to do to me?

"Answer me, you stupid slut, have you fucked any of those guys?" Spit hits my face as he screams at me.

"Yes," I squeak out. I want to hurt him, but I also want him to stop.

"What the fuck did you say?" He lets go of my throat so that I can speak. Kane takes a step back, watching me.

"Yes, I have, and you know what, every single time I was with you, I wished it was him." *Fuck you, you fucking cunt*, I scream in my head. I reach for my throat to rub it as it starts to throb from where he had gripped me. Kane looks calm as his face turns to stone, his entire body stills.

"Which one?" he asks calmly.

"Does it matter?" I throwback, pushing myself away from the wall that he had me pinned against. I make my way back to the kitchen under the guise of grabbing a glass of water, but I'm looking for a weapon.

"Yeah, it does, humor me, Ness." I frown at his request.

"It was Christian, I met him the same night I met you." The vein on Kane's forehead starts to throb, and he cracks his neck to each side. My heart starts to race. *Fuck, what have I done? You never poke the beast, Ness. So fucking stupid. But I wanted him to hurt just the same way he hurt me.*

"Christian? The same Christian you spend all your fucking time with? The same Christian who you travel with? Your best friend, Christian?"

Putting the kitchen island between us, my eyes dart around the kitchen looking for something to protect myself with in case Kane blows up again. I see something change in Kane's eyes before he launches at me. He's too fucking quick, and I get a couple of steps away before he's on me, tackling me to the ground.

"You fucking bitch, you're nothing but a goddamn slut! You are no better than those whores who suck my dick," he snarls.

His hands are all over me as he grabs at my pants, trying to get them down my hips. I try my best to kick, punch, and scratch him to defend myself.

"Get off me. Get your fucking hands off me!" I scream, tears filling my eyes. *Who the hell is this man? Why is he doing this to me? I thought he loved me.*

"You give up your pussy so easily for everyone else, why not me?" His hand breaches my panties as his fingers thrust into me. "I am *going to fuck you until all you can think about is me. I'm going to wipe Christian from your mind."*

I twist in his arms as he's distracted for a second, trying to finger me again. I punch him hard in the face making him drop his hand. Thankfully, shock registers on him, allowing me time to scurry away.

"You fucking bitch, you're going to pay for that." I bolt through the house, trying to get to the front door, but he's so fast, tackling me again, my head hitting the floor hard, stunning me. Then I feel his fist in my face. Fuck, I think I see stars. I swear he just broke my nose, maybe my jaw.

"How fucking dare you disrespect me like that!" Kane screams into my ear.

I flinch as the roar rocks through me. He's so loud and menacing that the sound of his voice rattles my bones—another fist, this time to the stomach, making me curl up into a fetal position. I can only hope it will help to protect me from his onslaught. The fists keep coming one after another until I pass out, and the darkness swallows me up.

I embrace it.

"Ness, can you hear me? Wake up, please. I need you. I miss you." *I know that voice. I could pick that voice out anywhere. Christian! Why can't I talk? I don't understand. I try to move my hand but nothing, so I try and move my fingers, and slowly they wiggle.*

"Ness, Ness. Nurse, she's waking up." *I hear footsteps run into the distance. Where am I?*

"Baby, come back to me, please." *Lips whisper against my ear. Using all my strength, I try really hard to move my body, but nothing happens. I focus on just trying to open my eyes, bit by bit. I can feel them twitch until I see a sliver of light trickling in. More light appears as my eyes try to focus, but I can't see anything.*

"Welcome back, Miss Roberts," *a female voice says.* "Take

your time, you have been out of it for a while. Don't try and push yourself."

Finally, the room comes into focus. I can hear the beeping of a machine in the distance, a bright fluorescent light shining in my eyes. My whole body aches. What the hell happened to me? Turning my head, I see Christian standing beside me. He looks pale, and I notice the bags under his eyes. He doesn't look well at all. He smirks at me as he catches me looking at him.

"Thank God, you're awake." He rubs his hand against mine.

"What?" I try to speak, but my throat is all scratchy.

"Here, sweetheart, take a sip of this," the nurse instructs, giving me a straw as I take a sip of water from the bottle she's holding. "That might make it better. You will find it hard to talk for a while as your throat is bruised." Why is it bruised?

"Do you know why you're in the hospital, Ness?" Christian asks me, and I shake my head. His whiskey-colored eyes look at the nurse. He looks worried.

"There's been no brain damage, Mr. Taylor. She might just be a little groggy from the drugs." Nodding at the nurse, his eyes turn back to me.

"Kane attacked you." My body tenses, and the machine starts to beep louder and faster as I remember exactly what happened. No, no, no.

"V, calm down, it's okay. I'm here. I've got you, you're safe," Christian says, pulling himself up onto my bed's side, wrapping me in his arms, protecting me as my tears start to flow.

How the hell did I let myself get into this position?

"Babe, the police are here, and they want to talk to you?" Christian wakes me from my nap. As the two young police officers come in, I sit up in my bed, their eyes widening as they see

Christian and Axel from Dirty Texas sitting with me in the hospital.

"Miss Roberts, we're here to interview you regarding your injuries," one of the officers says.

"Thank you, I appreciate you coming down, but I won't be pressing charges. Nothing happened." The two officers stare at me with a blank look on their faces.

"What do you mean you're not pressing charges? That fucker deserves to pay for what he did to you, Vanessa," Christian angrily protests. Ignoring the pissed-off rocker, I look to the officers.

"I'm sorry, but I won't be making a statement."

The other officer speaks, "We can help you, miss. You don't have to be afraid of him anymore." His kind, brown eyes look at me. He can see the injuries that have turned a lovely deep purple over my body.

"You can't help me. The man who did this is too high-profiled. He'll never come to justice, and he has vowed to ruin my life. I have too much to lose. I just can't. No one will believe me, he's a fucking god in people's eyes."

Tears threaten because it's the truth. No one would believe Kane Bennett hits women. He's a football star who wins Super Bowl rings, donates to charities, and feeds the homeless. No one would ever believe me.

"Ness, he can't get away with this." Christian looks at me with pain in his eyes.

"I'm sorry, Chris, I just can't." I turn my face away from him because I can't look at his disappointment anymore.

"Chris, just leave it," Axel says, comforting his brother.

"Miss, here is my card. If you ever need to talk, please give me a call," the officer with the kind eyes offers as he leaves the card on my bed. A few moments later, they walk out the door.

"I'm sorry, Chris, I just can't. It would be a PR nightmare for you and the label. The paparazzi and the media would have a field day with this. It would follow me around forever. I just can't." My tears start to flow again.

Christian pulls me into his arms, "Shh, babe, don't cry. I'm sorry, we don't have to do anything. I just want to protect you, okay?" Looking up into his eyes, I can see how much Christian is hurting by all of this.

"I don't want to let you down, Chris. I know I should report him, so it doesn't happen to anyone else. I know this, but I just can't."

Christian wraps himself around me. "I love you, Ness, and I'll support you with whatever decision you make." Christian loves me. My heart feels like it's going to burst.

"Shit, never thought I'd see the day my brother pronounced his love for another woman other than Mom," Axel jokes.

"Fuck off, dickhead, thanks for ruining the moment," Christian curses at him. Axel walks out of the room, flipping his brother off.

"I do love you, Ness, you're my best friend. I don't have any female friends because... well, you know... my incredibly good looks and huge dick always get in the way." This makes me laugh.

"But you're special. We just click. Seeing you in here, thinking I'd lost you, it drove me crazy. I realized I'd never told you how I feel, that you're as close to me as Axel and the rest of my family are. As much as I want to bone you every day because, let's face it, we're both fucking hot, I understand we can't. Fuck, I still jerk off thinking about that weekend we had together all those years ago." This shocks me, but it makes me smile.

"What I want even more than that is your friendship. I love hanging out with you doing boring shit like cooking dinner or hanging out at the beach. I love that I'm the person you call when your car isn't working or need a tap fixed in your house. So, if the only way I can keep you in my life forever is to have you as my best friend, then I'm okay with that."

Leaning over, I kiss Christian on the lips. It's supposed to be just a small one, but his words kind of struck me, and before I know it, we're making out. "Fuck, Ness," he whispers, resting his forehead against mine.

"I love you, too, Chris, and I agree sex complicates things. Honestly, I don't want to lose you. I love having you around even if you're annoying as shit."

"Yeah, but you love it," he says, giving me a mischievous smile.

"Yeah, I kind of do. Thank you for hanging around over the past couple of days at the hospital." Christian looks a little embarrassed by my compliment.

"It's what friends do."

10

CHRISTIAN

"Home sweet home." Camryn smiles, opening the door for Vanessa, who's tense in my arms. Walking through her home's doors after what she experienced here is tough, but Camryn and I have redecorated the space. We rearranged the room that Kane destroyed. We purchased new furniture, repositioned things around the room so that when Vanessa sat down to watch television, she didn't have to relive the horror that happened here.

"It looks different," Vanessa says, taking in the new look of the home.

"Yeah, Christian and I did some redecorating. Hope you like it." Camryn sounded like a perky cheerleader, but I know she's just nervous about today. Vanessa's eyes look around the room, and she smiles at us.

"Looks nice. I'm just going to go lie down for a while, I'm tired," she says as she walks toward her bedroom. Once she has gone, I turn to Camryn.

"Fuck, do you think she's okay?"

"It's an adjustment coming back here. I guess it will take time."

"Should I check on her? That woman standing here earlier with us isn't our Ness."

"I hate being in this house because of what happened, I can't imagine how she feels. Yeah, I'd check on her even though I know she'll hide whatever is going on in her head."

Maybe it's a mistake bringing her back here. I should've taken her back to my place. I walk down the hall to Vanessa's room. Lightly knocking on her door, I announce, "Ness, it's me."

A mumbled, "Come in," filters through the door. Opening the door, I find Vanessa curled up in a ball crying into her pillow. I race over to her, pulling her onto my lap, rocking her as her entire body shakes.

"I can't stay here, Chris. I can feel him all around me." She's shaking like a leaf.

"Angel, you don't have to stay here. Come live with me. I can move all your stuff to my place, and you can stay with me for however long you want or even forever, I don't care."

Her green eyes look at me. "You're a good man, Chris."

"Shh, don't tell anyone. I don't want them to know, it will ruin my reputation." Vanessa gives me a weak smile. "Come on, pack a bag. I can get Isla to organize the rest of your shit. We can be roomies," I joke, hoping to put her at ease.

"Thank you," she says, wrapping her arms around my neck.

"I can't believe you and Vanessa are still roommates. I thought she'd have moved out running and screaming after a week." Axel laughs as we head toward the studio to wait for the other boys to join us.

Vanessa has been living with me for the past couple of months, and it's been great. Well, for me, anyway. It's nice having someone else to knock around the house with. Being a twin sucks because you're always so used to having someone with you, but there's no way in hell I could live with that fucker anymore. It's hard enough working with him.

"She's not much of a cook, which sucks because I thought all women could cook." Axel chokes on his beer.

"Seriously, man, how the fuck are we related. I can't believe some of the shit that comes out of your mouth sometimes." I flip him the bird. Eventually, the rest of the boys join us, and we start the jam session in my studio.

There's a knock on the door, and Vanessa enters the room. The boys all say hello.

"Christian, do you have to leave your strays around the house because I just found a naked woman in the fucking pool?" My eyes widen. Shit, I thought I got rid of her this morning. How the fuck did she get back in?

"Y'all, I've got to go see this." Evan laughs and runs out the door. I can see Vanessa isn't impressed, and I feel bad because she doesn't need to see my conquests naked in the pool.

"Sorry, angel, I thought I got rid of her." Vanessa just shakes her head at me.

"Next time, make sure Sammy escorts them out of the house. You don't know what these women can do. They could be stalkers, they could be press, they could go through your shit and sell it on eBay."

She's right, it was fucking stupid. Jumping off my chair, I head out to the pool to deal with my situation. I find the blonde doing laps in the pool as if she belongs here. Who does that after a one-night stand? I walk over to where she's trying to catch my attention.

"Hey, darlin', um... whatcha doin'? Her chocolate eyes look up at me, then behind me when she realizes she has an audience.

"I was just cooling down, waiting for you to finish, so we could continue again." My eyes dip down to her naked breasts in the pool. She was a very enthusiastic lover, bendy as well.

She's a dancer, not a stripper, as she likes to point out. Even though her job requires dancing in a club on a pole, she's an entertainer.

"Well, darlin', I'm kind of busy. I explained that this morning when we said goodbye, and I thought you understood." I feel someone beside me. Sammy, his stony face, not giving anything away except the twitch on his cheek's side as he tries to hold back a smile.

"You're really kicking me out?" Her cheeks glow red, looking at the stony-faced Samoan bodyguard. She swims toward the steps, pulling herself out of the water, her amazing body on display as she grabs a towel to wrap around herself.

"Sorry, it was fun while it lasted." Really what else could I say?

"But we're meant to be together, Christian. You told me last night I was the best you ever had." The boys behind me snigger as Sammy escorts her out. "You're making a mistake, Christian. I'll let you stick it in my ass next time… please." Her declaration makes everyone laugh.

"Seriously, Christian, how could you turn that offer down?" Vanessa questions. I shoot them all the bird as I walk away from the commotion.

Fucking groupies.

11

VANESSA
A YEAR LATER

"Derrick," I greet, answering my phone. I look at the time as it has to be early in Australia. It's the night of Sienna's thirtieth birthday party. They're probably drunk-dialing me, letting me know how much fun they are having without me while I'm stuck touring with the boys. These boys have been grumpy as fuck lately, the never-ending traveling is wearing them all down.

The constant paparazzi, the fans, the microscopic attention is full-on. Once the boys finish this American tour, they only have the European tour to go before their Montgomery Records' contract ends. Hopefully, they can move onto bigger and better things, whatever that may be. While I'm sad about our time ending as I've been devoted to these boys for the past four years, it will be fun to start working with a new band.

"V, something's happened." Derrick's voice cuts through my daydream. Shit, he doesn't sound right.

"What happened? Is everyone okay?" I can feel the panic rising through my body.

"Si just busted Beau with another woman."

I drop my phone. Shit! "Sorry, D, are you still there?" I ask, picking it up off the floor. No way, there's no way in the world what he just said is real. "Are you joking right now?" Derrick is a trickster, but this is low if he's drunk-dialing me with some kind of bullshit.

"Fuck no, I wouldn't joke about something like this. It was with Diana. Beau's been fucking around with Diana," Derrick yells down the phone. Of all the people Beau could cheat with, it had to be his high school ex-girlfriend. During Sienna's entire marriage, she has had to compete with that woman. Beau's parents always wanted Diana to be his wife. He's a fucking bastard.

"I'm going to fucking kill him, D."

"Well, I almost did. We got into a fight, but it felt so good punching the son of a bitch in the face." Derrick laughs, he's such a loyal friend. I wish I could be there with her.

"Good on ya, D. I'm high-fiving you through the phone. How is she?"

There's silence on the other end of the phone, and I pull it away from my ear to check if he's still there. He is.

"I think it's really going to hit her tomorrow. She told Beau to fuck off when he came running after her, telling her it was a mistake, but she wouldn't listen. Then when she found out the woman was Diana, she lost it. There's no way she'll take him back after this."

"I wish I were there, but I can't get away," I groan into the phone, feeling totally helpless. Maybe I could get there for Christmas while the boys have a break. There's a knock at my hotel room door. "D, I have to go. Keep me posted, okay?" He agrees, and I hang up.

"Come in," I call out, and in walks my assistant, Sarah.

"Ness, um... we have a problem." She hands over her tablet to me, the black and white article blinking in my face. It takes me a moment to realize what I am looking at. Of course, this would happen now. I'm going to fucking kill them.

"What the hell is this?" I yell, shaking the tablet at the Dirty Texas boys. They are all looking at me bleary-eyed after I woke them up. I'm greeted by silence. Yeah, I'm ready to castrate each of them with the mood I am in now.

"How many fucking times do I tell you boys to be vigilant of your surroundings?"

"Queen V, I'm sorry, but how was I supposed to know that there'd be cameras in the VIP section of the club?" Christian smiles, and I hate that even after all these years, the way he looks at me still has some effect.

"You shouldn't be having your dick sucked in the middle of a club, Christian." It doesn't get any easier after all these years seeing him with other girls.

"If you helped a brother out, I wouldn't have to find groupies to do it. Which means I wouldn't get myself into trouble all the time. See, win-win, V." Christian laughs.

Rolling my eyes, I say, "Seriously, Christian, I'm surprised your dick hasn't fallen off from any diseases… it's a fucking miracle."

I hide my feelings through sarcasm, especially where Christian is concerned. It sucks having feelings for your best friend. It sucks watching him get blow jobs under a table in the middle of a club. It sucks that I want to take up his offer to help him out. Goddamn stupid morals, they genuinely suck sometimes.

"Just because you're Dirty Texas doesn't mean you can keep getting away with this shit." I shake the tablet in my hand again. I'm over this bullshit as I begin to pace around the living room of the suite. "Do you guys realize how much work it takes looking after you?" They stay silent—typical males.

"Cleaning up the same shit every day. Repeating it over and over." God, Ness, don't crack now. I try to hold all my anger in, but it doesn't work as I feel my eyes begin to water. Not in front of the boys, I think to myself. "You're not twenty-year-olds anymore. You can't keep doing this immature shit.

People are getting sick of it, namely me." I can feel myself begin to crack.

"V, are you okay?" Axel asks, his whiskey-colored eyes reminding me so much of his brother's. His question breaks me, and the floodgates open as tears run down my face. Shit, I never cry and mostly never in front of the boys. Embarrassed, I rush out of the room away from five pairs of freaked-out eyes.

I feel better after Evan came in and checked on me. The poor guy looks like he wanted to be anywhere else rather than dealing with a teary-eyed woman. I did notice his interest piqued when I showed him photos of Sienna. It would totally make her day knowing Evan Wyld checked her out. She's always had a crush on him. There's a knock at the door.

"Come in," I call out.

"Hey, I heard what happened, are you okay?" Christian asks, walking toward me.

"Yeah, poor Evan, he copped most of it." I give him a weak smile.

"That guy sucks at rock, paper, scissors." This makes me laugh as Christian sits down beside me on the couch.

"Evan says you want to go home for Christmas." I nod, it's the truth. Sienna is like a sister to me, and I need to be there for her.

"That sounds like a good idea, but it's going to suck not spending Christmas with you this year. You know Mom and Dad are going to be disappointed that they missed you."

Over the years, I've spent Thanksgiving or Christmas with the Taylor family, seeing as mine live thousands of miles away. I love Christian's family—they are so amazing and welcomed me with open arms. His mom confessed that I was the first girl either of the boys had brought home, so she was excited, even if it was only a friend. Viv is so lovely. Anytime she's in LA, we always spend the day shopping up a storm.

"I know, I'll miss them, too, but I can't wait to go back home. It's been too long."

"So, how's your friend doing?"

"Not sure yet. I spoke to Derrick, he's one of our friends she's crashing with. I guess I'll hear from her in a couple of hours when she wakes up." Christian's whiskey-colored eyes sparkle at me.

"You know I'm here for you," he states, putting his arm around my shoulders and pulling me into his side. "If you need to talk or anything, I'm here." He places a kiss on my head. "I promise I'll stop doing stupid shit, so I don't add to your stress, okay?"

Looking up at him, I reply, "You should stop doing it for yourself as well. When you eventually find the right woman, she's going to have your past conquests thrown in her face at every turn."

"Who's to say I haven't already met the right woman?" he says, giving me a cheeky smile. I can feel my heart start to race with the way Christian is looking at me.

"I'm talking about someone to marry, to have babies with, to do all those things."

He rolls his eyes at me. "Why can't we do all those things?"

"You can't tell me you're ready to settle down, to give up everything for one woman?"

He just shrugs. "Maybe."

I have to laugh because, in all honesty, I don't believe him. I meant last night he was getting his dick sucked by groupies under the table. He's so not ready for commitment.

"How about we revisit this conversation when we are thirty-five? If we're both still exactly where we are now, why don't you and I have a baby together?"

Has Christian been drinking the crazy Kool-Aid? Babies together? I'm in shock.

"V, just think about it. My parents aren't getting any

younger, and I want to give them grandbabies. They deserve it. I don't want some random who I have to put up with for the rest of my life. You're the only choice, you're already part of my family, and I know I can trust you. I know you're not after my money, you wouldn't sell me out to the press, plus we already live together." Maybe I'm high because Christian is making sense.

"But…" I have no words.

"We have five-plus years till we reach thirty-five. Who knows, maybe you'll find some hotshot, fall in love, and leave me behind." Rolling my eyes at him, I doubt his statement to be true.

"I'm not looking for love, you know that. After Kane, I can't ever trust myself to fall in love with someone ever again."

Christian tenses when I mention Kane's name. He eventually got put away for his crime a couple of years later. The paparazzi caught him hitting his new wife while on their honeymoon. It blew up into a major scandal. Sponsors dropped him, the team dropped him, and the evidence was crystal clear. The images splattered all over the media were unmistakable.

It wasn't long after that exposure that a couple of ex-girlfriends came out saying they too had been hit by him. That's when I also finally stood up. I gave my statement with the support of the band and the label. Seeing him again was hard, but I told my story, and even though the court case gave me closure, I still feel like I can't trust my instincts when it comes to men.

"I wish I could've taught that motherfucker a lesson," Christian growls. I rub his arm in comfort because I know seeing me bruised and battered changed him.

"Justice was served. He lost his career, he went to jail, and his wife divorced him and got all his money." He looks at me with a weak smile.

"I promise I won't ever let that happen to you again." I snuggle into him.

"Chris, it wasn't your fault, and believe me, it won't ever happen again." I quickly change the subject because I hate talking about Kane. "I'm going to be missing Evan's thirtieth in Mexico. I'm going to need you to behave," I order, elbowing him in the ribs.

"Come on, V, it's Mexico," he says with a broad smile. I raise my eyebrow at him because I'm not amused. "Okay, fine. I promise to make sure anything crazy we do is in the privacy of our villa and not public." He puts his hand on his heart.

"Fine, but please be careful, okay?" I stress, giving him a stern look. Christian just laughs and nods.

12

CHRISTIAN

"Welcome to paradise, boys." We enter the private house we have rented for Evan's thirtieth and our New Year's Eve celebrations. Waiting to greet us are a couple of gorgeous women wearing nothing but bikinis, holding a tray full of tequila shots.

"Hope they are my birthday presents." Evan chuckles, making the girls blush as he takes a shot from the tray.

"Actually, man, your present will get here a little later, and I think you might enjoy it a little bit more." Little does he know I've organized the two hottest porn-star twins to be his birthday present for the weekend. If you have enough money, you can buy anything.

"You guys are disgusting!" Isla pipes up, picking up a shot glass from the tray and walking toward the pool area. Isla should be used to it all by now. Fuck, she's been our assistant from day one, plus she's known us just as long as we have known Oscar.

Isla's only two years younger than her brother. She and her girlfriends have always hung around watching us play. From day one, Oscar warned us not to touch his little sister, or we'd see his fists. That was fine by me. Even in high school, he was a six-foot-six guy built like a linebacker. He looked like he just stepped off *Vikings'* set with his long, blond hair and beard. His parents are Scandinavian and moved over from London during high school, his dad working in the oil industry. They were exotic to us Texans, all of us coming from totally different backgrounds. When we all met up in music class, we could see that he played bass like a pro. We knew then he'd be a fantastic addition to our band.

"Your sister is such a buzzkill, man," I groan to Oscar. He flips me off and heads toward Isla.

The house is spectacular. It opens out to the pool area, then leads directly to our own private white sandy beach that melts into the turquoise ocean. I promised Ness when she left for Australia that we'd behave, so I found, actually, who am I kidding, Isla found the perfect place for us to party paparazzi-free in paradise.

Speaking of Ness, fuck, I miss her. I'm so used to having her around, I feel like I am missing a limb now that she isn't here. Moving away from the group, I pull out my phone. I have no idea what time it is in Australia, but I press her name into my phone while I search to see what time it is. Shit. It's six in the morning, fuck, that's early. She's going to kill me if I call her, but she's halfway across the world, so she can't hurt me from there. I make my way toward the beach, so I can't be disturbed. I press FaceTime on my phone's screen. It rings and rings and rings until it finally picks up with a groggy Ness on the other end.

"Morning, gorgeous." Vanessa let's out a groan, the room is dark, so I can't see her.

"Do you have any idea what time it is, Chris?"

"Yep, it's about six in the morning, I think, give or take. Get up, lazy bones." I hear another groan as she jumps out of bed. I watch her move around the room and pull open the curtains, and bright sunlight fills the room. My jaw drops. She's wearing a white slip that's so thin I can see her nipples through it. I suppress a groan as my dick twitches to life, her caramel hair is all messy from sleep, she rubs her eyes, walks out of her room, and sits down outside.

"So, you made it to Mexico, then? I'm guessing that's why I got an early-morning wakeup call." She's smiling now, so that's good.

"Yeah, we did. Hey, Ness, I'll show you mine if you show me yours." I catch her off guard with my random comment. Vanessa raises her eyebrows until she realizes what I mean—the view—she turns her camera around to show me where she's staying. Her parents own some exclusive health retreat in the rainforest somewhere in Australia, and she's currently there with her best friend, Sienna. I can see lush green valleys and the ocean in the distance. Swinging my camera around, I show her the white sandy beach and turquoise sea.

"I'm so jealous, that looks gorgeous." I turn the phone back so I can see her again.

"It's pretty nice. Wish you were here, I've been missing you," I confess.

"Yeah, I miss you, too. I'll be home in a couple of weeks. But I bet you aren't going to be lonely for long." She wiggles her eyebrows at me.

"It's not the same, Ness, no one compares to you." I've had a crush on her for the last four years, but we both agreed that we'd just be friends, and honestly, I'm kind of happy it's turned out the way it has. I'd have eventually fucked up, and she'd have ended up hating me. She'd have changed jobs and looked after another band, which meant I wouldn't have her in my life. So, I pass the time with groupies and easy lays because I can't have the woman I want.

"Well, I'm sure you will still find something to entertain you until I get back." I always do.

"I've bought Evan the best birthday present ever." Vanessa

groans. "Hey, don't be like that, he's about to turn into an old fart."

"Um... Chris, hate to break it to you, you're not as young as you used to be. You're only a couple of years behind him."

Ignoring her point, I continue, "Anyway, I thought he should start his thirties with a bang, so I bought him twins." Vanessa is quiet for a moment.

"Twins?"

"Yeah, there are these porn-star twins, and you can hire them for private shows and stuff, so I did. They are his to play with for the weekend." She makes a gagging sound at the end of the phone.

"Chris, that's gross. Thank fuck I'm not there to witness this."

"Yeah, me, too. I'm pretty sure you're not going to like what I've got planned."

"Don't worry, I'm sure Isla will fill me in." Of course, she will.

"Whatever, I'm going to get her drunk, and hopefully, she'll just pass out, and we can party without her telling on us," I grumble. I love Isla, but the fact that she rats us out to Vanessa whenever she can is annoying, but I know she's just protecting us. We've done some stupid shit in the past, and Ness has saved our asses because Isla has filled her in sooner rather than later.

"Go easy on her, okay, she never gets a break from you guys. Buy her a massage or something like that, help her relax. I'm sure watching your brother fuck a million groupies night after night will make anyone tense." Great idea, Isla needs to get laid. Oscar is like a Rottweiler around her. Any guy who shows Isla interest, he looms over, cracking his knuckles like some caveman.

"Yeah, Ness, I think you're right."

"Of course, I am. Your life is so much easier when you follow what I say." I chuckle because it's the truth. "I better go,

Ness, there's drinking to be done." I look at the boys hanging around the pool with more bikini-clad staff.

"Yeah, yeah, okay. Well, have fun. Stay safe, and... I miss you." Hearing those three little words, I miss you, makes my heart ache a little. Fuck, not a little, a hell of a lot.

"Miss you, too, Ness." Then she's gone, and I feel it deep in the pit of my stomach. Shaking off my darkened mood, I join the rest of the boys by the pool.

"HAPPY NEW YEAR," Vanessa screams down the phone with her friends filling up the small screen. It's early in the morning here after another huge night, and I guess Ness is getting me back for waking her up early the other day. She looks drunk but happy as she parties on the beach with what looks to be a million other people.

"Happy New Year, guys," I shout back, unsure why I'm shouting when it's dead quiet here. Thankfully, I'm alone in bed. Otherwise, that would've been embarrassing. A lot of women don't like it when Vanessa calls me, and if any of the women give her shit, they are out the door.

"Here's Derrick, talk to him," Vanessa says, shoving the phone toward some guy. Derrick apparently is Sienna's best friend and our soon-to-be new tour stylist.

"Hey, sexy." Derrick smiles at me, but his attention is pulled away, his eyes widen. "What the fuck are you girls doing?" he yells, making me sit straight up in my bed. I'm now fully awake.

"Derrick, what's going on?" I try to get his attention, which is hard when you're sober and the other person is drunk. I can hear people screaming and having a good time. "Derrick," I shout again, trying to get his attention.

"Oh shit, sorry, Christian, I forgot you were there. Um... the girls have decided to do a nudie run into the ocean." My jaw drops to the ground. What the fuck? No! No one is supposed to see Vanessa naked, that's not fair.

"Derrick, turn the fucking screen around," I yell. This seriously can't be happening. He slowly turns it around, and all I see is darkness. Finally, two shadowy figures come into view, and I can make out their womanly physiques walking toward Derrick. When they come into the light, I'm speechless. Fuck me. There she is naked as the day she was born with one arm crossed over her nipples and the other cupping her pussy. My dick is standing at attention. This is like a wet dream I've had before.

"Vanessa, put some fucking clothes on!" I scream through the phone, making her laugh. She drops her arms, and I can see her fully naked body, her eyes locking on me as she slowly bends down and picks up her dress, her lush tits on display for the whole fucking world to see. I'm not amused at all. Looking at her bare pussy glistening from her ocean dip, I can see the water running down her taut stomach over her mound, and I want to chase it with my tongue. Not soon enough, her body is covered again, and I can let out a steady breath.

"Happy New Year, Chris," she says, blowing a kiss into the camera, then she's gone, leaving me with a fucking hard-on the size of Mount Rushmore.

13

VANESSA
MONTHS LATER

Sienna and Derrick arrived from Australia yesterday, and I can't believe their ugly mugs are here. It's a lifetime ago that Sienna and I were single together, and now I have my girl back. I couldn't be happier. I'm throwing them a welcome to LA party tonight. Hopefully, it will help them settle in here before we start touring. Fingers crossed, Si will want to stay on, and we can hang out again just like the old days.

Sienna looks stunning tonight, and I hate that I have to walk out on her, but stupidly, I'm on my way to pick up Nick, my cougar bait, as Christian calls him. Yes, he's a lot younger than I am, but seriously the boy is hot as fuck. His body is nothing but muscle, and his dick is the size of my damn forearm. It sucks that he has no idea how to use it. Maybe men with big dicks don't have to try compared to regular guys. It's a shame, really. I'm trying to subtly train him so that I can get some benefit from his stamina.

I'm currently driving to his house because he's over an hour late to the party, and last I heard, he was going to take a nap after catching the red-eye from New York where he had a photo shoot. Nick is an indie actor, just starting to make the big time.

He'll begin filming on a new television show soon, which has an incredible buzz around it, with some really well-established actors as part of the team.

I pull up to his Hollywood Hills home that he shares with a motley crew of actors in various stages of their careers. It's one big frat party most of the time. Jumping out of my car, I walk along the crushed stone path. They always forget to lock the front door, so I turn the knob, it opens, and I walk into a quiet house, the only sound is the click-clacking of my heels across the tiled floor. Where's everyone? There are usually a couple of guys playing video games or working out in the gym they have set up on the back deck. Maybe he's still asleep?

I make my way toward his room as I notice his jeans at the bottom of the stairs, then his shirt, and boxer shorts. Messy fucker. Then my eyes see along with it a black dress and black lace panties. My heart begins to race. You little fucker! Tension runs through my body as I reach the top of the stairs. That's when I hear the sounds, porn-star moaning coming from the bedroom. Pushing the door open, I find my 'kind of boyfriend' balls deep in his new co-star. She's riding him like a cowgirl, putting on an Oscar-worthy performance in the fake orgasm category, one I'm very familiar with.

"Shit, Ness," Nick screams, seeing me standing in the doorway. I should be pissed and upset, but I'm not, which is the upsetting part of it all. How the hell have I become the girl who isn't crying over her pseudo boyfriend fucking someone else?

"That's quite a performance you're putting on, sweetheart. I now understand how you won an Emmy." I turn on my heel and walk back out the door.

"Ness, wait. Babe, I'm sorry it sort of just happened... we were practicing lines and..." Turning in the middle of the glass staircase to look at him, I had to question how smart he was, seriously. Was he saying that he was practicing lines, and then his penis just accidentally fell into her?

"Nick, save it. It is what it is. Good luck." I continued my descent.

"Ness, shit, I'm sorry. I'm so fucking sorry. Can we, you know, still catch up?" The nerve of that fucker. I flip him the bird as I slam his front door.

Jumping into my car, the false bravado I held onto crumbles as I burst into tears, banging my head against the steering wheel. Seriously, how the hell could I have been so fucking stupid? Pulling into my driveway moments later, I stay in my car trying to collect myself before entering the party.

Eventually, I get out of the car. I straighten up my shoulders, push my head back, hold it up high, and walk through my home's front doors. But the one person I wasn't expecting to see straight away is Christian.

"Hey, Ness. Where's cougar bait?" His whiskey-colored eyes look around me. This man knows me so well that there will be no way I can hide how I'm feeling.

"He was busy with his co-star apparently practicing lines," I say with a steely tone, mimicking air quotes around the practicing lines bit of that sentence. Christian understands what I mean.

"That little fucker, I'm going to kill him." He balls his fists at his side.

Grabbing his fist and holding it in my hand, I soothe him. "He's not worth it." I give him a weak smile.

"Yeah, but you are, Ness. You're too good for that little fuck." I smile. I love how Christian always has my back. A tear trickles down my cheek. No, fuck no, he doesn't deserve my tears. Christian pulls me into his arms, his hard chest pushes against my breasts, his strong arms holding me in place. I feel safe wrapped around him and finally sag against him and start to cry.

"What the hell is wrong with me, Christian? Why am I never good enough for anyone?" Christian ignores my question but continues to hold me tight. "He was crap in bed. I could totally tell she was faking it when I caught them."

This makes him laugh. Pulling my face away from his chest where I had it buried, I look up at him. "Do you have any idea how long it's been since I've had good sex, Chris?" I feel his body tense, those whiskey-colored eyes dilute as he looks at me.

"Months, if not years. Thank God for fucking vibrators keeping me satisfied. Fuck, maybe I need to buy one of those fake male sex doll things. At least that would be better than wasting my time on fucking duds. Can you buy me one for Christmas?" Christian is still quiet, holding me tight. "No, fuck it. I need to hire a gigolo. At least they know what they are doing."

Before I know it, I'm traveling backward, my back hitting the hallway's white walls, and Christian's lips are on mine. My best friend is kissing me, and it feels so fucking good. My brain is a bundle of fuzz, and his kisses are short-circuiting my mind.

"Fuck, Ness, there's no way in hell you're going to a fucking gigolo when I'm just a couple of feet away." Our foreheads press together, his breath labored after our kiss.

"But..." My words are silenced by another kiss.

"No, Ness, I'm your best friend, I can help." Huh, what's he saying? He can help? "I'm your best friend, and friends look after friends, no matter what." He kisses me again.

I've missed feeling his heaviness against me. I've forgotten his strength, the way my body burns with desire when he touches me. Those skillful lips tasting me, teasing me, enticing me. I can feel his excitement pushing against me, and I want more, more of him, more of this.

14

VANESSA

Christian grabs my wrist, pulling me along the hallway, past the front door I had just entered and toward the bedroom wing of our home. I look around, making sure no one we know sees what we're doing. The house is empty as most of the party-goers are out the back hanging around the pool. Christian pushes his bedroom door open, then slams it behind us, making me jump. He turns to look at me, his eyes wild with desire.

"Take off your clothes," he commands in a low, stern voice, which sends shivers over my body.

"Chris, um..." I hesitate even though I'm totally turned on right now. Christian stalks closer to me, and I tentatively take a step back from him.

"That was the wrong answer, Ness." Tilting his head to the side, he pauses for a moment giving me an appreciative look, and my skin flushes with goosebumps from his penetrating stare. He surprises me by grabbing my waist and turning me around in his arms, pulling me flush against his aroused state.

"Christian," I squeal.

"Shh, angel," he whispers into my ear. One of his strong arms snakes around my waist as he starts to unzip my dress.

"Chris." Not sure if I'm pleading or wanting him to stop as the cold air hits my fevered skin.

"When I ask you to do something in my bedroom, V, I expect you do it." Warm breath tickles my ear. Shit, that's hot, Christian going all alpha on me. My body shivers with desire and anticipation as his fingers run down my bare back following the zipper line. I bite my bottom lip, suppressing a moan.

"Ness, am I making you ache?" Warm lips touch my neck.

"Hmm," I mumble incoherently as my body is on the edge of utter frustration and desire. The straps of my dress fall slowly from my shoulders and pool at my feet. I'm standing in nothing but my lacy underwear.

"Nice, very nice, V," he whispers, liking the white lingerie set I'm wearing. Calloused hands skim over my exposed skin as he traces every dip and curve of my body. "Don't move," he commands. I'm so turned on that I automatically obey.

All thoughts of this being wrong have totally evaporated from my mind. All I feel is molten, white heat all over my body. His body heat disappears from my back, and I follow his movements as he walks slowly around me, viewing me like some precious artwork. He disappears again behind me, and I dare not move. Soft kisses move down my spine, and the ache he's creating between my legs is growing the further he moves down my body.

"Fuck, you're so beautiful, Ness," Christian murmurs against my skin. He has moved further down from my spine, feather-light kisses rain over the back of my hips toward my ass. Ever so gently, he sinks his teeth into the juicy flesh of my ass cheek. I let out a groan, making him laugh.

"Turn around," he demands. I do so and find him on his knees in front of me, his whiskey-colored eyes shimmering with desire. It's intense, and I move to cover myself feeling slightly exposed.

"Don't you fucking dare, Ness," he commands while grabbing my arms from covering myself. "Let me see you." Biting my lip, I nod. "Unhook your bra, let me see those magnificent tits I've missed," he asks, sitting back on his heels. I hesitate for the slightest of moments, but I catch his heated stare and instantly drop my bra, throwing it to the side. He gives me an appreciative smile for a long moment, just taking in the view. His eyes roam over my body, my dusty pink nipples standing at attention, pointing directly at him.

"You want more, don't you?" he questions me. Of course, I do and nod in agreement. He chuckles.

"Take a couple of steps backward." I take a deep breath and do as I'm told, my legs hitting the edge of his bed, stopping me.

"Sit down, Ness." I do so and feel the softness of his bed. He crawls over toward me on his knees. "Open your legs." His hands touch my knees, making me automatically open them for him. He gives me a wicked smile.

"Good girl." He shuffles between them. Leaning forward, he blows across my sensitive nipples, his mouth capturing the nipple he has been teasing, and my back arches as his tongue swirls around the puckered skin. My hands fist his hair as he plays with my breasts.

"V, I've dreamed of sucking your tits for so long."

"I've wanted your lips on them for just as long as well," I confess.

"Why have we been wasting time, then?" he questions me as his calloused palms massage my heavy breasts. I let out a strangled moan as a hand squeezes and twists my sensitive nipples.

"I need you, I don't care about whatever rules we're breaking tonight." I can't believe I'm pleading for my best friend to fuck me. See, this is what happens when you put up with bad sex for so long you lose your goddamn mind.

"Thank fuck, V," he murmurs against my chest. I watch as he quickly throws off his shirt, then tosses his shoes and socks to the side.

"Wait," I say as he touches his belt, his chest is heaving with desire, a look of frustration across his face. "Let me," I purr. He gives me a wicked smile. With shaky hands, I start to unbuckle his belt, and one by one, I pop the buttons of his jeans. Shit! Christian's gone commando. His thick cock bounces free of its restrictive cover. He's fully aroused, and I can tell by the glistening head in front of me. Moving forward, I lick the pre-cum off his slit.

"V," Christian moans, his hands automatically finding my head. Looking up at him as I take him in my mouth, our eyes lock on each other. I can feel his heartbeat pounding through his body, matching mine. I take him further down my throat as I hollow my cheeks. Christian's head rolls back, and a deep guttural moan falls from his lips. I do it again, loving the way he's responding to me.

"Shit, no, no, I can't," he mumbles, taking a step away from me, his cock falling from my mouth with a pop. Fuck, he's having second thoughts. Shit, this was a stupid idea. I quickly jump up to find my clothes. He must have seen the confusion across my face because he grabs me, and our lips are locked again. His forehead rests on mine.

"I don't want you to stop, Ness. It's just..." he pauses for a moment, "... I'm so fucking turned on right now that if you kept on going, I'd have blown my load, and I ain't in high school anymore. That shouldn't happen." Christian's confession makes me chuckle. "You think that's funny, V, that you have the power to make me lose control so easily?"

"No, but I like knowing that I have that kind of power over you," I whisper, giving him a seductive smile.

"You always have, V, always." He reaches out to me, his hands gripping my hips, and we take a couple of steps back toward his bed. "Knowing you have been next door suffering in silence kills me." My legs hit the end of the bed again, and he pushes me to sit, his cock bouncing in front of my face. I lick my lips in anticipation.

"All these years wasted when I could've been doing this to you." He pushes me, so I fall back against his bed and grabs my legs, stretching them wide, his thick fingers moving the tiny scrap of fabric that's my G-string to the side. He leans over me, and his tongue touches the outside of my glistening folds. Shit, that feels amazing. "Stay still, V."

Placing his hand against my chest, I willingly stay, sinking into the softness of his bed. His tongue teases my pussy with each slow lick, savoring me like a fine wine. Never tasting the same spot twice, my needy clit is throbbing in heated frustration as his tongue circles around it, never giving me what I want. It's like a fever has taken over my body. He has me squirming with each lick until finally, he touches the magic spot. The sudden feeling against my clit makes me grab his head to hold him in place.

"You taste so good. I've never forgotten the taste of your sweet pussy after all these years." One finger, then a second enter me, filling me as he keeps me on the precipice while my body wants to crash over the edge. His fingers find my delicate nerves inside of me, and with a few more sucks, he has me well and truly crashing over that edge.

"Christian!" His name fills his room. Crawling over me, he pulls my lifeless body further up the bed.

"Fuck, I love hearing my name on your lips when you come, I need to hear it again."

"No." Halting him, a small frown falls on his face. "It's your turn now, Chris." Pushing him onto his back, he willingly lets me. "Where do you keep your condoms?"

"Bedside drawer." Reaching over him, I fiddle with the drawer as my tits hit him right in his face. His lips wrap around my breast, making me buck and moan. Grabbing the piece of foil, I let him suck and nibble my breasts while I sheath him. Steadying myself over his cock, I slowly sink onto him.

"Yes," he hisses as my pussy engulfs him. Slowly, I rise off him again, almost letting him slip out as I sink back onto him, listening to his strangled moans with each thrust. I feel so powerful. "You feel so good, Ness," he says with a dirty grin on his face as I ride him hard, taking all my sexual frustration out on him. "That's it, baby, ride me."

My tits bounce with each thrust, my clit rubbing against his skin. I can feel his thickness inside of me, filling me. It's been so long since I've fucked someone who knows what they are doing. His skillful hands are roaming all over my body, fingers twisting my aching nipples, thumb circling my throbbing clit, hands slapping my ass as I ride him. So many sensations. I can feel another orgasm coming deep from within, so I rub myself harder against him until I explode and see stars. He flips me onto my back, making me squeal.

"As much as I love your sweet pussy riding me, now it's my turn, sweetheart." He thrusts harder into me, over and over, feverishly. I have to hold on for dear life as my hands roam over his hard body. Finding his perfectly shaped ass, I squeeze it, urging him on.

"Yes, Ness, yes," he screams as I grip him harder until he shudders, and a deep groan falls from his mouth. Careful not to squash me, he rolls over onto his back, taking me with him, not breaking our connection. Pushing my hair back from my face, he stares at me. "Ness, you're so fucking perfect." He kisses me, making my heart ache. I push any negative thoughts to the back of my mind and just enjoy some of the best sex I've had in a long time.

"Thanks, just what I needed." I giggle nervously because it's kind of awkward to have your best friend's penis still lodged inside of you.

"Are you going to be weird now about this, Ness?"

"No, it's just a quick fuck between friends." Christian frowns.

"Just so you know, the night's not over yet."

I smile. "Yeah, I know there's a party going on outside." Shaking his head, he looks at me with a frown. "No, what I mean is, you and me, we haven't finished. Do you seriously think that after all these years, now that I finally get you back into my bed, I'm going to let you go?"

"Christian."

"Ness." He looks at me sternly. "I had fun, you had fun, so why can't we have fun together?"

"Because we're friends, and sex always complicates things."

Rolling his eyes at me, he continues, "Ness, if you're worried I'm going to fall in love with you, then don't because I already have."

Slapping him, I reply, "Don't say that while your dick is still inside of me, that's just weird."

"Fine." He rolls me off of him, quickly disposing of the condom in the bin beside the bed. Pulling me back into his arms, he says, "Is that better? No penis in you, can we now have a conversation?" Looking at him, I nod.

"Look, I had fun, and you had fun?" I nod in agreement with his statement. "Then why can't we continue to have fun tonight, just you and me?"

"Just for tonight?" I wanted to make clear that's what he meant. Christian just shrugs. "Christian!"

"Yeah, yeah, just for tonight or anytime you have an itch you want to scratch, okay? No more dumb fucks like Nick. You need sex, you come into my room and jump me, okay? It's what friends are for."

I slap him again. "Don't be silly." Christian rolls me over

onto my back, pressing me into the bed, looking at me seriously.

"I mean it, Ness. I'm your best friend, and we live together. If you need a non-vibrator-induced orgasm, please knock on my door. It will always be open to you." His lips ever so softly touch mine.

He's serious. "Sex ruins things, especially between friends."

"Yeah, for most people, but we're different... you and me. Not many girls act like men when it comes to sex, but you know the difference between love and sex." That was the truth. "So, I trust that you and I can handle it." It sounds like a recipe for disaster.

"You want to add friends with benefits to our arrangement even though after all these years, we have kept it platonic?" I question him.

"We're older now, Ness, more mature." I burst out laughing.

"Hey, don't be a bitch," he whines as he starts to tickle me, knowing the right spots to deliver maximum tickles.

"Stop," I scream in between breaths.

"Okay, okay." Christian stops.

"So, we have a deal?" Christian smirks.

"Fine, I promise if I need the D, I'll call the C." We both burst out laughing.

"Sounds like a plan, and if I need the V, I'll call the V," he says, frowning before we start laughing again.

"That doesn't sound as good." We fall into another fit of laughter.

"When you need the P, call the V," I say, giggling.

"Okay, V, I need the P," he whispers into my ear.

"Okay, C, give me the D." I smile at him as his lips descend onto mine.

15

CHRISTIAN

"Play that bit again," Axel asks Evan and me to play our song section. We're gearing up for our European tour, so we're getting in some studio practice. We are also writing some new songs for our new label, which we'll be launching once we get back from this tour. But my mind is on the fact that Vanessa has gone out on a girls' night. Not sure why it's bothering me now, it never has before.

"Dude, where's your head at?" Oscar punches me in the arm. I'm groaning at the Viking's strength.

"Nowhere, man, just thinking."

"Don't think too hard there, you might break something," Axel teases. I throw a bottle of water at him, which just makes him laugh.

"I'm just thinking about our future. That's all, about the end of the tour and about the label… shit like that." The room goes quiet, and the boys all look at me.

"Shit, I think our little boy is growing up." Evan laughs. I flip him the bird.

"I get what you mean," Finn pipes up. "I've been thinking about the same things. We have all been together professionally for the past ten years, and before that, every day after school. This will be the first time we all kind of go our separate ways."

"But we'll all be working at the label together," Axel adds.

"Yeah, but we will all have different roles. Things are changing, and we're moving on to the next phase of our lives," Finn adds. Shit just got real.

"Fuck, when did you all become such pussies," Oscar curses us all.

"What? We can't have a grown-up conversation about life?" I question him.

"I don't know what the fuck they have done with the old Christian but bring him back. This one is scaring the shit out of me. Are you sick, man?" Oscar grabs hold of my shoulder, shaking it.

"Fuck off, man. I was just thinking, that's all," I bite at him, feeling angsty.

"Chris, you all right?" Axel asks.

"Yeah, everything is changing, that's all." I don't know why I am being a little bitch or why I'm contemplating life so much, but I am. "Ignore me, guys, I must be getting my period or something." I try to shake my thoughts away. The guys just keep looking at me. "Come on, let's play some music." I change the subject, hoping they will forget this conversation.

Thank fuck they all agree, and we launch into it for the next couple of hours.

I'M LYING HERE STARING at the ceiling, trying to get to sleep, but I can't because I know Vanessa is out on a girls' night with Isla, Sienna, and Derrick. I don't like it. I keep wondering if she's hooking up with someone. It never bothered me before—okay, that's a lie. This time I have a friend-with-benefits thing going on with her, and I don't want to sleep with her at the same time she's seeing other people. Rolling over, I punch my pillow a couple of times, trying to get comfortable.

I haven't been able to get Vanessa out of my head since the party last week. I knew it was stupid kissing her, knew it would open up old wounds, and bring all those dormant feelings to the surface again, but I hated her feeling like she wasn't good enough. She deserves more, and I want to give her more. She's so damn stubborn about keeping business and pleasure separate. Just thinking about her makes my dick hard.

Grabbing the remote, I turn on the television and search for some of my favorite porn. I need to forget about what she's up to tonight. My eyes widen as two blonde beauties start kissing, can't go past some lesbian porn to make me forget about Vanessa. Pushing my sweatpants down, I fist my cock, watching the girls moan as they touch each other. Glossy lips sucking on pert nipples, fingers disappearing between tanned thighs, listening to their moans, my dick thickens as I watch the scene in front of me. I'm in a steady rhythm as I watch the girls start to eat each other out, high squeals of delight filling my ears.

"What the fuck!" I scream as Vanessa bursts into my room, looking like a fucking vision. Dressed in a fire-engine red off-the-shoulder dress, a perfect 'V' showing off her rounded breasts. Vanessa's green eyes zero in on my hand stroking my dick, then flicks to the screen as the two blondes start coming, their orgasms filling the room.

Her eyes glance back to me as her hand reaches behind her and starts unzipping her red dress. My eyes are transfixed on the strip show happening before me. I don't care about the reasons why she's in my room at this moment because all I care about is seeing what's underneath that red dress. Vanessa takes her time, her eyes never leaving mine as she shimmies out of the tight dress. I watch as it hits the floor. My eyes follow her curves and linger on her bare breasts, a white G-string and red heels complement the view in front of me.

"What are you doing, Ness?" My words are shaky because fuck, I hope to God she's here to have some fun.

"What are you doing, Chris?" Her eyes are looking at my cock, my hand still groping it. I smile at her as I watch her lick her lips.

"Trying to forget about you." Her eyebrows raise at my words.

"Why?" Her voice is husky.

"Because I didn't want to think about you with other men." She's silent for a moment as she turns back to the television that has now gone blank. Not even a second later, her eyes are on my cock again.

"And you thought you would take matters into your own hands?" she asks, smirking at me.

"Yeah, I guess you could say that." I chuckle. Shaking her head as she slinks toward the bed, my eyes follow the bounce of her breasts and the curves of her hips. Kicking off her red heels, she kneels on the edge of the bed in between my legs. My eyes are unable to move away from her.

"What did you tell me the other day?" Her eyes are locked with mine. My brain has stopped working—there's nothing but emptiness knocking around between my ears.

"I don't know, Ness. I'm finding it hard to think at the moment with you naked in front of me." She smiles seductively at me.

"You said that if I ever had an itch to scratch, all I needed to do was knock on your door." I vaguely remember saying something along those lines. "Well, Christian, the same goes for you." Her hand reaches out and wraps itself around my cock just above my fist, her warm skin teasing my aching cock.

"Ness, what are you doing?" I ask breathlessly.

"Helping you. That's what friends are for, isn't it?" She licks her lips and starts moving her fist along my cock in a perfect rhythm that has me arching my back into her grip.

"Fuck," I groan, my eyes rolling back into my head. Vanessa giggles as she keeps jerking me off.

"I couldn't wait to get home tonight," she confesses.

"Yeah, darlin'?"

"Yeah." Shimmying closer to me, my eyes look down to her white lace G-string. I'm itching to touch her, but something about how she's taking control makes me wait her out. Bending down, her wet lips wrap around the head of my cock, her warm breath tickling my sensitive skin. Her tongue circles under the lip of my cock's head. Fuck me, it feels like heaven.

"Ness, Ness." I tap her on the shoulder. She looks up from her place between my thighs, her mouth still wrapped around me. "Darlin', as much as I want your perfect lips around my cock, I need your sweet pussy on it instead." Picking her up under the arms and pulling her flush against my naked chest, she lets out a tiny squeal.

"I wanted to give you a mind-blowing blow job, Chris," she pouts, straddling my chest.

"I want nothing more than to keep those lips wrapped around my cock, but I feel like this is a dream, and I'm about to wake up before I get to sink deep inside of you, Ness."

Vanessa's breath hitches as her lips land on mine. The kiss is frantic, wild, hot, and desperate. Her fingers run through my hair forcefully, pulling me closer to her, the pain mixed with the pleasure of her lips feels fantastic. My hands find her tight ass, squeezing it hard as she starts to grind on me, the lace of her G-string rubbing my aching cock with each sweep against it. My fingers push the flimsy material to the side, so her bare pussy is exposed. Finding her wet and wanting, my fingers move back and forth through her slickness. Vanessa bites down on a groan as my fingers enter her. Grinding against my fingers, our lips stay connected as my cock thumps against my stomach because he's missing out on all the fun. Pulling my fingers out of her, Vanessa whimpers at the loss, but I fill her again. Fuck, sinking into her, feels fantastic.

"Chris." I feel her tense.

"Yeah, babe?"

"You forgot the condom." Vanessa's green eyes stare at me. Shit, I got so caught up in the moment.

"Baby, I know you're on birth control, and you know I'm clean." I really don't want to pull out of her. That hot pussy is clenched so tight around me.

"I trust you, Chris," she says, smiling.

Our eyes are locked on each other as I start to move, my hands finding her ass as I push her harder against me, getting deeper inside her. Feeling her bare with no barrier between us heightens what we're doing with each other. We become frenzied at the new sensations. Rolling her onto her back, lifting her leg over my shoulder, I go as deep as I possibly can inside of her.

"Fuck, Chris," Ness screams as my cock hits her deeply. I pound into her, I'm strung so tight. Sucking her pert nipples into my mouth, my tongue teasing each of the little buds, my thumb finds her aroused clit and pushes against it, giving her that pressure and friction to bring her closer to the edge. Her pussy tightens around me as I work her body over. "Oh my God," Vanessa screams as she comes, a small line of sweat on her brow.

"Fuck, V, I felt every inch of that orgasm." Her glassy eyes look at me as I continue to pump into her.

"Fuck me, Christian, please hurry up and fuck me," she begs, her green eyes gaze into mine. Her fingernails are trailing down my back, digging into my ass, urging me on harder, faster, those pert tits bouncing with each thrust. I feel the tingling up my spine, through my balls until I finally come.

"V," I cry as I empty myself into her. A couple of moments later, she smiles at me.

"Thanks for that."

"I think it's me who should be thanking you." Cause that sure beats jerking off to porn. My forehead lands on her shoulder, my teeth gently bite her tanned skin, her pussy clenches around me again, and delicate fingers glide up my back. I don't want to pull out of her, but I can feel my dick softening. She probably wants to get cleaned up. Vanessa pushes my hair out of my face and just looks at me for a moment, then smiles.

"So lesbian porn, huh?" She giggles, making me roll my eyes at her.

"Um... hello? Two hot girls touching each other as if that doesn't get any straight guy going." We're both quiet for a moment. "Have you ever been with a woman? Because fuck, that would be hot." Vanessa laughs.

"I've kissed some girls. I think most girls have." My brain just short-circuited. Seriously, Vanessa with another woman? I can feel my dick hardening just imagining those things.

"Tell me everything," I pant, making Vanessa laugh.

"You know the story, one too many drinks, guys daring you to kiss, so, of course, you do it to prove them wrong. No big deal."

No big deal! I groan, "Fuck, I'd pay good money to see that."

"Some guys did." Vanessa giggles.

"What do you mean, pay?" My entire body tenses at the thought.

"Some guys would dare us with cash to kiss. We were broke university girls, so, of course, we'd take the money. We needed the cab fare." I'm stunned silent.

"Have you kissed Sienna?" Sienna is hot as fuck, and now she's single. They might do it again. I'd pay good money to see that. Vanessa starts giggling.

"Yes, a couple of times." My cock stirs. I love it when it's buried deep in Vanessa, especially while we're having this conversation. Her hands glide back and forth easily over my back as she talks.

"Can I get a repeat performance?" I ask, hopefully. She slaps my ass, stunning me.

"Dream on, Chris, dream on." She's smiling at me now. My heart is thundering in my chest. I want to stay like this for the rest of the night, maybe have another round or two.

"I better go get cleaned up." Vanessa starts pushing me off of her. I don't want to pull out from her, but I do slowly. I grab my T-shirt from the floor, giving it to her so she can clean herself up.

"Stay, Ness." Vanessa stops what she's doing and looks at me.

"The rest of the guys are here, probably not a good idea," she says, wiping herself clean. The boys like to crash at my place from time to time even though they have houses not far from here. We're all so used to being around each other all the time. I built the studio first, so they all stay here when we're working in it.

"But I want to have more sex." I flutter my eyelashes at her, doing my best puppy-dog face, hoping it works. I'm sprawled out naked on my bed. I watch as her eyes dip to my twitching dick and back up to me.

"Fine, but we need a shower first. I'm not going to sleep with your stuff pouring out of me." I choke at her words. We both burst out laughing, making our way into the bathroom.

16

CHRISTIAN

Lathering Vanessa up in a mountain of bubbles, my hands explore every curve and dip of her body. It feels right, washing each other like this in my shower. Her hands explore my body, up and over my chest, down my back, even between my ass cheeks, which surprises me. It makes her laugh.

"I can't see you anymore." She giggles through the clouds of steam and mountains of bubbles filling the shower.

"Here, is this better?" I take the shower head off its dock, hosing her down. The sudden hit of water has her screaming and flaying around the shower.

"Chris, you motherfucker," she screams as I wash away the suds until all I see is her naked form in front of me. God, she's gorgeous. Dropping the shower hose, I launch myself at her. She lets out a shocked squeal as I push her against the tiled shower wall.

"Fuck, Ness, I need you again," I groan, pushing myself into her. The shower hose sprays us with water as it runs wild like some sort of possessed snake. We forget about it, lost in each other.

"WHAT THE HELL ARE WE DOING?" Vanessa asks after another night spent in my bed.

"We're having fun," I tell her, kissing her cheek.

"You turned down going to that party?" She raises her eyebrow at me.

"Yeah, because why would I go to that party when I have you here in bed with me," I explain, nuzzling her neck.

"The boys were shocked. They know something is up." She twists in my arms, forcing my attention back to her face. I exhale a heavy sigh and straighten up.

"So fucking what?"

"So fucking what, are you serious?" She gets up on her knees. A vein throbs in her throat, and her cheeks are flushed. Ness is pissed.

"Yeah, I don't care that they know we're hooking up." It is the truth. It's been five fucking years, and I haven't told any of those fuckers about Ness. I promised her, plus I never wanted them to think of her any differently. Well, except Axel, he's in my head most of the time, so technically I didn't tell him, he just kind of knew.

"But I care, I fucking care about my reputation, Christian. I told you about what happened in London all those years ago. I thought you understood."

"You're irreplaceable, Ness, no one would care anymore." Letting my finger run down her arm, I try to get her to relax. She flinches. Shit, that's not good.

"You don't get it, do you? Why would you? You being a fucking slut is something to be proud of. Everyone worships the amount of pussy you get. But as a woman, I don't get to revel in that kind of treatment." She's now jumped off the bed and is starting to get dressed. How the fuck have we ended up with our sex session coming to an abrupt halt?

"Ness." I jump up naked out of my bed, chasing after her. "What's going on? Talk to me." I don't understand what has her so spooked.

She takes a deep breath. "I think we should sleep with other people."

My whole body stills at her words. "You want to fuck other people?"

"Yeah, and I know you do as well." I shrug because it's the truth, I'm a male. I'm not going to lie, but in all honesty, I haven't really looked at another woman now that Vanessa and I have been hooking up again.

"But I kind of want to keep fucking you, I like fucking you. Now that I have your taste on my lips again, I crave it, Ness." That's the God-honest truth. Well, actually, the truth is I'm so fucking scared about my feelings for Vanessa surfacing again. Now that we have stopped our platonic relationship, all those feelings I had for her years ago are bubbling up to the surface again.

It took me a long time to get over her, an exceptionally long time. So long that Axel sat me down and told me that I needed to move on and forget about her. That shit hurt hearing him say it, but it was the truth. One night he eventually convinced me to go with him to The Paradise Club, an elite sex club in LA. It's where the young, rich, and famous could meet and party hard, do anything they wanted, and there'd be no prying eyes of the paparazzi or journalists getting word of it. It took me a while, but eventually, those feelings for Vanessa disappeared.

Who the fuck am I kidding? I just put a big-ass Band-Aid over the top of my emotions. Stupidly, I ripped off that Band-Aid, and now I have a gaping wound in my chest. I mentally need to dip inside that medicine cabinet and find an industrial-strength Band-Aid and get it ready to place over my wound and hope to God that it sticks, permanently this time. Vanessa is looking at me, and I can see the wheels turning in her head.

"I like fucking you, too, Christian." My heart starts to skip a beat. "I have a suggestion." I nod enthusiastically because this time, she isn't saying no, but I just don't want to get my hopes up. She sits back down on the bed, and I join her, my leg twitching in anticipation.

"Do you think we can do the whole friends-with-benefits thing?" I nod because yes, yes, I think we can. Honestly, I'll say yes to anything if it means I can keep sleeping with her. "Eyes up here, Christian." Moving my chin up, I'm no longer looking at her breasts but instead into her green eyes and take in all her beauty.

"Do you think you can handle us sleeping together but also other people?" I ask.

"We both know we aren't cut out for relationships," Vanessa muses. Well, I'm a rock star. I haven't ventured into a relationship because there's too much temptation around me. I've been cheated on in the past, and it sucks. I don't want to do that to anyone.

"Okay, I agree with the relationship thing." Vanessa smiles.

"You and I have a crazy kind of chemistry."

"Fuck, yeah, we do, best sex of my life." *Dial it down, Christian.* Vanessa blushes at my enthusiasm.

"Agreed, I'm not going to deny that, but..." Oh shit, I don't like buts, well not that kind of but, although I do like ladies' butts, those are gorgeous little peaches—concentrate, man. "We have a policy of no hooking up with staff, remember that," Vanessa reminds me. Oh yeah, that one, we used to fuck around with some of the staff every now and again while on tour, and well, the shit sometimes got real, things went down, and now we have a rule—no fucking the staff.

"Ness, you're different, you're part of the band, you're family." She was, everyone loves her, she's like the sixth member of Dirty Texas.

"That's sweet, but it's still a rule, and you know how much

of a stickler I am for rules," she reminds me. I know her rules, especially when it comes to fucking, and I don't like any of them.

"Well, I'm prepared to break it, but... I think it's best that we keep this casual. I mean, you can hook up with groupies, and I can still hook up with guys, but if we have an itch and there's no one else around who can scratch it, then we can with each other." She smiles at me as if this plan is the most fantastic in the world.

"So, what you're saying is I get to sleep with you and other people?" I just want to be clear because this seems like I'm being set up or something.

"Yeah, and don't forget I can as well," she adds. Yeah, yeah, Ness, you don't need to remind me that you can fuck other dudes.

"I don't know," I confess, scratching at the imaginary hole in my chest.

"It's just an idea. Otherwise, we can go back to being platonic friends again, but if I'm honest, I am going to miss your cock and those fingers and your mouth." I grin.

"Yeah, babe, you going to miss all this," I say, waving my hand around my naked form, my dick coming to attention at hearing Vanessa say she'll miss him.

"Yes, Christian, I'll miss all that," she says, waving her hands all over me. "But I also want my freedom."

Since Kane, Vanessa has definitely enjoyed her freedom, and I suppose I understand. The guy was a controlling, manipulative bastard, and I hate that he has spooked her out of ever wanting a relationship again. But if this is the only way I can have Ness in my bed, I'll have to accept her terms. Maybe seeing me with another woman might make her rethink her feelings for me. Might force her to admit that she has them.

"Okay, Ness, you have yourself a deal. You and I are in an

open friends-with-benefits relationship." Giving her my hand, she ignores it, launching herself at me instead.

Oh, I think I'm going to like this arrangement.

How fucking wrong was I!

17

VANESSA

The first stop for the next three months is good old London town. I'm relishing that I'm back here again with the world's biggest band, Dirty Texas, as my client. It's been fantastic having my bestie around with me also.

Sienna has been coping relatively well in LA, but I have a feeling that might have something to do with a particular celebrity crush she has on Evan Wyld. I see the way he looks at her. He promised me he wouldn't touch her, and I believe him, I think. If flirting with Evan gives her the confidence to get back out into the world as a newly single woman, then more power to her.

My open friends-with-benefits relationship with Christian hasn't really been available to anyone else since we agreed upon it. We have been too busy getting ready for the tour and hanging out with Sienna and Derrick, so we haven't had much time to meet new people or even date others. With the tour starting, the groupies will be all over him, and I know how much Christian loves those groupies. I guess tonight we'll see how this open friends-with-benefits thing will work and if either one of us will get jealous.

. . .

IT DOESN'T TAKE the guys long to have a gaggle of beautiful women commanding their attention in the VIP area of the club. Christian currently has two blondes wrapped around his arm, and yes, I'm jealous. Their hands are touching his chest, and their oversized lips are touching his skin. Things that were mine not twenty-four hours earlier when we were wrapped in each other's arms at home, our home, or the quickie in the airplane toilet on our way to London while everyone was asleep, are now someone else's.

Thankfully, Sienna and Derrick enter the club with Isla hot on their heels to save me from my brooding thoughts. "I need a fucking drink." I grab Sienna by the arm. Christian looks at me, gives me a dirty smirk, and continues talking to the blondes. Bastard!

I've had the best time tonight. After a couple more champagne bottles, I've stopped worrying about Christian and his groupies and started to enjoy myself, especially having my closest friends around me for the first time in years. Letting ourselves go on the dance floor, we enjoy our time together, even reveling in some dirty dancing with some of the guys hovering around the dance floor.

My tongue is firmly stuck down the throat of some young football player at the moment. His muscles are bulging through his expensive white button-up, and my fingers love the feel of his body as they roam over him. I can feel an impressive bulge somewhere else as well. His hand is firmly stuck to my ass as I grind on him. One of his friends taps him on the shoulder, whispers something in his ear, and that's when his eyes peer over my shoulder to something behind me. He stiffens, then slowly disentangles himself from me.

"Sorry, love, I've got to go, early morning training session." Then he's gone, poof, just like that. Turning around, I see Evan's back heading toward the restroom. I shake my head in disbelief. Well, fuck him, he's probably crap in bed, anyway. Walking back to our table to get another champagne glass, I spot Isla sitting with Sienna and Derrick.

"What are you guys doing sitting at the table? I thought you were all busy with someone," I ask my friends who all look miserable.

Isla looks at me. "Mine quickly made his excuses and left."

"So did mine," Sienna added.

"Yeah, that just happened to me as well," I say, taking a sip of bubbles. Strange.

"I think the boys may have something to do with it. I noticed Evan say something to one of the guys on his way to the bathroom," Derrick adds.

"Men!" I look over at the booth, where they are all happily getting it on with girls. "It's okay for them to fuck everything that walks, but they won't let us have any fun. Well, screw them," I announce. "Let's show them we can't be tamed."

I jump up on the table, urging Sienna, Isla, and Derrick to join me. We all start dirty dancing with each other, and it's like a giant two fingers to the boys. We have created a bit of a commotion with our moves. There's currently a crowd of lustful men watching us dance on the table together.

Out of nowhere, my legs come out from under me. Screaming as I fall toward the ground, I'm saved by a solid shoulder under my stomach. Trying to lift my head, I see Sienna and Isla in the same fireman's hold like me, screaming blue murder at the boys as we're carried through the club's gapping crowds. I hear the sniggers and gasps as we pass people in the VIP section. "Let go of me, Christian," I yell, thumping on his solid back. I can tell that ass from anywhere and give it a hard slap.

"Keeping doing that, V, you know how much I like a good slap and tickle." His hand comes down hard on my semi-exposed ass. Ouch, fucking bastard. I wiggle, trying to pull my dress down, so my ass isn't exposed to the masses. "Stop wiggling, V. I promise no one can see anything. Seriously, do you think I'd do that to you?"

"I didn't think you would throw me over your shoulder and kidnap me from a club, either." Christian chuckles. Asshole! Before I know it, my ass is hitting the plush leather seat of the limousine with a seething Sienna and Isla beside me.

"We were just having fun," Isla whines, playing with her bag.

"So, it's okay for you boys to have girls all over you, but when we get some attention, you haul us all away like fucking cavemen. We aren't your women who you can do this to," I fume.

"Exactly, you boys had perfectly willing women in your laps all night. You didn't have to grab three unwilling ones," Sienna adds, crossing her arms defensively in front of her.

"Don't forget you ladies work for us, and when we say we're ready to go home, that means we *are* ready to go home," Evan yells, shocking us with his tone. The other two fuckwits nod their heads in agreement. Getting in the limo, they sit opposite us where they start texting God knows who. Ignoring the boys, the three of us girls fume huddled in the corner as far away from them as possible.

"I'm seriously pissed, how fucking dare they." The blood is pounding through my veins.

"And Evan pulling the fucking boss card. That was a dick move," Isla grumbles.

"I'm so fucking embarrassed," Sienna huffs.

"It's okay for them to have fun with all those women, but when we do, they act like they own us as if we're their property or toys. Obviously, they don't like other men playing with their toys. Well, fuck them, they don't own us," I huff, crossing my arms angrily in front of me. The girls nod in agreement. We sit in the limousine in silence, getting more and more worked up with every mile.

Eventually, the car arrives at the house the boys are renting while in London. Getting out of the car in silence, each of us women stomp through the quiet house. Yes, I am having a tantrum, but fuck it, I'm pissed. Walking up the one flight of stairs toward my bedroom, I turn my head and see the boys talking at the bottom of the stairs, their eyes watching three pissed-off women move through the house. I slam the bedroom door, the loud noise vibrating through the house. My point has been made.

Kicking my shoes to the side, I start unzipping my dress, throwing it into the corner. I walk toward the bathroom in my underwear and start getting ready for bed—wiping my makeup off, then brushing my teeth—the night's events running on a loop through my mind making me angrier. I head back into my room as I hear a faint knock at my door. I storm over toward it, open it, and find a smiling Christian. His whiskey-colored eyes trail down my nearly naked body, and a smirk crosses his face.

"Were you expecting someone else?" he coos, raising his eyebrows at me. Looking down, I realize I'm standing in my underwear, but fuck him, he can stand there and stare.

"What do you want? I'm about to go to bed."

"What do I want?" he questions, raising his voice as he pushes through the door, slamming it behind him, the sound piercing the quiet night air. "What I want, Ness, is you." He stalks toward me. Shaking my head, I hold my hands up in a defensive manner.

"No!" My answer stills him.

"You had me out of my freaking mind tonight, Ness." He walks closer toward me. "Dancing on that table, those killer legs of yours on display. I could see the drool falling out of those men's mouths as they watched you girls dance. Your dress was so fucking short, with each hip movement, I could see your panties, and so could everyone else in the club." *Oops.*

"It was driving me crazy. Those men don't deserve to see that part of you. A man has to earn it." Christian is standing in front of me, his eyes tracing my breasts' curves and his finger running along the lace's edge of my bra.

"I hated the wicked thoughts they were having about you dancing on that table. I could see it in their eyes." Another sweep across my breast, this time his thumb catches my sensitive bud, sending electricity over my body.

"Christian, I'm not yours to worry about," I remind him.

"Yes, you are." His large palm grabs my breast. I let out a hint of a moan, damn traitorous body. "See, I know what you like, Ness. I'm the only one who understands your needs." He pulls back the lace of my bra, his mouth catching my nipple.

"Fuck," I groan, arching my back. The champagne is making the world all bubbly and fuzzy, or maybe it's Christian's lips. My hands automatically go to his hair, pulling him harder into me.

"See, Ness, I know you." I nod as he starts on the other breast giving equal attention to it. "No one will ever be good enough for you." Maybe he's right because, at this moment, nothing feels better than the way Christian is playing with me.

"It's been too long, Ness." A hand makes its way down my body toward my panties, large fingers slipping inside the delicate fabric, and then inside of me.

"See, I know what you need... and you need me, don't you?"

I whimper because, at this point in time, I don't care. His hand suddenly stills, and I almost cry out.

"Say it, Ness, tell me you need me." His eyes are lit with fire. He looks at my flushed face, my heart is racing, and I know I should say no. I know I should push him away because I'm pissed at his actions tonight, but I've had too much champagne, and his magic fingers are currently teasing my aching clit. I want that orgasm that's just out of reach. Looking at him, our eyes never wavering from each other, the room melts away with its intensity.

"I need you," I confess.

"Thank fuck," he groans as his lips capture mine, his fingers continuing their sinful work on my clit.

"Ahh, Christian," I call out as my orgasm takes over, and my entire body turns to jelly. I slump against him. Strong arms wrap themselves around me, lifting me. The room moves in a blur of movement and color until my back is hitting the bed. I watch as Christian kicks off his shoes and socks and pulls his shirt over his head, leaving his naked torso exposed with his ink wrapping around his impressive body. I let out a sigh making him laugh. "Like what you see, angel?" He raises his eyebrow at me.

"Hmm." My eyes are feeling heavy. Maybe I'll just shut them for a moment. I feel the bed dip, and then Christian's body heat beside me.

"V, are you asleep?" I mumble something incoherently.

"Fuck," Christian curses. "It's okay, princess, you get some sleep, it's been a long day," Christian mumbles into my ear.

Rolling over so that my face is nuzzling into his neck, I whisper, "I'm still pissed at you even though you made me come." Christian's chest rumbles with laughter.

"Okay, noted, V." His arms wrap around me, his spicy scent of man and sweat swirls under my nose.

"I hate that you can make me come." Another rumbled laugh falls from his chest.

"Really, I'm pretty sure you just enjoyed it." Peeling my eyes open, I try and focus on him.

"It confuses me." Christian stills.

"Yeah, why?"

"You give me the best orgasms, but you're my best friend… that's not supposed to happen."

Looking down into my eyes, he murmurs, "You make me hard every time I'm around you, and you're my best friend. I don't think that's supposed to happen, either." He presses his lips to my forehead. "But I wouldn't change it for the world, Ness. It may be confusing, but I think it's just us."

"Why couldn't you be ugly? It would make it easier to be your friend." This earns me a deep baritone laugh.

"Good to know you're only my friend because of my good looks. Had no idea you were so shallow, Ness."

I punch him lightly in the chest. "Dick."

"Go to sleep, you can be mad at me in the morning." And I do. I slowly fall asleep, wrapped in his arms.

18

CHRISTIAN

We're back in London three months later after finishing our European tour and only a couple of days away from finally being free. Life is fucking great. I can't wait to let loose and relax. Everyone is buzzing. I still can't believe we have finally finished the tour. Our very last one for a fucking long time, and it feels incredible. My brother has been busily organizing shit for our lives after this tour, namely our new record label—Dirty Texas Records.

It pains me to say it, but he's a fucking legend. All the numbers and projections he has estimated for our profits are impressive—he's like rain man when it comes to business stuff. When we get back to LA, we'll start work on setting up our new studio. It's pretty exciting. I'm excited about the change as all of the guys are. We won't ever stop making music, but ten years of constant traveling and touring wear you out after a while.

Significant changes are happening at Dirty Texas. Evan, the fucker, got his girl. He and Sienna have been loved-up since being busted a month ago, being all sneaky and shit. Who knew Evan Wyld would be the first one of us to drop from the market?

"Cheers, you bastards, to another tour well done, and to never having to see your ugly mugs ever again," Vanessa jokes as we all clink our glasses together in celebration of a job well done. "Shit, does that mean you're going to be home all day, every day?" Vanessa asks, turning to me.

"Sure thing, queen V. You will finally have me all to yourself, every single day. I know how much this idea gets you hot," I joke with her, kissing her on the cheek, making everyone laugh.

"Actually, V, we want to ask you something." Axel looks serious, but we all know what's coming. We turn toward Vanessa, who's looking a little uneasy, but we have her attention. As much as I hated the idea, there's a part of me that thought, finally, no more excuses after five years. There'd be nothing coming between us anymore until Axel suggested this, and fuck, I couldn't deny her this opportunity. There's no one else better suited for the job.

"We were wondering if you would like to be the new PR Director for Dirty Texas Records." The table erupts, but we soon realize Vanessa hasn't answered.

"You want me to run the PR for your label?" She's looking a little shocked. The guys all nod in unison to Vanessa's question. Tears well in her eyes, which is pretty rare for Vanessa.

"Hey, V, no, no, why are you upset, sweetheart?" I wrap my arms around her while the rest of the boys look on with worried looks.

"There's no one else in the world we'd trust. You're family, V, and family sticks together," Axel states matter of factly. Vanessa's green eyes look up at him with wonder and pride. Her face lights up into a huge smile.

"Hell, yeah, let's do this." The table erupts into cheers again.

We're all trashed by the time we get back to our hotel room. Evan's gone off with Sienna, probably to go make babies, they are so loved-up. Oscar and Finn have gone off with some chicks. Derrick's disappeared somewhere with some guy, Isla's probably gone back to her room, so that leaves Axel, Vanessa, and me in the hotel room. Axel and I both collapse onto the couch while Vanessa runs around getting us something to drink. She's in the mood to party tonight.

"Can you believe we have finally finished?" Axel asks, turning to me. It's like looking into a mirror some days, except a slightly different version. His scruffy five o'clock shadow darkening as the early morning light filters through our penthouse windows, his light brown hair is now a little longer than mine.

"It feels good, it feels like the right time." My eyes are watching Vanessa walk around, her assets bouncing with each step.

"She's a beautiful woman." Axel admires Vanessa as she skips around the room. I nod in agreement. It's the truth, and then I notice how my brother is looking at her. I can see the hunger in his eyes, and I'm not sure how I feel about it. I'm jealous that he's checking her out. We've shared women in the past and enjoyed it, but this is Ness—I shake those stupid thoughts from my head. Fuck, I must be drunker than I thought.

"I found the tequila, boys." She smiles, waving the bottle in front of us.

"Come join us," Axel coos. What the fuck? That's his sex voice. No, he's never used the sex voice on Vanessa before. The atmosphere in the room changes, and I'm not sure what's happening. It's like I am a bystander. I don't know if I like it. Vanessa slowly walks toward us, her hips swaying. I feel my brother adjust himself as she closes in, but she stops in front of me, her knee nudges mine, and she steps in between my legs.

"Open up," she says, pouring a shot of tequila into my mouth. I swallow the acrid liquor, her eyes still on me. Bending down, her pink tongue darts out, tasting my lips, then my mouth. I hear my brother groan beside me, but he doesn't make a move. Vanessa turns her attention to Axel, handing him the tequila bottle, giving him a flirty smile before turning back to me.

Vanessa has a mischievous look in her eyes. She takes a couple of steps back from me, her hand disappearing behind her. Axel and I are both frozen as we watch what's happening before us, not quite believing it. The sound of her zipper unfastening slowly fills the silent room. Each undoing of the metal teeth adds an extra layer of sexual tension in the air. Her eyes never leave mine as she seductively undresses—my heart is racing. I don't know what the fuck is going on, but I can't seem to move. Axel hands me the bottle. I take another swig of tequila, hoping it will calm me down.

Vanessa's dress hits the floor. She's standing before us in black skimpy underwear and heels. I hear Axel mutter under his breath, but I can't take my eyes off her. She moves again toward me, placing herself between my legs, her emerald eyes sparkling like jewels as she takes a moment to look over me hungrily. Vanessa places a knee either side of my lap, and her tits are now staring me in the face. What the fuck is going on? This is the hottest thing I've ever seen in my life, but there's the elephant in the room, namely Axel, sitting right beside me watching.

"I want to fuck you, Christian," Vanessa purrs as those luscious lips touch the skin below my ear. My body is now firing on all cylinders. Vanessa's words make my body hum.

"I don't mind that Axel is here. In fact, it's kind of hot. I can put on a show for him." Axel lets out an audible groan when he hears Vanessa's dirty mouth.

"It's up to you, Christian... how far you want to go," she whispers. My heart is racing, but I'm unsure. I get to fuck a beautiful woman, but only if my brother watches. I chance a look at Axel, whose eyes are focused on Vanessa's body, his hand gripping his crotch. Vanessa's finger moves my face back to her.

"But just so you know, I don't want him." Her eyes glance to where Axel is sitting, then back to me. "I want you. I want your cock inside of me. You're the only one who knows what I like." Is she trying to kill me? Vanessa's voice drops to a whisper, "But the thought of him watching me fuck you..." she pauses, a hand disappearing down toward her panties, "... makes me fucking wet... feel me." She grabs my hand, pressing my finger against the damp material. Fuck, she's soaking. I look at my stunned brother. He has a fist in his mouth, trying not to make a sound.

"Axe, she's drenched," I whisper. He silently nods, his eyes focused on my finger running back and forth against Vanessa's underwear. My eyes look up to Ness, they are sparkling with desire, but they are focused solely on me.

"Axel, feel how wet she is." I pull his hand toward Vanessa. He's hesitant for a moment. I can feel him pulling against my grip. I give him a reassuring nod that I'm okay with it. Finally, Axel moves, his fingers tentatively touching her. Vanessa lets out a whimper at his touch.

"Fuck," Axel groans. "She's wet." He slowly rubs the lace of her underwear back and forth, feeling her.

"Axel, Vanessa wants me to fuck her, and she'd like you to watch."

"I don't know, bro. I want to stay because fuck, Ness, you look so fucking hot at the moment, but I kind of think I should leave because um..." His voice trails off.

"There will be no sharing," I state.

"I wouldn't want to share her either, she's so beautiful." Axel is in awe. I guess he now understands why I'm hooked on this girl.

"She is." I look up at her, and Vanessa's smiling at me. She hasn't glanced at Axel during this whole exchange. Fuck, I'm so torn. There's some part of me that wants to share Ness with my brother, so he can understand my feelings for her, which sounds so fucked-up, but then I don't want him ever to get to experience her, either. Fuck, I wish I wasn't so drunk and horny because it's messing with my head.

"Are you okay with me touching her?" Axel prompts. I nod, I can handle that. "Are you okay with her touching me?" I nod again.

"Yes. I think I'm okay with that." But a part of me has concerns. Maybe she wants Axel. Perhaps she wants to fuck him. That thought makes my heart ache. Her hands are on my face commanding my attention. Pulling my face toward hers, she stares at me with an impish smile on her lips.

"I only want to fuck you, okay?" I nod, looking at this beautiful woman before me. "But I don't mind putting on a show for Axe." Her eyes don't even move to where he's seated. "It's your cock that I want to be buried deep inside of me, do you understand?" Yeah, angel, I fucking understand, I say to myself.

"Fuck!" Axel let's out a startled breath, I know exactly how he feels. Vanessa has a dirty mouth. I fucking love it as I sit up and capture her lips.

"Thank fuck, I don't think I can handle you fucking or kissing my brother." Turning my attention to Axel, his face looks flushed from all the sexual tension swirling around the room. "Axel, no kissing and no fucking, everything else I can handle," I tell my brother. Axel nods. I'd agree to fucking anything if I were in his position as well.

"Now, angel, let us ravage you," I growl as my mouth captures her lips again.

19

VANESSA

"Holy shit." My whole body is stiff, and I'm overheating. Large tattooed arms are wrapped around me, and my leg is draped over a leg in front of me. What the fuck happened? My head feels like I've been hit by a sledgehammer then dragged through a sandstorm. Looking up at the ceiling, I try to remember what happened last night. We were celebrating the end of the tour, the boys offered me a job, and we got really drunk. Christian, Axel, and I returned to the hotel room.

Fuck!

I sit up quickly, realizing I'm in bed with Axel and Christian, who are snoring soundly beside me. Lifting the white bed sheet, I look underneath it. Fuck, they are both naked! I look a little longer because I need to remember this—last night feels like a blur of limbs and orgasms. These boys really are twins even down to their dicks. I try and stifle my giggle at the craziness of it.

Then Mother Nature hits me. I really need to pee. I quietly remove myself from Christian's strong arms and tiptoe into the bathroom to relieve myself. I jump into the shower, hoping it will loosen the hold my hangover has on me. My body aches but in a good way. I feel the warm water wash over me, and the craziness of last night haunts my thoughts.

"Now, angel, let us ravage you." Christian smiles as his lips caught mine in a kiss that's so searing hot I could've combusted right there. I feel movement behind me, rough hands touching my skin, sending flames spreading over my body. I rub my aching clit against Christian's rigid denim—it was alleviating the ache, but only just. Then unfamiliar lips touch my shoulders while the familiar ones nip at my bottom lip.

"You're so beautiful, Vanessa," Axel's gravelly voice murmurs against my skin. It never occurred to me that Axel found me attractive. I can appreciate Axel's good looks because I'm not blind, but he never got my stomach fluttering like Christian did. Is that because Christian met me first? If I had met Axel first, would it have been the same? I doubt it.

Axel's fingers slide under the strap of my bra and carefully pulls the straps down my shoulders, all the while raining sweet kisses over my heated skin. Christian's palms grab my ass as he pushes me against his denim-clad erection, grinding me against him. I feel like a goddess being worshiped by two Adonis. It's so erotic that it feels taboo. Having fun with twins is such a cliché. I know they have done this before. I never understood the sharing bit, until now. I fucking get it!

My hands start to unbuckle Christian's jeans. I need them off. I can feel he's toeing off his shoes and socks. My hand finds him commando in his jeans. Fuck, I love discovering him like that, it's a fucking gift ready for you. My thumb runs over his wet slit, making him hiss. He gives me a heated smirk as our eyes meet.

"Axe, I think she needs to be in a more comfortable position," Christian addresses his brother behind me as his fingers dig into me.

"Sure, do you mind if I take her?" he asks, and Christian nods his agreement. Axel's strong arms lift me out of Christian's lap, and I wrap my legs around his waist, his erection pushes against my underwear's thin material. He groans when I press against him, those whiskey-colored eyes looking at me. Christian said no kissing, and I thought I wanted that, but at this moment, I could kiss Axel. I think he senses it as well. Bending forward, he sucks my neck instead.

"Fuck, Ness, you taste so good. I've always wanted to taste you, but my brother..." The words trail off as he carries me toward the bedroom. Gently, he lays me down on Christian's bed, kicks off his shoes, and toes off his socks. Ever so slowly, he pulls his T-shirt over his head.

"Fuck!" I watch the material fall to the floor. Standing before me is Axel's naked torso. He works out but not as much as Christian, his six-pack is defined, a light dusting of hair crosses his chest, his blue and white Japanese style tattoos hiding his muscular arms. The further I look down, I follow the dark happy trail that disappears down under the denim. I wonder if he's commando as well? I wonder if their dicks look the same? What a crazy thought, they may be twins, but they would be totally different, wouldn't they? Christian now joins us standing in the doorway, his jeans unbuckled and hanging open from where I had undone them. His whiskey-colored eyes are watching me intently, maybe trying to work out what I'm thinking.

"Strip." Who the hell said that? I've never heard that tone from myself before. "I want you both naked in front of me." I sound like a damn dominatrix. Oh shit, that reminds me of that sexy dream I had once. They both look at each other and quickly remove their clothing. I can't believe that standing before me are two of the world's hottest men. I can feel drool pooling in my mouth, and some further south as my eyes ravish them both.

"Shit!" I sit up on the bed, I probably left a wet patch underneath me, but I don't care.

"I think it's your turn, babe." Christian smiles. I shake my head.

"No, I want to try something tonight. It's the only time I think we'll ever do something like this."

"You want to control us? Tell us what to do? You want us to be your slaves, Vanessa?" Axel's voice caresses my skin. He understands precisely what kinky thoughts are going through my head. "You know I don't give control over to just anyone, don't you, darlin'," Axel adds. I know he and Christian go to sex clubs. I wonder if Axel is into more than just sex. He's so domineering at work that I can only imagine he'd be the same in the bedroom.

"Trust me, you will want her to take control," Christian chuckles. How strange is this situation? Christian, my best friend, telling his brother to let me control the crazy sex we're about to have because it's going to be good. Thank fuck I'm drunk. Otherwise, I think I'd be utterly embarrassed by the way I am acting at the moment. I raise an eyebrow to double-check Axel is on board with me calling the shots.

"I'm at your service," he says, smirking. Fuck, it's hot.

Shit, now what? I quickly try and retrieve any threesome porn scenes I've watched recently on Tumblr, so I look like I know what I'm doing. Two hot men watching me, waiting for my command, I feel drunk from its power, or maybe it's just the tequila. Getting up onto my knees, I crawl to the end of the bed where they are standing, waiting for me, their large palms holding their hard, long cocks. My heart is thumping through my chest. I swear the whole room is vibrating from it. I'm now kneeling in front of them.

"Darlin', I think you need to lose your clothes." Christian arches his brow at me as he looks over me with hunger. He's right. My hand undoes the back of my bra, and it falls to the floor. I hear both men audibly inhale, their eyes so similar admiring what's before them. Christian is the first to reach out and touch my breasts, lightly fondling them. Axel's teeth sink into his bottom lip. My hand comes out tentatively to grab hold of his firm dick. Is it wrong that I'm comparing them? Axel and Christian share the same length, but Christian has more girth—they are each stunning in their own way.

Axel gasps at the first contact of my hand. Christian's fingers find my nipples and give them a light twist sending electricity shots directly to my clit. I drop Axel's cock and move to stand up, placing one unsteady foot *after the other onto the carpeted floor, bringing my body in direct contact with each of them.*

"Christian, get on the bed," I command, pushing him toward it. I watch as he sits on the edge. Slowly bending over, I take his cock in my mouth. I can feel his saltiness on my tongue. I spread my legs, hoping Axel understands what I'm asking for. A couple of moments later, I feel him behind me, his large fingers pushing the lace of my underwear to the side, his knuckle playing with my wetness before a large finger enters me. I moan around Christian's cock.

"Do that again, Ness," Christian groans. Axel sinks another large finger inside of me, making me feel full. "Fuck. Shit," Christian swears, grabbing my hair, pulling me harder against him. Axel's expert fingers are slowly going back and forth through my slickness. It feels amazing. I haven't had many threesomes in my life, and by far, none have ever felt this incredible. It's not long before I feel my underwear slowly move down my thighs.

"I don't think we need these anymore." Axel laughs as my panties hit the floor.

"Fuck, Ness, you taste so sweet." I look behind me and see Axel sucking my wetness off his fingers. I could come from that image alone.

"Ness, sit on my face," Christian commands. So much for me taking control of the situation. Who fucking cares as long as we all get off in the end, right? Christian lies down where he is on the edge of the bed, his back flat on the mattress, and his legs curve over the edge. I wiggle my way up over his body, making sure to rub myself over his bare chest. "Axel, jump onto the bed and kneel, Vanessa is going to need something to keep her quiet," Christian chuckles. Axel hops onto the bed and kneels near his brother's head. Christian pulls me close to his mouth.

"Ness, I can smell how turned on you are. This will be fun." He gives me one long lick, and I let out a moan. Fuck me, that felt good. He does it again and again. My eyes catch Axel kneeling before me, pre-cum lacing the tip of his cock. I smile at him as I bend over and lick the salty drop.

"Yes," Axel hisses. I look up at him, giving him a wicked smile before I sink his cock into my mouth. "Fuck!" Axel's hands go directly to my head, holding me in place, but Christian works his magic on my clit before I can get good suction, and I'm bucking and moaning.

"Jesus woman... Christian, do that again," Axel growls. And he does it again, making me hum over Axel's cock. "Yes, yes, yes," Axel groans as I keep sucking him off. Christian pushes me away.

"I need you to come on my face, babe," he mumbles as he continues to work his magic. I can feel the orgasm start in my toes, moving up my legs, and they begin to shake. I still have Axel's cock in my mouth, and I swear it's getting bigger the closer I'm getting to my orgasm. Christian places his thumb against my puckered hole, putting the slightest pressure against it, making me go off like a firecracker. I almost swallow Axel's dick in my mouth as I convulse over Christian's face. He slaps me hard across my ass.

"That's my girl." Christian laughs as he wiggles from underneath me, leaving me on all fours. Axel's dick falls from my mouth with a pop. "Now it's your turn to see if you can make her come." Christian challenges Axel with a predatory smirk.

"It would be my pleasure," Axel cockily states, moving into the position Christian had just left. His large hands pulling my hips down toward his mouth, Axel gives me a quick lick, and I almost shoot off his face. My clit is sensitive from Christian's orgasm. "Fuck, she tastes so good," he hums against me.

"I need those lips wrapped around me, Ness," Christian prompts me, his large, thick erection bobbing in front of me. Yes, they do need to be wrapped around him. Eagerly, I start licking him. Axel's technique is different from Christian's but equally as magical. It doesn't take long to make me come.

"Fuck, so fucking good." Axel smiles between my legs. This is so surreal. Moving off Axel, my eyes follow Christian across the room to his jeans, where he pulls out a condom. Yes, I need him inside of me.

He walks back toward the bed and lies down. I help him with the condom.

"Now, sweetheart, I'm going to need you to jump on," he orders, smiling as he lays back on the bed. "I want you reverse cowgirl, looking at Axe." My heart is thumping but in a good way. As I'm told, I slowly sink onto Christian, both of us groaning as he fills me. Axel smirks and moves closer. "Hold her still for a moment," Axel asks while bending down and taking a nipple into his mouth. Rolling his tongue over it, he sucks it deep into his warm mouth, using his teeth to send crazy sensations all over my body. Axel spends his time driving me crazy, playing with my nipples. It's not long before a finger slowly dips in-between my legs. Fuck, now that's hot, Christian's cock filling me while Axel's finger is touching me. "I think we can get another out of you," Axel growls.

"I need to move, man," Christian grumbles. "Let's see if she can come on my cock with your fingers." The double sensation is making me crazy. Bright lights are flashing before me. Christian is moving slowly underneath me, Axel's large fingers are playing with my clit, his warm mouth wrapped around my breasts. Rock stars are great at sex, not because of all the groupies but because they can keep their rhythm, each of them in tune with the other as they bring me higher and higher to ecstasy.

"Fuck," I scream, my whole-body convulsing, tears touching my eyes from the orgasm's power.

"Shit, I felt that in my bones," Christian mumbles underneath me.

"You okay?" Axel asks. My face is flushed, my skin has broken out in a slight sweat, my body feels like it's floating in some sort of heaven, yet I want more. Axel shuffles back, and Christian pulls out of me, making me whimper.

"Get on your hands and knees, this is about to get rough," Christian growls. I'm drunk on orgasms, they could tie me up and do anything to me, and I wouldn't care. It's the most magical feeling I have ever felt. Christian positions me on my knees, his hands are on *my hips as his cock nudges my entrance. He teases me until I'm making some sort of frustrated, crazed whimper. When he enters me, everything feels right again.*

I reach out, grabbing Axel's cock, stroking it in time with Christian's thrusts, which start out slow and torturous, but his thrusts become frantic within moments. It's not long before Axel's cock is in my mouth, and my body starts to shake again as Christian fucks me hard. Shit, his girth stretches me, his length finding the perfect places inside of me that make me want to soar.

I can feel the saltiness of Axel's arousal in my mouth, my hands find his balls, which start to tense. He's close. Christian's thumb finds my puckered hole again as he thrusts into me just as Axel's cock hits my throat. The sensation is overwhelming, and I come again. My orgasm spurs Christian on to find his release, and not long after that, Axel comes down my throat. We all collapse in a shaky, sweaty, blissful mess of limbs.

I think I just came again thinking about last night, my cheeks are flushed, and my body is humming.

"Morning, gorgeous," Christian calls out.

"Shit, you scared me, Christian," I squeal, trying not to fall over. The bastard chuckles as he joins me. "How are you this morning?" His eyes run hungrily over my body.

"Fine, just a wicked hangover. How about you?" I understand what he's really asking—if I'm okay with what happened between Axel and him last night.

"It was hot, but do I want to do it again? No." I could see the vulnerability in his eyes, wondering if I wanted to be with his brother. Wrapping my arms around his neck, I rub our noses together.

"Not sure how last night happened. I think we were riding on some sort of high, the tequila probably didn't help, but honestly, I'm happy with the memories. It was erotic, and it has left me with enough spank bank material for a lifetime."

Christian chuckles. "How did I get so lucky to have you in my life, Ness?"

"I think it was some kind of cosmic kismet that brought us together." My lips touch his as I feel his arms tighten around me.

"I think you might be right." He nuzzles into my neck, pushing me a couple of steps back against the shower wall. "I need you again, Ness, just you and me. Is that okay?"

"Yes." Christian turns me around in his arms, pressing my chest against the cold tiled wall. He enters me in one swift movement. We lose ourselves in the rawness of the moment, my oversensitive body doesn't take long to come, and I scream as Christian takes me.

"Morning," Axel says, smiling as we walk out into the kitchen. Room service has delivered our breakfast, and it's waiting for us on the table. My cheeks flush, looking at Axel standing there, his hair pulled up into a man bun, his gray sweatpants hanging low on his hips. He's not wearing any underwear, thank God for the dick imprint in his sweatpants. I bit my lip remembering last night.

"Okay, is this going to be awkward now?" Axel asks, looking between Christian and me. We both shrug. So yeah, I guess it's going to be awkward.

Axel walks toward me, and I can see that desire in his eyes. He grabs my face and kisses my cheeks, thank fuck. He turns to Christian, who looks like he's ready to skin his brother for touching me and slaps him on the back.

"Last night was fun, thanks." He sits down and starts eating his scrambled eggs. Christian and I look at each other and follow suit, and we eat in silence for a while.

"Seriously, guys, is this going to be weird?" Axel asks again, looking at both of us. We're still both silent. See what I mean—awkward.

"Okay, I guess I'll have to spell it out because both of you are incapable of forming words. Vanessa, you're a beautiful woman, and I find you extremely attractive, especially this morning listening to you come in the shower. Fuck, you made me come in three seconds flat, which is rare for me when jerking off." I choke on my eggs as does Christian.

"Last night was some freak break in the matrix or something like that. I know us, and we'd never have done something like that before, probably was a full moon or something. Now... do I want to repeat that again? Yes, because I'm a male, and it was sexy as sin, but in all seriousness, no, I don't because now, it doesn't seem right in the cold light of day. I know I'll think about last night many times as I jerk off as you both will. But know this, Chris, you can trust me around Vanessa, okay?"

I hear Chris let out an audible breath. "I know."

Axel smiles. "And... Ness, know this, I'll turn you down if you come onto me. Unless, of course, I have written permission in blood from my brother."

This makes me laugh. "Keep dreaming."

"Oh, I will, don't you worry, so let's just think of last night as some magical little anomaly never to be repeated." And with that, we continue eating our breakfast as if last night never happened.

20

CHRISTIAN
PRESENT DAY

Now is the time.
    I'm taking the most significant chance of my life by telling Vanessa about my feelings. We're huddled together waiting for the clock to strike midnight to ring in the new year together. Evan and Sienna got married today. It was beautiful, those two looked so happy, and I want that happiness with Vanessa.

    Having our families spend time with each other on this trip really sealed the deal for me. They just meshed. My parents love Vanessa. Mom would love for something more permanent to happen between us, so hopefully tonight, we can start the new year off with a bang as a couple. I'm nervous as fuck. We have had such a great time while being here. Vanessa has been so relaxed, showing me around where she grew up, especially that hidden waterfall where we basically spent the day fucking in the sun in the middle of nowhere. Heaven, it was fucking heaven.

    "Happy New Year," everyone screams as the fireworks go off around us. I kiss Vanessa with everything I have, hoping that by some miracle, she feels the same way I do. Breaking our kiss, we turn and watch the light display.

"Vanessa, I love you," I whisper into her ear.

"I love you, too," she answers. I maneuver her around in my arms so that we're face to face when I explain to her what I really mean.

"No, V... I love you." I don't think she gets what I mean because we say that all the time to each other, but it's usually friendly. Now I'm suggesting it in a more-than-friends kind of way. "Not as the best-friends- forever kind of love, more like..." I pause for a moment stumbling over my words because I am nervous as fuck. "I love you as in you-are-the-one kind of way." Vanessa laughs. She must think I'm joking and isn't taking me seriously.

"Ness?" I prompt her because she hasn't answered me.

"What?" She responds as if I haven't just declared my deepest feelings for her.

"You don't have anything to say?" I question, feeling annoyed by her reaction. She's silent for a moment then reaches out and pinches me. "Ouch," I groan, rubbing my arm. What the hell did she do that for?

"Chris... no," she finally answers, and I can see that she's freaking out, and I don't blame her because if the roles were reversed, I'd probably be doing the same thing.

"V, look at me," I command, trying to get her to concentrate on me in front of her, not everything else that's going on in her head. "Ness, stop freaking out and look at me," I demand again when she refuses to meet my eyes. "No one can compare to you, Ness." I want her to understand exactly how serious I am about her. "I tried, I tried so much to get over you, but you're so far under my skin." I can see the panic on her face.

"But... we live together."

Ugh, that same old excuse I've heard through the years, I'm over it. "And yet, that doesn't stop you from crawling into my bed most nights," I taunt, not meaning to get annoyed with Ness, but I am.

"Don't," she whispers.

"Doesn't stop you from straddling my dick on the couch during a movie or..." Her soft, warm hand covers my mouth, silencing me.

"I never hear you say no," she bites back.

"Why the hell would I, Ness? You're fucking hot, and I love you." My hand lightly runs down her arm, trying to keep the connection between us going.

"But... you're my best friend." Another excuse she has made over the years.

"Don't you think that's a great foundation to start a relationship?" I look at her, daring her to disagree.

Shaking her head at me, she replies, "Chris, you weren't supposed to fall for me."

"How could I not, Ness? You're beautiful, sexy, you look after me, and that accent of yours does things to my dick. I trust you, and there aren't many people I trust. You also swear like a biker, drink like a sailor, and fuck like a pro." Pushing a hand on my chest, she takes a step back from me. I'm a little confused by her reaction.

"Wow, what a glowing reference." She sounds angry. "Why the hell would you want to be with someone like that? I don't sound like a woman you want to bring home to your family."

"My family loves you, Ness, and you know it." She looks at me, shaking her head.

"It would ruin everything we have worked so hard to build, and you can't go and change the goalposts now."

"What? Haven't you liked being in my bed all of these months?"

"Fucking you is different from being with you." She quickly covers her mouth when she realizes what she has said. I'm not going to lie, it fucking hurt. I feel my anger bubble to the surface.

"Okay, I get it. I'm good enough to fuck but not good enough to date. I'll only ever be one of your many fuck toys you play with." My heart is racing. "I never thought you were like that, Ness. I never thought you saw me like that." I cross my arms defensively in front of me.

"Christian, you're more than that to me, and you know it," she whispers.

"Are you sure about that, Ness?" I say sarcastically.

"I thought it was always going to be you and me, having fun, messing around. I never thought there'd ever be... more." This woman makes me so angry, and I don't understand how she can say all these things to me. I thought what we have together was something special. I get that she has had some fucked-up relationships, which have made her cautious about love, but this is me. I've been around her for so long, she should know by now that I'm trustworthy enough, that I'll never hurt her. I just don't get it.

"You thought for the rest of our lives we'd just fool around?" There's silence between us. She thought we could just continue fooling around, no commitment. Like what? Until we're sixty or seventy, or until one of us is dead? "I'm sorry that I finally had the balls to say how I feel, Ness, about you and I have between us. It's once-in-a-lifetime stuff. We're meant to be together, and you know it." I pull her to me so she can see how serious I am about her.

"I want happily ever after with you, and I'm sorry if that makes you feel uncomfortable. These feelings I have for you scare the absolute shit out of me, but I'm willing to give this a try." I smile at her, hoping that will show her how much I mean what I'm saying. "Someone needed to be honest with their feelings here. Five years we have been in and out of each other's beds, and yet we haven't become sick of each other. That must mean something." Vanessa pulls herself out of my arms, and my heart sinks.

"I'm sorry, Chris, but I can't. I can't love you like that. I don't think I can love anyone like that." What? Does she not realize she already does love me that way every single day?

"Nothing? You feel nothing for me?" I ask, thumping my chest. I notice a single tear falling down her cheek. I know her heart isn't made of stone.

"I can't give you what you want, Christian. I'm sorry." Fuck, this woman makes me so mad.

"You're a fucking liar, Ness. Don't forget, I know you. I can tell when you're lying to me, lying to my face. Have you forgotten what it feels like between us?" I need to show her, remind her, she's so fucking stubborn sometimes.

I grab her face and pull her to me and let my lips do the talking, hoping she can't deny the physical reaction she has to me. It's working as she grabs my body and pulls it closer to her. How can she ignore what happens between us? Finally, I relax a little, hoping that our kiss has enough power to change her mind. Resting my forehead against hers, I whisper, "I felt exactly how much you love me in that kiss, Ness."

"I can't. Why is that so hard for you to understand? I have my job, we live together, our friendship. I'm sorry, I'm not risking all that for some fantasy life you think we can have together." I am physically stunned by her words. "I'm not capable of loving you the way you want me to." My heart sinks deep down inside of me. "I'm sorry, Chris, it's not worth the risk."

There it is, she just doesn't love me as much as I love her. I can't continue on like this, loving someone who will never love me back. I've wasted five years chasing after a dream that will never happen. I'm so fucking stupid.

"Okay, Ness, I hear you loud and clear. I'm not worth the risk. All I am to you is a convenient cock." I am pissed, I am hurt, and I am lashing out. I take a couple of steps toward her before spitting out, "I'd have made you happy if only you had the guts to take a chance. Don't worry, V, I won't make that mistake again. As I said, I hear you loud and clear." And with that, I turn on my heel and head back toward the party, leaving the woman I love behind.

"Sorry, excuse me, are you Christian Taylor?" A petite blonde catches my attention as I stomp my way through the gardens. She's one of the waitstaff at the resort.

"Sure am, darlin', and you're exactly what I've been looking for."

21

VANESSA

ONE MONTH AFTER THE WEDDING

"Things can't possibly be that bad?" Derrick questions me as we drive to my home.

"Just you wait, I mean it, D. I don't think I can live with him anymore." Christian is refusing to have anything to do with me since he confessed his love and asked for a future chance. I wanted to say yes, but I couldn't because fear stopped me. It's stupid to be so scared of being in a relationship, especially with him.

But now, the way he's treating me, the way he has totally cut me out of his life, is hurtful. This is why I couldn't chance it because of this exact reason. Christian has been partying hard since the wedding. Photos of him stumbling out of clubs with many women on his arms have been landing on my desk at work.

And don't even get me started with the working situation. Apparently, we need a mediator because that's the only way we can communicate with each other. He refuses any one-on-one meeting I have requested to help clear the air. Poor Isla is caught in the middle of us, and the entire band is at a loss as to why he's acting the way he is toward me. I've never seen him so cold toward me in the five years I have worked with them.

Evan was the only one that knew something was up. He pulled me aside one day and asked me point-blank if I had said no to Christian. I was pretty shocked that he knew about us. He explained that he was the one who pushed Christian to declare his feelings for me, and now he feels bad that he might have ruined us. Of course, it wasn't Evan's fault. It was Christian's wounded pride that had taken a beating. Yeah, I was kind of a bitch to him, but I thought we could at least be civil until those hurt feelings had gone away. I was wrong.

There's music coming from the house as Derrick and I exit the car.

"This should be interesting," I say to Derrick, pushing open the front door. Derrick and I walk through the foyer toward the living area, which is empty. We then hear voices out near the pool. My stomach sinks. This isn't what I want to see when I get home. Christian is sitting on a pool lounge, getting his cock sucked by some blonde. Several naked women are lounging by the pool, oblivious to what's going on around them. Christian looks up from the blonde sucking his cock, and gives us a wicked smile.

"You're a disgusting pig," I spit out, wanting to throw up. The girl sucking his dick turns around and looks at me with a death stare.

"Ignore her, I do most of the time," Christian snarls. The blonde turns back and starts working his dick again.

"What the fuck, Christian?" Derrick blurts out. "I have no fucking idea who this guy is in front of me. The Christian I know would never treat his best friend like this."

Christian frowns at Derrick's comment, then quickly composes himself. "You two going to stand there all night watching, or do you want to join in?"

Derrick just shakes his head. "Fuck you, enjoy loneliness,

you fucking prick because that's where you're heading if you keep up this attitude." Christian blanches at the heated words Derrick spews at him.

"Come, V, you don't need to be subjected to this," Derrick states, waving his hand at the wannabe porn scene in front of us. Grabbing my arm, he whisks me away and toward my room. "Come live with me," Derrick says. "I'll not allow you to subject yourself to some man-child tantrums. He needs to fucking grow up." I give Derrick a weak smile.

"But I did this to him." I feel ridiculously guilty over not saying yes to him.

"Look at me, V." Derrick grabs my arms and holds me still, those dark eyes sparkling at me. "You were honest with your feelings to him. He's just upset that you turned him down. I don't think anyone has ever rejected that boy, which must be a new feeling for him. He's screwing around with groupies to feed his ego, to show you that he is desired, and that you made a mistake. He's trying to hurt you because he can't have you, and he doesn't know what else to do." I feel sick.

"But I love him, D," I confess.

"I understand you love him because he's your best friend." Derrick nods his head at me. I can't look at him. "Ness," Derrick growls at me. That's when I break down in his arms.

"I love him, D… but I'm scared, and naively, I thought we could go back to the way we were, just like we had for the last few years. This time, I think he's done with me." Derrick is quiet for a moment. I can hear his heart thumping in his chest.

"I think what might be best for the two of you is time apart. I don't think you're ever going to rebuild your relationship if you have to live here and watch him fuck these cheap imitations of you." I nod in agreement. "So, let's pack a bag for tonight, and then we can organize for you to move the rest of your stuff over on the weekend."

This sounds like a good idea.

EARLIER TODAY, we collected all of my stuff from the house. I've been waiting for Christian to leave, so I wouldn't have to run into him. Isla told me he had planned some boys' time in Vegas this weekend, so that's when I organized to get the rest of my things from his home. Luckily, he hasn't changed the locks on me.

"It's our one-week anniversary as roomies." Derrick pops a bottle of champagne for this very special occasion. He moved into this charming 1920s bungalow in West Hollywood not long after we returned from Paris. It's perfect for him—he's close enough to the action, but far enough away to feel like living in the suburbs. He has a gorgeous little garden where we have had one too many crazy barbecues.

We're heading out on a girls' night with Stacey, Isla, and Charlotte to celebrate. I finally feel up to a night out after this Christian debacle, which still hasn't sorted itself out. I miss him. I'm so used to talking to him every day. It's been ages since he's uttered a single word to me. "Cheer up, buttercup, I have an awesome night planned," Derrick says, smiling at me.

We've had such a fantastic night tonight, starting off with delicious Mexican food, continuing on with copious amounts of cocktails, and ending up with a party back at Derrick's place. The ratio of men to women is heavily tipped in our favor.

I'm currently chatting with a very handsome Australian actor called Darcy. He's funny, charming, and great company. Derrick met him when he was asked to style him for an up-and-coming Australian star in Hollywood magazine article, and they hit it off straightaway. Now I'm standing in Derrick's backyard flirting with this much younger man and loving it. I put all thoughts of Christian behind me.

"I'm glad Derrick introduced us." He smiles at me, his blue eyes sparkling in the moonlight.

"Me, too," I reply as we stand huddled together at the back of the garden.

"You're beautiful, Vanessa," he compliments me, making me blush.

"You're not so bad yourself." Seriously, I feel like I'm back in high school with these kinds of flirtatious comebacks. Darcy moves closer to me, his breath is on the edge of my neck.

"I really want to kiss you," he confesses into my ear.

"Me, too." I feel the butterflies in my stomach. I watch as he moves closer to me, his lips touching mine hesitantly. Slowly, we start to explore each other. A tentative tongue comes out as his large palm caresses my head holding me as we softly kiss. It's a beautiful kiss, not too passionate but not dull either, the perfect amount to leave you wanting more. We smile at each other once it's over.

"Stop!" I hear Derrick yell as there's a commotion behind us.

"Get out of my face, D." Is that Christian's voice? Turning around in Darcy's arms, I see a very pissed rock star with a menacing look across his face.

"Christian," I gasp. What the hell is he doing here? He stalks over to where I'm standing with Darcy, and before I know it, he has punched Darcy in the face. The poor guy falls to the floor, blood pouring out of his nose.

"You fucker, I think you broke it," Darcy screams through the blood.

"What the fuck, Christian?" I yell at him, pushing him square in the chest. "What the hell have you done?" I crouch down near Darcy, whose hand is covered in blood. Someone hands him a towel to clean himself. As he does, he winces. "You need to go to the hospital," I say, helping him up from the floor.

"Yeah, no thanks to your fucking boyfriend," he hisses.

"He isn't my boyfriend, he's... he's..." I'm not sure what he is anymore. Darcy just frowns and storms off with his friends.

"How fucking dare you!" I push against his chest, making him take a step back.

"How dare I? You're the one who packed up your shit and left me, Ness. I came home and found your room empty. All your shit is gone. How dare you just pack and leave me." Christian looks hurt by my actions, but that doesn't excuse him coming into Derrick's home and punching out some guy.

"I'd have told you if you actually fucking spoke to me instead of giving me the cold shoulder." Christian rakes his hands through his disheveled hair.

"Do you even care about my feelings? I guess not because here you are making out with some young punk," he spits out.

"I don't give a fuck how you feel anymore because you sure as hell didn't give a fuck about how I felt. On several occasions, I walk in on you fucking random sluts on our couch or getting a fucking blow job by the pool. I came home to some goddamn kegger in the backyard. As far as I'm concerned, you can go and get fucked," I spit at him. I'm so fucking angry. Christian takes a step back as if my words have physically assaulted him.

"You didn't want me, Ness. I'm a single fucking man, and who I fuck is none of your business." His words are full of anger, and I hate that he's so angry at me. I walk up to him and poke him in the chest.

"And who I fuck is none of your business, either, yet here you are punching out guys, laying them out, bloodied on the floor."

"You're right, Ness. I don't give a shit, you can fuck whoever the fuck you like," he roars, then walks away as if nothing happened, leaving me shocked and confused.

22

VANESSA
ONE MONTH LATER

"Oh my God, Si, he's beautiful." I cuddle my soon-to-be godson, Ryder Hayes Wyld. Touching his little fingers, I look at his tiny little toes, those gorgeous puckered lips, and chubby cheeks. Dammit, he is so cute he's making my ovaries clucky, but I'm so far from having kids, it's not funny. Sienna's a trooper, spending all day in labor. Seeing her finally live out her dream of becoming a mother, I cried. I cried when I saw her holding her beautiful baby boy. Mind you, I wasn't the only one. Sienna and Evan's parents were equally smitten with little Ryder.

Christian turned up to the hospital with the other guys to greet the new addition to the Dirty Texas family. I still haven't spoken or seen him since that night at Derrick's. My hands are sweating, I'm nervous seeing him again. He looks good dressed in a hooded sweater and jeans, his golden-brown hair has grown a little longer, and he's gotten rid of some of the scruff on his face. I notice the dark circles under his eyes, he doesn't look like he's been sleeping well. Probably all the partying he's been doing.

We may not talk, but I read the gossip magazines. I see the

reports on *TMZ*, and I have a vague idea of what he has been up to. I also noticed how he's keeping himself separate from everyone, even the boys. That's just so not like him. He's usually the life of the party, the one who brings the group together. Now he doesn't look like he gives a shit. When he leaves, I relax again.

"Hey, how are you?" Axel asks as we stand outside the hospital room.

"Yeah, good, really good," I say, shuffling my feet from side to side.

"You like living with D?" Axel asks.

"I do, we have lots of fun together." Axel nods and falls silent again.

"I'm sorry about my brother, he's just…" He lets his words fall away.

"… having a tantrum," I finish his sentence for him.

Axel chuckles. "Yeah, he's used to getting the girl, and the one he wants isn't interested." He gives me a pointed look.

"Look at the way he's acting, Axe."

"You know he's just acting out. His ego is hurt, Ness. I know he still loves you. The question is, do you still love him?"

I can feel the tears threatening. I don't want to cry, but they fall, anyway, down my face, over my cheeks, falling with a splat onto the hospital floor.

"Of course, I do, but not the way he wants me to."

"Seriously? You never saw yourself with him in any other way other than as a friend?" Axel questions me.

"I don't want to talk about it, Axel." I push off from the wall and walk away from Sienna's hospital room and head toward the little hospital garden.

"Ness." Axel follows me out into the garden.

"What?" I turn around, sounding mad.

"Why are you so afraid of my brother's feelings for you?" I

can't talk to him about this because I don't really understand why I'm so afraid of Christian.

"Please, I don't want to talk about it," I plead with him.

"No, I need to know." He pushes the subject.

"I'm worried that if I take a chance on him that we could destroy what we have? That he'd eventually get sick of me or cheat or move on, then what? My heart would be broken. I'd have to leave the job that I love and leave the city that has become my home. I have too much to lose to take that chance, Axel."

"And yet, you already have lost him," he says, shoving his hands in his pockets as he turns and heads toward the door, leaving me in the tiny courtyard with my thoughts. "Have you ever thought about how much you could've gained if you had said yes?" And with that, he leaves me stunned.

"Hi, Mum," I say into my phone.

"Hey, beautiful, how's things?" Concern laces her voice. She knows what's going on between Christian and me.

"Same old stuff, haven't seen Christian, but I hear the gossip."

"I'm sorry, sweetheart. He's a good guy, just probably hurt and lost and doesn't know what to do with himself." I let out a long sigh, it's frustrating, but I don't know how to fix our relationship. I never thought it would ever be this broken.

"How is little Ryder doing?" she asks.

"Oh, Mum, he's gorgeous. He is so perfect."

"I've seen so many photos of him. He is gorgeous."

"I'm sure you have. Enough about them, I need to know about your results."

Over Christmas, Mum told me she was going to get the BRCA test done because we have a strong family history of breast cancer. She found a lump, and thank God, it was benign, but it was the push she needed to get the test done. All the women in our family have had some sort of cancer, breast cancer being the majority. It sucks that we have some faulty genes in there.

"I got the results back, sweetie." My heart is racing as she sounds so ominous. "It's positive." No! I think I'm going to throw up.

"But what does that mean?" I stammer out.

"It means if I am not proactive, then I'm going to get cancer." I can't lose my mum. "So, in a couple of weeks, I've scheduled a double mastectomy and a hysterectomy because of my age. I think my baby-making days are over," she jokes.

"I'm coming home." She needs me there, and I need to be there. It's major surgery.

"Oh, sweetie, no, you don't have to come home. It's routine, I'll be fine. You're so busy with your job, stay, you can't do anything here." As if I'm going to get any work done worrying about her.

"No, Mum, I'm coming home and helping Dad look after you." She knows how stubborn I am, mostly if I have made up my mind.

"Fine, sweetie, but can you do me one thing before you come?"

"Anything." And that was the truth.

"I want you to take the test. The results take a while. There's a big chance you have this faulty gene as well, and you need to catch this early to put measures into place. I want to be a grandma someday. You have a long life to live, and this way, you know instead of it being a ticking time bomb."

I'm silent, my mind is rushing around trying to work out what this means for me. I didn't even contemplate having the test thinking it was something for older women to do, but if all the women in my family have this faulty gene, shit.

"Vanessa," Mum calls out to me, realizing I have zoned out. "Sweetie, please do it for me, it's important."

"Of course, Mum. Of course, I will."

I booked myself in for the test as soon as I could. It would take about six weeks for the results to come through. Fingers crossed everything is okay.

23

CHRISTIAN

"How are things going, man?" I greet Evan, slapping him on the back.

"I'm so fucking tired, Chris. So fucking tired," he groans as he walks to the man cave with his little bundle wrapped in his arms. "Kids are hard work. Ryder doesn't stop screaming, and the amount of shit that comes from this tiny little human is unreal. Like how the fuck does he make that much crap?" Evan hands over the baby to me. I look down at the sleeping child. He's so tiny. Fuck, it takes my breath away that Sienna and Evan created him.

"He's going to be a lady-killer when he grows up, just like his Uncle Chris," I joke.

"Speaking of lady-killer, how are things going with Ness?" Evan asks, placing a beer on the side table.

"I wouldn't know. I haven't spoken to Vanessa in weeks." I ignore the pang deep in my heart because one of the closest people in the world to me is now a stranger to me.

"So, guess you don't know that she's in Australia, then?" My whole body stills.

"What did you say?" Ryder squirms in my arms, feeling the

tension in my body. Evan puts his beer down and takes the child from me.

"Sienna told me that Ness left for Australia the other day. Her mom is having some major surgery, and she went to be with her. She's gone for a month, dude. How the hell did you not know about this?" Running my hand through my hair, I take a big swig of beer from the bottle and fish around for my phone. I quickly unblock Vanessa's social media and start cyber stalking her.

"Is her mom okay?" Fuck, I feel like a real asshole, not knowing her mom is having surgery. This is the kind of stuff where I'd have been there for her. I would've been in Australia right beside her, no questions asked.

Evan nods. "Yeah, Sienna said she had a mastectomy and hysterectomy, so she doesn't get cancer or something like that." Shit, that's a big deal. Ness and her mom are really close.

Little Ryder starts fussing. "He's due for a feed, give me a sec, and I'll palm him off to Sienna." It doesn't take Evan long to return.

"So, you over your fucking mantrum yet or not?" Evan asks. I'm a little shocked by his tone.

"Mantrum?"

"Yeah, fuckface, mantrum, you know man-tantrum. I still can't believe you're this hung up over some chick not wanting to be your girlfriend." I just stare at my best friend. Is he serious right now? "Are you seriously happy with the situation and how it's turned out?" he questions me.

"She hurt me, man. She broke my fucking heart into a million pieces, then stomped on it." Evan raises his eyebrow at me.

"Boo fucking hoo. You have been treating her like shit for the past couple of months. So much so that she packed her shit and moved in with Derrick after years living with you."

"But she doesn't want me." How the fuck does he not understand it, I'm heartbroken?

"No, Christian, that's not what happened. She wasn't ready for something more, not yet. I'm sure she was shocked by your declaration, and instead of giving her the time and space to maybe see you in a new light, you took a torch to that love. Now look at what's left... nothing but ashes." I'm in shock, but I think he might be right. Peeling the label off my beer, I refuse to acknowledge what he just said. "It's not too late, man," Evan tries to convince me.

Resting my head in my hands, I whisper, "I fucked up big time, man. I hurt her so badly. The shit I pulled... I'll never forgive myself for that. All because my ego got bruised."

"Do you still love her?" Evan asks.

"Yeah, man, I do. Fuck, I miss Vanessa so fucking much. I feel like a limb is missing, I'm so lost without her."

"Yeah, that's love, man. It sucks, but we wouldn't have it any other way," he says, slapping me on the back. "Now go and get your girl. It's going to be a long journey because you fucked up big time. Start by sending her mom flowers or some shit like that. You were close with her family, send something to show her you still care. Slowly get back into her life and stop fucking groupies in front of her." I smile at my wise friend.

"Shit, man, becoming a dad has turned you into Yoda. How the fuck did you get so wise?"

"Fuck knows, now go and do something and stop being a pussy." He shoves me out the door.

IT'S EARLY, and I can hear my phone ringing, I try to find it, but I'm tangled in my sheets. It stops ringing. Dammit, when I read the name on the missed call, I could kick myself. Vanessa. Shit, I missed a call from her. Instantly, I FaceTime her back.

"Hey," she says, picking up the phone. She looks beautiful, her hair is pulled up in a ponytail, and she's wearing a low-cut black dress, her perfect breasts almost spilling out of it. My dick twitches to life.

"Hey, sorry I missed your call. I couldn't find my phone."

She smiles. "Sorry, it's early, I'm just getting ready to go out with friends." My body tenses. Hopefully, she isn't going out with any single guys. Not like you have a say, anyway, you fucked it all up.

"Thank you so much for the flowers, Christian, they were beyond beautiful, and Mum loved them." I had organized for an orchid bouquet to be delivered to the resort. I remembered Vanessa telling me it was her mom's favorite flower. I may have gone over the top with how big the bouquet was—you know size matters and all. I also sent a bouquet to Vanessa with an apology. It was the least I could do for my behavior.

"I'm glad. How is she feeling?"

"She's sore but getting stronger every day. I'm glad I am here for her." I can see the emotions written across her face.

"I'm glad you are as well." We smile at each other. It's been too fucking long.

"Ness, we need to talk."

"Yeah, I know. But not now, I have to go." My stomach sinks.

"Okay, well, have fun." Reluctantly, I let her go.

"Thanks, I will." She shoots me a wide smile. Then she's gone. I can feel the distance between us. I need to make it right.

"Been a while since we've done this," Derrick says as we start our ascent up Runyon Canyon. Derrick is my go-to workout partner, and I have been shunning him because I thought he chose Vanessa's side in our fight.

"I'm sorry, man, I just..." I pause, not knowing what to say to him. There's no excuse for my behavior.

"Come here and give me a kiss." Derrick grabs me and plants a wet kiss right on my cheek. "I still love ya, even when you're the biggest dickhead on the planet." He chuckles.

"Yeah, I know," I reply, kicking the dirt under my feet.

"Well, say you're sorry and move on." Derrick makes it sound so simple.

"I don't think Ness is going to accept it," I tell him as we start to run. I can feel the endorphins pump through my body. This is what I need. Sweat is pouring out of me as if purging me of my sins. We finally reach the top, and I bend over, trying to catch my breath.

"You did good," Derrick praises me. The man hardly looks like he's puffing after that half-hour run.

"How... the... hell... are... you... not... dead?" I pant.

Derrick slaps my ass. "I have been looking after myself, plus I have stamina." I roll my eyes at him. "You have been partying too much lately," he states, giving me a pointed look. I take a seat and look out over the LA skyline.

"Yeah, I know. Shit, I'm sorry, man." Derrick sits down beside me.

"No need to apologize to me, but I think you owe Ness a big one," he informs me as he takes a long sip from his bottle.

"Yeah, I do. I spoke to Vanessa the other day."

"Really?" Derrick sounds surprised by that little bit of information.

"Yeah, she thanked me for the flowers I sent." I take a long gulp of the cold liquid.

"Well, that was nice. Ness was so worried about her mum. Thankfully, the operation was a success." I nod in agreement. Actually, I'm still panting because I don't think I'll ever get my breath back. "So... what are you going to do about Ness?" Derrick asks me.

"Slowly win her back," I tell him through gasps.

"You're going to have to get down on your knees at some point, I think she deserves that level of groveling."

"I know, I fucked up, but I was hurt." I try to excuse my behavior.

"You know what? I don't blame you." I'm in shock. Someone actually agrees with me.

"And if you tell Ness, I'll deny it all." I laugh. "But I get why you're pissed. From what Ness has told me, you two have been on and off since Sienna and I arrived in LA." Yeah, he was right about that. "And you two have been living together for years." Yeah. "You have worked together since day one, you lived together, traveled together, and took holidays together." I keep nodding because he's right with everything he's saying. "You probably haven't been any closer to anyone in your life?" he questions me.

"No, maybe Axel, but he's blood, so it doesn't count."

"And when the person you trusted over everyone else tells you you're not what they want, it's only natural you're going to be pissed, hurt even." Yes, yes, that's it. "Imagine if the person you loved, you relied on, suddenly turned their back on you and purposely did things to break your heart."

My stomach sinks. I don't think he's talking about me being in the right anymore. "Imagine if the person you loved more than anything in the world but was too scared to take a chance on brought random girls home and tainted every surface, every memory you had there with that person. Imagine how that would feel?"

Fuck! I feel like shit, the scum of the earth. "D," I say, taking another big gulp of water. "She's never going to forgive me, is she?" Looking up at him, I'm hoping that he can give me the answers.

"Honestly? I don't know."

Shit, shit, shit.

"But... I think there's enough history between you two that maybe you can build back your friendship, anything more I don't know. I don't know how she's going to be able to forget the things she has seen."

"I can't lose her, D. I'm going to make this right."

"Ness is stubborn, Chris. So, don't push her, I know you're in a very different place now, just give her time to be in the same one, okay?" He looks at me sternly. I nod my head.

"Okay, I promise I won't push."

"Good, now come on. The last one to the bottom gets to be the bottom." Derrick winks at me.

24

CHRISTIAN

I am so nervous. Today, I'm seeing Vanessa for the first time since her visit to Australia. My stomach is twisted in knots. It's inevitable that we'd see each other again. I mean, we work together, and our best friends are married and have a baby together, so no matter what, we'd always be in each other's lives for significant events such as today, little Ryder Wyld's christening.

Here I am sitting in the church with all our family and friends, and I'm having really lustful thoughts about the beautiful woman standing up at the altar. She's dressed in a demure, yet sexy, white lace dress with a cream cardigan and her trademark high heels, her caramel hair is pulled up into a perfect bun, and her makeup is flawless. She looks like the angel I remember her to be. I sit uncomfortably as the service continues, watching her every move. Looking at her holding little Ryder claws at my heart because at that moment, I had a vision, a vision that it was us. I groan audibly at my crazy thoughts.

"Be respectful." Axel elbows me in my seat.

Shaking my head, I whisper, "Sorry."

Axel leans into me. "Are you okay?"

"Yeah, it's weird seeing V again." He follows my eye line. Vanessa quickly looks away when she spots the two of us staring at her.

"She looks beautiful up there, doesn't she?" Axel states as he questions me. I clench my fists at my brother's comment, but I don't say a thing. "Her holding a baby looks good on her, don't you think?" Fuck, this twin shit gets on my nerves sometimes.

"Yeah, she does," I huff. Axel chuckles at me before elbowing me in the side again, trying to get my attention.

"Well, then, sort that shit out. Mom is so disappointed in you, and so am I. You have kept up this tantrum long enough, so get over yourself. I'm sick of this bullshit, brother. Your attitude is affecting everyone."

I sink further into guilt over the way I have been acting. I nod in agreement with Axel, he's right. Everyone's been pulled into my mess. I've made them feel like they need to pick sides. I've been an absolute dick about the whole situation, and I mistreated her because she didn't feel the same way I did.

Taking a deep breath, my attention turns back to the ceremony. I watch as Charlotte and Jake light a candle handing it to Derrick and Vanessa, who then place it on the altar, all of Ryder's godparents working together in the name of love.

When Vanessa takes her place beside Derrick, I chance a look at her again. Looking back at me are those jade-green eyes, so I smile at her. My heart thumps when it's returned. Maybe there's hope. I swear baby Jesus has come down and anointed me. My body feels like it's glowing just from receiving one of her smiles. It's been a long time since I've seen that smile, and I've missed it.

"I'm the godfather." Derrick turns and looks at Jake. "And I am going to make you an offer you can't refuse." Derrick wiggles his eyebrows at Jake. Jake just laughs and pulls him into a man hug.

"Congrats, you guys," I say, catching Evan and Sienna as

they wander around the backyard of their Hollywood Hills home, Ryder happily gurgling away in Evan's arms.

"Thanks for coming, man." Evan smiles at me.

"How are things?" Sienna asks, her eyes flicking behind me where I know Vanessa is standing.

"It's okay... weird."

She smiles at me. "It will all work out. Just talk to her, she might surprise you. You both have a long history together, and you can't erase all of that so easily, no matter how much you try." Maybe Sienna is right. Turning, I look at Vanessa, who's chatting with Derrick, Jake, and Charlotte.

"I guess there's no time like the present than to fix the shit-storm I have created." Evan and Sienna give me words of encouragement as I make my way toward the group. "Hi, guys," I say as I join them, my eyes not leaving Vanessa's.

"Hey, Jake, where are Mom and Dad?" Charlotte asks quickly.

"Not sure, let's go find them," Jake agrees, not so subtly.

"Oh, look at all the hot guys over there," Derrick adds as the trio quickly leaves me alone with Vanessa. We both stand there awkwardly for a couple of moments, not knowing what to say, which is weird because this woman has been a part of my life for so long. Why does she feel like such a stranger now? "So... um... did you want to go for a walk and talk?" I ask.

"Sure," Vanessa agrees. We head toward the back of the garden, away from the rest of the party. I can see the guys watching us as we disappear over the garden's edge and toward the chairs that look out over the sprawling view.

"How's your mom?" I start the conversation off on something neutral.

"She's good, really good. I'm happy that she's all better. She is one tough old lady. Thanks for sending all those flowers, she loved them so much." I watch Vanessa's silhouette as she talks, noticing that she can't look at me, and it guts me that she doesn't feel comfortable anymore around me. But I did this, I'm the one who pushed her so far away. I don't know if I'll ever get her back again. Moving my hand to hers, it stiffens under my touch, but she doesn't move it.

"I'm sorry." The words stick in my throat.

Vanessa slowly moves her hand away from mine. "I know." Turning and looking at her, her face is expressionless, there's nothing there. I have really fucked up. I turn my whole body, so I'm facing her.

"No, Ness. I'm so fucking sorry for everything. For the way I treated you, for throwing those groupies in your face, for hurting you." My heart feels like someone has it in a vice grip as I plead with her to understand how truly sorry I am for everything. Those jade-green eyes meet mine, a single tear falls down her cheek, and I want so badly to wipe it away, but I'm frozen by her stare.

"I'm sorry I hurt you, too, Christian." I'm shocked. What's she apologizing to me for? Grabbing her hands in mine, I shake my head.

"No, you were just honest, but my damn ego got in the way, instead." She gives me a small smile.

"Yeah, you do have a pretty big ego." This makes me laugh. Her making jokes is a good thing, I think.

"It's not all that big." I wiggle my eyebrows at her. Shit, what was I thinking, flirting with her like that? But she surprises me and laughs.

"You haven't changed." She smiles.

"I'm sorry, Ness, so fucking sorry." I try to hold back the raging emotions inside of me, but I can't, and I too release a couple of tears. Vanessa moves forward with concern in her eyes.

"Shit," she says, holding my face within her palms. "Chris, please, don't..."

"I miss you, V, I miss you so fucking much. It's like a part of me is missing. I'm kind of lost without you." There it is. I've laid it out on the table for her. My damn tears fall again. Her hands fall from my face as she wraps them around my body, pulling me into a hug.

"I've missed you so much, too, Chris. The one person I needed when Mum was having surgery wasn't there. I have never felt more alone than I did then." She starts crying as I wrap myself around her, comforting her.

"I'm sorry, Ness, so fucking sorry. I wish I were there for you. I fucked up so much. I don't understand what came over me, I wasn't myself." We hold each other in a comfortable embrace for a long time, just absorbing each other.

"It's going to take a while to get back to where we were, Chris," she says, moving out of my arms. My heart sinks again.

"I know, I'm just happy that you're back in my life, I don't care about its capacity."

Vanessa smiles. "I think it's for the best that I continue living with Derrick for a while." I nod in agreement. It sucks, but I'm happy with baby steps. "And just so you know, I may have forgiven you, but I haven't forgotten, just give me... us, time, and we can get back to where we once were." My heart bursts into a thousand pieces hearing that she's willing to give me a second chance. Time, it's just going to take time.

"Come on, we better get back to the party, you know they are all waiting nervously for our return." She stands up and takes my hand, linking her fingers with mine. It feels so good, it feels right, and I never want to lose her again.

25

VANESSA

"Oh my God, you need to come with me. I've been accepted as the newest member of The Paradise Club. I can't go alone." Derrick jumps up and down excitedly.

"No way. No way in hell am I going there, D." That place makes me feel sick.

"Ness, I know the history it has with you in regards to Kane." Hearing his name makes me stiffen. "But maybe it might give you some sort of closure going there." I glare at Derrick, he can't be serious. Closure, I got that when the fucking bastard was sent to jail. "Look, Stacey and Isla are coming as well. You won't be alone. Girls' night!" Derrick is giving me puppy-dog eyes. How the fuck can you say no to Derrick when he's looking at you like that?

"Stop it, stop being so fucking cute." Derrick pulls me into his arms.

"Look, if you want me to play with you tonight, I will if it makes you feel better." I'm lost for words like I totally lost the ability to speak.

"D, you don't like vaginas." He makes a face at the word vagina.

"No, they are gross, but I'm willing to take one for the team if it means you come with me." I burst out laughing at him.

"Wow, you must be really desperate to check this place out if you're willing to play with my vagina."

"Yeah, I kind of do. I want to try all those naughty things Christian has told me about what goes on there. It would be like my fifty shades of fantasy coming to life." I let out a groan on hearing Christian's name.

"Please tell me he isn't going to be there?"

Derrick just shrugs. "And so, what if he is? You guys have made up." I roll my eyes at him. Yes, we may have technically made up at Ryder's christening, but we're still not one hundred percent there on the friends' front, and we are most certainly not there on the sex front.

"Yeah, but don't you think it will be awkward if he's there? Don't you think I have seen him having sex with enough people to last a lifetime?"

Derrick shakes his head. "Um... maybe awkward for him having to watch all the hot guys drooling over you or watching you suck some hot guy's cock." He gives me a sly smile. Maybe he has a point.

"Fine, I'm in."

"Shit, yeah! Now come on, let's get you dressed. Tonight we're finding Vanessa's inner sex goddess."

"WELCOME, MR. JONES," the tuxedo-dressed doorman greets us at the door. He's standing behind a leather-studded reception desk with two suited-up bouncers on either side of him. "Congratulations on becoming the newest member of The Paradise Club, here is your card." He hands over what looks like a gold credit card. "Swipe this when you want to move through the different floors. Each level has a security door, and you will need this to get to the next level.

"Miss Roberts, Miss Ferguson, Miss Eriksen, here are your temporary cards. It has the same access as Mr. Jones' but only for one night." The doorman hands us all a white version of Derrick's card. It's kind of exciting like we're about to step into a new world.

"And here are your bands," he advises, handing us multicolored bands. "Each color represents what you are interested in. Pink if you're into exploring with women, blue if you are into exploring with men, white is no sexual intercourse, but all other play is okay, red is if you're happy to explore sexual intercourse in the club, yellow is looking to explore with just one person, green is looking to explore experiences with more than one person, purple is okay with playing in public, and orange if you would prefer to play behind closed doors.

People will know your interests by looking at these bands. It makes everything more open and honest when you're chatting with other people. Also, there's a black band as well, which means no play at all and a lot of the staff members will have one on, but you will also see some staff members with colored bands. You will be able to ask them to play at any time, and they will."

Wow, playing with the staff as well. The bands make sense, I suppose. He hands them over to each of us. Curiously, we all look at each other. I decide to go with all the bands bar the white one. The others are pretty much in the same boat. Oh my God, my friends are a bunch of kinky fuckers.

"Drinks and appetizers are complimentary, but the club is very strict on drunkenness. You can be ejected and your membership revoked if you mess up," the doorman tells us, then launches into all the rules regarding the club. We all nod in agreement. The golden doors open, and a beautiful woman dressed in an emerald evening dress walks toward us.

"This is Lucy, she'll walk you through the club showing you where everything is." Lucy gives us a blinding smile.

"Welcome, Mr. Jones and party, please follow me." And we do, we follow her through the golden doors and into the club.

Wow, this place wasn't at all what I thought it would be. In my mind, I thought it was some dark, scary den of debauchery, but in actual fact, it feels like we have stepped onto the set of *The Gatsby*, and Leonardo DiCaprio could appear at any moment around a corner, which could happen because I bet he's a member.

We're standing in a large room where many people are milling around, all still fully clothed as if this was just another exclusive nightclub in Hollywood. Black leather booths line the walls of the room, sizable ornate gold chandeliers hang from the ceilings, the walls painted black with gold art deco designs swirling across it, and soft jazz music is playing through the stereo system. It's like stepping through time to a 1920s old Hollywood jazz bar. I love it.

Lucy guides us toward the studded leather bar, and I notice curious eyes following us as we walk. The stunning bar staff hand over a couple of glasses of champagne to us. "This level is the safe room. There's no nudity allowed in this area. Later in the evening, a DJ will play, and the dance floor fills up. It doesn't take long for people to move onto other areas of the club." She gives us a flirty wink.

We follow our sexy guide to the back of the safe room where there is a grand staircase leading to the next level and two elevators with bouncers guarding the area.

"There are five levels of play. The further you ascend, the more intense the levels get." All four of us are quiet, not a single peep out of any of us as we take it all in. Derrick squeezes my hand as my heart is thumping. I'm not sure what's going to happen tonight and how far I am willing to go, but I also feel kind of excited by that prospect as well.

We slowly take the stairs to the next level. "This level is for voyeurs and exhibitionists." Lucy points to a large glass cube room. Peering inside, Derrick and I are shocked to discover a threesome happening, two women and a male. He's lying on his back with one girl riding his cock and the other riding his face as they kiss. I'm mesmerized as are Isla, Stacey, and Derrick. A light flutter tickles my belly. Shit, I'm getting turned on. "I'll be leaving you on this level. You have your map. Please know that at any time, you can use the club's safe word, 'paradise.' When it's used, everything stops. If it doesn't, then one of the bouncers will make sure it does." Lucy points to the many men dressed in black, strangely hidden in plain sight. Then she leaves us.

"Okay, I'm trying not to freak out, but we just watched people have sex." Isla giggles nervously.

"I know, it's kind of hot," Stacey confesses, and we all burst out laughing at the craziness we have stepped into.

"Maybe we should go back down to the safe room, have some drinks, and then work up the courage to continue our journey," Derrick suggests. We follow his lead and head back downstairs and straight toward the bar. "Tequila shots, kind sir," Derrick flirtatiously asks the handsome bartender.

"Coming right up, sir," he flirts back at him.

"Not yet, but maybe later I will be," Derrick fires right back.

"Sounds like something I'd like to be a part of," the bartender states, showing off his wrist's multicolored bands. Derrick's in luck as I spy blue. Our tequila shots arrive, and we all slam them down quickly, nerves getting the better of us.

"Is it going to be weird if... you know, we see each other doing something?" Isla asks.

"Maybe, I don't know, just as long as you don't ask to join me, we should be fine," Stacey says, making us laugh.

"Well, I wouldn't mind watching Derrick and the hot bartender later on," I confess, elbowing D in the ribs.

"I know you want all up in this, Miss V. But check the bands, girl, no pink on this wrist." He shakes his bands in front of my face.

"Ew, I don't want to join in, but I wouldn't mind watching." I giggle, confessing to one of my closest friends that I wouldn't mind watching him have sex. What the hell was in that tequila shot? I mean I'm probably not the only one thinking it. Derrick is fucking hot, and his body is impressive, like a damn cover model, and the bartender is equally desirable, plus I love gay porn, and this would be live—two hot men making out, hands roaming, tight bodies, two dicks. *Win-win.*

"You're only human." He grins. "Fine, I can handle that." Putting his arm around my shoulder, he pulls me closer beside him. He leans down and whispers in my ear, "If you hook up with Christian tonight, let me watch, please. I have been trying to see him naked for ages, just once I want a little peek. Pinky promise."

"What?" I gasp out loud, making the others look at me. I wave them off and turn my attention back to Derrick. "Seriously?"

He nods. "You know I have the biggest crush on him, and this is probably the only chance I'll get to, one, see him naked, and two, feel what it's like to fuck him." I'm stunned.

"Honestly, D, if Christian does turn up, I highly doubt we'll be having sex. We're still on rocky ground."

"Yeah, you're right. Would you mind if I watched him with someone else, then?" My stomach sinks. Shit, if Christian turns up, does that mean I'd have to watch him have sex with someone else? Why did I not think of this before? Breathe, Ness, breathe. It's going to be okay.

"I take it from the constipated look you have on your face you aren't so happy with that idea?" I roll my eyes at him. "Fine, out of loyalty to you, I won't watch. Fuck, who am I kidding? I'll take a peek, just a tiny one, then I will huff away in disgust, how does that sound?" Derrick makes me laugh, taking my mind off the prospect of running into Christian.

26

CHRISTIAN

"Welcome back, Mr. Taylor, Mr. Connolly, Mr. Eriksen, and Mr. Taylor," Jerome, the doorman, greets us. "Here are your bands. Have a good night."

"We always do." Finn smiles as we walk in through the golden doors into the safe room.

"Come on, let's grab a couple of drinks before we all go our separate ways," Axel says, leading us to the bar.

"No fucking way," Oscar growls as he walks off from us. I look to see what has caught his attention, and I see Isla. What the hell is she doing here? My eyes bounce to where Stacey, Derrick, and Vanessa are standing, all laughing and chatting away at the bar. Axel grabs my arm.

"Relax. Don't freak out, okay?" We head over toward the group.

"What the hell are you doing here?" Oscar asks his sister.

"I'm here having fun." Isla stands up as tall as she can, but she's no match to her Viking brother.

"I don't want you here," he tells her.

"Too fucking bad. Derrick invited me, and I'm determined to have fun, so you can fuck off." She crosses her long arms over her chest.

"Sorry, Ragnar," Derrick interrupts, using his nickname for Oscar. "Little sis is here to have fun. You need to let the leash go, or maybe not, depends on if we make it to the BDSM level." Derrick bursts out laughing at his joke, which Oscar doesn't find funny at all and glares at him.

"Isla, it's a little awkward for us to be in a sex club with you," Finn adds. Isla walks up to Finn and pushes her finger into his chest.

"Then you can fucking leave. You are a member, and you both can come anytime you want. But for me, this is my one and only night. So, you either stay and see something you might not like, or you can both fuck off." I have never seen Isla so angry before.

"Fine, I'll go," Oscar says. "Finn, stay, keep an eye on her. Make sure no fuckers mess with her, okay?" Finn nods in agreement, but Isla is shooting daggers at her brother as he walks toward the entry and disappears through it.

"Okay, now that matter is over with, let's get our freak on," Derrick cheers.

"I'm sorry, this is awkward," I mention to Vanessa when I can get a moment alone with her at the bar. Those big green eyes stare at me, where I can see her cheeks are rosy from the alcohol.

"It's no different to coming home and seeing it." Her barbed quip hits me squarely in the gut.

"I said I'm sorry, Ness, for all that shit." Vanessa's shoulders sag in defeat.

"I know." She takes a deep breath, turning her body toward me. "But like I said, it's not so easy to forget sometimes." And with that, she moves away from me.

Dammit, I'm just going to have to make her forget.

"Chris, you haven't played at all tonight," Axel states. "Everything okay?" We're currently on the voyeur level, where we watch an orgy taking place. Usually, I can feel some kind of movement downstairs, but tonight, nothing, my dick is on hiatus.

"It's Vanessa. I can't stop thinking about what she's up to."

Axel nods. "Thought that might be the case, but just so you know, she has only been watching scenes. I haven't seen her participate in anything, yet." I turn to my brother.

"How do you know this?"

He chuckles. "I've been following her for you. I knew you would be worried. I care about her as well, and I know you would've hated seeing her with someone else." Sometimes my brother is kind of all right.

"Where is she now?"

"She's on the floor walking around the open viewing rooms. Go find her before someone else does." I nod at him. "Oh, and Chris, let me know if you want to share again." He smirks at me. I flip him the bird. There's no way in the world if I ever get a second chance with her, that I'm sharing her.

"Hell, no! One-time deal only, remember?" He just smiles and tells me to go find her.

Moments later, I find her watching three men in one of the rooms playing with each other. Slowly, I walk toward her, so I don't spook her. She barely registers me when I stand beside her, lost in the action taking place in front of her.

"Does this turn you on?" I'm curious to see what she says.

"Yes, I think it's hot," she answers without even looking at me.

"What do you like about it?"

"The fact that three hot guys are fucking each other." This makes me chuckle.

"Does it turn you on knowing that they like you watching them, that they are performing for you?" She intakes the smallest of breaths, and I notice her cheeks are flushed. She's turned on. Shit, my dick twitches to life, finally. Vanessa's concentration is still stuck on what's happening in front of her. I move back behind her. One of my hands rests lazily on her hip, the other on the window of the room we're watching.

"Christian," she scolds me but doesn't move from my embrace.

"Shh, let me enjoy watching you watch them." Vanessa lets out a heavy sigh and continues watching what's happening between the three men. A few moments pass, and I notice the slight movements she's making, trying to stem the ache that I know is happening between her legs. I work up the courage to push the boundaries a little with her.

Leaning in, I whisper into her ear, "An ache has started between your legs. Your skin feels like it's on fire. Every nerve ending has come alive. Am I right?" Vanessa lets out the barest of moans and nods. "If you were at home right now, you would have your hand down your pants, circling that aching little bud, wouldn't you, angel?" Vanessa lets out a whimper as she nods her head in agreement. "You like watching these men together, don't you?"

"Yes," she whispers.

"I remember what turns you on, Ness, this exact scenario does it for you."

"God, yes," she moans as the men continue their playing. I press myself against her.

"Do you need some help, Ness? I bet your clit is throbbing as we speak." I push myself into the curve of her backside. Vanessa doesn't answer me, but she doesn't push me away, either. "I can help, Ness," I whisper into her ear. Her face turns slightly to mine, and her steady breath has increased somewhat. "You can watch them while I help relieve the ache that's building between your legs." I watch as her teeth sink into her bottom lip. Fuck, she's so turned on. "Let me help you." We stare at each other for what feels like hours. I can see a multitude of emotions fly across her face.

"Only because I'm so turned on that I can't think or see straight, I need something..." Her words trail off as she's distracted by the scene again.

"I understand what you need, I can help you, Ness." She gives me the barest of nods, permitting me to play with her. My lips touch the sensitive skin of her neck, her throbbing vein pulsating against my lips as I suck against her heated skin. She audibly gasps at my contact.

My hands follow her body's path over her hips and down toward the hem of her dress sitting mid-thigh. Moving under her dress, my hands find the scantiest bit of fabric covering her. I can already feel the heat radiating from her.

"Spread your legs, angel, and let me get to work." She does as she's told, moving her legs fractionally wider for me, never letting her eyes fall from the erotic scene before her. My knuckle skims the edge of her underwear, feeling her wetness. "You really are aching, sweetheart."

My fingers slip underneath the fabric and sink into her wetness. Vanessa lets out a moan as her teeth sink into the bottom of her lip. "Eyes on them, Ness. Whatever you do, don't stop watching them." She groans again as I start slowly pumping into her body, her tightness engulfing me. "Look at the way he's fucking him, the look of pleasure on his face as the other man takes his hardened cock in his mouth, look at them, Ness. Look at how much pleasure they are enjoying." I push a second finger into her. "Do you want to hear what they sound like?"

"Yes," she groans. I turn on the microphone switch to the room, which sits beside the door, and the sounds of slapping flesh, moaning, and groaning fill our little empty corridor. "Listen to them, Ness. Listen to the way their flesh sounds against one another." I notice that now she can hear them, she has closed her eyes. My fingers are still working her, moving back and forth. "Listen to their pleasure." The moans increase with the quickening thrusts of one of the men.

"Yes, yes, yes." Vanessa lets out the faintest of replies as my hand quickens in time with the man's thrusts. Her cunt tightens around my hand, and I know she's close. One man explodes with his climax. He lets out a loud moan as he fills the other man with his cum. Moments later, another climax explodes as another man comes in the man's mouth being fucked from behind. Soon Vanessa joins them in their chorus and comes all over my hand, her forehead sagging and pressing against the cool glass.

The men continue playing with each other as Vanessa comes down from her orgasm. She pushes my hand away from her, which annoys me. Turning around, Vanessa presses her back against the window, those jade- green eyes sparkling. Grabbing my hand that was inside of her, she guides my fingers to her mouth and sucks herself off them. Shit, it's the hottest thing I have ever seen in my life. My dick is ready to burst.

"I think I want to see more," she purrs at me.

"With me?" I want to double-check that she's comfortable with me. I cross my fingers and pray that she does. Wrapping her arms around my neck, she pulls me to her, her hand running through my hair, her warm breath on my face.

"I want to go into one of those rooms. I want people to watch us. I want to put on a show for others. Knowing that they are getting hard over watching us is fucking hot." Her lips press against mine as she talks. "I want people to see how fucking hot we are together. I want women to envy me as you push your cock into me. I want men to wish that it was their mouths wrapped around my nipples." Fuck me, dead! I'm going to come in my pants if she keeps talking like that to me. "One night, Chris. I want one night of wild abandonment. I want to forget about everything except pleasure."

"Your wish is my command, V." With that, I lead her away to fulfill her fantasy.

27

VANESSA

I can't believe I let Christian do that to me, but that scene was so hot, and I needed relief. Now that the lust has subsided, I'm worried that I might be leading him on as he holds my hand and leads me to one of the voyeurs and exhibitionist rooms. Thankfully, the hallways are dark, and people can't see my face. *Don't you think the time for embarrassment is over? You just let Christian finger bang you in a public hallway while you watched a threesome, then requested he fuck you in front of people.*

We stop, and Christian swipes his card against the security door. We enter a vast room. It looks like we stumbled onto the set of *Cleopatra*. Everything is gold, and there are even hieroglyphics on the wall.

"This is one of the themed rooms, the Cleopatra suite," Christian explains. Looking around the room, there's a large king-size bed, a couple of large chaise lounge beds as well, and a curtain that runs from one side of the room to the other. My heart starts to beat rapidly. Shit, what the hell was I thinking?

"Ness," Christian calls from behind me. "Do you still want to do this?" he asks, walking around to where I stand staring at the golden curtain. I'm sure that just behind it, there are people eager to see what will happen in the room. I try and swallow, but my mouth is dry.

"I need a drink," I stammer. Christian rushes over to where there's a hidden kitchen, reaches into a bar fridge, and pulls out a bottle of water. I take it from his hand and take a large gulp of the refreshing water.

"Are you okay, Ness?" Christian asks, watching my mini freak-out. "Because we don't have to do anything. I never expected you to let me get that close to you ever again, so I'm happy to call it a night. We can walk out and head down to the safe room and talk or dance, whatever you want."

My eyes finally meet his, and he gives me a weak smile. Damn, he looks good dressed in a white button-down shirt and dark denim jeans, his golden-brown hair pulled up into his trademark man bun. The dark circles look like they are still there but not as visible. He's even shaved tonight as he isn't as prickly like he usually is. Those whiskey-colored eyes stare at me with such uncertainty. I should be more pissed at him, no, I am, but there's just something about Christian Taylor that's so far embedded under my skin that I can't seem to let go of him. I put down my drink on the side table and walk a couple of steps toward him.

"Do you like this sort of stuff?" I question him.

He frowns for a moment. "What, sex?" I roll my eyes at him.

"No, voyeurism and exhibitionism? Is that what you come here for?" I ask because I realize how well I know this man standing in front of me, but I don't understand why he comes here?

"Yes, Ness. I love the feeling I get when I'm with a woman, and there's another man on the other side of that window, and he wishes that he was me, that he wishes his tongue was lapping at her sweetness, that his cock was plunging into her, and that her screams were for him. That, to me, is a potent aphrodisiac, Ness." I cross my legs because my body most definitely appreciates that imagery. "But, what about you, Ness. Why are you here?" Christian asks me. My mouth feels dry again,

"I'm here…" I try to find the right words to explain to him why the hell I ended up at a sex club. "Honestly, I was trying to get over you." Quickly I cover my mouth because that wasn't at all what I wanted to divulge, especially not to him.

"Ness." Christian's voice is low as he takes a couple of steps toward me. "Why?" My heart is racing now, my face feels like it's on fire. This isn't the place where I wanted to have a deep and meaningful conversation.

"Because you hurt me. There was a part of me that wanted to come here and fuck as many men as I could right in front of you. So, you could feel exactly how I felt walking into our home."

The tears start falling down my cheeks. Who the fuck cries in a sex club? Christian's strong arms surround me, holding me tight. I hate that he's seeing me so vulnerable. He is supposed to be seeing me as a cool and confident woman who doesn't need him in her life, who isn't affected by him. My emotions had other ideas. I thump against his chest, "I hated it. I hated seeing it. I hated you," I confess.

"Let it out, Ness. Yell, scream, say anything you want to me, and I'll take it. I deserve it." He lets go of me and takes a step back, giving me space. "Punish me, Ness, if it's what you want and need."

His eyes flick to a wall of sex toys, then back to me. My heart is almost beating out of my chest. I walk over to the wall, eyeing all the instruments. I have no idea what half of this stuff is or what you're supposed to do with it. I find a riding crop—this I know what to do with. I spent my childhood riding horses on our property, so I'm familiar with this. Turning and feeling the leather in my hands, I notice that the golden curtain has been pulled, and I'm shocked to see faces staring back at me. Then I look at Christian.

"I have closed off the sound so the people watching can't hear, I also locked the door indicating that we don't want anyone to join us." I relax a little as I twist the implement in my hands. "You can say whatever you want to me, and no one will hear it but me."

I look around the room again, taking in its richness, and my attention falls back onto Christian. "You can use the safe word at any time, V, and everything stops," Christian reminds me. I nod in understanding.

"I want to control things tonight. Are you okay with that?" I know how much Christian hates not controlling situations, but I hope tonight he'll give that to me. I need it.

"Yes, Ness. I'm all yours." That thought alone made my panties wetter.

"And you will do anything I say, no matter what?" I just want to double-check.

"Yes, of course. I know I can always use the safe word to get out of a situation, so I'm sure." I let the tension that has filled my body relax by his answer.

"Take off your clothes," I command. Christian undresses ever so slowly, kicking his clothing to the side. My heart is racing, but I feel kind of powerful. This beautiful man is standing before me, naked, his beautiful cock standing at attention. Fuck, how I have missed it.

"Turn around, bend over and put your hands on the window, but don't look at anyone." Christian nods and does precisely that, his taut white ass staring at me. I bring the riding crop up and hit him ever so slightly, my hands shaking by the situation. "That was for being a dick to me." His ass tenses at the tiny sting of the crop across it.

I lift it again, bring it down, this time harder, and the quiet room's sound reverberates. "That was for refusing to deal with me at work." The sound of the crack and the pink tinge coating his tight ass makes me feel powerful. "That's for punching Darcy." This time it was harder and the sound louder, but still Christian takes it.

My eyes look up and catch the curious faces in the crowd. I can see people are in various stages of undress, some people are kissing, and some are just watching. I bring the crop up again and down hard against him. "And that was for fucking other women in front of me." Christian's ass is now bright red, and I feel a little guilty for it.

"Shit, Chris. I'm sorry, I didn't mean to hit you that hard, I just..." I throw the riding crop to the side. Christian moves from the window and looks at me. "Do you feel better?" he asks. My eyes flick down to his still hard cock, then back up to his handsome face.

"Yeah, I kind of do, but I also feel guilty for hurting you." And I'm not just talking about the riding crop either. My emotions have bubbled to the surface, and I don't think I can push them back down again.

"We hurt the ones closest to us." Christian gives me a weak smile. "I'm willing if you are to put the last couple of months behind us once we leave this room tonight. I need your forgiveness, Ness. I am so fucking lost without you, I can't sleep, I'm not eating right, I don't even feel like making music. My world has dimmed because you're not in it anymore." My heart skips a beat by his words. "I fucking miss you so much, Ness, and I'll do anything to have you back in my life. I mean, I let you flog me, naked, in front of a room full of strangers." This makes me giggle.

"So that goes to show that I'd do anything to get you back, to say I'm sorry. I need you, Ness, so fucking much. I feel a part of me is missing, and it hurts, I am so sick of it hurting."

I see his pain.

I'm over this rift between us.

I want my best friend back.

That's when I launch myself into his arms, surprising the people watching us. They are probably expecting us to be fucking now, but this is so much more intimate than that.

"I've missed you, too," I mumble into his neck, tears falling down my cheeks.

"Thank fuck." His hold tightens around me, and we stay like that for several moments. I'm sure this is quite boring for the voyeurs out there, but I don't care. My eyes catch Derrick's in the audience with his bar friend, and I have a bold idea.

"Chris?" I unfold myself from his arms.

"Yeah." He looks down at me with a stupid grin.

"Can I ask you to do something and not to question it no matter what?"

"Okay," he says, without skipping a beat.

"Can you turn around and face the window and give your cock a couple of strokes for the audience." He gives me a crooked grin.

"Anything for you, sweetness." As he turns around and does it, it makes me giggle when I see Derrick's reaction. I think he'll faint, his eyes are bugging out of his head, and he's fake-fanning himself. Then I press the button, letting the curtain fall, covering the window.

"Get dressed," I tell Christian. He stands there for a moment looking at his clothes scattered around the room and then to his hard cock, he raises an eyebrow at me, silently asking for something.

"Keep dreaming, friend," I say, which makes him chuckle. He silently gets dressed and slings an arm around my shoulder as we head for the door.

CHRISTIAN

It's been a week since Vanessa and I kind of hooked up at The Paradise Club. We're taking it slow, friendship-wise, anyway. Things at work have become a lot less chaotic with us not fighting anymore, and the staff looks a lot more relaxed about it. Most nights, I have been heading out to open mic nights with the boys, looking for the next big thing tucked away in some stale beer stank hole. Throwing my keys in the bowl, I notice a message on the machine, which is random because if people are after me, they call my cell. I press play as I grab myself a beer.

"Hi, Vanessa, this is Tracey calling from Dr. Jensen's office. He has your test results and would like you to schedule an appointment if you could please call the office at 533-2311. Thank you."

What the fuck? Test results? Why the hell would Vanessa need test results for? Fuck, is she pregnant? My heart is racing, I don't understand. Before I know it, I've jumped in my car and headed to Derrick's. I don't care how late it is. I need to know what's going on with her? I take a deep breath and knock on the door. It's late, but Derrick's always up doing something. He's very much a night owl. As predicted, Derrick answers the door.

"What are you doing here?" Derrick frowns, looking me up and down as I stand in the moonlight.

"I need to see Ness." His brown eyes bore into me with so many questions.

"If this is some sort of booty call, then you need to turn that fine ass around and go back to where you came from," he says, crossing his arms defensively.

"What the... I'm not here for a booty call, are you serious?" He just shrugs his shoulders. "I need to see Ness, it's important." He looks me over again.

"Fine, come on in, then. Don't make me regret this." Pushing my way past him, I run to Vanessa's room, and without knocking, I barge in, falling over a stray bag on the floor and end up on my knees.

"Christian, what the hell?" Vanessa screams at me. She looks beautiful, so fucking beautiful. She's dressed in short shorts and a tank top, her hard nipples pressing against the thin fabric as she lays in her bed reading.

"Are you pregnant?" I blurt out. Vanessa looks at me in surprise.

"What the hell are you talking about? Are you high?"

"Well, are you?" I press her again as I find my feet and stand looking down at her in her bed.

"No, I'm not fucking pregnant. Why the hell are you asking me this?"

"Who's Dr. Jensen?" Questioning her. Vanessa stills, and I can see the color drain from her face.

"How do you know about Dr. Jensen?" She sounds angry.

"They left a message at home, your results are in, so I'm going to ask you again... Vanessa, are you pregnant?" We're almost toe to toe. I don't even know when Vanessa sprang up out of bed, but we have naturally gravitated toward each other like magnets.

"Fuck you, Christian." She pushes me away from her. I catch her wrists and hold them to my chest as she tries and wiggles out of my tight grasp. Eventually, I let her go.

"If you're pregnant with my baby, Ness, then I need to know... unless it's with some douchebag you are seeing. Do you not know who the father is?"

Slap.

My face feels like it's on fire.

"You bastard! How dare you come back into my life after all these months and accuse me of being knocked up and not knowing who the father is. How fucking dare you!" She spits fire at me.

"Well, that's the only logical explanation for a doctor to be leaving a message regarding test results."

"Why? Because I'm some fucking slut who fucks all these men with no condoms?" She hisses at me, and my eyes look to the floor. Shit. Lifting my chin, I look into her green eyes, and I can see a world of hurt behind them.

"No, Ness, I don't."

"Because the only guy I have never used a condom with is you." I suck in a startled breath, unsure why that bit of information makes me feel good, but it does. "And to clarify once and for all, I'm not pregnant." A heavy weight feels like it has been lifted from me.

"Okay, so you're not pregnant, then who's the doctor?" Vanessa takes a deep breath. The room is silent as she mulls over what she's about to say next.

"Come sit down," she says, patting the edge of the bed. I follow and sit in front of her. "You know about Mum and how she had her surgery." I nod in agreement. "There's a family history of breast cancer in our family, so Mum wanted me to do this test to see if I'd get it."

My stomach sinks. What the hell? No, I can't lose Ness, not now that I just got her back. "It's called the BRCA test." I shake my head in confusion. "You know, the one Angelina Jolie did?" Oh shit, yeah, I remember reading something about that. "Mum was diagnosed positive. Because of her age, she decided to have the mastectomy and hysterectomy to give herself a five percent chance of getting cancer instead of an eighty percent chance.

Fuck!

I rake my hands through my hair. "But why are you getting it done?"

"Because the gene is in my family, so the chance of me getting breast cancer is high, Christian. I need to know." I see her tears. Vanessa breaks down, so I pull her into my arms, and she wraps her arms around me. It feels so good to have her in my arms again.

"I'm here for you, okay?" I kiss her feather-light kisses all over her face, trying to calm her down. "I'll come to your doctor's appointment. You can't do this alone." Vanessa sniffles, and those big green eyes look up at me.

"You would?" She sounds surprised.

"I'd do anything for you, Ness." I bend down to kiss her lips, but she turns her head at the last moment.

"Sorry, I just…" I pull myself out of her arms. "Please let me know when it is, and I'll be there." She nods, I get up and leave her room. I ignore Derrick's barrage of questions and walk out the door and drive home in a daze.

29

VANESSA

I'm nervous as we wait in Dr. Jensen's waiting room. I watch as the nurses sneak glances at Christian, who's playing on his phone. They whisper behind their hands. I've noticed that some of them have done some primping while we have been waiting. It's kind of rude seeing he has one of his strong hands holding onto my leg, the one that won't stop bouncing from the nerves. He could be my boyfriend for all they know.

I let out a frustrated sigh at these women, it's not like I'm not used to it. Thank God, he is here with me. He's the only one I have told about this. It's nice having him back in my life again, I've missed him. Things are still a little awkward, but at this moment, the last bit of frost between us had thawed because he's here with me now when I need him the most, and that's the most important thing.

"Calm down, babe." Christian smiles, squeezing my thigh, instantly calming me down.

"Sorry, it's just..."

"It's going to be okay." He smiles at me, and he looks beautiful. His light brown hair has grown longer, and he has it pulled up in a top knot. He has the perfect five o'clock shadow prickling his jaw. Those whiskey eyes staring at me remind me of all the fun times we have had together.

"Vanessa Roberts," Dr. Jensen calls my name. I smile and get up, Christian takes my hand, and we follow him down the corridor. "Please take a seat." Dr. Jensen is hot for an older, distinguished guy—think Gibbs from *NCIS*. "Okay, I won't delay the results any further as I'm sure you're eager to find out." No shit. "You have tested positive to the BRCA gene." I suck in an audible breath. Fuck!

"What does that mean?" Christian asks, his hand holding tight against mine. Thank fuck, he's here because, at this moment, all I hear is white noise.

"It means that her risk of getting breast cancer is about forty to eighty percent in her lifetime and getting ovarian cancer is sixteen to forty-four percent. Christian squeezes my hand tightly at those figures. Shit, they are really high. The men start talking amongst themselves while I have a mild, no, major freak out. I will get cancer. This little test is like a crystal ball telling me what I have to look forward to.

"So, if she has the surgery, her chance of getting cancer is like five percent?" Christian asks. Wait, what surgery? Why are they talking about surgery? Am I going to have to lose my breasts? No way, Vanessa. Just like Angelina Jolie, she got her boobs taken off so they wouldn't kill her. Shit, I am Angelina Jolie!

"I'll do it," I blurt out in the middle of the conversation. "Take them off, I don't want my boobs if they are going to kill me." The room goes quiet.

"Babe, why don't you think about it?" Christian advises me calmly.

"There's nothing to think about, Chris. I want them off so I can live." I turn my attention to the doctor. "Am I able to get new ones at the same time, or do I have to have a different surgery for that?"

"Miss Roberts, we can remove the breast and reconstruct it with a new one all in the one surgery."

"So, that means I can choose new boobs?" I ask.

The doctor laughs. "Yes, you get to choose new breasts." I turn to Christian and wiggle my eyebrows at him, making him laugh. "Miss Roberts, you need to know about the risks of having a double mastectomy."

"I understand, my mum just had this done a couple of months ago. I helped with her recovery." The doctor explains everything to me, anyway. It's part of his job, I guess. Until he's satisfied that I understand everything about the surgery and diagnosis, we don't leave his office. "Okay, well, let's see when we can fit you in." He fiddles with the calendar on his computer.

"Are you sure about this, Ness?" Christian whispers while the doctor is distracted.

"How is there a choice, get cancer and die or get new boobs and live." Christian looks at me intensely.

"Just so you know, I'm coming with you to pick out the new boobs. You really should have an expert with you, and I just happen to be one. I'm brilliant with boobs." I elbow him in the side, making him grunt. He gives me a brilliant smile helping ease my fears.

"So, in a couple of months, you will be getting some new boobs," Christian jokes as he drives me back to Derrick's after the doctor's appointment.

"Yeah, I guess I will..." I let my words trail off. "Thank you for today, Chris, I couldn't have done it without you."

"Hey, what are friends for?" he shrugs as he pulls into Derrick's driveway. We sit there in silence for a while, staring out the front window of the car.

"I really couldn't have done it without you." I break the

silence. He turns and looks at me. His hand moves toward me, pushing the hair away from my face.

"Thank you for letting me be there." Just the tiniest of touches has ignited my body. I can feel my breathing has changed as his thumb gently strokes my cheek. "I don't ever want to lose you, Ness." My heart aches at the way he's looking at me. "If this surgery is the only way I get to keep you for longer, then I'm all for it." Tears start to run down my face, and my heart hurts.

"I don't want to die, Chris." The gravity of what the doctor has told me starts sinking in. Christian pushes his seat back, unbuckles my seat belt, and hauls me onto his lap. My legs spread on either side of his thick thighs, his large palms hold my face as those familiar whiskey eyes sparkle with emotion.

"You aren't going to die, Ness. This surgery is preventative, you don't have to go through it, but every six months, you will have to have mammograms and keep on top of things that way."

I know that's what the doctor told me, but what happens if they still don't get it in time. Ovarian cancer is harder to detect, usually when it's too late. I want to have kids. Fuck, I might not be able to have kids. That's when I start to have a panic attack. My chest feels like an elephant is sitting on it and crushing me.

"Ness, Ness, breathe, it's going to be okay." Christian is yelling at me, trying to help me out of my attack. "Eyes on me, angel, eyes on me." I try and focus on his face, looking over his square jaw and the stubble that covers it, his long neck, those apple-bud cheeks, those eyes, those eyes that can see through to my soul. My breathing slowly starts to abate.

"That's better." His hands are still holding my face. "Want to tell me what that was all about?" Just thinking about kids makes my heart start to race again. "Ness," Christian growls, forcing my attention onto him. "Tell me."

"Kids, I was thinking about kids." Christian frowns, trying to work out my train of thought.

"What about them?"

"I want them, but I don't think..." My words trail off as I'm lost in my thoughts. Warm lips touch mine, my mouth automatically opens for them, hands hold my face, the kiss is soft and gentle, loving even. Eventually, Christian pulls away, smiling at me, making my stomach do cartwheels.

"Remember how we had that conversation a long time ago about turning thirty-five, and if you haven't found someone, then we'd be it for each other." I frown, because yeah, I kind of do, but I swear he must have been high when he said that. "We can hit fast forward if you want. You and I can have a baby together." My whole body stiffens. "You don't have to say anything now, just think about it, okay?" I nod because I'm too stunned to say anything.

30

CHRISTIAN

I'm not going to lie, I've been freaking out about Vanessa's diagnosis. Cancer is fucking serious. What she's considering is a matter of life and death. I know she has age on her side, but I understand where her worries are coming from. To be able to look into a crystal ball and see into the future would suck, but I'm trying to be strong for her.

I listen when she calls me in the middle of the night in a panic, I soothe her, letting her know everything will be okay. She's asked me not to tell anyone. She doesn't want any of our friends to know just yet. I understand she's scared, but our friends will only want to be there for her, support her. She asked me to swear not to say anything to anyone. Of course, I agreed.

"I'm glad I am here today. I told you I am a boob enthusiast." My hands play with some silicon breasts in the plastic surgeon's office.

"Stop molesting the breasts, Chris," Vanessa snaps at me, but her smile lets me know she isn't angry.

"Ness, I'm feeling them up, making sure they are the right fit. You don't want something too small, and you don't want something way too big. You need them to be just right. Like these." I throw a pair of DDs at her.

"Chris, these look so huge. I don't want to look like one of your stripper friends." She throws them back at me.

"Babe, you would be a high-class stripper with these." She rolls her eyes at me.

"Miss Roberts, thank you for waiting." The doctor waltzes into the room. He walks straight over to where Vanessa is standing. "If you could open the top of the gown so we can have a look."

Vanessa's eyes glance over to me, where I'm seated with an excellent view. She glares at me, and I ignore her. It's not like I haven't seen her tits before or feasted on them or licked or nipped or—fuck, I'm getting a half chub in the doctor's office. This isn't good.

Vanessa sighs and opens up her green hospital gown to show the doctor her perfect breasts. Fuck, I'll miss them. The doctor starts touching them, moving them as he talks about breast tissue and what happens with reconstruction, some sort of bullshit, but all I see is red. Calm your tits, Christian, he's a doctor, and this is his job. Pretty fantastic job, really. I look around and realize he touches boobs all day, then before I know it, Vanessa has closed her gown again. The doctor is showing her different sizes and explaining the benefits of them. "I recommend your natural size, which is a C cup. If you want, you could drop down to a B if your old breast size gave you problems."

"No, V, don't do that," I quickly interject, and they both look at me funnily. "Don't go to a B, where's the fun in that size? No, you need at least a D. Look at them. They are perfect." I hold them up for reference.

"I'm guessing your partner likes the original size?" The doctor asks with a smirk.

"He's not my partner, he is a friend," Vanessa adds. Not

going to lie, her confession hits home that I don't really get a say in what size boobs she should have because I won't be the one playing with them. So, I distract myself with some samples instead.

"I've decided to go for a C cup if you were wondering." Vanessa nudges my shoulder as we head toward the parking garage.

"I'm sure someone will love them." My tone is sulky. I can't help it.

"What's the matter?" I continue walking in silence.

"I'm just sad knowing I won't get to play with your boobs ever again." When I turn around to gauge her response, she's stopped walking and is looking at me strangely.

"Are you seriously upset about not getting to say goodbye to my boobs?"

"Yeah, Ness, I am. I've loved those boobs for six years. I consider them mine. But some other guy may be playing with them, and they might be the last one who gets to."

This conversation is getting weird. Quickly I unlock the car, and we both jump in. Vanessa stays silent, which is probably for the best. Not being able to stand the awkward silence anymore, I break it.

"I'm sorry, Ness, I didn't mean to get weird about your boobs. They're your boobs, no one owns them but you." She nods in agreement, and we both stay silent as we continue back to Derrick's place. It's not until we pull up that she talks again.

"Would you like to come inside?"

"Um..." There's a long pause, and I notice Vanessa is acting nervous all of a sudden. Shit, maybe I have freaked her out.

"Sure, I could use a glass of water," I say. Vanessa nods, and we both jump out of my truck and head inside in silence.

"Derrick's at work," Vanessa tells me as she fixes me a drink.

I smile and say, "Thanks," as she hands me the glass of water. Then the awkward silence is back. What the hell is going on? Maybe she's freaking out over everything. Today was a big day for her, making it all seem real. I turn my back to her as I place my glass in the sink. She probably needs time alone.

"I should get going," I say as I turn around, but I'm in shock because Vanessa is taking her top off. "Ness?" I question her, my heart is racing, and my dick is getting excited.

"I thought about what you said about my boobs and how you have known them for a while, and I think you should say goodbye to them," she says, standing there in pink lingerie. Her hand goes behind her back and unclips her bra. I watch it flutter to the floor. Fuck, fuck, fuck, there they are right in front of me. My mouth goes dry.

"Um... Ness, I don't know if this is right." Why the hell am I a gentleman? I don't want to be a gentleman.

"You're just saying goodbye to some old friends," Vanessa adds with a smile. She's right, I kind of am.

Taking a step toward her, I take in their curves, running my hand over their fullness. I hear Vanessa's breath hitch when I touch her skin, my finger continuing underneath her breast following the circle. I can feel the heat radiating between us. I touch the other breast and follow the same path around the outside of it. I move in a little further and start that same path, around and around slowly and softly until I reach her hard, puckered nipple. My thumb ever so gently rubs around the bumpy skin, my eyes look up, and Vanessa has hers closed. Her teeth are biting into her bottom lip, her cheeks are flushed, and her hands are gripping the counter hard, almost cutting off their circulation. I pinch her nipple.

"Ah," Vanessa groans.

"I'm going to miss you." I talk to her breasts, my heated breath blowing on them. I bend over and let my lips kiss the top of them, and I softly kiss my way around them, taking my time until I find her pink nipple again, and I land a kiss directly on it.

"Hmm," Vanessa hums, her eyes still closed.

"These have been the perfect breasts. My palms are weeping because they will miss holding you while their master sleeps." Vanessa's eyes open, and our stares meet each other. I smile at her as my tongue darts out and starts its turn around one breast. Slowly, ever so fucking slowly, I trace the same route committing it to memory, feeling the tiny bumps of her areola on my tongue, moving onto her nipple where I swirl it around my tongue.

"Fuck," Vanessa exhales on a shaky breath. My lips sink over her nipple, and I give it a hard suck. "Christian, you're going to make me come if you keep doing that." I smile as I keep working her breasts, moving from one to the other until she finally pushes me away, her face flushed, and her breathing has accelerated. I step closer to her, pushing her body against the cabinets.

"Thank you for letting me say goodbye." I move off the cabinet and walk away from her, hoping that she realizes that the chemistry between us is hard to beat.

31

VANESSA
WEEKS LATER

"You can't hide this anymore, Ness," Christian reminds me.

"I know, I just..." I let out a sigh, "I don't want everyone to treat me differently."

"I get it, but you're about to have surgery, your friends are going to want to be there for you." I know he's right, but I'm scared. The more people I tell, the more real it feels, and that's scary.

"Fine, okay. Come on, let's organize a team meeting."

"Want me to call next door to Wyld Jones and get them to come over? You can do it all at once." That's not such a bad idea.

"Is everything okay?" Axel asks as the Dirty Texas boys sit in the conference room.

"Christian didn't knock you up, did he?" Derrick questions, the whole room goes silent.

"What, no!" I squeal. Christian frowns at me.

"Then why are we all here?" Sienna asks, "You're not sick, are you?"

My whole body stills. She knows me too well. I fiddle with

my fingers, everyone's eyes are on me, and the room's tension is unbearable.

"Um... I don't know where to start." I fumble over my words. Christian squeezes my hand, giving me silent encouragement.

"You two didn't like get married or something?" Evan asks, looking at our entwined fingers.

"No, God, no," I add quickly.

"Hey," Christian retorts. I shake my head, trying to find where to begin.

"You know how my mum had that test, followed by the surgery she had to have so she wouldn't get cancer?" I watch as everyone's heads nod as they all remember. "Well... um... I'm doing the same thing." The room falls silent. Every single person's face looks worried.

"You're having a mastectomy?" Isla asks. I nod my head. The room erupts into noise with everyone hurling questions at me all at once.

"Hey, hey, everyone shut the fuck up," Christian yells, silencing the room. "I get you all have questions, and Ness will answer them, but one at a time." He gives me a tight smile.

"What's going on, Ness?" Sienna asks. I can see the concern on her face, so I take a deep breath.

"There's this test you can do if you have a family history of breast cancer. Mum did it, and that's how she found out she was positive to the BRCA gene, so she begged me to do the test, and I did. It came back positive." Tears threaten, but I try to hold them back. I have to be strong.

"But, but... what does that mean?" Derrick asks.

"It means that there's a ridiculously high chance that I'll get breast and ovarian cancer." I hear the crowd gasp in shock.

Christian grabs my hand again, giving me the strength to continue. "So, in a couple of weeks, I'm going to have a double mastectomy, just like Angelina Jolie did, and I am going to kick cancer's butt before it kicks mine."

Sienna starts to cry and rushes toward me, pulling me into her arms. Derrick joins her, and one by one, everyone in the rooms takes a turn hugging me. "Guys, please don't treat me any differently. It's just a little surgery, and I'm getting new boobs while I am under as well."

"I helped pick them out," Christian adds, lightening the mood.

"So, everything will be okay, then?" Stacey asks.

"Yeah, fingers crossed."

"I'M SO NERVOUS." I'm standing in a small studio space in the basement of Dirty Texas Records wrapped in nothing but a very thin robe.

"You look beautiful," Derrick coos as he fusses with my hair.

"It's just the closest people to you, Sienna and Derrick," Charlotte says from behind the tripod.

"If it helps, I'll be whipping my boob out every five minutes to feed Ryder." Sienna laughs. It's the truth, I have caught sight of her naked boob so many times. That's why Evan makes all the men leave the room if Sienna has to feed. He doesn't want any of them getting a quick look at her tits, even if it's for the reason they were designed for. Caveman!

"Yeah, but you haven't seen my vajayjay before," I moan, any excuse to not drop this robe.

"Well, if it makes you feel any better, seeing your vajayjay will give me nightmares," Derrick adds. I elbow him in the ribs as he plays with my hair.

"Take your time, Ness. I understand this is hard. Most people don't feel comfortable being naked in front of the camera. How about I put some music on, Derrick can pop some champagne, and we relax a little." That sounds like a good idea.

It was because one bottle of champagne later, I let the robe go and enjoyed the experience.

Charlotte is doing some sexy boudoir photos for me. I want to have some beautiful images of my breasts before they are gone for good. I know I'm getting fake ones, but they might not look the same, they most definitely won't feel the same. I can't believe I let Christian say goodbye to my breasts. What the hell was I thinking? I had to make him stop because I was moments away from pushing him onto the kitchen bench and straddling him. It was the single most erotic thing he has ever done to me—the slow, measured strokes of his tongue, lips, and fingers. There was no hurry with him, he took his time committing my breasts to memory, and it was fucking hot.

"Brilliant, V, that's a wrap," Charlotte squeals as Derrick covers me with the robe again. "You did so well," she says, smiling.

"You looked so sexy. I think my dick twitched." Derrick smiles, kissing me on the cheek.

"Wow, D, what a compliment," I joke as he gives my ass a hard slap. "Ouch."

"You did so well, babe. I'm so fucking proud of you." Sienna hugs me.

"I couldn't have done it without you all, thank you."

"Okay, I have to go because I'm slightly turned on after this, and I need to go ravage my husband." Sienna laughs as she grabs all her baby shit and walks back upstairs to where the boys are.

32

CHRISTIAN

"Everything is ready," Camryn advises me. I walk out into my back garden, looking out over a sea of pink. I called in the cavalry to organize this party for Vanessa. She goes in for surgery on Monday, and I know she's freaking out, so I wanted to do something nice for her.

I have decided that I'm going to woo her with everything I have. We have been spending heaps of time together again, and it feels right. I like having her back in my life again, hanging out, watching movies, going out for dinner, having lunch in the office together—just mundane normal shit. I wish it meant bedroom time, but I'm a patient man, just having her back in my life again means more to me than sexual gratification. Fuck, thank God, none of the boys can hear my thoughts because they would totally call me a pussy for that kind of talk, but it's true. My hand is a poor substitute for Vanessa's pussy, but it has to do for the moment until we get back to where we were before things went pear-shaped.

Today is a surprise. She has no idea what I have planned. It was only a couple of weeks ago that Vanessa had the courage to finally sit everyone down at work and tell them what was going on. She was so scared, but it went really well. Of course, everyone is worried about her, they want to help, but they also give her the space she needs. No one hovers, no one treats her any differently.

Her parents flew in this weekend, and I have put them up at the Four Seasons in a beautiful suite with a car on standby to use at any time. They are bringing her tonight under the guise of us all catching up for dinner—they are totally in on the surprise. I've asked them to text when they are close. I got their text five minutes ago, so they shouldn't be far.

"Okay, listen up, she should be here in five minutes, everyone take your places and remember to yell 'surprise' when she walks in the door." Everyone nods and goes off to find their hiding spot. Moments later, the buzzer of my front gate goes off, alerting everyone that she's here. Checking the security camera to make sure it's them, I buzz them in. "Places, everyone," I call out as I head toward the front door. They are all just getting out as I open it. "Welcome," I say warmly as I greet Vanessa's parents. It takes a few moments before we all walk into the foyer.

"Surprise!" The room erupts, and poppers of pink confetti shoot all over my home, showering it in pink dust. But I really don't care. Vanessa looks taken aback until she sees the big sign hanging up saying,

Goodbye Boobies, Hello Tatas

Her eyes are watering, really badly, and she looks like she's in shock. She looks at me and then runs to kiss me in front of everyone, like a full-on-rips-your-clothes-off kiss, to which the entire room erupts into hoots and hollers.

"Um... Ness," I say, interrupting our hot kiss. "Everyone is here."

Her eyes don't look around the room. "I know, and I don't care." She smiles at me.

"You did this, didn't you?" Of course, I'd do anything for her. "And that's why I kissed the hell out of you because only you would throw a proper goodbye party for my boobs." She bursts out laughing. "Thank you, Christian, thank you so much." Her arms are still wrapped around me.

"You know I'd do anything for you, don't you?"

She nods her agreement. "Yeah, I know." Her lips touch mine again. This time it's lighter. My heart is racing. What does this mean? Is she just being thankful, or is there a chance for us to take things further? "I'm staying tonight, okay," she tells me.

"Of course, and just know that if you do, I might never let you go." I put my heart on the line again. She gives me a huge smile that lights up her entire face.

"I think I can handle that."

"Okay, stop making out, you love birds, Sienna and I have something to give Vanessa in honor of her boobies, but you have to follow us," Derrick says very secretively. We excuse ourselves from the party for a moment as we follow them into her old room, where there's something hidden under a sheet.

"We wanted to give you something extraordinary to commemorate your boobs." Sienna smiles as her hand is poised on the sheet. "We hope you like it." She pulls the sheet away, and there, staring back at me is a pair of bronze tits.

Vanessa's jaw drops. "Are they mine?" Derrick and Sienna nod. "But how?" she asks. I may have gone over and run my fingers over Vanessa's deliciously bronzed breasts, feeling the cold metal against my fingers' pads.

"Stop that," Derrick says, slapping my hand away from the tits. "This isn't your new sex toy. You will not hump the monument," Derrick adds. I'm insulted, my mind hadn't even thought of that, but maybe I would. Just once, I could jerk off over the bronzed tits.

"We asked the plastic surgeon to do the mold. He told you it was part of the surgery," Sienna adds.

"No, fucking way, you guys are sneaky. I love it. Look at my boobs, they're hot." She squeezes them with a honk-honk, making us all laugh.

"So, the dream team is back together again?" Derrick asks, looking between the two of us. We're both silent, not knowing what to say. Putting my arm around V's shoulders, I stand tall.

"I'll take her any way she wants me, I'm a patient guy. I know what it feels like to lose her from my life, and I'm not willing to lose her again." Sienna and Derrick both sigh at my words. They are the truth. Vanessa leans over and kisses my cheek.

"Um... we shall leave you two alone with the boobs," Derrick says, pulling Sienna out of the room.

"They are crazy." Vanessa laughs as she puts her arms around my neck.

"They just love you, that's all. We all do."

The party is a roaring success. I may have gone overboard with the boob theme, but seriously, when in my life am I ever going to be able to have a party dedicated to boobs, boobs, and more boobs!

Camryn has outdone herself. The whole house is covered in pink. There are boob cupcakes, lingerie cookies, pink flowers, pink cocktails. You name it, we have it here. Of course, this is a Dirty Texas party, and it continues well into the night. A friend of ours set up a DJ booth and was spinning tracks by the pool. It wasn't long until people were stripping and jumping into it.

"So, you got the girl," Axel states, sliding up beside me on the pool's edge, all our friends running around having fun.

"I'm not sure."

"Seemed that way when she walked through the door."

"Yeah, that surprised the shit out of me." I chuckle.

"So, you thinking of doing all that through-sickness-and-in-health stuff?" My body stiffens. What's my brother getting at?

"Huh?"

"I'm not talking marriage, I'm talking about looking after her while she's sick. That kind of puts a lot of pressure on a relationship." Why the hell is Axel talking like this?

"I'd move heaven and earth for that girl, and you know it. Even if things were the way they were before and we were just friends, I'd be doing the same thing."

Axel smiles. "Good, I just wanted to check."

"Really? You were just testing me? You're a bastard." I push him into the pool, he falls in spluttering, flipping me the bird as he swims off. Vanessa swims up in between my legs as I sit on the side of the pool. I look down at her. She's swimming around in the skimpiest of bathing suits, and it's driving my cock hard. I noticed some of the Sons of Brooklyn boys checking her out earlier. I wasn't impressed. I was ready to rip her away from those little punks, their greasy little eyes all over her, but she was having fun, and she deserves no stress before her surgery.

"Having fun?" I question her. Her hands move up my legs and disappear under my board shorts, her fingertips touching my balls. "Sweetheart, you might want to stop that. Otherwise, I might have to pull you out of this pool and fuck you in front of everyone." Vanessa visibly gulps and yanks me into the pool. She's laughing when I surface above the water again. Vanessa wraps her legs around my waist and her arms around my neck.

"You could fuck me in this pool, and no one would know," she whispers into my ear, sending shivers down my spine. She's been drinking, I can tell by the rosy glow on her cheeks.

"Ness," I growl. She really is testing me. We haven't been this flirty in a long time. It's thrown me off as to how affectionate she is toward me. I thought I'd have to work much harder to get her like this, who knew all I had to do was throw a goodbye party for her boobs. My fingers slip into her easily, and she wiggles closer to me, pressing her body against mine. Luckily, the water is neck height, and you can't see much. Back and forth through her folds, I go.

"I'm going to make you come in front of all these people, sweetheart." Her eyes are glazing over as I magically play with her clit, but there's a hint of a challenge behind those green irises. Pushing my thumb harder against her throbbing clit, over and over again, I add a couple more fingers filling her up, in and out, in and out. Vanessa's cheeks are flushed, and she's so close. I capture her scream with my mouth, kissing her while she rides my fingers slowly as her orgasm subsides.

"Fuck, that was sexy," Axel says beside us.

"Fuck off, Axe," Vanessa says, splashing water in his face. He quickly puts his hands up, surrendering.

"Have fun, you two," he comments as he swims away.

"Sorry about him, he's such a voyeur."

"We know that's true." She giggles, remembering what she saw at The Paradise Club.

"You like being a little exhibitionist, don't you, angel?"

"I think so."

"I'll take you back to the club when you're all healed if you like." She smiles, kisses me quickly on the lips, and starts swimming away from me.

"Ness, Ness, where are you?" I call out into the empty home. Everyone has finally gone home, and I'm shattered. I just want to curl up with Vanessa and go to sleep. Maybe if I'm lucky, we might get to do something else, but I can't seem to find her anywhere. Then I hear it, very faint sniffling coming from her old room. When I see her, she's sitting at the end of the spare bed, her tanned shoulders hunched over and crying. The closer I get, I realize there's something in her hand. It looks like a book she's flipping through the pages of.

"Ness." She jolts and looks up at me with red eyes. "Babe, what's the matter?"

I scoop her up in my arms, holding her tight against me. She opens the book again. It's black and leather-bound, and the white pages are thick cardboard style. Turning the pages, my eyes are mesmerized by what I see—tasteful pictures of Vanessa in various positions and nude. My heart is beating faster and faster as I turned each page. "Ness, you look beautiful." I turn her face to mine, and I can see the concern lacing it.

"I look good now, but what happens if I'm no longer attractive? When I have too many scars?" Vanessa looks at me. She seems so fragile and vulnerable.

"I'd still find you the most beautiful woman in the world, scars or no scars. I don't care, it's what's inside that counts, babe." She hiccups as her tears fall.

"Easy for you to say when all those hot groupies are throwing themselves at you with their perfect bodies and skin, then you come home to me." Was she serious? Grabbing her face, I make her look at me.

"You're it for me, Ness. There has been no one else inside my heart but you. It's always been you." Shit, I hope that doesn't freak her out.

"You really think that?" she asks quietly.

"Yeah, I do, babe." I kiss her cheek. She gives me a timid smile, and that's when I know she gets it. She gets that I'm not playing anymore.

33

VANESSA

My parents and Christian are here in the waiting room with me. I'm freaking out. Christian's mom has flown in as well. She's staying at the house and getting things ready for me. Christian is quite adamant that I'll be staying with him during my recovery—well, in all honesty, I haven't left his side all weekend. We spent the time together lazing by the pool, watching movies, and making love.

Yeah, it might be stupid because I could totally die on the operating table, and if I did, I want my last moments on earth to have been filled with mind-blowing orgasms and the best sex of my life. Christian paid careful attention to my breasts, really giving them the best send-off he could think of. Mainly it was jerking himself over them, claiming he was marking his territory.

I'm so happy that Christian is here with me at the hospital. He's my rock and has been throughout this whole process over the past month. Holding my hand while I am dressed in a horrible hospital gown and hairnet, I watch as the nurses walk past and take him in, and why wouldn't they? He's a rock star, and even if he weren't, heads would still turn.

His light brown hair is longer and wavy as if he has been at the beach all day. Those whiskey-colored eyes dance with mischief, and that body is a body made for sin—sculpted arms that should be on a Greek god, colorful tattoos covering his tanned skin, washboard abs that deserve to be on a billboard, and that cock, that beautiful, silky cock that brings the most fantastic pleasure you could ever imagine. I may have done something good in a past life because, for some reason, he has chosen me to give his heart to. Me, the woman who's losing her breasts, a piece of me that makes me feel like a woman, the same woman who broke his heart when he had the balls to tell her how he felt.

Fuck, I really am a fool. A fool who's too scared to see what's right in front of her. My eyes fall to his beautiful face, the same one that smiled up at me this morning as he snuggled me in bed. I just stare at him, committing everything to memory, so if I don't wake up, I can dream forever about his beautiful face.

"Are you okay, Ness?" he whispers, noticing me staring at him.

"Yeah, I just..." I take a deep breath, "... just can't believe how lucky I am to have you by my side." He wraps one of his massive arms around me.

"I'm just as lucky, angel, to have you back in my life." He places a kiss on my forehead. My heart bursts, totally overfilled with love for this man, but before I get a chance to tell him how I feel, the orderly comes in with a hospital bed and asks me to get on it as he'll be taking me down for the surgery. The shit's about to get real.

I kiss my mom and dad goodbye. I can see the worry on my mother's face. She tells me I'll be okay and to look forward to a long and healthy future. The panic is rolling over my body. Christian helps me get into the bed. He holds my hand as we walk down the corridor, his beautiful smile looking down at me, his brown hair pulled back while a couple of wisps of hair have escaped.

"I'm going to be waiting for you right here, okay?" he says firmly.

"I'm sorry, sir, this is as far as you can go," the orderly tells him.

He looks down at me, and I can see he's holding back his tears, trying to put on a brave face for me. What happens if I don't wake up? He won't know how much I fucking love him? Why the fuck did I ever say no to this man? He's so far in my soul that it hurts.

"Christian," I call his name and ask him to bend down. "Can you give us a moment, please?" I ask the orderly, who nods and moves away from us.

"Chris, I need to tell you something, just in case something happens." I try and keep the tears back, but I can't because I'm so fucking scared.

"Babe, don't think like that, everything is going to be okay, you hear me." I nod, but the lump in my throat feels like it's trying to choke me.

"I need you to know something before I go in." Christian nods, giving me his full attention. "I've been so scared of my feelings for you, and fear guided my decisions before. I wanted to say yes to you at the wedding when you bared everything to me. The way you make me feel consumes me. I was worried that if I took that chance, that if anything happened, breaking up with you would end me. There was no coming back from that kind of heartbreak, so I chose fear." I can see tears welling in Christian's eyes. It's the first time we have spoken about that night. He goes to speak, but I silence him.

"What I want to say is, I love you. I love you so fucking much that my heart can't contain it." I hear Christian's audible gasp and see his eyes widen. "I need you to know if you're willing to take a chance on me, I want it all, Chris, I want it all with you. It's always been you." Christian's lips come down on mine in a heated kiss, his tears falling onto my cheeks.

"It's you and me against the world now, babe." I nod in agreement, trying to hold back my tears. "I fucking love you so much, Ness, and I can't wait until you open your eyes again after this surgery, and we can spend the rest of our long lives together." Now it was my turn to gasp. He just smirks.

"That's right, angel, you and me, forever and ever." He kisses me one last time. The orderly clears his throat.

"Sorry, we have to go." Christian holds my hand until the last possible moment, then he's gone, and I slip into a deep dark abyss.

"We're going to get married, have babies, and grow old together," I mumble through the haze.

"Damn right, we are." I hear that voice, that deep timbered voice that warms my body.

"I can't wait to get you home and ravage you, Chris," I slur. Then I hear laughter, and it sounds like my mum.

"Mum?" I call out, my eyes feeling too heavy to open, and my mouth so very dry.

"I'm here, sweetheart," she answers, squeezing my hand.

"I'm alive, I made it." I marvel as I realize I am alive, and that something horrible didn't happen to me in surgery.

"Yes, sweetheart, you're alive. The doctor said everything went well, and he's delighted with the results." I sink back into the fluffy pillows. Thank fuck.

"He said your boobs look great." I hear Christian from beside me and turn my head to where his voice is coming from. Willing my eyes to open, they finally move, and I blink at the bright light when I see Christian's face staring back at me, his beautiful face.

"You're so hot." The words tumble out of my mouth, damn anesthetic.

"You look pretty hot yourself." He moves closer to kiss my forehead.

Over the next hour, I slowly come out of my fog, and I can see everything a little clearer. I realize I can't move, and the pain of the surgery comes into play. The doctor finally comes in and runs me through the procedure—how they took my breasts but saved my nipples, they had to play around with different size breasts because of the skin elasticity and actually ended up settling on a D cup, much to Christian's delight. I'll be in the hospital for about five days to ensure there's no infection, and I will be discharged once all my vitals are in order.

Christian advises the doctor that he has organized twenty-four-hour nursing care for me when I'm at home, which seems like overkill, but it's probably for the best. Poor Christian, he doesn't need to wipe my ass for me.

34

CHRISTIAN

V's been home for about a month now, and she's definitely stronger than she was when she first came home. Seeing her in pain, the tears falling down her face all because she'd forget she couldn't lift her arms or she would roll over in the middle of the night, forgetting she had surgery, those blood-curdling screams at night were scary. Thankfully, we have nurses on call because I was a complete mess.

Seeing the woman I love in that much pain ripped me to the core. I want to help her, but Ness hates being dependent on me, even though I told her that I'd be by her side the entire time. Thankfully, our mothers are still here helping with her recovery.

Sylvie, Vanessa's mom, has been helping the nurses with her day-to-day well-being, and my mom has been cooking up her famous southern comfort food for me, which I have missed living in LA. I've probably gained one hundred pounds from her cooking, but I don't care because it's so good. Mom is a retired nurse, and she's explained to me what Vanessa is going through in basic terms so that I could understand.

I've found Vanessa crying by herself, and I try to help her, but nothing seems to work. Mom told me what signs to watch out for in case Vanessa sinks into depression, which apparently is typical for a woman when losing her breasts. She explained that for a woman, it can feel like losing the very essence of herself, her femininity, her beauty, and no matter how much encouragement I give her, she needs to process the loss herself. So, I let Ness cry herself to sleep some nights, which kills me, but I notice that she appears stronger when she does have these mini breakdowns. I hope I'm doing the right thing.

"Mornin', darlin'," Momma says, handing me a steaming hot coffee as she sits down beside me in a pool chair. "How ya feeling?"

"I'm good, Ness is good. She's got most of her movement back, and her pain is finally subsiding."

"But how are you doin'?" she asks, being a concerned mother.

"Yeah, I'm all right." I sip on the piping hot liquid.

"So, what are your plans?" she asks, peeking over her coffee mug at me.

"What do you mean?" I question because I know exactly what she means.

"What are your plans with Vanessa?" She gives me a piercing look. "Are you going to make an honest woman out of her?" I choke on my coffee.

"Mom!"

"Don't you 'Mom' me, I want to know if there's a chance I'm going to be a grand momma or not?" I'm in total shock. "You love her, boy, so hurry up and put a ring on it," she states firmly.

"Mom, I finally got her to confess her feelings for me. She's been through a lot, so we're taking it slow."

"You have spent the past six years taking it slow, now's the time to go grab the bull by the horns." I love my mom, I really do, but she's kind of desperate for grandkids, and now that there's a slight chance that could happen, she's on full baby alert, especially as she has been spending time with Ryder while's she's been here.

"Don't worry, when the time is right, I'll put a ring on it, okay?"

Mom nods.

"I knew the first time you brought her home that she was the one." I roll my eyes at her. She always says this. "Don't you roll your eyes at me, boy, it's the truth. You both gravitated toward each other. Everything was natural between the two of you. I could see your connection then, even though you were both fighting it. I understood, especially as a woman in the workplace." I'm close with my mom, so she knows how Ness and I met and everything between us. "I knew she was the one because she only had eyes for you, not your brother."

It sucked when a girl I was interested in was way more interested in my brother. Most girls liked the brooding poetic vibe that Axel oozed. I'd bring a girl home, and their focus would be on Axel when he was around, listening to him sing, watching him write music, or play his guitar. He'd always have them eating out of his hand by the end of the day.

I had no need not to trust him, he was my brother, but when I came home from football practice early one day and found my first serious girlfriend in bed with him, I was fucking hurt. She later confessed that she was curious to see if we both fucked the same. I punched my brother out that day, and we didn't talk for a long time. He eventually told me he did it to test her and that she was no good for me. After that incident, I gave up trying to have a relationship with anyone because I was worried they would secretly want my brother.

"I know. I promise, Mom, you will be the first to know when we get engaged, okay?" She leans over and kisses my head.

"Perfect, now hurry the hell up." She ruffles my hair as she takes our cups back inside.

"I'm so fucking turned on, Ness," I whisper in her ear as we sit patiently at the doctor's office for her check-up. It's been nearly five weeks since Vanessa and I have had sex, and my blue balls are killing me.

"I just want the all-clear from the doctor first." She runs her hand along my thigh.

"The plastic surgeon said it was okay," I moan.

"Yes, but I'm just waiting for my oncologist to give me the all-clear, then I'm all yours, I promise." She smiles, winking at me.

"Miss Roberts." The doctor calls her name, and we make our way into his office. The doctor looks over her test results and examines her. What he asks next totally floors us. "So, Vanessa, have you decided what you're going to do with your ovaries?"

"I'm sorry, what?" Vanessa asks.

"If you're going to have a hysterectomy? Saving your eggs and implanting later? Or are you thinking about not having kids?" Vanessa stiffens. "You are in your prime birthing years at the moment, and each year increases your risk of ovarian cancer due to your genetics."

Fuck, that was heavy, and after everything Vanessa has just been through, she now has to think of this as well. "I know this is a lot to think about, and you probably haven't broached the subject with your partner, but you really need to think about it and start planning. I suggest you go home and talk about your options," he says as he hands us both a stack of brochures and information.

"No need to talk, doc. We're having kids, just need you to give Vanessa the all clear, and we can get started."

"Christian," Vanessa scolds me.

"Don't look so shocked, angel, you and I are in this for the long haul, and if you have to have a baby now so you can have a hysterectomy later, so you don't get cancer, then that's what we do." I cross my arms over my chest. I want to have babies with her, just like Evan has with Sienna. I want to play football and baseball in the backyard with my son or teach him to play guitar.

"But…" Vanessa splutters.

"There's no discussion, babe, you need to have a baby, you need my sperm. Quite frankly, look at me, I'm one hundred percent all male, you can't do any better than me, so why would you not want to breed with me?" There's that gaping fish face that Vanessa seems to have mastered in the space of five minutes.

"Anyway," the doctor interrupts awkwardly. "I'll let you two discuss this at home. You're free to resume normal activities, but still be careful in some areas," the doctor advises us. Right, be careful, but sex is a go.

"Come on, let's get home and make a baby," I say as we walk out of the doctor's office.

"You can't be fucking serious, Christian," Vanessa yells at me in the car.

"What, to want to have a baby with you?"

"Yes. Do you even want kids?" she yells, sounding frustrated with me.

"Never thought much about it—" She cuts me off before I get to finish what I'm saying.

"Ha, see you're just thinking of sex and not the consequences of all that practicing," she states as if she has found the secret codes to mankind, crossing her arms over her chest confidently.

"Oh, believe me, Ness, we're going to have so much practicing for this baby." I smile at her as we drive back to our home.

"You seriously want a baby?" Now she's looking at me like I'm some weird social experiment gone wrong.

"Honestly, I never thought of having a kid until I knew there was a chance that I could have one with you." Vanessa is silent in the car. I glance over to her because a silent Ness is a scary one. Then she bursts out crying. "What the fuck, V?" I keep flicking my eyes at her.

"I never thought I wanted kids until I found out there was a chance that I couldn't have one," she sniffles. My hand finds her thigh, and I squeeze it.

"And now?" I question, wondering what her answer will be because I never thought I wanted kids until I met her. Her hand rests over mine on her leg.

"I think I want one..." She pauses for a moment, "... with you," she whispers. I turn and look at her.

"Really?"

"Fuck, this is crazy. I mean, I just had a double mastectomy so I wouldn't get cancer. I'm not even married. It feels all kinds of messed up and backward, planning a baby when you and I are..." she pauses, "... you know, trying to find our way."

"If you're worried about us, then let me spell it out for you. One day we'll be getting married, that's a given, and I'm not taking no for an answer. I love you, Ness, and I want to spend the rest of my life with you and only you." My eyes flick to where Vanessa is sitting stunned in the passenger's seat.

"Regarding kids... is it sooner than I would like, probably, but it doesn't change what I want. What I want is you and me and babies, there's no one else in the world that I'd want to mix eggs and sperm with." This makes her laugh. "It's the truth, V, we'd make beautiful children. It's really unfair that the world should miss out on our beautiful offspring."

"That's true. Oh God, imagine if we had a boy, he and Ryder could be best friends."

"They would get into so much trouble, and they would pick up so many chicks together." We both laugh about it.

"Imagine if they started up their own rock band, it would be Dirty Texas 2.0." She laughs.

"That would be awesome, our kids all playing in a band together just like their old folks, fuck yeah!" My heart is racing because I can totally see it. "So, judging by that smile on your face, you think the idea of breeding with me is kind of hot." I wiggle my eyebrows at her.

"I'm not a fucking animal to breed with, Chris," she laughs. I grab her hand and kiss her soft knuckles as we make our way back up into the Hills.

"It would make me the happiest man in the world to be the one to knock you up."

"Now that's more romantic. Christian, I can't wait until you fuck a baby into me." I almost crash the car with Vanessa's statement. We both burst out laughing.

35

CHRISTIAN
ONE MONTH LATER

It's my thirtieth birthday, and we're off to Vegas, baby. The whole crew and, of course, Axel, seeing as it's his birthday too. I'm sitting inside our private jet on our way to Las Vegas with all the people I love around me. It's funny how things have changed. This time last year, I never thought that I'd be celebrating my thirtieth birthday with the woman I love and trying to get her knocked up. Fuck, life is crazy sometimes.

Currently, I'm cuddling Ryder, giving Evan a break from the little man. Looking at his little fingers wrapping themselves around my large ones, the tiny gurgling sounds he makes soothe my heart.

"Don't tell me you're getting broody?" Axel asks me, spotting me mesmerized by the baby in my arms.

"Fuck you, I don't think it would be too bad," I say, much to Axel's horror.

"Seriously?" I shrug as if it's no big deal.

"I'm happy for you, man." I can see the sincerity in his eyes. He has no idea that we're trying for a baby, no one does. Vanessa doesn't want anyone to know. She thinks they won't understand, and she doesn't want to jinx it.

"Fuck, my little bro is going to be a family man." He laughs.

"Hey, I'm like a minute younger, dickhead."

"What happens if you have twins?" he asks. I still. Fuck, I never thought of that, shit! I was getting used to the idea of just one baby, but two?

"Don't curse us, please. Fuck, man. I don't know how to look after one baby, let alone two."

"Can I have my child back now?" Evan asks as he walks over. I hand over Ryder to his dad.

"You're looking a little melancholy there, Christian." He smiles. Shit, I need to start hiding these feelings. Otherwise, I'll let the cat out of the bag.

"Please keep your spawn away from me. It has magical powers turning former players into sappy wusses," Axel jokes, before quickly hightailing it out of there.

"Ha-ha, his time will come," Evan states with a smile. "So, are you wanting to knock up Ness?" My eyes look over to where she's seated with the girls laughing, her caramel hair pulled up in a ponytail. She's dressed in fitted jeans that mold to her tight rump and a plain white T-shirt that shows off her very perky and generous assets.

"Yeah, man, I kind of do," I confess.

"Well, I can't wait until you join the club, man. Kids change you. They are hard work, man, but fuck, the love you have for that tiny little human… nothing I have ever felt in my life comes close to that feeling."

We both look down at little Ryder, who's growing bigger and stronger every single day, growing from a baby to an active little guy. Evan's mom has flown in from Houston to look after Ryder so that Evan and Sienna can have some free time together. They were not ready to leave him alone overnight.

"I'm happy for you, man, for finally getting your girl." He smiles at me.

"Yeah, I finally did, and I couldn't be happier." Looking at

Ness, I smile like a fucking Cheshire cat. It's still early when we arrive in Vegas. We all head to our suites at the Palms Casino Resort to get ready for dinner and drinks. I've booked Vanessa and me into the erotic suite to have some alone time now that we're a couple. I know Axel's booked the two-story sky villa for him and the single guys. He's sharing with Oscar, Finn, and Derrick. We decided to have dinner in their suite tonight, then head out to the Sons of Brooklyn's after-party. They are playing at the Hard Rock Cafe.

"Oh my God," Vanessa squeals as we enter the red and black suite. She runs through it enthusiastically, touching all the gadgets. We have a round bed that rotates, a stripper pole in the middle of a massive shower, a Jacuzzi in the other bathroom, a bar, a million televisions scattered around the room, and a kick-ass sound system.

I find her playing with the remote control on the rotating bed. I watch as she spins around. "Hope I don't get dizzy." She giggles as she slowly turns. I notice each time she passes me, she's losing an item of clothing. Standing at the end of the bed, I start to follow her lead and ditch my clothing. She smiles, seeing my hardening cock bobbing in front of me.

"Come join me." I jump on the bed, making her squeal. It feels very unnatural with the bed moving, but I put it out of my mind as my lips capture hers. Vanessa's hands make their way over my skin lightly as we enjoy just making out. I'm trying not to put any of my body weight on top of her because I know she's still sore from her operation.

She sucks my bottom lip in her mouth, knowing how much I like it. Small nibbles start down my neck, then her tongue glides up my neck and back into my mouth. This feels so good. Usually, we're so feverish with desire that we are ripping each other's clothes off as soon as we see each other.

"Babe, we have to be quick. We need to get ready for dinner," she explains, breaking our blissed-out trance.

"Fuck it, it's my birthday. We can be late." I start licking her collarbone.

"That's true."

I make my way down toward her chest. The frustrating thing for Vanessa now is that she has lost all sensation in her breasts. Before I could make her come just from sucking on her tits, but now there are no nerves there, so she feels nothing. I can see it in her eyes when I'm playing with them that she misses the feeling. I have to distract her from worrying by sinking a finger deep inside of her. Her tits look and feel amazing to me, but they are hard. I miss the softness of her natural ones, but I'd much rather have her in my life than a pair of tits.

Making my way down her soft body, my tongue guides me toward its final destination. Pushing her legs apart, I can smell her arousal. I kiss my way along each of her thighs, and she wiggles in anticipation. Her hands shift to my head, and she runs her fingers through my hair. The closer my tongue gets to her sweet spot, the harder her fingers pull. I like feeling the burn. My five o'clock shadow prickles against her skin, adding friction against her clit. Finally, my tongue sinks deep inside of her.

"Yes," she hisses, pulling tight on my hair. I lap at her, back and forth, rolling my tongue over her tightening bud, losing myself in her divine pussy. I sink my finger back into her, and another moan hisses from her mouth. My thumb ventures behind her and finds the puckered skin of her tight asshole. Lightly, I press against it, feeling the resistance. Vanessa arches her back at the sensation. I add another finger inside her slick center, stretching her, getting her ready for me. I press harder against her back entrance, trying to gain access.

The harder I push, the harder her cunt tightens around my fingers. The dirty minx loves a little bit of anal play, she's thrashing around the bed, and I can feel she's getting close. I suck hard on her clit and press harder against her hole. She arches off the bed, her body spasming from the orgasm. I lightly flick my tongue across her sensitive center one last time, the aftershocks make her body twitch. Slowly, I withdraw my fingers, and Vanessa groans at their absence.

"Don't worry, sweetheart, you'll be full again soon." I move between her thighs, lining up my hardened cock. Gradually, I sink into her wetness, inch by glorious inch, and she engulfs me with pleasure.

"Fuck." We both moan as our bodies become one, those green eyes looking at me with a sexy smirk.

"That's the best feeling in the world, Chris... feeling you inside of me." I groan as her inner muscles clamp down on me.

"You're killing me, Ness." I don't want her to stop. Vanessa raises her knees so that they are almost at her chest. This allows me to go deeper into her. I didn't think I could get any deeper inside of her, but I was wrong. Thank fuck, I have been working out. Otherwise, trying to keep myself off her chest would be hard. I find my rhythm as I enter her.

"Ness, look at us." My eyes drift to where we're joined, she looks up, and her eyes widen as she watches me enter her. "I'll never get sick of this, of being with you," I whisper, her eyes looking up at me, and she smiles. Before I know it, she's flipping me onto my back.

"How about this view?" She starts riding my cock like a damn cowgirl as my eyes watch as she slides up and down. Fuck yes! She reaches behind her and starts playing with my balls, making my eyes roll back into my head. Yes, yes, yes. A stray finger starts moving further south, um, no, no, no. Her thumb pushes against the virgin territory as she squeezes around my cock while putting just the right amount of pressure against my hole. I feel it, I feel it so deep down in my balls.

"Do that again," I pant. She indulges me with more. "Yes," I say, arching my back this time. Her thumb pushes a little further and infiltrates momentarily, and my dick stands at attention.

"Want me to keep going?" Vanessa questions me. I do, fucking hell, I do, but honestly, I haven't let anyone touch my backdoor before, not because I think it's gay or anything, but because it feels intimate and none of the girls I have been with ever deserved that right.

"Yes," I whisper, and Vanessa's finger sinks in. She finds this bundle of nerves that I have never felt before, her finger moving back and forth, and I swear I see stars floating around her head. She does it again, still while riding me, and I'm gone, so fucking gone. Some glorious sweet spot she has found makes me explode into a thousand tiny little pieces. I swear she makes me blow the biggest load of my life. I can't move, I'm dead. She slowly moves off me and lays on her back with her feet in the air.

"What the fuck are you doing?" She looks like a dead cockroach.

"It's peak ovulation time, Chris, I'm not wasting that load." I burst out laughing. "Isn't that an old wives' tale?" I ask, genuinely curious and also a little worried.

"Maybe, I don't know, but it makes sense holding it all in for as long as possible." I crawl up beside her. She turns and looks at me.

"Sweetheart, how about I just keep filling you up every single day? I think that might be a little more enjoyable than pretending you're a dead cockroach on the bed." She bursts out laughing.

"You're right," she sits up, "It's just..." Her words fall away.

"Just what?"

"Now that we both kind of want to have a baby," she says this quietly because it's still kind of strange thinking about it, "... I kind of want our baby to be close in age to Ryder," she confesses.

My eyes widened. "Really?" She nods.

"We could have playdates and things, you know, going through the same kind of stuff together."

"I guess all we can do is try, sweetheart, and if you want to lay down like a cockroach after sex, then I can handle that." She leaps into my arms with a hard oomph knocking the air out of me as she starts kissing my face all over, laughing.

"I love you, Christian Taylor." She giggles, and it's the best sound in the entire world.

CHRISTIAN

"Okay, today I have planned a special guy's day. A day to separate the boys from the men." Derrick looks at us like a drill sergeant, dressed in some sort of couture army gear standing before us in our hotel suite. Honestly, I'm a little scared, especially if he has organized the day.

"You're going to have fun." Vanessa walks over, placing a kiss on my cheek. The girls are heading to the spa. Wrapping my arms around her, I nuzzle her neck.

"I kind of had planned on staying in bed with you all day, licking you all over." I feel her shiver in my arms.

"Later, we have plenty of time for that." She kisses me. "I'm off with the girls."

"Come on, boys, fall out," Derrick yells, setting us in motion downstairs to the lobby where we're greeted with several army Humvees. "We are going to have so much fun." He rubs his hands with glee as we all pile into the cars.

We ride through the streets living out our inner GI Joe fantasy—it's actually pretty sick. We pull up to a warehouse, and we're greeted by the owners. We follow them inside and are ushered to a wall of guns. We are talking about every possible weapon you could imagine from handguns to rifles to sniper and army-style guns. We're kids in a candy shop.

"As you have hired it all for yourselves today, you can choose any gun to shoot." The owner launches into a big spiel about all the guns on display. I think I might have drooled a little. Eventually, we all choose a gun to shoot first, and us being boys, we all go for our fantasy gun first. My first choice is a Thompson M-1928 SMG, always wanted to shoot a Tommy gun like a fucking mafia gangster. I shoot up my target in no time. I swear I got a hard-on. I'm used to being around guns growing up in Texas. Dad loved his guns and always took us down to the range to learn how to shoot.

We spend the next couple of hours going crazy, living out every gun fantasy there is. Once we had finished shooting, we were taken out into the back parking lot area and told that the next part of our boys' day is driving an army tank over a car and crushing it. Fuck me! Climbing into the tank, touching all the nobs, the instructor spoke to me about safety, and then he let me take the wheel. The rumble of the tank is vibrating all over my body as we lined up the car. *Boom,* up and over. Hearing the glass windows crush underneath us was terrific. Fuck yeah! I felt like Rambo.

"Now, who's up for more action?" Derrick asks once we've all had our turns in the tank. We nod enthusiastically because so far, so good with Derrick's ultimate guy day. A large party bus turns up at the shooting range, and we file in. We sit and talk about the day, hyped up on adrenaline. It's a quick journey, and we're pulling up to a construction yard where diggers and excavators are sitting.

"Are we playing with them?" Finn asks. Derrick's face lights up with a huge grin.

"Bob-the-Builder fantasy, anyone?" I have no idea what he's talking about, but hell yeah, it's like we have reverted back to being kids again playing shoot-em-up and now playing with machinery. Best day ever!

"Now, don't think the day is over just yet," Derrick says cryptically as we enter the party bus after playing with all the machinery. "We have another stop, and I think you're all going to love it." We travel a little further and arrive at a race track. Lined up is a flotilla of supercars—Ferraris, Lamborghinis, Maseratis, Porsches, and Aston Martins, all in a rainbow of colors. Holy shit, they are pretty. I run my hand over the red gloss of the Ferrari as I check out the black leather of the supercar. Hell, yeah, I'm taking this baby for a spin.

"Now this ultimate guy day is coming to an end, and I know you're all sad because today has been kind of awesome, because hello, I organized it." Derrick chuckles. "But we're moving on to the last stop, and I think this is going to be your favorite stop yet."

"Okay, boys, this is our last stop." The bus parks in the back of an empty alleyway. We all look at each other, not really sure this is where we're supposed to be until a door opens, and Nate Lewis, owner of The Paradise Club, greets us.

37

VANESSA

"Spa day," Sienna whisper-yells as we all meet at the hotel's luxurious spa. The boys have gone out on some ultimate guy-day thing Derrick has planned for them, and us girls are going to have a girly day of catching up and relaxing. Sienna is bouncing up and down. She's super excited. "I have been looking forward to this day for so long." I give her a look. "Don't look at me like that, just wait until you have kids one day, ladies. You have no idea how much you crave your own personal time and space. Having a kid is so claustrophobic, Ryder is always on me."

"Lucky he's cute," Charlotte adds.

"Yeah, he is," Sienna giggles.

The spa director comes out, greets us all, and directs us to the VIP spa area. We're welcomed into our own room with a heated spa, a champagne bottle, and a tray of chocolate-dipped strawberries waiting for us. We strip off our robes and lay down on the beds beside the pool. We're each given a glass of champagne. "Please press the buzzer when you're ready for your treatments." She points to the button on the wall, then she disappears.

"If I fall asleep, ladies, I apologize now because this is so relaxing, and I'm so tired," Sienna moans as she sinks her teeth into a chocolate strawberry.

"So, you and Christian seem to be doing well?" Isla asks, sipping on her champagne.

"Yeah, we are. He's been brilliant, especially with the whole boob and cancer thing."

"That's because he loves you, Ness," Sienna states.

"Yeah, he does. It took me a long time to realize I felt the same way, but I'm finally there. I am one lucky woman." The girls all give me a girly clap and cheer with excitement.

"Thank fuck because having you two at war sucked," Isla moans. Poor thing, she was caught in the middle of everything. Isla was in charge of keeping the two of us apart during that bad time.

"Yeah, sorry about that," I say sheepishly. She waves me off as if it's water under the bridge.

"So, when are you two going to get married?" Charlotte asks, and I choke on my champagne.

"Um..." Fuck, we haven't really discussed it, so I just shrug my shoulders.

"Please, you two will be married by the end of the year, that boy is so desperate to lock you down," Sienna adds.

"I think you will be pregnant again before Christian and I walk down that aisle." I wiggle my eyebrows at her.

"Oh, fuck off. Evan is hounding me for more babies. I'm like, no way, our life has just started to slowly settle down. Ryder's crawling, and that creates so many hazards, throw in another baby and fuck me dead," she groans, and we all laugh because she's so going to be knocked up by the end of the year. There's no way in hell Evan will let her get her way. He wants babies and lots of them.

"And what about you and Blake?" Sienna asks her sister-in-law.

"Being on tour with them sucks," Charlotte groans. "We're both so busy. He's got shit going on in his home life, and we are both young. I don't want to lock myself down yet."

"Sowing your wild oats, are you?" I ask.

"Yeah, something like that. We're friends, and that's kind of how I want to keep it. My career comes first." And she has been doing so well. Her photos are amazing, especially her touring ones have been selling out.

"And what about you and Finn?" I ask Isla. She just shakes her head.

"Nothing's going on there. In fact, my crush is one hundred percent done and dusted." We all laugh because we know it isn't.

"What happened to Wes?" I ask. He owns The California Bros. Brewery in Venice Beach, and he's good friends with the Dirty Texas boys. She's had a couple of dates on and off that I know of.

"We're just friends, he's a nice guy, but you know..." She twists her glass in her hand.

"He's just not Finn," I add.

"I hate it, I hate that he has this hold over me, and I can't get over him. Why the hell can't I get over a man who isn't interested in me." Isla's eyes fill with tears.

"Hey, hey, don't cry over him," Stacey says, sitting beside Isla on the couch.

"He's a guy, and guys suck. They are so blind when it comes to a good woman."

Isla nods. "Is that what you think of my brother?"

Sienna and I still, what the hell is going on between Stacey and Oscar?

"Your brother's cute, but you know..." Stacey sighs.

"Back this train up, you and Oscar?" Sienna asks the question I've been thinking.

"I didn't tell you because it was nothing. Oscar and I hooked up at your wedding." Holy shit, that was nearly a year ago, that dirty little bitch holding back with that information.

"So, it was like a one-time thing?" I ask because I want the details.

"No, I've done it a couple of times since being back in LA but nothing serious. Sorry, Issy, close your ears," she warns Isla, who just rolls her eyes. She's used to her brother's antics. "Your brother is kind of kinky. We have an understanding."

"So, you're saying you're kinky as well?" I question Stacey. She gives us a cheeky smile.

"Maybe."

"Come on, don't leave us hanging," Sienna pushes.

"There's nothing to tell. Just that I like to... you know... experiment with things, and I'm okay if that's with a guy or a girl." The room goes quiet.

"You like girls?" Charlotte asks quietly. Stacey shifts a little in her seat, looking a bit uncomfortable about her admission.

"Yes." She looks around the room. "I'm not looking to date a woman, I'm heterosexual in that aspect, but sexually, I like to play with both. Is that going to make things awkward?"

"Hell, no, babe." Sienna gets up, sitting beside her, placing her hand over hers. "We still love you. We don't care who you're sleeping with as long as you're happy. And who hasn't kissed a girl and liked it?" Sienna giggles quoting Katy Perry.

"Thanks, guys." Stacey laughs.

"Girls, forget about rock stars, we're in Vegas. I'm sure three sexy single ladies can find some hot men or two or three to play with." I raise my champagne glass to them.

"Yes, give those boys a taste of their own treatment," Sienna adds.

"Take it from us, one thing those rock stars hate in the world is sharing their women." I chuckle.

CHRISTIAN

"Fuck, what are you doing here?"

"This is my club," Nate states as we head toward the entry. I've been to many of his clubs worldwide. I've even been to his Las Vegas club, but this one I have never seen before. "It opens next month. Thought I'd let my best customers check it out first." He smiles at us. What the hell has Derrick planned?

Giving us a change of clothes at the club, we're all dressed and refreshed as we follow Nate down a long, dark hallway where he escorts us toward a room with a stage and a couple of stripper poles. Oh shit, no, no, no. I quickly try and search for my phone, but I've left it with my dirty clothes. Shit!

"Derrick, this better not be strippers?" He looks at me and smiles.

"Dude, we're in Vegas, and it's your birthday. Of course, you're getting strippers." He smiles at me.

"No, I don't want to be here, I won't do that to Ness," I tell him, his face softens.

"Dammit, I just lost a twenty-dollar bet. Ness told me you wouldn't be into this, but I thought no way in hell. I honestly thought you would be up for strippers just like the old days." The spotlights on the stage turn on, and out walks Vanessa with two strippers, each carrying a chair. They place them back to front in the middle of the stage.

"Axel, Christian, your ladies are waiting," Vanessa calls to us. To say I'm confused is an understatement, but I blindly follow my brother up the stairs and take my seat. "It's okay, you can enjoy it. Just no touching," Vanessa whispers into my ear. I turn around, and she saunters off the stage and back behind a curtain.

The music starts, and the two blondes start dancing around us. The lights dim a little, and more ladies come out from behind the curtain to entertain the guys sitting in the audience. The blonde is rubbing her hands all over me, her ass is wiggling on my crotch and nothing, my dick can't even manage a half chub.

"You doin' all right there, bro?" Axel turns to ask me.

"It's not really doing anything for me, honestly." I smile at the gyrating woman. She's beautiful, but my dick just doesn't care.

"Get up and find your woman then, and leave this one for me. It's my birthday, after all." I look up at the blonde, then out into the audience where my friends are having a good time, except Evan, who's standing off to the side on the phone.

"I'm sorry, darlin', I need to find my woman." She stops what she's doing and gives me a wide smile.

"Took you long enough, sugar, go find her," she purrs, handing me a swipe key with a red sash attached to it. Pushing off the chair, I quickly run behind the black curtain and am met with an endless number of black doors. What the fuck? How the hell do I know which one she's in? I start opening the doors, hoping she is in one of the first ones because my cock has been resuscitated with anticipation. I've opened six doors now and nothing. I continue on to a couple more until the green light flashes, and the door opens. Yes!

Opening the door into the darkness, I call out, "Ness," my ears picking up high heels in the distance.

"Take a seat, Christian," Vanessa commands from somewhere in the room. I can't make out where her voice is coming from. There's a sliver of light streaming underneath the door, and I stumble toward the chair in the middle of the room. My hands feel the soft leather of the chair, and I sink into it. Vanessa's heels click-clack along the cement floor. I'm blinded for a moment as she flicks the lights on. A red glow fills the room, then the music begins to play through the stereo system.

Vanessa's dressed in the sexiest black, silk dressing gown, my eyes trail down to the lace detail on the edges. I notice the sheer black stockings she has on underneath with black stilettos. Her caramel hair is pulled up into a messy ponytail, and her lips are painted scarlet red. My dick throbs, thinking of how that lipstick would look coating my shaft. Her curvaceous hips sway to the music's beat, hypnotizing me as she glides across the floor in front of me. Manicured hands playing seductively with the gown's tie, teasing me, I get a tiny glimpse of black lace underneath her gown. She does a turn for me, her fingers touching my shoulders as she sings along to the song about not keeping her hands to herself, and I'm quite happy to have them on me.

"Get your cock out," Vanessa purrs into my ear. I quickly start to undo the buttons on my jeans, and my hand pulls out my hardening cock from my underwear. I feel the cool breeze of the air conditioning against my heated skin. There's a drop of pre-cum glistening on the tip, and I use my thumb to wet my cockhead. Vanessa turns away from me, my eyes focusing on her hips like a pendulum back and forth they go, my hand on my dick keeps in time with her. Then the gown is gone and slowly flutters to the floor. My heart stops, I'm dead.

"Fucking hell!" I groan as I see what she's wearing underneath the dressing gown, some sort of lace bondage-style lingerie with a garter belt attached to her stockings. She gives me a flirty smile and a shimmy, then slinks back toward me. My hand starts its assault up and down my aching length, watching as she prowls toward me. Dragging her fingers over my shoulders, humming away to the music, she kicks out my legs so she can stand in between them. "You look so fucking unbelievable," I breathe out.

"It's all for you," she whispers, moving closer to me now, her breasts dangling deliciously in my face. "Now remember, no touching the dancers." She giggles, turns around, and wiggles her ass in my face. I bite it. "Ouch." She jumps away from me.

"You said no touching." I give her puppy-dog eyes.

"No biting, either... until later," she tells me as she raises her eyebrow at me. My cock twitches a little more. Poor guy, he really wants to get in on the action. I give him a short choke to satisfy him until the main event.

Moving to the music's beat, I watch as Vanessa's hands move over her body, sliding down her arms over her soft skin, up her chest, and over her breasts. She walks closer toward me, her fingers playing aimlessly with her body as she does some salsa hip movements, her hands rubbing over the swell of her ass. Like a snake charmer, she's mesmerizing me with her hips.

I'm so focused on her hips that I haven't noticed her slip off her bra until it lands in my lap. My head whips up, and there they are, her gorgeous tits, the same tits she tries to hide from me every time we make love because she's worried about the scars, and she's worried about their firmness and lack of sensitivity. But all I see is a survivor, a damn sexy survivor. She drops her tight little ass over my dick, swaying it from side to side, the lace of her underwear touching me, it feels so good. My hands automatically come out and hold her hips still as she hovers over me, rubbing herself on me.

"I said no touching," she clucks with her tongue, moving away from me, just enough that she's out of arms' reach. Turning around, she dances for me. I huff out a frustrated breath, and she sways again in front of me. I watch as her fingers slowly sink beneath the lace, then her panties start rolling down her legs. Giving herself a shimmy, she throws them at me.

I look to the heavens. Thank you, Lord, for this beautiful creature. I have no idea what I have done to deserve her but thank you. I look at her as she moves toward me again with a wicked smile on her face. Her eyes drop to my lap, where my dick is currently pointing sky-high. She licks her scarlet lips, then drops to her knees in front of me.

"Fuck, Ness, I want to see those red lips wrapped around my cock," I hiss as she moves closer to my lap.

"Of course." She smiles, her warm fingers wrapping around me. Fuck, it's incredible. My dick is excited that he's finally getting some action. I watch as her red lips close over the aching head of my cock, red lips wrapped around my length. Yes, yes, yes, this is what I've dreamed about.

She starts sucking, and my brain loses all rational thought, my eyes stay fixated on my cock going in and out of her mouth. My hand wraps around her ponytail, and I give it a hard tug, pulling her perfect mouth off of my cock. My cock bobs around, trying to search for her mouth that was rudely taken from him.

"I need you to fuck me, Ness. You have me wound up so fucking tight with this little seduction, I need to release the pressure building up. Please, baby, help me come." I plead with her, never have I ever wanted a woman as much as I want Vanessa. She nods, and I let go of her ponytail.

Vanessa stands up slowly, lifts one leg over my thigh, her sexy garter, stockings, and heels are still in place. She then places her other leg over my other thigh. She's hovering over me, right above my cock, her hands hold onto my shoulders for balance, and my hands have her hips. I move one of my hands down between us, rubbing my twitching cock through her wet folds. Vanessa mews as I rub back and forth across her clit, back and forth through her slickness until we're both panting for more.

In one swift move, she sinks down on me. We both freeze, enjoying the fullness of our coupling. Vanessa starts moving slowly up and down, getting into a rhythm. She's bouncing on my dick enthusiastically, her tits bounce in my face, over and over again, my thumb finds her clit, and I press on it as she rides me.

"I'm coming," Vanessa screams, and I can feel her tight, little cunt clamping down on my cock, and with white-hot sparks, I come not far after her. She's still bouncing on me like I'm her personal pogo stick until we both come back down to earth.

"Happy birthday, Christian," she says, kissing my lips.

"Fucking happy birthday to me!" I grin.

39

VANESSA

I need to pee. I stretch out in the world's comfiest bed and stumble out of Christian's tight grip and make my way to the bathroom to relieve myself. I look like a red, hot mess staring at myself in the bathroom mirror while washing my hands. Last night turned crazy. The night is a blur. Nate let us all enjoy the pleasures The Paradise Club had to offer.

Christian and I tried some light bondage, which was fun. We skipped the voyeur room as we weren't in the mood to watch our friends fuck. Nate organized some beautiful ladies to play with the single guys there, and from what I saw, they were having a good time, especially those Sons of Brooklyn boys who joined us a little later on. Kinky little fuckers.

Washing my face, trying to feel a little more human than a zombie, something catches my eye in the fluorescent light. What the fuck? I stare down at the massive diamond on my finger. My heart starts to beat faster, my empty stomach sinks. What the hell? I have a bad feeling about this that we might have done something stupid. We were all pretty wasted.

I hear one of our mobile phones go off. I ignore it. It's not important. What's important is this damn rock on my finger.

Now that I have noticed it, it feels heavy on my hand. I quickly run back into the bedroom and check Christian's hands. FUCK! His hand is sporting a titanium silver band.

No, no, no, please don't tell me, Christian and I became a Vegas statistic and got married. I think I'm having a heart attack, my heart is beating furiously through my chest. I'm surprised the next room can't hear it. Christian's phone rings again, and I notice **MOM** across the screen.

"Chris, Chris." I shake him trying to wake him up. "Your mom's calling." He ignores me and rolls over, grumbling about it being fucking early, and it's his birthday, and he can sleep if he wants too. "Wake the hell up, birthday boy," I scream at him. He startles awake and sits up quickly, his brown hair a messy bird's nest, his square jaw peppered with stubble. He rubs his eyes and focuses on me.

"Darlin', what the fuck?" He squints, trying to look at me.

"Did we get married last night?" My voice sounds a little hysterical. Christian bursts out laughing as if I have gone mad. I shove the massive diamond ring in his face, and that makes him stop laughing.

"Shit!" Then he notices his wedding band. "Fuck, Ness, we got married last night."

"No, shit, like how the fuck did this happen?" I question him as if he's the gatekeeper of all things matrimony and wasn't as plastered as I was last night.

"Fuck, this wasn't how I envisioned our wedding." He rakes his fingers through his hair, his whiskey-colored eyes looking at me with a hint of sadness.

"Huh, what are you talking about our wedding?" I question him.

"Ness." He tuts at me. "You and I both know we were always going to get married, but you deserved the wedding of your dreams, not some Vegas ceremony," he coos, taking my hands in his. "I want to give you the world." He smiles now, looking down at our hands, the ones currently joined with two symbols of a lifetime commitment. "At least in our drunken state, I got you a nice ring. Do you like it?" He sounds concerned.

My ring is the least of our concerns. I look down and really take it in, turning it around in the light. Fuck, it's so pretty, and the diamond band beside it fits so well. It would've been the ring I picked out if money was no object and if I didn't care what others thought of the ostentatiousness of such a huge diamond.

"Of course, I do, look at it, it's beautiful, but I can't keep it." Christian's face falls.

"And why not?" His tone sounds hurt.

"Because I don't remember any of it happening." That's the truth. I never thought I was a traditional person until now. I'm sitting here with the love of my life, who I can't remember marrying. "It doesn't feel real or right."

"But the thought of being married to me isn't the reason, is it?" Christian asks with such vulnerability that it hurts my soul. I grab his face and kiss him passionately.

"It would be an honor to be your wife, one day." Christian suddenly jumps up out of bed. He's dressed in only a pair of black boxer briefs as he gets down on one knee.

"I have loved you from the moment you fell into my arms all those years ago. You bewitched me. It may have taken us a long time to get our shit sorted and finally be together, and I know what it's like not to have you in my life. I know what it's like to fear losing you, and I never want to experience that loss ever again. You make me the happiest man in the world, and I want to grow old with you, Vanessa. I want to have babies with you. I want to spend the rest of my life on an adventure with you because you make my life better. Will you marry me again?" Tears are running down my face, and I don't even hesitate.

"Yes, yes, of course, I'll marry you." I jump into his arms, kissing the ever-loving shit out of him. "Maybe that should've been, yes, I want to stay married to you, seeing as we might already be married."

We both burst out laughing at the craziness of what we have done, but it doesn't matter because I love this man so fucking much. Christian's phone rings, and it's his mom again. "You better get that, it must be important if she's calling." I snuggle into his side.

He picks up the phone off the floor. "Hey, Momma." I hear yelling down the phone. Shit, she's pissed. "Mom, I'm sorry you had to find out via *TMZ*, but honestly, Ness and I don't remember getting married."

This makes me sit up, shit, how the fuck does *TMZ* know about this before we fucking do, the people who supposedly got married. I listen to Christian try to placate his mom on the phone. I look down at my own and see a million missed calls, messages, and emails. Oh shit! All of a sudden, the knocking starts at the hotel door.

"Open the fuck up," Axel screams. I jump up out of bed and quickly rush to the door. I see a fuming Axel standing in front of me and a bemused Evan, Sienna, and Derrick.

"Is Christian decent?" Axel seethes.

"He's on the phone with your mom," I tell him. Axel pushes past me and heads toward the room where his brother is located, trying to calm down his mother.

"I might just check on Axe." Evan slinks past me, following the furious steps of Axel.

"You dirty bitch, sneaking off and getting married, not inviting us. You've broken my heart," Derrick mocks.

"Well, if it makes you feel better, I don't remember inviting myself, either." I try to laugh, but it sort of comes out on a hiccupped cry.

"Hey, hey, hey." Sienna wraps her arms around my sagging shoulders. "It's going to be okay. You're not the first couple to get married in Vegas, and I'm sure you won't be the last, either." She tries to soothe me while rubbing my back, but the tears fall freely now.

"I have totally fucked up, this is going to be a PR nightmare for the band and label."

"Are you fucking serious?" Sienna starts to get into me, but then we hear shouting from behind us. Across the room, Axel has Christian by the neck and is screaming in his face. I run toward them. Evan is trying to pull Axel off of Christian.

"How could you fucking do that to Mom?" he screams at Christian. "I had her in tears on the phone this morning? Do you even care that she had to watch you drunkenly get married by some Elvis impersonator on *TMZ*?"

"I know, bro, I know I fucked up, okay!" Christian pushes Axel off him, and I run to his side. It's as much his fault as mine. They should be pissed at me too. Axel's glaring at both us.

"Axel," I call, grabbing his arm. "We're sorry, okay. But honestly, we don't remember last night. Do you know how that feels not to remember your wedding?" His whiskey-colored eyes look down at me, the tension subsides a little.

"What the fuck were you two thinking?" Christian tries to interject, but I shush him.

"Honestly, I don't know, Axe, but I can tell you this. Your brother proposed to me this morning, properly." The room falls silent, and Axel's eyes widen. "I said yes because I love him. I love him with all my heart. After everything we have been through over the years, there was never anyone else who could compare to him." Axel's face softens, a smile slowly forming.

"You want to be married to this fool?" I start nodding.

"I can't wait to spend the rest of my life with that man." Those damn tears start running down my cheeks again.

"Fuck, Ness, come 'ere." Axel opens his arms for me. "Welcome to the family." He hugs me tight. I feel another large body wrapping their arms around me, and I smell Christian's musky scent.

"Don't worry, we're going to get married again, and we are going to do it right."

"Oh my God, another fucking wedding," Derrick squeals as he joins the Taylor family hug.

"Derrick, man, you better not get a boner," Axel states.

"You're no fun, Axe," Derrick chuckles. Finally, parting from the man sandwich, Sienna rushes over toward me.

"You're getting married, you're fucking getting married," she screams.

"Wait, does that mean you're going to have kids as well?" Derrick questions me. I nod, giving them a sly grin.

"Oh shit, you two have already started, haven't you?" Sienna guesses correctly. My eyes bug out. How the fuck did she guess that?

"Damn right, we have," Christian announces to the room. I give him a piercing look, but the bastard ignores me. "But we wanted to get married first, you know, to make an honest woman out of her." He jokes, forgetting that Sienna and Evan were not married when they were pregnant with Ryder. "Oh shit, Si, I mean..." His words trail off in awkwardness.

"Please, Evan and I hardly knew each other. You two, on the other hand, it's taken you bloody long enough to get your shit together, we don't have time to wait anymore," she says, smiling.

"I'm sorry we have created a PR nightmare. I promise I'll sort it all out." I remember the million calls on my phone.

"Fuck that shit, it's your wedding day... no, post-wedding day. We need to celebrate. Tonight, you will have the wedding reception you missed out on. I'm sure Derrick can whip up a wedding in a couple of hours," Axel muses.

"We need to get you a dress to wear tonight, your hair done, and we need new clothes. There's so much we need to do." Derrick's tone sounds panicked.

"If you don't mind, D, I'd like to have some alone time with my wife before you whisk her away." Christian wiggles his eyebrows at Derrick.

"Oh, for fuck's sake, fine, go fuck your bride. We'll be meeting downstairs in three hours, okay?" Derrick points his finger at me. I nod because Derrick looks serious. Our friends finally shuffle out of our room, and Christian and I both fall into bed together.

"Let's check out our wedding video, see if we can remember any of it." We settle in on the bed and play around with the TV until we find *TMZ*. And there it is in all its glory, our wedding video, and what the fuck? It already has two million views.

Christian presses play, and the grainey footage starts. There's Christian and I dressed in our clothes from last night. We look like we stumble a little and giggle as we walk down the aisle toward Elvis. The sound is low, someone has filmed us from behind a curtain. No one looks aware of what's going on—what a low-life scumbag. Elvis pronounces us husband and wife, and then we kiss. Wow, that kiss was kind of borderline porno, groping hands and stuff. We sign some papers and skip out of the chapel happily.

"What a beautiful wedding," Christian fake cries. I punch him in the arm.

Christian and bride shop for rings.

That's the name of the next video. We both look at each other confused. Again, there's someone secretly filming us as we waltz into a twenty-four-hour jewelry store. We're all over each other. You can see me visually trying on rings. Looking down at my ring, shit, I picked well even completely plastered. Then the video cuts out. "Oh, the memories." Christian laughs.

"I can't believe we did that and don't remember."

"At least we looked happy, though. In our drunken subconscious state, we thought it was a good idea." Christian smiles. This was very true.

"Now, wife," Christian growls in my ear. Hearing him call me his wife sounds kind of hot. "Come service your husband."

Continue on for a bonus novella.

40

CHRISTIAN

"Jump on, angel," I say, holding my arms out for Vanessa.

"What? No," she says, giving me a look.

"I want to carry my new wife over the threshold."

"Chris." Vanessa rolls her eyes at me. "I've been here before." She gestures to my home. I know she has lived here with me for years, but this time it's different. This time she's walking into my home as my wife. Well, maybe that should be 'our' home now, seeing as everything I have is now hers.

"Please, babe, I just want to carry my wife over the threshold."

Vanessa steps into me, wrapping her arms around my neck and gives me a slow, sensual kiss.

"Who knew Christian Taylor is a traditionalist? I hope you aren't expecting me to be a traditional wife." She raises an eyebrow at me.

"Babe, I know your limitations." She slaps the back of my head. Ouch.

"I'm joking. I'm joking. I only married you for your cock-sucking skills."

Vanessa lets out a gasp, then bursts out laughing.

"And I only married you for your big dick. So, I guess we're a match made in heaven."

"Damn right, we are," I growl. I have been waiting years for this moment, the moment she's truly mine, and I want to savor it. I press my hips against hers, showing her how excited I am that she's my wife. "We need to get inside so we can consummate the marriage."

"Haven't we already done that?"

"Yes, but I think we need to do it again, just in case. I want to make sure everything is good and legal."

She giggles, then jumps into my arms, wrapping her legs around my waist. "Take me to bed... husband."

Shit, I love hearing her call me her husband, it gets me so fucking hard.

"I want you to make sure the neighbors know exactly who the hell I am. I want them to hear that you're mine, and I'm yours."

"I'll make sure they do." She captures my lips with her own. I don't move for a moment as our insatiable hunger takes over. Finally, my shaky legs move, and I punch in the door code, missing a couple of times due to my wife nibbling my ear. The front door swings open for me, and I take the next few steps over the threshold. Knowing that she is my wife makes me harder and makes me realize this is it, Vanessa and I are about to start a life together, forever. I kick the door shut, and it echoes through the quiet house. Vanessa hasn't let go of my lips as she grinds herself against me.

"Welcome home, wife." I turn and push her up against the cold, hard wall beside the door. "You're stuck with me now, babe. We've crossed the threshold, you can't get rid of me now." My voice is low, making sure she understands me.

"I have no plans of getting rid of you," she whispers into my ear, sending shivers over my body. "But maybe your shirt..." Her hands start to push my T-shirt up and over my head, her lips moving over my skin as I dry hump her in the middle of the foyer. "You're stuck with me, Christian."

"I want these tits stuck against me."

Vanessa's eyes darken with lust. Her hands fall from my bare chest, and she slowly unbuttons her white shirt, each button exposing her brand-new tits, the ones that I love because they saved her fucking life, and I get to have my forever with her. The shirt falls open, exposing her white lace bra. I love her tits. Leaning forward, I lick a path along the edges of the bra. I don't concentrate too much on them anymore as she has no real sensation after the surgery. She's still getting used to that.

"We need to continue this in our bed. I want to fucking christen it." Pushing myself harder into her, she wraps her legs tighter around me.

"Yes." She sounds breathless with need. Placing my hands on her tight ass, I awkwardly maneuver her around the furniture, which is hard when your cock is tented in your jeans. Moving through the foyer, past the living area, we head toward the bedroom when we hear a female voice piercing the quiet.

"What the hell were you thinking?"

Vanessa screams, sending me deaf in one ear. My eyes look over the top of Vanessa's head, and there's my mom, tapping her foot, not looking happy at all.

"Please tell me your mum isn't standing in our living room," Vanessa whispers into my ear.

"Mom is standing in our living room… and she looks pissed," I whisper back. Vanessa tightens her arms around me.

"Do you have any idea how upset your mother is finding out her son got married via *TMZ*?" Dad adds. My eyes shift to where my father is walking out of the kitchen with a beer in his hand, making himself at home.

"Um… what the fuck y'all doing here?"

"Excuse your language, son," Dad scolds me. I grimace.

"Chris, we need to get dressed," Vanessa whispers into my ear.

"Excuse us." I make a hasty escape back to the foyer where my shirt is lying on the floor. Vanessa clings to me like a damn baby koala, her nails digging into my back.

"Fuck, Chris," Ness whisper yells at me as she buttons up her shirt.

"How the hell was I supposed to know they would be here?" I shove my T-shirt over my head.

"We were two seconds away from screwing in front of your parents. I'm mortified. How the hell am I ever going to look them in the face again?" Vanessa looks like she's about to throw up.

"Babe, it's going to be okay, I promise they didn't see a thing. You still had your shirt on." Vanessa looks up at me and gives me a tight smile. "We're going to walk in there and pretend like nothing happened."

Ness nods at me and takes my hand—united we stand. "We're in this together." She smiles at me as we head back to the living room.

"Mom, Dad, this is a surprise."

Mom still doesn't look happy. Dad has settled in on the sofa with his beer. I can see a glimmer of a smirk crossing his face.

"Viv, Frank," Vanessa addresses my parents. "We're so sorry that you had to find out about us getting married like you did." Mom turns her attention to Vanessa, her features softening. "My parents are just as upset."

Mom huffs in response, but Vanessa keeps talking. "I don't regret marrying Christian, I don't even regret marrying him in Vegas." This surprises both Mom and me. "But what I do regret is that you and Frank weren't there..." This gets my mom's attention. "And that my dad missed out on walking me down the aisle..." Mom nods her head in agreement.

"That our friends didn't get to witness Christian and I declaring ourselves to each other." Dammit, she's making me feel like shit. "But I love Christian…" She turns to me and squeezes my hand. "I love him, and I'm so honored to be his wife." I swear I fall in love with my wife all over again.

"Oh, damn," Mom cries as she launches herself at us both, wrapping her little arms as far as she can around us. "Welcome to the family, Ness." Mom starts bawling. "I'm so happy," she sniffles as she holds us both tight. "I just wanted to experience it with you both… after everything you have been through. I just…" Looking at my mom's red-rimmed eyes, my heart hurts.

"Don't worry, Mom, we'll have another wedding."

Vanessa stills, her jade eyes finding mine, looking shocked at my confession. "I want all our family and friends there."

"Really?" Mom looks at us both hopefully.

"Yes, of course," Vanessa adds.

"Good, at least this time, you'll remember it." She's right, I kind of want a do-over. This time, I want to marry Ness right. I want to show the world how much I love this woman and showing that via a drunk Vegas wedding isn't how I saw Ness and I starting our lives together.

41

VANESSA

"I guess congratulations are in order," Lucas Edwards greets us with a frown and a hard handshake. He's Dirty Texas Records' lawyer, but with his blond hair and gray eyes that pierce you with their intensity, most days, you could easily mistake him as a male model who looks like he has stepped straight off the pages of a *GQ* spread on hot lawyers. He's always dressed in some kind of designer suit, a hair never out of place. He seems very standoffish, but he's good at his job, and I guess that's all that matters.

We both take a seat in one of the brown wingback chairs as Lucas sits back down behind his wooden desk, which is perfectly neat, not an item out of place. I think he has OCD. I have a sudden urge to mess up the neatly-stacked papers on his desk.

"So, what the hell were you two thinking?" His words shock us. We sit there in silence, staring at him, not quite believing his tone. He's worked with us for a year. The boys poached him from Montgomery Records when they branched out. Monty wasn't happy at all, but Lucas had wanted to go out on his own for a while. He couldn't progress any further in the legal department at Montgomery Records as his bosses there were not leaving anytime soon. Monty made their jobs worth it to stay.

"Really? Nothing. You have no answer for this?" He looks between the two of us, his steely gray eyes molten with anger, maybe even disappointment.

"We kind of weren't thinking at the time," Christian says, anger lacing his words.

"Christian, do you have any idea how fucked you are?" Lucas' hand slaps the hard surface of his desk, the sound echoing across the quiet room. "You didn't sign a prenuptial agreement. This night of not thinking could end up costing you everything you have worked for."

Christian stiffens beside me. "Excuse me… are you insinuating that Ness is going to take my money?" Christian stands up, his fists balled tight together, looming over the irritated lawyer. Lucas sits back in his chair as if an angry rock star staring him down was an everyday occurrence—maybe it is with his attitude. "Vanessa isn't a gold digger," Christian growls.

"No, shit, Chris." Lucas sits up straight in his chair, his eyes flicking to me, then back to Christian. "I know Vanessa isn't one now, but what happens ten years down the road when you aren't so loved-up, or you cheat?"

My body stiffens at his words, no fucking way. Christian would never cheat on me, and if he did, he knows I'd chop his fucking balls off.

"I love her. How fucking dare you say that," Christian spits at Lucas as he still looms over him.

"Babe, sit down." Grabbing his forearm, I pull him back toward me. He looks like he's seconds away from flattening Lucas.

"I have seen so many loved-up couples walk through my doors that have ended up in divorce court… years, even decades later. Do not think that people don't play games when they are hurt. Don't think the person you married will remain the same." He looks at both of us.

"I'll sign whatever you want me to sign," I tell Lucas. Christian looks at me, shocked.

"No, Ness, you won't," he argues back.

"Chris, this is stupid. You have worked so hard for your money. You need to protect it. I love you, I'm not after your money, and I truly believe it's for the best, for you and the band." This is his life's work, and having a prenup, or is it a postnup now after the fact, doesn't make it any less romantic.

"No, I trust you. I love you. You're the one who helped build us up to where we are. You organized our band's promotion, got us the gigs, the airtime, the magazine shoots. You did all of that. If we had any other PR manager, I don't think we'd have been as big as we are." Looking into Christian's whiskey-colored eyes, I can tell he means it.

"Thank you," I reply as I put my hand on his arm. "But please, for me. Let's just sign a prenup and hope that we never have to use it."

Christian frowns at me. I can tell he doesn't like this idea.

"Lucas, put together the paperwork, and I'll sign it."

I ARRIVE HOME from a busy day at Dirty Texas Records absolutely exhausted. Finalizing the first-anniversary party of Dirty Texas Records and Wyld Jones boutique has me working longer hours than usual. We decided to do something completely different and have two parties together. It's a great PR move on both parts, merging fashion, celebrities, and music together. It's the perfect fit.

I'm so lucky one of my closest friends is an event organizer.

Camryn's here from New York helping me. We want to create something exciting like Victoria's Secret fashion show, where we mix live acts with fashion.

"Christian," I call out into the dark, empty home. I wonder where he is? Kicking off my shoes in the foyer, I drop my bag beside it and head toward the kitchen to see what I can find for dinner. Flickering light catches my attention as I pass the living room. The pool area is all lit up by hundreds of tea lights.

"Christian," I call out again into the quiet house, my feet propelling me toward the light. I open the sliding glass doors and notice the cabana has twinkling fairy lights wrapped around it, and it's been set up for a candlelight dinner. Looking around, I try to work out where Christian is.

"Christian," I call out again. I hear movement behind me, and there he is, dressed in a pair of ripped jeans, a classic white tee, and his shoulder-length hair all wet, smelling of fresh soap.

"Evening, sweetheart." He smiles, giving me a chaste kiss.

"What's going on?" I gesture to the table. He smirks at me.

"What, can't a husband treat his wife to dinner?" Wrapping his arms around my waist, he pulls me against his hard chest, my hands resting on his tight, muscular shoulders.

"I'm not complaining, believe me, after the day I've had, this is exactly what I need." I snuggle into his warm chest.

"I know, angel." Running his large palms over my body, he continues, "I thought you needed some pampering."

My heart flutters. Seriously, is this man really mine? "Yeah, and what kind of pampering do you have in mind?"

"V," Christian growls at me, my hands moving over his tense shoulders, down his muscular back, the thin T-shirt doing nothing to hide his firm muscles. My hands grab a big, meaty chunk of his ass, giving it a hard squeeze.

"I'm so tense, babe, I need you to relax me," I purr into his ear. His large palms sink into the fleshy globes of my ass as he picks me up, forcing me to wrap my legs around his waist.

"That's my job to look after my wife." He smiles at me as he walks back through the house toward the bedroom. He enters our bedroom and passes the king-size bed, still rumpled from our morning lovemaking. He strides past it and into the steaming ensuite. The oversized marble bathtub is filled to the brim with bubbles and rose petals while candles flicker in the room in the corner.

"Christian." My feet hit the ground as I slide down his hard body. "You did this for me?"

"I know you've had a hard day, I just wanted to make it better for you." My husband is looking a little shy by his generous gesture.

"Thank you." I kiss him on the cheek.

"It's my job to look after you, Ness." Christian grabs my face in his calloused palms. "One that I was born to do." He gives me a slow, sensual kiss. A smile laces my face as I look into those whiskey-colored eyes, which I love so much.

"It's also my job to undress my beautiful wife." His hands move down my body, tracing my curves. Fingers unzip the back of my skirt, the material pooling by my feet. Those hard hands caress my exposed ass cheeks, my tiny G-string not covering very much. Christian's hands move to my front to start unbuttoning my blouse. One by one, he pops the small buttons as he concentrates hard on his task. I notice his teeth sinking into his plump bottom lip. It's hot. My blouse joins my skirt on the bathroom floor. I am left in my nude-colored underwear, and goosebumps prickle my skin in anticipation. "Fuck, I'm a lucky man." Christian looks over my nearly naked body with such divinity that I feel unworthy of it.

I take a step closer to him, bringing my body against his. "I'm just as lucky." My hands land on his chest, and my fingers move the material of his T-shirt. Realizing what I'm asking, he pulls it up over his head, the way men do, which is utterly hot, his muscles rippling with each movement. My hands go to the buttons on his jeans and start making quick work of them, his hardening length pressing against his boxer briefs' thin material. I push the offending material down his thick thighs, and he steps out of them. I drop to my knees.

"Ness," Christian hisses as his cock springs free of its restraints.

Of course, he deserves a thank you for this. I take the thick head of his cock into my mouth, savoring his saltiness. Christian's fingers trail through my hair. The harder I suck, the harder he grips my hair. "Ness." He lets out a strangled moan as my hands work up his length. I gently hum against his velvety skin. "Ness," he calls out my name again, making me smile.

The fact that I can make this man come undone excites me. Before I can finish him off, he's pulling me up by the arms. "I need you, Ness. I need to be inside of you." His words sound desperate. Spinning me around, I brace my hands on the side of the marble tub. Christian makes quick work of my bra and shreds my G-string, and before I know it, he's thrusting inside of me.

"I'm so fucking lucky," Christian groans as he continues a punishing cadence into me. I arch my back to take him deeper. "Fuck, my wife's pussy is so fucking tight." I swear he thickens even further inside of me as he tells me all the dirty things he loves about me, his wife. He wants to do everything to his wife, especially how he can't wait to knock me up. That's it. I combust into a loud screaming orgasm, and Christian comes not far after me. His heavy weight resting against my back.

"I'm feeling really relaxed now." I giggle as his dick twitches in me. He slowly pulls out, picks me up, and places me in the hot bath, settling behind me. "Christian," I squeal as I watch a tsunami of water rush over the tub's edge.

"It's all good, babe. Now just lay back and relax." He pulls me back against him as the warm water washes over us. Christian's fingers find the tense muscles in my shoulders, the warm water loosening them as he slowly works on relaxing me. We lay there in silence as I feel the tension slowly leaving my body.

"Ness, can I ask you something?" He sounds a little hesitant. I turn around and look at him.

"Of course, you can." He looks serious for a moment, my stomach sinks.

"Hey, it's not bad." His thumb flattens my frown as he gives me a cheeky smile. "It's good, actually, but..." The frown comes back. "I just don't know how you feel about it. We haven't spoken about it since Mom left." I have a feeling I know what he's talking about. I maneuver myself so that I'm straddling his thighs, my hands running over his warm, wet skin, urging him to continue what he was about to ask. "I love our Vegas wedding, but—"

"But no one was there," I finish his sentence.

"Yeah." His hand brushes against my face. "And you deserve a proper wedding."

"You know I'm not one of those girls, babe. I never dreamed of a big wedding day."

Christian smiles at me. "I know, that's why I love you. You're low maintenance." This makes me laugh. "But I kind of want the day."

"Has Christian Taylor, womanizing bad-boy rock star, always dreamed of a white wedding?" I tease.

"Yeah, he has, the moment he laid eyes on you." My breath hitches at his confession. Goddamn him. Leaning forward, I give him a loving kiss.

"You're such a romantic," I say as our foreheads press together.

"Yeah, I guess I am. Evan and Sienna's wedding was kind of awesome, and I want that. I want all our friends and families to be witnesses to us declaring our love for each other. I know we don't need it, but I want it, Ness. I want to show the world how much I love you." Wow, how can a woman say no to that kind of declaration?

"Yes."

Christian is silent for a moment, trying to work out why I'm saying yes.

"Yes, I want to marry you again," I tell him as I smile at him.

"Seriously?" Christian questions, looking a little vulnerable.

"Of course. Why wouldn't I want to marry you again? I already did it in Vegas."

"I worry that you regret that night," he whispers, his hands nervously playing in the water around me. My heart aches at his vulnerability.

"What? You seriously think that I regret marrying you?" I ask, a little shocked at his confession.

"We were drunk…"

"So what! That doesn't change the fact that I love the fuck out of you." Grabbing his face and making sure he sees the way I feel, I ask, "Have you really been worried about this?"

He nods.

"Christian," I gasp, my heart hurting that he has been worried about Vegas. "I love you so much. You're my person, and you have been my person for years. I was just so goddamn scared to take a chance. But when I finally got over myself and let myself love you, that was it. I was all in, no matter what. Vegas was perfectly crazy, and that's us. I'm kind of glad that you and I had that wedding, just the two of us. Now I want to share that with everyone else."

Christian's face breaks out into a big grin. "Yeah?"

I nod my head. "Yeah, I do. I want all those women out there to know that you're mine, and I don't share." I move my hips against him, getting him into the right position so that I can sink down on him. "You're mine, all mine." This makes him chuckle as he pushes up into me.

"Mine," he growls as we rock against each other.

"Forever," I remind him.

"Forever," he agrees as we make love in the rose petal bath, not caring about the mess we're making as the waves of water crash around us.

42

CHRISTIAN

"Why am I blindfolded?"

I have whisked Vanessa away from work for the next couple of days before things get any crazier than they already are. I know it's not the best time for her to go away as she's in the middle of planning a huge event, but isn't that what delegation is for? She's got a great PR staff, plus Camryn's team is looking after the event side of things, and Isla will be there manning the fort as if she were Ness.

We haven't had a chance to have a honeymoon yet. This wasn't exactly my first choice of places, because, in all honesty, I want to take her away to a tropical island where we can spend weeks lying naked on the beach together. Unfortunately, my impulsiveness, when getting married in Vegas, means that now isn't the best time to be taking time off, so my dream location will just have to wait. Zander, our tattoo artist at The California Bros. in Venice Beach, told me about the cabin that he has up at Big Bear Lake. Big Bear is kind of the perfect location not far from LA, no paparazzi, secluded, romantic, and Wi-Fi for my wife, but I'm going to make sure that she's naked and too exhausted to even think about work.

"Last time I was blindfolded, I ended the night married to you. I'm already marrying you a second time, not sure if marrying you a third might be pushing it." Vanessa chuckles to herself.

"Babe, patience, just relax, we'll be there shortly." Vanessa huffs at me, but it's not long before she's asleep. Ness has been working so hard, lately, I'm kind of glad we're able to have a break. She needs it. I haven't been to Zander's home before. We usually party at his Venice Beach place. He told me this is his private getaway. Not many people get invited to his sanctuary. So, I'm very grateful he's letting us use it.

A couple of hours later, we're pulling up to Zander's home in Big Bear Lake. Nestled behind a forest of trees stands an imposing log cabin, secluded and beautiful, and right on the edge of a lake.

"Babe." I give Ness a gentle nudge. She grumbles a little before opening her eyes, blinking rapidly as she realizes where she is.

"We're here?" she asks, looking out the window, a small smile graces her lips. "This looks beautiful," she says as she admires the cabin before her.

Taking a step out of the car, there's nothing but silence. All we hear are the squawks of some bird flying by. I grab our bags out of the trunk and move toward the cabin. Punching in the security code that Zander provided, we step inside.

"Wow," Ness gasps. It's pretty impressive. The rooms are large and open, and natural light filters through the cabin from the large triangular windows overlooking the lake and the forest beyond. Zander, in true guy style, has fitted it out in what I'd call rustic, lumberjack style. There are a few deer heads hanging on one wall, tartan lounges with oversized blankets, and an enormous stone fireplace sits in one corner. "This place is amazing," Vanessa croons as she moves further inside.

"Yep, and it's all ours." I wrap my arms around Ness as she has her face plastered against the window.

"Look." She points to some deer that have run in front of the cabin and have stopped to nibble on the fresh grass.

"All I see is my gorgeous wife before me." I nuzzle into her neck.

"Yeah, is that all you see?"

My hands glide down her arms, making her shiver. "Hands on the glass, angel, and spread your legs." She quickly presses her hands against the cool glass. There's no one around, so what I have planned will be okay. My hands find the zipper of her dress, and I slowly pull it down, the metal teeth echoing through the quiet house, nothing but our labored breaths filling the void. I push the fabric over her creamy shoulders, letting it fall to the floor.

I take a step back and admire my wife, dressed in sexy black underwear and heels, spread out before me. I'm one lucky son of a bitch. She turns her head, and I can see a smile across her face, those jade eyes sparkling with desire. I quickly shed my T-shirt, kick off my socks and shoes, and jump out of my jeans. My cock is standing at attention—he knows it's his time to perform. My hand fists him a couple of times, preparing him. Vanessa wiggles her butt in my direction, not so subtly, telling me what she wants.

"You want me, Ness?" My voice is dropping low, my need overtaking my body now. Her eyes meet mine, and they are filled with desire as she gives me a cheeky smile.

"Yes, Christian. I'm waiting for you." I let out a groan as her fingers reach between her legs, her eyes flutter shut as she teases herself. My cock twitches in my grasp as I fist him tighter, watching my wife pleasure herself. I can't take her whimpers any longer. I fall to my knees and spread her legs even wider. She lets out a squeak of surprise as my tongue is there, replacing her fingers. Her sweetness hits my tongue, and my entire body shivers. I could stay here forever, my face between my wife's thighs. Her fingers painfully dig into my scalp as I feast on her.

"Yes," she moans as I tease her bud. My fingers dig into her soft thighs, pushing them wider, allowing me access to heaven between them. Vanessa presses harder against my face, chasing that orgasm that I know is starting to take shape. I feast on my wife like a starving man. Never will I ever get sick of her. I'm happy to stay here forever, and I damn well will because this beautiful creature above me chose me to be her one.

Me! She chose me to be the father of her children. She chose me to be the man to build a family with. She chose me to be the man who she grows old with. She chose me to be her forever.

"Yes, yes, yes," Vanessa screams as her orgasms rises through her, her fingers tightening in my hair, holding me in place as she quakes above me. I never let up savoring her sweetness as she slowly comes back to earth. I jump up from my place between her thighs, my cock standing at attention. He knows it's his time to shine now. My hands run down her back, sending shivers over her body, my fingers grip into her fleshy hips as I position myself at her entrance. She's still breathing heavily from her orgasm. I slowly run the tip of my dick along with her wetness, and a low hum falls from her lips.

"Hang on, baby." I slip in my cock, and we both gasp at our joining. Slowly, I pull myself back out, relishing the easy slide through her wetness and push myself back into her with a grunt.

"Yes," Vanessa hums.

"Keep your hands on the window, Ness." She follows my instructions as I enter her again. Over and over, I tease her with my slow, yet hard strokes.

"Please," she pants, turning her head to the side. I just give her a smile. I can see the begging behind those jade eyes as I push into her hard with each long thrust. I love teasing my wife. I love watching her become so needy that she loses control. I'm slowly getting her there. She's now pushing back against me, her greedy cunt searching for my cock.

"Harder, Chris, harder," she pants. I piston into her faster, my fingers gripping her hips harder, probably bruising her, but I know she won't care. She loves it a little rough sometimes. She clenches down on me, which she knows drives me wild. The first tingles of my orgasm start as she clenches again, and my balls twitch. Yes, I'm chasing that release. Ness turns her head again, giving me a saucy smile as she clenches one more time.

"Fuck," I grunt, losing myself in a mind-exploding orgasm. Vanessa giggles as I collapse against her back in a sweaty, exhausted mess of a man. My legs feel like they are about to give out as aftershocks pulse through my body.

"Now, that's a great way to start our honeymoon." Vanessa smiles at me. I just nod against her back, making her laugh.

"I WANT TO MARRY THIS BATH." Vanessa moans as she sinks into the large Jacuzzi in the master bathroom.

"Please, as if this bath is better than your current husband," I mock as I sink into the heavenly, hot bath as well, letting out an appreciative moan as I do. "Okay, now I get it." I pull Ness against me as we watch the steam float above us. The Jacuzzi is situated in front of a large glass window that overlooks the lake and forest. We take a sip of our red wine as we enjoy the sheer luxury of the awesome bath.

"We need one of these at home."

"I one hundred percent agree. I think we need to renovate as soon as we get home and put this in our bathroom." Resting my head against the edge of the tub, we both sit in silence, taking in the scenery around us.

"We should get married in a place like this," Ness suggests.

When Mom surprised us after Vegas, we told both of our parents that we were going to get married again, properly, and not by an Elvis impersonator. With everything going on in our lives, we haven't really talked about it again.

"Really… you want to get married in the mountains?"

Ness is quiet for a while. "Honestly, I have never thought about my dream wedding. I was never one of those girls. I never wanted to get married." My entire body stills, and she feels it. "Hey," she says quickly, turning around in my arms. "That was before you." She smiles, kissing me.

"And now?" I ask, a touch of my vulnerability showing through.

"And now, I'm looking at this place and am thinking of our dream wedding."

"You've been having lumberjack fantasies again, haven't you?"

Vanessa giggles. "Maybe, hopefully, this weekend, I can watch you chop wood and do some of that manly stuff that I know you can do," she says as she starts rubbing herself over me.

"Me doing manly things gets you going, does it?" She nods.

"So what, me playing guitar and being one of the sexiest rock stars in the world isn't manly enough for you?"

Ness rolls her eyes. "I guess that's manly in its own way."

"What?" I pull her flush against me. "Take that back, I'm a goddamn rock star, it's the manliest thing in the world," I argue as I start to tickle her.

"Stop, stop," she protests as I continue my tickle assault on her.

"Not until you take it back," I demand.

"Fine, fine," she relents, my fingers stop.

"Fine, what?"

"Fine, rock stars are the manliest men in the world, and I

bow down to your manliness." She smirks. "Are you over your mantrum?"

"Yes, but you insulted my manhood. I needed to defend my honor... anyway, about this wedding."

"Yeah, well, I was thinking. I know we were all talking about a white Christmas this year, especially as my parents are coming over."

Vanessa straddles herself onto my lap. She takes a couple of sips of her red wine, then continues, "I know Si wants to show Ryder the snow also. All of our families are going to be together this year, so it kind of makes sense to have the wedding around the same time." My eyes widen. She's serious. Christmas isn't that far away. Well, it is, but I guess not in wedding months.

"So, you have been thinking about having it then?"

"Yeah, Derrick has been bugging me with a Pinterest board he has set up with wedding ideas that he has added all of us onto, everyone has been adding their two cents worth to it... so I guess I have subconsciously been thinking about it."

"And?" My heart is racing. I honestly don't care where we get married. The fact that she wants to do it again, and the first time wasn't a fluke, still blows my mind.

"Well, being here has kind of made a choice for me." We stare at each other, and her lips turn in a small smile. "I thought maybe we could go somewhere snowy for Christmas, rent a big house for all our friends and family, then maybe between Christmas and New Year we have our wedding. We can all continue on and celebrate New Year's together. If time allows, once all our families have gone home, we could... you know... go on another honeymoon."

Now it's my turn to smile. "Who knew you were a bridezilla underneath this hard exterior, Mrs. Taylor?" I pinch my wife's ass, making her yelp.

"I'm not going to be a bridezilla, thank you very much," she huffs, and I raise an eyebrow at her. "Just because I demand perfection from professionals does not make me a bridezilla." This makes me chuckle, my perfectionist wife thinks she isn't going to be a bridezilla. "Anyway, that's what Camryn is for."

That's true, Camryn is pretty scary when it comes to events, but she's the best of the best. "True, she can be scary when she wants to be."

"Exactly, she's the kind of person who you need to whip up a wedding in what... three months? Like that's normal, isn't it?" I shrug because I have no idea how long it takes to organize a wedding.

"Why do I already feel anxious about planning it? Please don't tell me I have been hit by wedding fever already." She looks at me, horrified.

"I have the perfect cure for your wedding fever." I twitch my cock that's hard and stuck between us.

"Oh, really?" She gives me a sly smirk.

"Yes, the groom's cock will most definitely help with getting rid of wedding fever. Jump on before it's too late." Ness moves around until she's hovering over me, she slowly sinks down on me, and we both let out a satisfied moan.

"I think it's helping, babe. The wedding fever is slowly disappearing."

"Why do you ever doubt me, wife?"

43

VANESSA

"Christian is such a romantic," Sienna says.

We're currently sitting in my living room with Chinese takeaway and bottles of champagne. The gang wanted to hear about my spontaneous honeymoon.

"It was so beautiful, quiet, and so relaxing." I show them the PG-rated pictures from our honeymoon.

"I can't believe you turned off your phone for a whole weekend." Isla chuckles.

"I bet Christian had his ways of keeping her occupied, am I right?" Derrick seeks a high-five from me, and, of course, I indulge him, and we slap hands.

"That's what you do on honeymoons, D, fuck each other's brains out," Camryn adds as she digs into her cashew chicken stir fry.

"It's still nice that he whisked you away for some alone time. I mean, you guys have been so busy since coming back from Vegas," Sienna adds.

"At first, I was having a heart attack because we had so much shit to do for the party."

"Yeah, but that's what I'm here for," Camryn adds.

"Exactly, that's why we hire the best."

"Damn right, bitch." Camryn gives me a high-five. What are we now, some frat brothers or something with all these high-fives?

"Well, you look utterly refreshed," Stacey complements me.

"Thanks, babe. I do feel fantastic. Actually, I have some news." The room goes quiet, and all eyes land on me.

"Shit, you're pregnant," Sienna whispers.

"Christian put a bun in your oven," Derrick adds.

"What? No," I quickly reply. Shit, I should've thought of my delivery better. "No, no, not yet, but we're trying." The room erupts. It's not like that's a big secret. Christian likes to tell everyone that practice makes perfect, and our kid is going to be pretty perfect with the amount of practicing we have been doing. Men!

"Well, you better tell us as soon as you pee on that stick, woman." Derrick's eyes narrow at me as he points his chopsticks my way.

I cross my heart.

"Of course, you'll all be the first to know. Well, I mean outside of my husband." They all nod in agreement and start digging back into their dinners. "But this has to do with our wedding." Everyone stops eating again.

"And?" Camryn asks.

I smile at them and continue, "And... I have the perfect idea for it." I explain to them how we were talking about having a white Christmas this year for the family and how everyone was going to be here, so why not have our wedding then, sometime between Christmas and New Year's. Obviously, New Year's Eve is out as that's Sienna and Evan's wedding anniversary, and I don't want to get married on Christmas Day, but one of those dates in between is fine.

"Oh my God, this is so perfect," Camryn squeals. "I have so many ideas."

"First, we need to pick a spot," Sienna suggests.

"Somewhere that snows a lot at Christmas," Stacey adds.

"And it has to be fabulous because there's no way in the world you two are getting married in some hick town," Derrick states.

"Do you want to stay here in the States or go overseas?" Camryn asks.

"I'm not sure. That's what I am struggling with? I have never dreamed of a wedding, and now that Christian is asking me to plan my dream wedding, I'm so confused. All I know is I want it to snow!"

Everyone goes quiet for a moment, all lost in thought until they start calling out places all around the world.

"Oh my God, I've got it. What about England?" Camryn suggests. "Doesn't Olivia have a family castle up there? I'm sure she'd let us borrow it."

Liv, or Lady Olivia Pearce as she's known to everyone else, met Camryn when she helped organize a party for her mother's charity in London, they hit it off, and we welcomed her into our merry little group of friends. We have spent time up at her family's estate in Northumberland, up in the north of England, which borders Scotland. It is beautiful, grand, and perfect for a wedding.

"Oh my God, I remember that place. Do you think she'd mind?"

"I'll give her a call and see what she says. We can only ask, and if not, we can try somewhere else," Camryn says as she walks away dialing Olivia's number.

"This place is amazing... old stone, endless manicured gardens, it's like walking back in time," I tell the others. I hope Christian likes the idea. Moments later, Camryn walks in with a sad look on her face. My stomach sinks, damn, just when I got excited about the idea.

"Guess who's getting married in a castle!" she shouts.

"What? No! Oh my God," I squeal as I launch myself into her arms. No way in the world. "She said, yes?"

Camryn is smiling. "Liv said she'd be so honored if you got married at her estate." I swing Cammie around.

"This is going to be incredible."

"It's going to be perfect, plus not to mention a total paparazzi-free zone seeing how large the estate is," Camryn adds.

Shit, in my excitement, I hadn't even thought about the damn paparazzi. They are going to have a field day if they realize we're getting married again.

"This is seriously going to be amazing. We need to start planning now because you only have a couple of months. We have to get a dress, suits for the boys, bridesmaid outfits, food, location, theme, honeymoon..." Camryn's endless lists continue, and the throbbing in my temple starts.

"Okay, well, first, let me start with my squad." I look at all of my closest friends with a smile on my face.

"Are you saying what I think you're saying?" Derrick is the first to catch on. I nod my head, and he squeals. The others all look around confused. "She's asking us to be her bridesmaids, bitches," Derrick shouts. The rest of the room turns into squeals and tears.

"What's going on here?" Christian walks in with Axel as I wipe the tears from my cheeks.

"Ness just announced her squad," Derrick states.

"Squad?" Axel questions.

Derrick rolls his eyes. "How do people not get this? Taylor Swift has a squad, now Vanessa Taylor has a squad. Us."

Christian and Axel look at Derrick, confused.

"I asked them to be my bridesmaids," I tell them.

"We're planning your wedding," Camryn adds.

"Really now?" Christian smirks at me, and I nod my head in

agreement. He walks over and takes a seat beside me, kissing me on my temple as he does.

"So, what are the plans?" he asks excitedly.

"A friend's castle in England." Christian and Axel raise their brows.

"I know people," I say, winking at Christian, making him smile.

"Sometime between Christmas and New Year's. A winter wedding, imagine watching the snow fall, cozied up together beside a roaring fire, all your family and friends around you." Camryn paints a magical picture.

"I love it, but can I add something?" Camryn nods at Christian. "I know it's a moot point having a bachelor party, seeing as we're already married, but I've been thinking."

"And you know that's scary when my brother has been thinking." Axel chuckles. Christian's arm comes out and punches him in the gut, making him wince.

"Like I was saying, I've been thinking, and if I could have the bachelor party of my dreams..."

I look at my husband with a frown, he seriously wants to have a bachelor party! I know the kind he'd want, probably filled with skanky strippers and stuff. I thought he had changed. "Angel, don't look at me like that." He's pouting at me. "I'm serious, I want something cool, and Camryn, I want you to organize it."

"If it's strippers, I'm going to veto it," she says, having my back.

Christian makes a face.

"Strippers! You think my dream bachelor party would include strippers?" He looks at us all, and we shrug.

"Yeah, we kind of do." Now he pouts, even more, folding his arms across his hard chest. "I'm so offended right now, guys."

"Bro, come on, most bachelor parties include strippers." Axel nudges him.

"Well, this one doesn't." The room falls silent. "Ah, that got your attention, didn't it? Now, I'll tell you. I want a James Bond-themed bachelor party."

"Hell, yes," Derrick yells.

Christian smiles. "In Monaco." Silence. Christian looks around the room at our shocked expressions. "No one has anything to say?"

"Fuck, yeah." Axel is the first to break the silence. "Count me in."

"All the boys in tuxedos, my dreams will be coming true." Derrick smiles at us.

"Babe, so what do you think?" Christian asks, squeezing my knee.

Turning, I look into his excited face. "I think that sounds awesome." I wrap my arms around his neck and give him a kiss of encouragement.

"What about the bachelorette party?" Isla asks.

"If the boys are going to Monaco, then so should we," Isla adds.

"We could be bond girls," Derrick suggests, which makes us laugh.

"I'd love to see your Pussy Galore," Christian whispers into my ear.

"And Yvette can do your dress, we could fly to Paris, then onto Monaco for the party," Sienna suggests.

"Oh my God, that's brilliant." Yvette designed Sienna's wedding dress and did a spectacular job. Of course, I want her to do mine.

"Sebastien could do the catering, he's a famous chef." Derrick winks.

"Do you mean Sebastien Sanchez?" Camryn asks, and I nod. Sebastien is Yvette's brother and close friends with Sienna and Derrick. Sienna also kind of hooked up with him after her divorce while she and Evan were just friends. "He's like one of the most sought-after chefs in the world, plus the man is stunning."

"Sienna knows all about that, don't you?" Derrick teases.

"Stop it." Sienna throws a fortune cookie at Derrick.

Camryn is looking between the two.

"Before she got serious with Evan, she hooked up with Sebastien," Derrick whisper yells.

"D," Sienna shouts.

"We only kissed, we were friends, plus my relationship with Evan was complicated then," Sienna nervously tells Camryn.

"Who cares, that boy is fine. Do you seriously think he'd cater the wedding?" Camryn looks hopeful.

Sienna shrugs. "I can always ask, no harm in it." Camryn looks very excited by this prospect.

"This is going to be the best wedding ever," Christian calls out, and I think he might be right. It's turning into something pretty epic.

44

CHRISTIAN

Ness hasn't been feeling well leading up to tonight's event. I told her she needs to slow down because she's going to burn herself out. I hate seeing the dark circles under her eyes. At least next week, she is off to Paris with the girls—wedding dress shopping, and hopefully, she can relax then.

My parents are so excited that the wedding is happening sooner rather than later, and if I'm honest, so am I. I know I had already locked down the finest lady I had ever met when we got married in Vegas, but this time feels like it's more official than that because we're declaring everything in front of family and friends.

The wedding is going to be pretty spectacular from what Camryn has been sending through to me. I know, I know, the groom shouldn't be involved in the planning of the wedding too much. It's usually the bride. But my bride is super stressed at the moment, and I want to take some of the burdens off of her, so I have been emailing ideas back and forth with Camryn.

"Christian, Christian," the paparazzi call my name as I

arrive early to the anniversary event. "How's married life?" one of the photographers asks.

"The best decision I ever made," I reply back. They continue asking questions about Ness being knocked up and how her health is, but I ignore them. I need to get to my girl. Jackson Connolly, our security director and Finn's younger brother, is waiting by the back entrance of the hotel for me.

"This way," he calls, ushering me away from the vultures.

"We need to push them back, they are blocking the door for everyone," I tell Jackson, who nods and speaks into his microphone relaying the message to his security team.

I see Ness standing out by the pool with Camryn, the girls, and Derrick. They're watching the construction of the stage and runway on top of it. It's a pretty cool idea, putting the clear cover over the pool then building the stage on top of it and the runway circling it.

"Hey, angel," I say, slipping my arms around her.

She jumps at the shock but then sinks back against me.

"Hey."

"How's it all going?" I ask, looking at the major construction happening before me.

"Great, just making sure this gets set up correctly. Most of the bands are here already hanging out in the cabanas." She points behind us, not taking her eyes off the workers.

Luxury cabanas line the edges of the pool. We have rented enough, so all of the lower level for the event is guaranteed privacy. Luckily, the hotel is set up for celebrity clientele, and discretion is key for them.

Tonight, those rooms are going to get a lot of action. I laugh to myself because I'd have been one of those using it with some random groupie. Actually, maybe I'll use one of those rooms, whisk Ness away from the party, pretend she's one of my groupies, and push her up against the wall, hiking up her dress and plowing into her hard and fast just the way she loves it.

Ness is always up for a bit of role-playing. I adjust my dick, but he's not listening. His mind is still stuck on my fantasy in the suite.

I hear a throat clear, Ness' bottom wiggles against my stiffening dick. Shit, that perks him up even more.

"Seriously?" she questions me.

"Not my fault, my wife is hot, and I was thinking about the dirty things I want to do with you in one of those cabanas." This makes her chuckle.

"It's a shame I'm busy."

"Do you really need to watch those construction workers put the stage together? I mean everyone else is here." I look over to where Camryn, Isla, Stacey, Sienna, and Derrick are standing talking amongst themselves.

"There's some serious eye candy setting it up, so we needed all hands on deck," Ness answers.

I pinch her ass, making her squeal.

"Oh, for fuck's sake, would you two stop your newly-wedded bliss," Derrick jokes.

"I was just trying to convince my wife to have a quickie with me in one of the cabanas."

"Christian," Ness gasps.

The rest of them giggle. It's probably totally unprofessional of me to say that, but my dick isn't deflating, and now I can't stop thinking of fucking her.

"You have ten minutes before I need her again." Camryn smirks at us. "Think you can be quick?" she challenges me.

"Normally, no, but at the moment, yes." I grab Ness's hand, and she lets out a squeak as I pull her along the tiled pool deck, our friends laughing as I haul my wife off. I head toward one of the cabanas, the glass door is wide open, which is perfect. I stick my head in and double-check it's empty. There are no bags or anything in it, so we're all clear. I pull her in behind me, slamming the glass door shut and pulling the curtain.

"Christian!"

"Shut it, Ness, I need you," I growl as I pick her up and press her against the cabana's wall.

"Chris, that was so... unprofessional..." She lets out a moan as I press myself against her.

"Babe, you're wound up so tight with stress, let me help you." I grind against her again, harder, pressing my denim-clad bulge against her delicate underwear.

"We have to be quick... I..."

"Babe, honestly, I can be done in five, and I know that's nothing to brag about, but..." Her hands are unzipping my jeans, heated fingers pushing my underwear down, letting my dick spring free.

"I don't care, Chris, just fuck me," she pants as she guides my dick into her, pushing her flimsy G-string to the side.

"Yes..." She moans as I enter her, closing my eyes, enjoying her heat. I start slowly, slicking myself up, pushing her harder against the wall, loving the way her legs wrap around my waist, pulling me in tighter against her.

"Please, Chris," she begs. I never get sick of hearing her beg. Ness isn't a woman who ever begs for something. If she wants it, she goes right for it. I love that I've cracked her hard shell and got her to loosen up and be vulnerable with me.

I increase my speed into her, shifting my hips, knowing exactly the right spots to hit to get her to where she needs to be. I piston into her harder, her fingernails grip into my ass, urging me on. "Yes, yes," she screams as I feel her spasm around my cock. I'm not far behind her, releasing into her.

"That was..." I pant, not able to think, and my legs start to wobble. I feel dizzy.

"Just what I needed." She smiles at me, running her hand over my heated skin, pushing my hair out of my face. "I love that you can perform quickly when needed."

"Pretty easy to come quickly when my wife is fucking hot."

This makes her giggle. We still can't believe we're married. Nothing has really changed. No, that's a lie, everything has changed because now we're open and honest with our feelings instead of hiding them from each other, too scared to take those chances. It has given us a much tighter bond, if that's even possible. Contentment has brought to me that we have each other's back no matter what, forever, and I can't wait to show my family and friends how happy I am that this amazing woman wants to be mine. I sound like a goddamn pussy, but I don't fucking care.

At least Evan's in the same pussy club as I am. He gets me. I get him. It has brought the two of us closer together because now he's not the odd man out in the group. I just have to hurry and knock Ness up, then I can join his baby club as well. My heart skips a beat thinking about becoming a father, and not in a panicked kind of way, either, that I thought I would. Maybe because it's Ness, or maybe I have finally grown up, but I'm looking forward to the next phase in my life. I can still be a rock god, make music, and be a husband. I can be all these things and more.

Before Ness, I thought having a wife would mean I'd have to give up my lifestyle, but now I know I can still be me. I mean, I've given up on the groupies, that's very much in my past. There's no way in the world any one of them could ever tempt me. Why the fuck would I give up Ness, this amazing woman, for a cheap thrill? I know what it's like to lose Ness, and never in my life do I want to experience that again. Nope, she's stuck with me.

"Babe," Ness pulls me from my thoughts.

"I have to go get cleaned up before my meeting." She smiles at me, and I lean forward to give her a slow kiss. "What was that for?"

"I love you, Ness, that's all." I move us through the room, kicking the bathroom door open and placing her bottom onto the vanity. Grabbing a washcloth from the rack, I slowly pull out of her and press the towel to her. I don't have time to savor looking at myself falling from her, but just knowing she's going to walk around with wet underwear all night because of me will keep me satisfied.

"Don't look so happy." Ness smiles at me. "I know what you're thinking, and it isn't as hot as you think. I'm going to have to walk around feeling like I've peed myself." I laugh as I take a leak. "You're such an asshole," she playfully scolds, throwing the dirtied towel into the bathtub.

"I know, and yet you still love me, want to make babies with me, and married me..." I joke, holding her hand as we walk out of the bathroom and through the cabana.

Ness laughs, "All true, what was I thinking?"

I slap her ass in protest. "Hey, you love being my wife."

She looks up at me, smiling. "Yeah, I do... but now I have to go and yell at some people." She kisses me quickly on the cheek. "Thanks for helping me de-stress. Love you." Then she's gone.

TONIGHT'S A SUCCESS. There are hundreds of celebrities, VIPs, clients, industry, and press at the party. They loved the idea of the fashion show and concert all in one. Tonight was also the launch of Wyld Jones men's collection. Derrick has been getting a lot more styling jobs for men, which, of course, he loves. This means we'll all be styled up with new clothes, and apparently, Derrick believes we need to up our style game. Of course, the ladies appreciated the male models walking down the runway just as much as we did the female models.

I see the Sons of Brooklyn boys hanging around with one of our newest artists, Gypsy Sisters, a talented Australian girl band Evan and Sienna stumbled on while holidaying in Byron Bay. I need to go and ask them all a favor.

"Christian," Johnny greets me wholeheartedly with a thumping man hug.

"Guys, you killed it tonight, thank you so much," I praise and watch as they all take it in. "But I have a favor to ask you all."

"Anything," Chance answers.

"Great, I'm glad you said that because I have written a song, and I want both of your bands to perform it at my wedding." Their jaws drop, and I hear silence.

"Really?" Indie, one of the girls from Gypsy Sisters, questions.

"Yeah, really. I think mixing both of your sounds together and performing it for Ness will be epic." They all nod their heads in agreement.

"This is such a privilege, Christian," Blake adds. "We won't let you down."

"Good, don't fuck it up. You have a couple of months to prepare. I'll send you all the words, and then you can play around with the music." They all nod enthusiastically. "Okay, well, enjoy your night, I've got to find my wife."

45

VANESSA

"I can't believe we're going back to Paris," Sienna says as we chill on Dirty Texas' private plane. "This time last year, I was getting engaged, and now you're here, married, and getting married again."

"And you have a baby," I add.

"Who would have thought it?" She giggles.

"And here I am still single." Derrick pouts.

"That's because you keep picking the wrong men," Sienna answers.

"True, but they are just so cute. It would be a disservice not to try out all of them," Derrick argues.

When the paparazzi spotted Derrick and Chance together one night, the rumors started about them, and Chance freaked out. He wasn't ready to tell the world he was bisexual. He told the media that Derrick was just his stylist, nothing more, which devastated him. He was heartbroken, but in all honesty, it was probably for the best. For nearly a year, Derrick and Chance have been fooling around, especially at The Paradise Club, where people don't bat an eye at what people get up to and who they do it with, but Chance is very much still in the closet. It's really a no-win situation for Derrick.

After many bottles of wine, Derrick confessed that he had had many threesomes with Chance as he was very much still into women. Derrick is most definitely not into women. He's one hundred percent gay, so for him to agree to bring women into their bedroom meant he really cared for Chance. I guess he was willing to do anything to make it work.

Derrick deserves someone special, and I definitely don't think it's Chance. He needs someone either the same age or older, someone who's comfortable with their sexuality and not a confused boy. He needs someone who can put up with his huge personality and also can handle his shit, and many men can't do that.

Don't get me wrong, I like Chance, he's a great kid, but he hurt Derrick. I know he didn't mean to, but he did.

In true Derrick fashion, he threw himself headfirst—pun intended—into The Paradise Club, the celebrity sex club the boys like to frequent, instead of taking a chance—no pun intended there—on dating. I doubt he will find a husband and a father figure to help him raise babies in a sex club.

Derrick also confessed after the Dirty Texas/Wyld Jones anniversary party and with his thirtieth birthday looming, he was hoping that by this stage, he had gained more from life. He wants marriage and a family—he wants what Sienna and I have. It broke my heart, hearing him confess his darkest secrets to us. I want this for him. He deserves it. He has no contact with his family. They treat him like he doesn't exist, so for him to have his own family and right the wrongs his parents did to him means a lot.

"There's someone out there for you, Derrick, and when you least expect it, you'll find him," Sienna soothes him.

"You know it's hard to tame all this," he replies, waving his hand all around him.

"Never know, he could be in Paris," Stacey suggests.

"Some hot European royal sweeps me off my feet, and you'll all have to bow down to my awesomeness."

We all groan and throw pillows at him.

"You need to come to New York. I'll hook you up with some hot billionaires," Camryn entices Derrick.

"Invite them for my birthday. They can be my present." He smiles.

"Oh, that's a brilliant idea. Let's invite all the hottest, single, gay men we know to your birthday party. You'll have a smorgasbord of hot men to choose from. You never know, one of them could be Mr. Right." Isla claps excitedly.

"Yes, please. Invite them all. Cammie, do you think we can fit more men onto that island?" He wiggles his eyebrows at her. Camryn is organizing Derrick's thirtieth birthday on a private island in the Caribbean. It will be crazy if Derrick has his way.

"For you, Derrick, anything." Camryn smiles, pouring herself another glass of champagne.

"Fantastic! It's my party, and I can fuck if I want to, fuck if I want to, fuck if I want to..." Derrick sings, making us all laugh as he gyrates his hips around the plane's cabin, dry humping any kind of inane object. Finally, after circling us a couple of times, he settles back down into his chair.

"So, Mousey, how are things going with Viking dick?" Derrick asks Stacey about Oscar.

Stacey just rolls her eyes at Derrick.

"I know you're holding out on us. I've seen you at the club sneaking away with Oscar."

"It's just fun, Derrick."

"La la la la," Isla sings, putting her fingers in her ears.

"Don't be a prude, Isla. You've seen your brother do way worst stuff than what Mousey is telling us," Derrick states.

"Yes, but never with one of my friends," she adds.

Derrick bursts out laughing. "As if he hasn't shagged one of your friends."

Isla just pokes her tongue out at him.

"So, you and Oscar just hook up at the club, then?" Sienna asks Stacey.

"Yes, well, you know my story..." Stacey's cheeks turn pink.

"It's always the quiet ones who are the kinkiest." Derrick smiles as he looks at Stacey.

"Oh, this sounds interesting? I want to hear all the dirty bits," Camryn says, rubbing her hands with glee. We're all a little tipsy from the numerous bottles of champagne we have consumed—things get a little interesting when that happens.

"Not much to tell, we're just friends."

"Who fuck," Derrick states.

"Isn't that why we go to The Paradise Club?" Stacey questions him.

Derrick is quiet for a moment. "Okay, fine, Mousey, you got me there, you and Viking dick do dirty, nasty things to each other." He turns his attention to Isla. "What about you, Isla? Is Finn just as kinky as his BFF?" Derrick asks.

Isla rolls her eyes. "I have no idea."

Everyone bursts out laughing.

Isla flips us all off. "You know I've been on a Finn detox, so it's been a while."

"Really?" Derrick pushes. "I don't know if I believe you." He pins her with a stare.

Isla confessed at Sienna and Evan's wedding last year that she was going to start the new year Finn-less. Seeing Sienna and Evan so happy, she decided that she needed to change the decisions she has been making with her love life. We thought this might mean she'd give Wes, The California Bros. Brewery owner, a chance as he had the hots for her, but she said they were just friends after their one and only date.

It's probably about time Isla got over Finn. Fifteen years is a long time to pine after a man. It still surprises me that Oscar never suspects his best friend is fooling around with his little sister.

But true to Isla's word, she has kept away from Finn this year, rejecting his suggestive texts, joining the online dating world, actually going out on physical dates with other men. To say Finn is happy about this is an understatement, but he doesn't have the balls to declare his feelings for her because he's scared of Oscar. I call horseshit on it. I think he just likes having his cake and eating it too. Isla deserves more than that. Maybe because I'm all loved up, I want my friends to be happy also.

"Fine, Derrick, like a damn junkie, I had a relapse. Finn and I hooked up in Vegas, it happened. I mean... it's all your fault, Ness." Isla points at me.

"Hey, what? How did I make you sleep with Finn? I was happily shagging my surprise husband that weekend." I'm not getting blamed for this one.

Isla huffs, "Goddamn Vegas and all its sinful delights."

"Vegas, huh?" I question her.

"You and your bright idea of hosting the boys' birthday party at a sex club. What the hell did you think was going to happen? I'm a goddamn Finn junkie, and waving him in front of my face like that wasn't fair. Of course, I was going to fail," Isla huffs. Laughter erupts in the plane at Isla's dilemma as good friends should. "Fuck you, guys, it's not funny." Isla grabs another glass of champagne.

"But as long as you have kept away since that slip-up, you should be fine," Sienna states.

"You have kept away, haven't you?" I ask.

Isla lets out a groan. "Okay, fine, I slipped up again after the anniversary party. It kind of just happened. You know... deserted cabana, lots of champagne... hot, chiseled, looks like sin rock star begging you for more, whispering dirty things into your ear. A girl can only use her vibrator so many times."

"Isla," Stacey squeals.

She hangs her head in shame. "I know, I know, I'm weak... so very, very weak, but it was the last time, honest to God." She crosses her heart. "It's been a couple of weeks since we last hooked up, so that's good." She looks at all of us for validation, and we all burst out laughing again. "Fuck you." She pouts, which makes us fall into fits of laughter even more.

Derrick puts his arm around Isla. "I'd find it hard saying no to Finn Connolly as well. That boy is fine." Isla bursts out laughing and flips him the bird as we crack open another bottle of champagne.

46

CHRISTIAN

While the girls have gone to Paris, we decided to make a boys' trip to Big Bear Lake. I'm taking a leaf from the Evan Wyld playbook and buying my wife a house. It's going to be a surprise. She loved it so much when we were up here for our mini honeymoon recently.

"You can't come up with your own ideas." Evan shoulders me, chuckling as he takes a seat in our private jet. I flip him the bird.

"We better not be neighbors," Zander adds. He's going to be our official tour guide for the weekend.

"No way in the world do I want to see your ugly face," I mock as I sit back into the leather seat.

"Still can't believe you're married, dude." Zander slaps me on the back as he takes a seat across from me.

"The best decision I ever made, boys." I raise my bottle of beer to them.

"Here, here." Evan clinks his bottle against mine.

"Aw, look, the married boys club," Axel jokes.

"Seriously, bro, don't knock it."

Axel huffs. "There's no way in the world I'm ever settling down."

Oscar, Finn, Zander, and Axel all clink their beers together, a stand of single solidarity.

"Never say never." I smile at them. "Y'all aren't getting any younger."

Axel groans. "Doesn't mean we have to settle down with one woman."

"There's no way on God's green earth I'd ever give up Ness for the endless supply of pussy you guys are talking about. None of that stuff could ever compare to what Ness and I have."

"That's 'cause you and Evan got the best ones," Zander adds.

"Damn right, we did," Evan says.

"Yeah, we got lucky, but that's 'cause we stopped searching through the easy pussy to get to the prime stuff."

"You know, Ness would kill you if she heard you talking about her prime pussy," Finn adds.

"Yeah, she would, and I wouldn't care because that woman is my life, and one day y'all might meet that one woman who makes you lose your breath and want more from life." The plane is silent for a minute, then the boys all burst out laughing at me. "Y'all a bunch of fuckfaces." I flip them all the bird.

"I like husband Christian, his words are poetic and shit." Zander laughs.

"Whatever, I'm just saying there's more out there than short-term kicks."

"Agreed," Evan adds.

"Oscar's been hanging out with Stacey a lot, he might be next," Finn confesses while Oscar shoots him daggers.

"Well, well, well." I smile.

"Fuck you, dude. We aren't a bunch of women gossiping about our sex lives," Oscar grumbles.

"Hell, yeah, we are. I want the gossip," I add.

"You've been around Derrick too long, you sound just like him," Oscar huffs. If Derrick were here, he'd so be getting the gossip out of these guys.

"Time to buckle up, boys, we're about to take off," the hostess advises us before disappearing again. The cabin goes quiet as the rumble of the jet starts, and we hurtle down the runway. Moments later, we're up in the sky, the plane evens out, and we all resume talking again. It's less than an hour to Big Bear Lake from LA, so it will be quick.

"Don't think I have forgotten what we were talking about before," I remind them.

"Argh, you're so annoying. Fine, Stacey and I like playing at The Paradise Club, and we're into the same things. She's very sexually adventurous, but other than that, I'm not looking for anything more."

"So, Stacey is just a fuck buddy?" I ask.

Oscar runs his hands over his face. "Yes... no... I'm not really sure. She's a cool chick, but she has never indicated that she wanted anything outside of the hookups we have."

"But you hook up with her a lot," Finn adds.

Oscar glares at his best friend. "Like I said, sexually, she's highly compatible."

"She's pretty hot at the club," Axel adds.

Oscar growls at him. "I know that you know."

My head bounces between the two of them as if I'm watching Wimbledon.

"What does that mean?" I ask.

Oscar's eyes look to the floor. "They have hooked up before." The plane goes silent.

"What the hell, bro." I throw a cushion at him.

"Hey, hey, Oscar allowed it," Axel defends himself.

"You allowed it?" I question him.

"Chris, you know Axel and I are into different kinds of things than you guys are."

Axel and Oscar have kinks, certain fetishes that they both like. They have women who like the same things, not that they don't do what they call vanilla from time to time. That's why The Paradise Club is good because they can find people who like those sorts of things without the press finding out about it.

"But why would you share Stacey with Axel? Was she okay about it?"

"Yes, of course. I shared her with another because she wanted a certain experience that one man couldn't give her. So, I asked Axel, who understood what she was asking for, and who I trusted to give her that experience."

"And now?"

"Axel joins in if she needs more."

"And you're okay with doing this?" I ask Axel.

"Oscar wanted to fulfill an experience that his woman wanted, I helped, and that's all there is to it."

Axel and I may be twins, and we're very similar in a lot of ways, but when it comes to sex, I guess we are poles apart.

"So, you don't do anything with her outside of the club?" I ask Oscar, who looks a little uncomfortable by my question.

"We both agreed that we keep what we have in the club."

"And you do?" I ask.

"Yes. Could you imagine if *TMZ* got a hold of this, especially after *Fifty Shades of Grey*? They'd have a field day. I don't need my family knowing what I get up to behind closed doors," Oscar explains.

"And you trust Stacey?"

"Hell, yeah, I do, she's a great girl, plus she's already in our inner circle. She's best friends with your girls, so that means something."

I nod in agreement. He's right.

"So, what happens if she goes to the club without you?" Evan asks.

"Then she has fun without me," Oscar adds.

"And you're okay with that?" Because I sure as hell wouldn't be.

"Of course, we're not exclusive." Oscar looks uncomfortable, explaining the Stacey situation to us. "We have an agreement. She's mine to do with as I see fit at the club, I'm helping her explore her sexual side. The one that's started to bloom since we've, you know..." He shrugs before gulping his beer.

"So, you're her boss?" Evan asks.

"Kind of, she tells me what she wants to experience, and I help her experience it. When we're together at the club, she is mine. She must ask for permission if she wants to be with another, and I must do the same."

"So, you're only exclusive at the club and only when you're together," Evan repeats.

"Yes."

"But you don't see her as anything more?" Finn questions. Oscar is silent for a couple of moments.

"Stacey may be the first woman who has made me question my stance on commitment." The plane falls silent.

"So, if you were committed, you would stop sleeping with other people," I ask, intrigued. Oscar turns to Axel looking for help in answering that question.

"Like we've said, Oscar and I like things a little different than you guys."

"If I could find a woman who let me sleep with other women, I wouldn't let her go." Zander chuckles to himself.

"It's not..." Axel starts, and I can see it on his face he's becoming defensive about their choices. I need to defuse things before they get heated.

"I guess as long as you all understand the rules, and no one is getting hurt, then it's all good." Oscar nods at me, and Axel lets it go. I'm getting a real education into my friends' sex lives today. Wait till I tell Ness.

"This is the one." I stand out the front of the sprawling estate.

The real estate agent rattles off the details of the home—ten bedrooms, twelve bathrooms. The coolest thing is the indoor sports center, including an indoor pool, sauna, spa, squash court, basketball court, games rooms, and pool room. Outside is another pool, swim-up bar, tennis court, equestrian center, and winter sports cabin. Inside also boasts some awesome things—a cellar, movie theater, an enormous master suite that looks out over the mountains, down past the valley where there is a river and lakes—the list goes on. It's also situated on ten acres of land.

"This is pretty cool," Axel says in awe, looking at the huge house in front of us.

"It's perfect for the extended family and us."

He just nods in agreement, staring at the imposing structure made of stone.

"The estate also has four luxury cabins sprawled out amongst the acreage for guests."

"There you go, boys, you each have a cabin." This is the place. I can see Ness and I coming up here in the winter with the kids, teaching them to ski. Even in the summer, we can come here to ride horses and go hiking. All our friends and family with us and the sound of kids laughing with excitement, this is what I'm looking forward to.

"I'll take it."

47

CHRISTIAN

It's Derrick's thirtieth birthday extravaganza, his words not mine, and we're taking the Dirty Texas jet to the Caribbean for the weekend. Like I said, extravaganza. If I'm honest, I'm kind of excited to be spending the next couple of days with my sexy wife on a deserted island, watching her prance around in a skimpy bikini, making love on the beach, making love under the stars, pretty much looking forward to spending the entire time in her.

"It's party time, bitches," Derrick squeals as he enters our private plane. The flight attendant has a tray full of tequila shots ready for everyone entering the plane. We all throw them back and spy the buckets of champagne on ice. The girls quickly get to popping them and pouring glasses for each other. I think it's going to be a wild ride the way everyone is knocking back the drinks.

"You should see my moves on the pole. I honestly don't understand why I am still single. I'm hot," Derrick mumbles as he grabs the stripper pole that's in the middle of the cabin. Long flights call for wicked fun. By this stage, we had drunk a lot. Most of us are pretty messy, including Derrick. But the girls urge him on as he swings around the pole.

"Take it off, take it off," the girls chant at Derrick.

"You like what you see, ladies," he croons. "What about you, Chris, want to see more?" he flirts with me. I love D, he's one of my best buddies, and I'm flattered he has a huge crush on me because Derrick is an extremely good-looking guy. If I liked dick, then yes, I'd most definitely like Derrick, but unfortunately for him, I'm strictly vaginal or is that virginal, no, that's not right. Fuck, too many tequilas making my head hurt.

"Take it off, take it off," I chant with the girls, which makes Vanessa giggle. My hollering spurs Derrick on, and he starts taking off his shirt, which he flings at me. Then he tries and takes his jeans off but is horribly unbalanced due to the large amount of alcohol he has consumed and falls over a couple of times, making us all laugh. Eventually, he pulls them off and throws them at Oscar, who doesn't look impressed at all.

"Ragnar, cheer up," Derrick slurs at Oscar. That's his nickname for him, after the famous Viking. Now he's standing in his boxer briefs, hip-thrusting the pole.

I lean over to Ness. "I'm so horny right now," I whisper into her ear.

"I didn't realize Derrick stripping did it for you."

"As sexy as he is..." I look over at Derrick, who's currently hip-thrusting against a chair, "... my dick only has thoughts of a sexy, hot Australian girl, who's married to a rock star."

"What? Your dick wants Sienna?"

"What? No," I shout, making the room go quiet. "Sorry, carry on," I tell Derrick. "You... I want to fuck you." I make sure she understands it's her my dick wants.

"I know, baby, I just like making you squirm." She smiles.

"That's it." I jump out of my seat and pick her up. She squeals as I throw her over my shoulder.

"You all right there, Ness?" Axel calls out as I pass the boys.

"I think my husband wants to show me something."

"I bet he does," Finn adds.

I flip him the bird as I carry Vanessa into the bedroom. Throwing her onto the bed, she bounces a couple of times. "Remember last time we were in here?" I ask her. She looks at me for a moment, her brain foggy from being upside down and too much champagne.

"On our way to London..." She trails off with a faraway look on her face. I think she remembers exactly what happened last time.

"Remember how everyone else was asleep..." I jump onto the bed, my body crawling up over hers.

"You had been teasing me the whole flight, wearing that dress, the one that made you look like a dirty librarian. It molded to the curves of your body to perfection." I press her into the bed with my body weight. "You were a naughty girl, walking past me, telling me you weren't wearing any underwear. Do you have any idea how fucking hard I instantly got?"

She gives me a wicked smile, her teeth sinking into her lip as she nods her head.

"You were doing it on purpose, I understand that now," I growl in frustration. "You liked to tease me back then, and it was hard because I couldn't always have you when I wanted."

"I know, I liked knowing that I affected you." She smiles, her hand reaching down against my jeans and palming my aching length. "Just like I do now." Her fingers rub against me, making me hiss.

"But it's different now, isn't it?"

She nods.

"Because I can have you anytime I want?"

She nods again.

"I want you, Ness." My lips come down upon hers in a drunken, lust-filled kiss. The kiss is full of passion as we frantically pull each other's clothes off. We work slower than normal due to the amount of alcohol we have consumed, but before we know it, we're both naked on the bed, her nails are ripping into my back, and my hands are palming her breasts. We're wild and frenzied when I slide inside her. It's quick and hard.

"You're as fucking tight as you were then. Fucking heaven." As I piston into her, the bed is creaking with the ferociousness that I'm taking her.

"Fuck me harder," Ness moans, and I oblige, my balls slapping her ass as I try to satisfy her the best way I know.. "Harder, baby, harder." Her fingers bite into my ass cheeks, pushing me to fill her all the way, my girth stretching her, making her mine all over again. "Yes, Christian, yes," she screams as my dick finds the perfect spot inside of her, the one that I know sets her off like a fucking firecracker.

"Fuck, Ness, fuck," I scream as I come not long after her. We both collapse into a sweaty, exhausted mess. Closing our eyes, we drift off to dreamland.

"HARDER, HARDER," Finn mocks when Vanessa and I join the gang back in the main area a couple of hours later.

"Fuck you, asshole." I flip him the bird.

"Oh my God," Vanessa shrieks at Finn's crude joke.

"Yeah, I think you said that as well." Axel laughs.

I clip him around the ear. He's an asshole too.

"It was hot." Derrick joins me. "You obviously know how to please a woman," he adds, winking at me.

"Hell, yeah, I do." I wrap my arm around a very embarrassed Vanessa.

"Shut up, all of you," Vanessa scolds all of our friends.

"It's all good, Ness, 'cause Evan and Sienna were singing the same tune not that long ago as well," Camryn adds. "You're not the only one worshiping God today."

. . .

It was probably not the best idea to have drunk so much on the plane because once we arrived at the airport, we had to catch a boat to the island. Let's just say a lot of people were hugging the sides.

"Thank God for land." Derrick falls dramatically into the white sand.

There's a traditional Caribbean steel band greeting us on arrival, but with the way we feel, we aren't the happiest of travelers. We're all a little green around the gills. The manager is there to greet us as well with fresh fruit cocktails.

"Welcome to Azure Bay. I'm sure you're all tired after the long journey." He looks at us, and yeah, we look like shit. "So, we will get you settled into the home, and then we'll leave you alone." We walk through the hot sand toward the palm trees, and there waiting for us is a fleet of golf carts. "The easiest way to get around the island is via these." He points to the carts. We all jump in, and I can already see this is going to be a bad idea.

"After you, my beautiful wife." I gesture to Vanessa as she steps into the cart.

"Thank you, husband." She smiles at me, color coming back to her cheeks.

"We're jumping in with you guys, I don't trust those boys," Isla says.

Finn, Oscar, Axel, and Derrick have all grabbed a cart each and zoom off before all of us. I can already tell that someone is probably going to roll one or fall out of it. Evan, Sienna, Stacey, and Charlotte are in the other. Camryn rides with the manager upfront.

"Please don't go crazy unless you want me to spew all over you," Vanessa warns as I start off with a little too much throttle. I ease off the gas and go at the same pace as Evan's cart. I can hear all the boys up front hollering and yelling abuse at each other.

"I bet someone gets hurt by the time we make it to the house," Isla says.

"Ten dollars, it's Derrick. He's pretty drunk." Vanessa giggles.

"So is Finn," I butt in. "True, but Axel is super competitive," Isla states.

"Oscar will probably sit back and watch them all fuck themselves over and win by default," I add, and we all laugh at that.

We pass through the palm trees lining the walkways, the gorgeous beach is on our left, and as far as the eye can see is a white sandy beach and turquoise water—sheer paradise. The rest of Derrick's party is coming a couple of days later, so it's just going to be our crew until then. We arrive at the most glorious architecturally designed house, all glass and wood, and the walls open to the elements and look out directly to the ocean.

"The accommodation is made up of three large buildings all connected by breezeways. We're currently standing in the main building. From here, you'll find your dining and living areas. There's a bar, games room, library, cellar, movie theater, also a sauna and spa area. The pool you can see here runs all the way around the three buildings. From most bedrooms, you can step out right into the pool. Of course, all views from your rooms look out to the ocean. Our chef and butler will be on standby, and when the rest of your guests arrive, we have a couple of extra staff to help with anything you want." The manager hands Camryn a folder and says his goodbyes.

"Okay, I have everyone's keys, luggage is being taken to your rooms as we speak." Camryn starts handing out the keys. "I hope you don't mind, but I put you married couples on one side of the house and the single guys on the other," she states as she hands out our keys.

I love my boys, but yeah, good idea. I can see that wing of the house is a total frat house. We all agree to meet up for dinner later. We say our goodbyes and head to our rooms. I push open the door, and before Ness can take a step inside, I sweep her off her feet and into my arms, making her squeal.

"Christian."

"Look, I'm treating this as a kind of honeymoon, so I am taking my wife over the threshold." This makes her giggle. She doesn't wiggle as I walk into the grand room.

"Oh my God, this is stunning," Vanessa gasps, and it is. No words can describe the beauty of what's laid out before us. The whole side of our room is one big glass wall, and all you can see is the turquoise water. Gently, I put Vanessa down as we walk toward the glass door. I pull it open, and we walk out onto the deck. The pool's water laps at the edge of it, and our room is screened off from the others beside us. Beyond the screen are palm trees, white beaches, and the ocean. "This is paradise," Vanessa marvels.

I wrap my arms around my wife, and we silently take in the view. A couple of moments pass, and I nuzzle her neck. "You know I'm so going to fuck you in this pool." This makes her laugh.

"I'm pretty sure we aren't going to be the only ones doing it in the pool." She laughs.

"Gross, on second thought... that king-size bed we passed looks pretty good as well."

"I need a shower, then a nap."

"I don't mind helping you with those things." I squeeze my wife's ass.

48

VANESSA

"I'm dying," Christian moans from beside me.

"We all are, bro," Axel groans.

"Such a bunch of lightweights." Derrick smiles as he drinks a cocktail by the pool.

"But it was the best night ever if I say so myself," Camryn also groans beside me, her Jackie O glasses hiding her hangover.

Last night we celebrated Derrick's thirtieth birthday, and you could say things got crazy and pretty wild, especially with all the extra guests around. Camryn and her business partner, Kimberly, who flew in from New York to help, had organized a stunning beach barbeque. There were long tables set up on the beach, a bonfire, cabanas set up in the sand decorated with white lace and fairy lights—it was magical.

She organized for Derrick to be carried out by four, half-naked men. Of course, she had designed a floral crown for him to wear and a throne for him to sit on. He looked like King Tut as he arrived at the barbeque, waving to his waiting subjects. I guess it could've been worse, he might have arrived via elephant.

At the outdoor bar there is a DJ duo, called Duo, who played the tunes. They were also recently signed to Dirty Texas Records. As the night progressed, Sons of Brooklyn pulled out their acoustic guitars and serenaded Derrick. It was sweet, even though you could see the strain between Chance and Derrick. True to her word, Camryn gifted him the hottest, single men she knew, and he most definitely opened up all his presents. It was his birthday, after all.

"You know what I'll remember most?" Derrick grins.

We all shake our heads because we have no idea.

"Christian's lap dance," Derrick says with a huge smile.

"Please tell me no one recorded it," Christian groans from his chair.

"I made sure no one recorded it, baby," I soothe, kissing him on his very prickly skin.

"You're a good woman," he mumbles, his large arms covering his eyes.

I asked Christian last night if he could strip to a G-string and give Derrick a lap dance. Let me tell you he wasn't keen on the idea, but I plied him full of tequila and then told him he could do whatever he wanted to me if he did this for Derrick. When you wave that flag in front of a bull's face, he's going to charge.

Well, did Christian put on a show! It was the funniest thing I had ever seen. He was dressed up as a policeman. I have no idea where he got the outfit from, and I kind of don't want to know. He pushed Derrick up against a palm tree and gave him a frisking he will never forget. He gave everyone a treat as he slowly started to strip out of his policeman's uniform as he pushed Derrick onto a chair and threw his clothes into his face. When he pulled off his pants and saw Christian had on nothing but a G-string, I thought he was going to have a heart attack right there. He was in shock as Christian's white ass twerked in his face. He did such a great job that I'm demanding he give me a lap dance at least once a week. My man's got moves.

"I think everyone enjoyed that." Camryn giggles as she snuggles up with Harris, her New Yorker boyfriend. He's totally Cammie's type—tall, built, and a workaholic. He has that air of East Coast privilege about him. It took him a while to loosen up, but when he did, he was a lot of fun.

"Hey," Harris scolds, capturing Camryn's lips against his. "You shouldn't be looking at your bestie's man."

"I don't think anyone had a choice. It was all out there," Axel adds.

"I know everyone appreciated my performance last night because look at me, who wouldn't." He's so modest, my husband.

"Please, your performance was definitely no Magic Mike. You were lucky Derrick was just mesmerized by your white ass to say anything," Axel goads his brother.

Christian sits up. "Really, really, you think you can do a better job than me?"

Axel shrugs.

"Oh no, you can't just throw that shit out there and not back it up. I dare you to give Derrick a lap dance and let him decide which of us is the better lap dancer," Christian argues.

"Oh, hell, yes," Derrick squeals from the pool.

"What? Now?" Axel stumbles over his words.

"Yes, brother. Now! Unless you can't handle it?" Christian pushes Axel.

"Oh my God, this is so hot," Derrick whispers to me.

"Okay, fine." Axel jumps up out of his chair. "Derrick, are you ready to be entertained?"

"Yes, yes, yes," Derrick squeals, quickly jumping out of the pool. He grabs a towel and dries himself off as he sits down on one of the sun lounges by the pool. "Give it to me, baby," he croons.

"Well, I'm going to need some music," Axel says.

Christian hands him his phone, and Axel plays around with it until he finds the perfect song—'Hot in Herre' by Nelly. He empties the bucket of ice into the garden then fills the bucket up with water. Not sure how much stripping he's going to be doing as he is only wearing board shorts.

The music starts playing, and Axel starts dancing around, and wow, can he dance. We're talking full-on boy-band dancing. I had no idea Axel had moves like that. He's gyrating around and hip thrusting. Everyone's eyes are drawn to each thrust when we realize he is commando under those board shorts. Derrick is clapping and wolf-whistling as Axel gives him a fantastic lap dance. He picks up the bucket and turns it over himself, the water running down every inch of his cut body, his board shorts becoming almost see-through.

"Yes, yes, yes," Derrick screams.

Axel is now hip-thrusting himself into Derrick's face, and he loves it. He turns around and does a slut drop on Derrick's crotch as he twerks his ass over him.

"You're giving me a hard-on," Derrick yells.

Then Axel starts untying his board shorts—next thing, he throws them in Derrick's face, and his hand is covering his junk. Well, not so much is covered as there's no way his hand can cover that monster between his legs. He lets Derrick slap his bare ass, and as the song finishes, he jumps into the pool naked.

"I think I need to join you." Derrick jumps in after him. "I need to cool down after that."

We all erupted into hoots and hollers after Axel's performance. Christian is clapping. "Still think mine was better," he says with a pout.

"You'll always be my number one." Derrick laughs from the pool.

CHRISTIAN

"I'm so excited," Mom whispers to me as we settle into our private jet. "All this is so luxurious." Mom and Dad are always amazed when they realize how much their kids can afford. Currently, the jet is filled with Evan and Sienna's parents, Vanessa's parents, my parents, Axel, Finn, Oscar, Jackson, Charlotte, Camryn, Isla, Stacey, and Derrick.

As we're heading to Monaco for the bachelor party, we are doing a quick pit stop in Paris to do some last-minute fittings for Vanessa's wedding dress and the bridesmaid dresses. Derrick is also taking us suit shopping. I told him I'd just wear one of my old tuxedos, which earned me his ire. "This is your wedding day, Christian Taylor. You're declaring your love for the woman of your dreams. You'll not wear a second-hand suit for that." Seeing as he's the expert on all things fashion, I have left it all up to him.

We are also celebrating Thanksgiving while we're here with a little bit of a French twist. Sebastien has graciously told us he'd host Thanksgiving at his restaurant, which Vanessa tells me is amazing.

Mom is so excited about Paris because she has always

wanted to visit there but has always refused the million times Axel and I have told her we'd fly her there. She says she's just a simple southern woman who doesn't want to cause a fuss. Like I believe that, but I'm glad she's here now. The parents are going to stay on in Paris and explore while the rest of us jet down to Monaco. Evan and Sienna's parents are on babysitting duties with Ryder, so they can have some fun this weekend too.

We have heaps of friends flying in for the weekend as well. Who would say no to a James Bond weekend in Monaco? Nate, who owns The Paradise Club, is letting us use his multimillion-dollar superyacht for our stay—nothing is more James Bond than a superyacht in the middle of the Mediterranean.

The plane ride to Paris is a little more subdued than the last one we took to the Caribbean.

"I'm so excited, thank you for suggesting this with our families." Vanessa snuggles into my side. It made sense. Our families were already here getting ready to celebrate Thanksgiving. We had to have this weekend away at some point. Why not mesh the two together, especially when we're running out of weeks until the wedding.

"I love seeing our parents experience our rock-star life, they get a kick out of it."

Vanessa lets out a big yawn and snuggles further into my side. "I can't believe how tired I am." She yawns again. My wife has been working too hard. This wedding can't come around soon enough just so we can have some extended leave together and relax.

"I can take you to one of the bedrooms if you like?"

She shakes her head. "I think they might be all occupied by the oldies." She giggles. "Plus, you're nice and squishy."

"Hey, there's nothing squishy about me." I flex my muscles, which makes her laugh. I know I haven't been working out as hard as I used to. I mean, we have been so busy. Shit, maybe I'm becoming squishy in my old age. Vanessa's giggles pull me from my freak-out.

"Your face is priceless. I can see the wheels turning in your head." She smiles at me. "I'd love you even if you were squishy." She gives my love handles a little squeeze. Right, I'm heading to the gym as soon as I arrive, and I need to start laying off the beers, or maybe start drinking low-calorie ones. Vanessa shakes her head at me.

"You're worse than a woman. Now recline this chair and let me sleep on you." She jumps into my lap, and I pull the lever to recline the chair back as she snuggles into me again. The flight attendant hands me a blanket as she passes. I wrap it around both of us, and we fall asleep to the hum of the jet.

"Welcome to Paris," Derrick announces as the jet pulls to a stop. We make our way through the private airport's immigration and then hop into the fleet of limousines that are waiting for us. Thankfully, no paparazzi are out waiting for us. The last thing we want is for people to know we're here. We head through the bustling streets of Paris, Mom's eyes wide as she takes it all in, and a smile is firmly plastered on her face.

"There's the Eiffel Tower." She points in wonderment.

"Look at those pastries." Dad points as we pass a couple of bustling boulangeries.

"Remember what the doctor said, you have to watch your cholesterol," Mom reminds him. Dad just rolls his eyes at her playfully. She squeezes his knee while smiling at him. Even after all these years together, my parents are still in love with each other. I hope Ness and I can have as many years together as they have. That would be the biggest blessing.

Eventually, we pull up to the apartment that we rented. We decided to rent one large apartment to fit us all in. I guess we're all so used to being stuck with each other when we travel, the habit is hard to break.

"Oh, sweetheart, this place looks amazing. Like something

out of a movie." Mom is mesmerized by the French architecture. Isla punches in the passcode, and we enter the three-story building. We're staying in the seventeenth arrondissement, not far from the Arc de Triomphe and Champs-Élysées, perfect for our family to explore Paris. We enter a marbled foyer. There's an antique-style lift to the left, and to the right is a beautiful marble staircase with an intricate gold handrail.

"Who's game for the lift of death?" Derrick asks. Most people shake their heads. "Fine, but if something happens to me, just know I'll haunt your asses." Derrick jumps into the lift.

We all trudge up the stairs, excitement filling the empty villa. The first level is the living area. I can see Mom enjoying the large entertainer's kitchen with its views over Paris, making us pancakes in the morning. Dad would head straight to the media room and try searching for a football game and probably curse the time difference. There are also two bedrooms downstairs, which my parents and Vanessa's parents claim. Dad hates stairs, plus he has a dodgy knee, so walking up and down too many flights of stairs will hurt him.

"Guess I'm going to get a workout with all these stairs." Ness smiles at me as we continue up to the next level. The Wyld family takes over this level with the large master suite, giving them more room for little Ryder. The rest of the girls and Derrick join them on that level, each one of them grabbing a bedroom for themselves. The rest of us continue up to the next level, where Ness and I, as well as Axel, Oscar, and Finn, will be staying. We have everything we could want up here with the most spectacular views over Paris.

"Wonder where this door goes." Finn pushes the small wooden door that's beside his bedroom. It creaks as he opens it, and we follow behind him, wondering where it goes. There's a metal spiral staircase, and we follow him up to it. Finn pushes another wooden door at the top of the stairs, and it opens out onto a stunning rooftop terrace garden. Bright green box hedges line the edges of the terrace. In one corner, a large lemon tree stands proudly, and it's ripe for picking. Another corner has a wall of herbs, the smell tickling my nose. Oversized outdoor furniture is also scattered across the terrace, which looks out across the rooftops of Paris.

"Oh my God, this is beautiful," Vanessa exclaims.

"We're so partying up here," Axel adds.

"Wow," Oscar admires as we all take in the view.

"I'm so going to fuck you up here," I whisper into Ness' ear. "Under the stars facing the Eiffel Tower." A shiver runs through her.

"I can't wait."

50

VANESSA

"Oh my God, you're here," Yvette squeals, greeting us at her exclusive boutique. We all hug her as we enter and introduce her again to our families. "I'm so excited. I can't wait to show you your dress."

Butterflies start to take flight in my stomach. I never thought that I'd be excited about a wedding dress, but now that I'm here, I kind of feel very bridal. There are bottles of champagne chilling in the dressing area along with delicate little pastel pastries.

"This is beautiful," Mum whispers to me, taking in the luxurious surroundings of Yvette's boutique.

"I think we should start with the bridesmaids first," Yvette says.

Sienna, Isla, Camryn, and Stacey head off behind the velvet curtains as I settle in with Mum and Sienna's mum, who's holding a wriggling Ryder. Moments later, the girls come out dressed in stunning black dresses. They consist of a black, long sleeve top with full-body tulle skirts.

"Oh my God, they are perfect," I say in amazement as each one of my girls models their dress for me. I'm getting a little emotional, and tears are threatening to fall from my eyes. What the hell is going on with me?

"I love them," I say, and I can see Yvette visibly relax at my words.

"I feel so sophisticated." Stacey twirls her dress around like a ballerina.

"I feel sexy." Camryn smirks as she thrusts her leg out of the hidden split, showing off a tanned leg.

"Well, I think I need to cut down on whatever I'm eating as I have gained some pounds since the last time I was here." Sienna moans as she turns around and shows me the half-unzipped skirt. I try and stifle a giggle, but I can't hide it. "You're such a bitch," Sienna moans, which makes me laugh even louder. She flips me off and storms away. Even her Mum is laughing now.

"Next, we'll do the bride," Yvette announces, and I follow her nervously back into the dressing room. I didn't trust Derrick when he suggested a princess-style dress, but my friends assured me that it would match the location. As Derrick says, 'You're getting married in a goddamn castle, when else can you be a princess.' He's right, and I decided on the dress that's so far from what I thought I'd ever get married in. Stepping into the dress, the yards and yards of sparkly tulle surround me.

"This is going to be fun going to the toilet in."

"That's what the bridesmaids are here for." Yvette smiles as she dresses me. I slip my arms into delicate, sheer long sleeves, and I can feel the heavy beading of the bodice. I catch myself in the mirror, and I pause. I look like a bride, I can't believe this is me, I look happy. A single tear falls down my cheek as my stomach flip flops with excitement and happiness.

"Um... Ness." Yvette stops zipping me up. "I don't mean to be rude, but... have you put on weight since our last fitting?" I still, I'm utterly horrified. I don't fit into my dress. This is a disaster, and panic starts to seep through me.

"Shit," I mumble, embarrassed.

"Hey." Yvette grabs my attention. "Weddings are stressful times. I can totally adjust the dress. But may I ask a personal question?" Yvette chews her lip nervously. "Do you think you might be pregnant?"

I go completely still. No, I can't be pregnant. I try to mentally calculate the last time I had my period. "I just asked Sienna the same thing, and she gave me the same look you're giving me," Yvette points out. "I just thought I'd ask. I know it's something personal if you are, but if you are, I can adjust the dress accordingly."

My heart is racing. There's no way I could be pregnant.

"Come, let me try the zipper one last time, and then you can show yourself to everyone outside." Yvette works her magic on the zipper and is able to just do it up. She pulls back the curtain, and my family and friends appear in front of me. I slowly walk out to where the stand is in front of them so that I can get a 360-degree look of myself.

"Oh my..." Mum gasps, seeing me for the first time. I look over, and she's bawling her eyes out, which, of course, makes me start crying, then the rest of the girls join in.

"You look beautiful," Sienna states.

"Like a princess," Camryn adds.

"Christian is going to faint when he sees you," Isla says with a smirk.

"Stunning," Stacey adds.

The girls come and stand beside me, and for the first time, I see my wedding party altogether. They all look so beautiful.

I'm truly blessed, and if Yvette is right, I might have some more good news coming my way.

51

CHRISTIAN

"Christian," Vanessa screams from the toilet. Fuck, I hope she's okay. We're getting ready for Thanksgiving at Sebastien's restaurant in Paris.

"Babe, what is it?" Turning the corner where Ness is in the ensuite, I rush the last couple of steps and see she's standing looking at something on the counter. I can see her face reflecting in the bathroom mirror—it's pale, and she's crying.

"Ness?" The uncertainty in my voice echoes against the bathroom walls. Her hands are shaking as she hands over a white pen-like thing. I take it from her and stare at it. I'm not sure what she wants me to do.

"Look at the screen, babe."

I frown and look at the little digital screen on the pen. There's a plus sign on it. I look up at Ness, then back to the pen. No, this isn't what I think it is, is it? My heart starts thumping in my chest.

"What do you think, Daddy?"

"You're using the word daddy in a non-sexual way, aren't you?" I ask, not sure if I can believe what I'm seeing in front of me.

"Yes." She smiles.

"We're having a baby?" I question, just to double-check because my brain isn't working at the moment. It seems to have left the building.

"Yes, babe. You and I are having a baby." Tears start running down her cheeks.

"Fuck!" I pull her into my arms and nuzzle my face in her neck. I can feel the tears falling down my cheeks. I'm going to be a dad. Me!

"Babe, are you okay?"

Lifting my head, I look into those jade eyes that I love so much.

"I don't think I could love you any more than I do right now. You have made me the happiest man on the planet. I thought the night you married me in Vegas was the happiest I could ever be, but no, right here, right now, you giving me this gift of becoming a dad, it trumps everything. How can I ever repay you for giving me this gift?"

"Christian," Vanessa whispers as more tears fall down her face. She wraps her arms around me. "We're so fucking lucky." She smiles at me, and my heart bursts, like literally bursts with love, and I can't contain it any longer. I smash my lips against hers in a heated kiss. I show her exactly how much I love her. My hands run down over her body feeling her curves, curves that I know are going to change each day with the growth of our baby inside of her.

"I can't wait to see you with a big belly."

Ness groans. "Are you still going to find me sexy when I'm waddling around the house like a whale?"

"Hell, yeah, I can't wait to have pregnant sex with you." I wiggle my eyebrows at her. She smacks me lightly on the shoulder.

"We shall see when I'm the size of a house whether or not you'll still want all of this?" She wiggles her body against mine.

"Babe, I'll want you when we're old and gray, sitting in the old folk's home, and I'll still be jumping your bones." Ness starts to laugh, then bursts out crying. "Oh, babe. What is it?" I ask as the tears stream down her face.

"I'm so fucking happy," She wails into my shoulder. Her reaction makes me laugh.

"Oh, babe. I'm so happy, too. But we're going to have to finish getting ready because we have to get going to Thanksgiving."

We both come down the stairs from our level in the apartment to find most people are milling around anxious to jump into the waiting limousines. But Vanessa sees Sienna and bursts out crying and runs back upstairs. Sienna is hot on her heels.

"What did you do?" Evan's eyes narrow at me.

"Hey, why do you automatically assume I did something?"

"Because your wife just burst out crying as soon as she saw her best friend, and in chick talk, that means you have had a fight." He crosses his arms over his chest. Then I watch as Mom and Vanessa's mom rush upstairs also.

"Oh shit, it's big, isn't it? The wedding is off? You got cold feet?" Evan asks.

"Fuck you." I punch my best friend in the arm. "As if I'd be getting cold feet."

"Who's got cold feet?" Axel asks, joining our conversation.

"Christian, he's got cold feet about the wedding," Evan replies.

"Are you fucking serious?" Axel clips me around the head.

"Ouch." I frown at my brother. *"I don't have cold feet,"* I shout at Evan and Axel.

"Okay, okay." Axel puts his hands up defensively.

"Then why was Ness crying?" Evan asks.

"Ness was crying?" Axel questions.

"Would you two fuckers just shut up for a moment and let me explain."

"This should be good," Evan huffs. I give him a death stare.

"It's early, but Ness just found out she's pregnant." Evan and Axel's jaws drop, both equally stunned by the news. "What, nothing to say now, fuckers?" I goad them. My question breaks their surprise, and they both congratulate me.

"Fuck... that means I'm going to be an uncle?" Axel looks pale as the realization of my news sets in.

I grab him on the shoulder. "You're going to be the best uncle there is." I can feel myself getting a little teary-eyed. Shit, can men catch pregnancy hormones? Axel pulls me into another hug, this time a little tighter as we both thump each other on the back like men do.

"I'm so proud of you, bro," Axel mumbles into me.

"I can't believe it, I'm going to be a dad." The words hitching in my throat.

"Fuck, I love ya," Axel responds, and for the first time in a long time, Axel and I are really connected.

"Welcome to the club, man." Evan hugs me. "And I guess if we're dropping bombshells... Sienna and I are having another baby as well."

Axel and I both stare at Evan in shock. "No way, man." I hold onto his shoulder.

"Yeah, we just found out, too." He has the biggest smirk rising on his face.

"Shit, what the hell was in the water in Vegas? Because you're both knocked up from it. Keep that voodoo shit away from me," Axel moans.

Evan and I both look at each and realize we both knocked up our girls while on holiday. We give each other a high-five. "We need to celebrate." Evan indicates for us to follow him downstairs to the sitting area where I notice our fathers are all set up, chilling and chatting away.

"Dad," I call out, seeing the old man reclining in the oversize lounge, watching football highlights on the big screen. He gets up and hugs me.

"Happy Thanksgiving, son," he says with a smile.

"Happy Thanksgiving, Pop," I reply, and my dad stills.

"What did you call me?"

"Or would you rather grandad or even grandpop?"

"What are you saying? Are you drunk?" He's not sure if I'm joking or not.

"Ness and I are going to have a baby." That's when I see it, tears quickly well in his eyes as he comes for me again, pulling me into a big, tight, dad hug.

"I'm going to be a grandpa?" he asks. I nod. "Holy shoot," he says with a shocked expression on his face. "I am so proud of you, son. So damn proud."

"Thanks, Dad."

"We were just about to celebrate," Axel adds.

"Sienna is pregnant as well," I tell Dad Evan's good news.

"No way, that's fantastic. Little Ryder will have a sibling." He congratulates Evan and his dad.

"I think this calls for a round of bourbon and cigars," Evan calls out from the bar, and we all agree.

THE THANKSGIVING MEAL WAS AMAZING. We looked out over the Seine, the Parisian skyline before us with all her famous icons. Sebastien put on an incredible feast, a totally new spin on our traditional Thanksgiving banquet, but no one cared as the food was to die for. If he cooks as well as this for our wedding, then it's kind of going to be spectacular.

Ness explained that she couldn't keep the news any longer and told her mom, Sienna, and Sienna's mom. She said that reality hit her when she saw Sienna with Ryder, that's why she ran back upstairs, realizing she was going to have a little baby in her arms next Thanksgiving. She couldn't believe Sienna was pregnant as well, and she was so excited that they would be having babies together. Ness started going on and on about baby stuff, and if I'm honest, I might have tuned out. My head was spinning just finding out I was going to be a dad, let alone all this crap I'm going to have to buy.

Last year, we started a tradition of standing up after dinner and telling everyone what they are thankful for, and so we have kept the tradition this year too.

"I'm thankful for the amazing opportunities that I have been given this year." Derrick starts off his list of what he's thankful for. This could be interesting. "I am also thankful that I look this good at thirty." We all chuckle. "I'm also thankful for Mr. and Mrs. Taylor for getting busy one night and producing Axel and Christian." My poor parents almost choke on their meal. "Because your boys gave me the most life-changing gift for my birthday, I'll never forget it." The room bursts out laughing.

"Awe, my boys were raised right. They would have given you something nice for your birthday." Her reply makes everyone laugh and Derrick grin.

"Oh yes, Mama Taylor, they knew exactly what I wanted," Derrick smirks, and Axel quickly places his hand over Derrick's mouth.

"It wasn't really anything worth mentioning," Axel adds. This makes the boys erupt into laughter. Mom and Dad look around at the teenage sniggering going on around the table.

"Love, I don't think we want to know what happened," Dad mentions to Mom.

It's my turn to stand up and tell everyone what I'm thankful for. The list is long. "I'm thankful that this beautiful woman beside me..." I turn to where Ness is sitting and take her hand in mine, "... decided that she wanted to take a chance on love, and I was the one she wanted to experience it with." Our mothers are lapping this up. "I'm also thankful that my wife is in good health, and that I get to spend forever with her." Vanessa squeezes my hand, and I can already see her eyes becoming glassy. "I'm also so thankful that she allowed me to knock her up." The table goes quiet as the words sunk in.

"No bloody way," Derrick screams.

"Yep, Ness and I are having a baby," I announce to our nearest and dearest. The whole table erupts into hollers of congratulations.

52

VANESSA

"I can't believe you two hussies are knocked up at the same time." Derrick pouts as the boys watch the Thanksgiving football game in the sitting room.

"What can I say, Vegas!" I sip my mineral water.

"You guys can have a joint baby shower," Camryn squeals.

"No, I don't want to take it away from Ness. This is her first baby, and she should get to enjoy it," Sienna adds.

"What? No, we can definitely have a joint party. It would be silly to have two separate ones when the same people would be going to both," I tell her.

"Yeah, I know, it's just…"

"Stop it, I don't mind sharing. It will be heaps of fun."

"I'm so excited. I don't get to plan many baby showers. I am planning your baby shower, aren't I?" Camryn asks.

"Um… hello, of course. Who else would I have plan it?"

"Oh my God, imagine if these two beans grow up and marry each other," Derrick adds.

Sienna and I look at each other and laugh. "That would be so cute," Charlotte adds.

"Looks like Dirty Texas 2.0 is starting to take shape," Isla jokes.

"That would be so awesome, the kids following in their daddy's footsteps," Stacey adds.

"No, no, no. I'm surrounded enough by egomaniac rock stars, I don't need my kids to follow in their footsteps." I shudder at the thought of a little Christian running around on stage, chatting up girls. Nope, no way, not for my boy.

"So, what do you think you're having?' Derrick asks.

"Um... a baby?" I joke. He flips me off.

"No, do you think you're having a boy or a girl?" he asks the question again.

I shrug. I mean, for months I have had no idea I was pregnant, let alone imagining if it's a boy or a girl.

"As long as it's healthy, that's all I want." I give my nonexistent belly a rub.

"Could you imagine Evan and Christian with daughters?" Isla asks. "It would be karma for all their womanizing years." We all burst out laughing at the thought, but I do have a small pang of excitement imagining me with a daughter, then flashes of a little sandy blond boy with whiskey-colored eyes filter through my mind, just like his daddy. I wonder what you are, little nugget?

"Imagine the fashion if they are girls," Derrick gasps. "I know Ryder rocks the coolest kid's clothes ever, but a little girl running around..." I can see Derrick salivating.

"You need to open up a Wyld Jones' children's boutique," Charlotte suggests. Sienna and Derrick go still.

"Why the fuck have we not thought of this?" Derrick turns to Sienna.

"Um... because we have been so busy running the boutique and your business, plus possibly trying to expand into the shop next door if we can get it."

Next door to the boutique is a two-story shop. Upstairs has

offices, and downstairs has a shop front. They found out that the owner has gone bankrupt, and the building is up for sale. Sienna wants to use the money that Beau gave her from the divorce to buy it.

"We could move the adult shop into the new building, and upstairs could be the styling side of the business, and the next door could be for the children's boutique." I can see Derrick's legs shaking with excitement.

Sienna pauses for a moment. "But we don't know anything about children's fashion."

The room erupts into laughter. "Si, the fact that Ryder has his own Instagram account with over a hundred thousand followers suggests you know about children's fashion," I remind her. She rolls her eyes at me.

"But, that's just taking cute photos of my boy, but doing business out of it?"

"Look at the Kardashian's. Once they started popping out children, people wanted to know about what they were wearing, just like Ryder, only he's way cooler," Derrick adds. "You're spending more money on children's clothes than you do your own at the moment. Think of all the rich mummies wanting to dress their kids in the coolest fashions just like Sienna Wyld."

Sienna smiles at him. "I do go kind of crazy looking for kids' clothing for him, and now with another on the way…"

"You could call it Wyld, instead of Wyld Jones, that way, it would be different branding to our adult shop," Derrick suggests. This gives Sienna a chance to pause.

"What, you don't want your name on it?" She looks a little hurt.

"Oh, no babe, that's not at all what I was thinking. I think it should be a separate brand under our Wyld Jones' banner. I could concentrate on the styling and adult side, especially now we have men's fashion, and you could concentrate on the children's side."

"There's a shit ton of money in children's fashion," Charlotte adds. "The amount of photography work my friends are doing for couture children's fashion is crazy."

Sienna listens to Charlotte's words. "But I just found out I'm having another baby, D. How am I going to deal with Ryder, buying real estate, and adding a new business to the mix plus everything else going on in my life?"

Derrick puts a reassuring hand on her knee and smiles at her. "We hire the best people, and we get good staff around us. We're already starting to amass an awesome team, and we can hire more people."

"Don't forget you have me," Stacey adds.

Sienna smiles at her.

"Stacey found our staff, she can do it again. Stacey could take over the running of all the other stuff, and you can concentrate on discovering the best brands for the boutique," Derrick explains to her.

"Plus, don't forget Ryder has amassed a huge following on Instagram, and they will all want what he has. I bet if you open up the children's boutique to online orders, you'll have a runaway success because all these mothers will want to dress their children like him." I give her my two cents worth.

"Ryder is pretty cute, and he does have awesome style." Sienna smiles. "You sure we can do this, D? I mean, it's a lot of work."

Derrick gives her the biggest smile. "I think it's kind of a perfect business idea. We can now dress the whole family."

This makes Sienna laugh. "When you put it like that, yeah, I guess it makes perfect sense. Okay, let's do it. Evan is going to kill me, but oh well."

"Just suck his dick, he'll be fine," Derrick adds.

53

CHRISTIAN

We just said goodbye to the ladies as they head off to their hotel. We're at the Monaco marina, where Nate is standing at his ship's tender waiting for us.

"Good day, fellas," he calls out in his crisp British accent, looking every inch the billionaire businessman that he is. "Welcome to your last weekend of freedom," Nate declares as I greet him.

"It's already too late for that, man, he's been married to Ness for months now," Axel corrects him.

"True, well, you can still enjoy the weekend, anyway." He slaps me on the back. Nate ushers us toward the luxury tender, all sleek and shiny with buttery soft leather. "Hold on, boys, this is going to be fast." One of his crew starts up the motors, the rumble vibrating through us as he slowly pushes the throttle weaving us between the multimillion-dollar yachts moored around us.

As soon as we hit open water, he pushes the throttle to full, and we zoom out across the waves. The freezing sea spray hits us as we bump over the waves. It's not long before we reach a super sleek, white, chrome, and wood superyacht, the kind young boys would pin onto their bedroom walls and probably jerk off to from time to time. Yep, the inner teenage boy in me is getting a stiffy over the vessel in front of me.

We pull up alongside the boat, and Nate's very good-looking female crew greets us, wearing long-sleeved, extremely fitted white polos with tight navy booty shorts that leave nothing to the imagination. Meaning it's bloody cold, and I don't need the wind to tell me that. "Welcome, Mr. Taylor," a blonde coos as she helps me from the bobbing boat.

"Thank you," I reply as I quickly let go of her soft hand. Don't want her getting any ideas. This may be my bachelor party, but I'm most definitely a happily married man.

"Welcome to Paradise, boys." Nate smiles, the gold word 'Paradise' scrawled across the side of the boat.

"I think I'm going to like Paradise," Axel mumbles as the brunette he's with gives him a flirty giggle. I roll my eyes because that used to be my life.

"God, I was a douchebag," I chuckle to myself as I follow Nate through the teak interior of the boat.

"Glad I'm not the only non-single guy here," Evan whispers to me as we walk.

"I got your back, bro."

"As long as Nate has told these ladies you and I are off their menu, it should be okay." I look at Evan freaking out over some chicks. It's kind of funny. It's amazing what a good woman can do to a notorious womanizer.

"This is the main saloon," Nate points out. And wow, everything is glass, chrome, or white, very sleek and modern. There's a bar set up to one side where a beautiful woman is making drinks. She gives us a flirty smile and continues working. In the middle of the room is a large U-shaped sofa, and in front of that is a big-screen television.

"Anything you need up here, Nadia will be happy to assist

you." Nate points to the bar lady, who waves at us. She seems to have lost a couple of buttons off her top, exposing her generous cleavage. Look away, Christian, look away.

Nate takes us back out into the foyer and to a set of spiral stairs. "These lead to your bedrooms. Each room has your name marked on it. There's staff on call any time of the day if you should need it. They can cater to anything you desire, and I mean anything."

"On the first deck, we have another bar," Nate states as he gestures toward it and points to another gorgeous female attendant. "The dining room is also on the first deck, and upstairs we have the play area." We follow him up the teak staircase to where we find the Jacuzzi, sun loungers, and another big-screen television.

"As this is Christian's bachelor party, and as he will not be partaking in the usual bachelor-style shenanigans, the rest of you boys are able to sample the delights that I have arranged for you. As you have guessed, my staff is very good-looking." Well, no shit, Nate. "That's because most of them are staff members from my European clubs, and I have asked them to join me on my boat to have fun this weekend with you. They all have Paradise Club wristbands, so you can see what they are into. Of course, you'll have access to my club here in Monaco whenever you wish to use it, ask any one of the normal crew, and they can arrange a tender to take you back to the marina.

"Now, Chris, I know you have more friends coming along later tonight who will be meeting you at the casino. If you wish to bring the party back to the boat, then that's fine. Of course, only people who have been vetted by myself will get access to the club if you so wish to party there as you can understand the need for exclusiveness." I nod, I don't really care about the club unless Ness wants to have some fun there, but now that she's pregnant, maybe it isn't a good idea.

"You guys are probably ready for some lunch. If you want to

take a seat down in the main dining saloon, lunch is ready to be served."

Okay, not at all what I was expecting for lunch. There on one of the tables is a naked lady, and she's covered in sushi. Nate smirks at me. The rest of the boys, except for Evan, are enjoying the sight as they start to take bits off her body. On the other side of the naked lady is another table set up full of man food. There are trays of buffalo wings, sliders, tacos, hot dogs, and no naked lady. Evan and I decide to tuck in over there.

"How's Ness feeling?" Evan asks.

"She's okay, no throwing up yet, but I'm guessing she might be a little early."

"Each woman is different. This time Sienna says she feels different, I mean our first baby was a surprise... we had no idea, and again this baby is a super surprise even though we have been trying. But this time, she's much more sensitive to smells. That's how we knew, she started to gag at the smell of coffee, then my cologne, and so on." He chuckles.

"Smells make them sick?" I question him. Shit, I had no idea.

"Yep, especially at the start. She will also go off certain foods, but I'll say they do get a hell of a lot hornier." My eyes widen, and Evan laughs. "I thought my dick was going to fall off with the amount of sex Sienna wanted. Man, I thought I had a high sex drive, but hers was crazy. I had to beg her to stop harassing me because I needed a break."

This makes me laugh. I remember now that I sent him a box of horny goat weed to help with his stamina. Shit, maybe that prank is going to come back to me. "I guess I better stock up on horny goat weed, then."

Evan elbows me in the side. "Not going to lie, man, I tried some of it, and it fucking helps. I still have a billion boxes left. I might send them to you, you're going to need it." We both burst out laughing.

"Do you want another boy?"

Evan smiles before saying, "Yeah, it would be great for Ryder to have a brother, but if it's a girl, I'll be happy with that. But man, I'm scared shitless if it's going to be a girl. I am going to have to carry a shotgun around because I don't want a fucker like me turning up trying to get into my daughter's pants." I start to laugh, then I realize Ness could be pregnant with a girl as well.

"Fuck, no way, man. No way in the world will I be letting a rock star date my little girl… nope, never."

"We'll both have to get shotguns then, and maybe I'll train Ryder as well so he can make sure no fuckers mess with his little sister." We both nod in agreement.

"Or we could have boys and then not worry about any of that stuff."

"True, but then we'd have to worry about groupies and gold diggers," Evan reminds me. Either way, we're screwed.

"Do you think I'm going to be a good dad?" I ask, feeling a little vulnerable about what a big thing this is, bringing a little person into the world.

"Man, if I can do it, you can do it. Those little fuckers change you. They are the best things in the entire world, even when they are screaming at two in the morning, or shitting themselves, or pissing on you, or vomiting God only knows what like a damn exorcist. Even dealing with all that, you still love them to death. So yeah, I think you're going to be a good dad, and don't worry if you don't know what you're doing, you'll work it out.

"Plus, I kind of take my cues from Si. She seems to know what to do most of the time. I think it's ingrained into women, this special knowledge on how to deal with kids. She's fucking amazing, and Ness is going to be the same. And when you see her with your baby in her arms, rocking them back to sleep, that's when you realize that everything else you have in your life means nothing or isn't worth as much as that moment is right there."

Evan clasps my shoulder and squeezes it. "I'm here for ya anytime." He walks off back toward the rest of the guys.

Shit, my life is about to change and for the better.

54

VANESSA

"Oh my God, you're here," Camryn screams, wrapping her arms around Olivia, one of our closest friends from London.

"I have missed you so much, it's been too long," Olivia says with the cutest British accent. Oh, how I have missed hearing it. "And you!" She points at me. "Marrying a rock star in Vegas, oh the cliché of it all." She smiles at me as she wraps me in her arms.

Olivia is this petite little thing. The perfect English rose with her silky, chocolate brown hair, porcelain white skin, and ruby red lips. But it's those doe-brown eyes that pull you in.

"It has been too long," I say, looking at my old friend.

"I know, I have been so slack."

"Please, we understand." Camryn squeezes her hands. Olivia is the oldest daughter of the Duke of Northumberland. Her father has been suffering ill health for the past couple of years, and she gave up her career in international business to come home and run the estate for him, with no help from her younger sister, Penelope, I might add, who's too busy living the life of a socialite.

Olivia has turned the estate around from financial ruin to a multimillion-dollar business. She has opened the estate up for visitors and functions, especially weddings in the stunning gardens surrounding the property. She moved her parents to Edinburgh, where her father can get full-time medical care, and she has been living in that big old estate by herself for the past couple of years while her sister lives this exciting life in London.

"I'm so happy you're here." Sienna steps forward.

"No way, Sienna, is that you?" Olivia smiles, hugging her.

"I know it's been a while." Sienna caught up with Olivia a couple of times when she visited us in London when she was married to Beau.

"Ness told me you're married to a rock star and had a baby."

Sienna smiles before confirming, "Yep, sure did, and couldn't be happier."

"The party is here." Derrick busts through the door with three very hot men behind him. "I have brought the entertainment," he smirks as the men enter our penthouse and make their way over to where the makeshift bar is set up. All the women in the room track their movements as they start taking off their clothes.

"Derrick," I squeal.

"What? Hello, this is a bachelorette party." Thankfully, the men stop at their boxer briefs. Each of them ties an apron around themselves and quickly pull off their underwear. My eyes widen, and I shoot Derrick a glare. He just smiles and blows me a kiss.

"Is this Lady Olivia Pearce I see before me?" Derrick asks cheekily.

"Is that Sir Derrick of Boner I see before me," she replies. A joke the two of them had when they would catch up in London. Derrick always believed he should've been a royal. He whisks her off her feet, the five-foot-nothing there is of her.

"Milady, I have missed you." He gives her a big wet kiss on her cheek. "I've heard my princess has been locked up in the castle for a while. Thankfully, Sir Derrick is here to save the day. I bet the princess is pretty horny."

"Derrick," she gasps, her cheeks turning a lovely shade of pink.

"Hmm." He scrutinizers her. "I can tell, sweetheart, it's been a while, hasn't it?" Olivia rolls her eyes at him. "And I'm not talking about the manual kind of play." Olivia turns a deeper shade of pink.

"Derrick, leave her alone." Camryn comes to her rescue.

"Cammie, this girl needs me. Look at my princess, she has been stuck up in that tower waiting for her Prince Charming to come along, but he has been waylaid by some skanky wench. It's my duty to help her."

Derrick is probably right. Olivia was always the good girl because of who she was related to. The media always watched her every move, and she never wanted to give her family any scandal, unlike her sister, who didn't care what people thought of her. Penny would regularly be on the news for dating married men, sunbathing topless in St. Bart's, and partying her way around Europe every summer while poor Olivia kept her in the lifestyle she had become accustomed to. If it weren't for Olivia giving up her life and turning the estate around, Penny would never have the money to fund her extravagant lifestyle, plus it doesn't help that her parents indulge Penny.

"Actually, Derrick, I'm engaged." The room goes quiet, and we all freeze.

"Engaged," Derrick says, slowing, nearly stumbling over his words.

"Yes, it's only just happened." Her cheeks go pink again.

"How the hell did I not know about this?" Camryn asks.

"Honestly, it's not a big deal." She shrugs her shoulders.

"You're telling me getting engaged isn't a big deal?" Derrick asks.

"No, well, not for me, anyway." Olivia frowns. "It's not like we got engaged because we love each other." You could hear a pin drop.

"What do you mean?" I ask.

"My father is dying..." Tears well up in Olivia's eyes, and she tries to push them back, but a couple escape.

"Hey, come here." Derrick pulls her into his lap and wraps himself around her. She gives him a weak smile.

"Dad's best friend is Duke of Roxburghe, and they believe if I marry his son, that will strengthen both of our estates. My father agrees with him, and so they have arranged for me to marry his son, Marquess Edmund Lumley."

"It's the twenty-first century, arranged marriages don't exist," Charlotte pipes up.

"Unfortunately, in noble circles, the practice is alive and kicking." She smiles sadly at us.

"At least tell me the man is good-looking and not old enough to be your father," Derrick adds.

This makes her laugh, "No, no, far from it." She takes her phone out of her bag and types into it, then turns the screen to Derrick. His jaw drops.

"I'd let him arrange anything on me." He takes the phone and hands it around. All the women agree, the man is hot.

"Yep, I could've done a lot worse in the looks department. But the problem is... he's a notorious womanizer, and I'm... well..." She lets the words trail off.

"You're what? A beautiful woman? A smart, intelligent, sexy woman?" Derrick answers for her.

Olivia blushes. "Thank you, but I mean, I'm... well... you know, not as experienced as he is. I have only been with a couple of men, and they were lackluster at best." Looking down at her hands, she twists them in knots, embarrassed by her confession.

"Then, it's lucky you have come to the right place, especially when we're partying with rock stars." Derrick smiles at her. "Think of me as your white knight of non-virtue here to corrupt you." This makes her laugh. "You want to learn things that will help you feel more confident in the bedroom with his royal hotness... then you're going to get the best education this weekend. I'm sure one of the Dirty Texas boys would love to show you the ropes."

"Just not Evan," Sienna pipes up.

"Or Christian," I add.

"Yes, yes, ladies, retract those claws, and Finn is off-limits." He looks at Isla.

"Remember, I'm staying strong," Isla adds.

"Yeah, not this weekend, you're not, I'm totally psychic, and you two are totally doing the nasty. And probably not Oscar 'cause he and Stacey have some *Fifty Shades of Grey* thing happening."

Stacey just shrugs and smiles.

"That leaves Axel. Yes, he's kind of perfect. I bet he'd totally be up for some sexual experimenting."

Olivia shakes her head. "He's too experienced for me."

"No, he is perfect, seriously, plus you're totally his type. He likes brunettes, and we all know Axel doesn't do relationships." Everyone nods in agreement.

"I'm pretty sure Axel could get any woman he wants. There's no way in the world he'd look at me," Olivia tells Derrick, who just laughs.

"Um... hello, have you not heard about Derrick Jones, stylist to the stars? I can so totally transform you, but you're already gorgeous."

Olivia gives him a big smile. "Okay, why not. It's the only

weekend I'm going be able to do something reckless, go big or go home," she says.

"That's what I like to hear. First things first, stand up." He pushes her off the chair. "Now, sit down right here." He motions her to take his place on the chair. "Seeing as Ness is already married and won't even look at another beefcake because... well, she doesn't have to as she gets to screw Christian Taylor every night." I give Derrick a high-five, damn right, I do. "I think Olivia should take her obligatory bachelorette lap dance instead."

The girls all agree, and Olivia looks like a deer caught in headlights. Derrick stands over her. "Do you trust me, princess?" She nods her head slowly. "I promise I won't push you too far, just enough to have some fun." Olivia slowly nods her head.

"Great, boys," Derrick calls out to the three naked waiters. "I need you to shake what your mama gave ya for this beautiful woman sitting here." He points to Olivia, who's sitting up so straight she's as stiff as a board. The three men nod, one of them plays around with his phone and connects it up to the stereo in the room. Stripper music starts pumping through the speakers.

The three men move closer to Olivia in time with the music. Her cheeks have turned pink, and I can see the red flush rushing up to her neck. The rest of the room is hollering and urging her on. Before long, I'm joining them. This is what friends are for—to corrupt the innocent.

We watch as a wide-eyed Olivia notices that the three topless waiters are naked under their aprons, and she lets out a gasp when one of them places her hands on his bare ass. This kind of sets us off into hysterics. Derrick is dancing around the room, encouraging her. He pours a couple of shots of something down her throat, which makes her wince. The men continue giving her a lap dance, their hands roaming all over her body, her hands slowly and cautiously, exploring theirs.

"That's it, princess, squeeze their butts," Derrick hollers at her. She does it, and it makes her giggle. "Now, test what's under the apron." Olivia stills and shakes her head, but one of the strippers grabs her hand and places it on his hardening dick. Olivia's mouth forms the perfect 'O' in surprise as the stripper moves her hand up and down along his length. Not sure what kind of strippers Derrick bought, but he obviously got the all-inclusive type. Olivia is shrieking and giggling and trying not to look at what her hand is doing. Derrick gives her a couple more shots, which loosen her up.

"What else do you want to do?" Derrick asks Olivia. She looks at him, confused. "These men are all yours for the night if you want them," Derrick tells her, and she shakes her head. One of the men leans over and nuzzles her neck, making her squeal, and she lets go of the other man's dick.

"Liv, you don't have to do anything you don't want to do," I call out to her over the music. She nods, and I can see she's looking a little shocked.

"Okay, fellas, we might take a break." Derrick pulls the music, and the gyrating men slow their thrusts. "I think we could do with some more drinks," he tells the topless waiters. They understand their duties and quickly make their way back to the bar. "You did so well," Derrick tells Olivia while she buries her face in her hands.

"His dick was so thick, that can't be real," she gasps, finally looking at us all. We burst out laughing. "What?" she looks at us, all confused.

"I think you have definitely been with the wrong men, then," Camryn adds, which makes Olivia groan.

"I'm such a reject."

"Hey, no. Remember I was married for ten years before I hooked up with Evan. I had such self-doubt because I hadn't been with that many people, but let me tell you when the sex is that good, it doesn't matter how inexperienced you are, human instinct takes over, and you just go with the flow," Sienna tells Olivia.

"Well, we all know I was a slut before hooking up with Christian, so I have no advice."

"Same here, babe, before Harris," Camryn adds, we high-five each other.

"Thanks, guys. I'm sorry to have kind of crashed your bachelorette party like this, Ness."

"Hey, I am most definitely not touching thick, stripper dick, so someone should be enjoying it."

55

VANESSA

We're back from our amazing weekend in Monaco, and all the craziness of the bachelor and bachelorette parties are over. Thankfully, Christian behaved himself, even though there were some strippers and naked women running around. I guess it was no different than the three naked waiters in our suite.

Today is an exciting day as we get to meet our little nugget. Our parents are still here and are at home, eagerly waiting for the first pictures of their grandbaby.

"I'm so nervous." I hold Christian's hand as we wait in the doctor's office. Today is the first day that we get to check out our baby, and I just hope nothing is wrong. Morning sickness has kicked in like the bitch that she is, making me throw up each time I brush my teeth, which defeats the purpose of cleaning my teeth.

"Everything is going to be okay with our little nugget, okay?" Christian reassures me. I know it is, but it's still kind of scary. I just hope the baby is healthy.

"Vanessa Taylor," the doctor calls my name, and we follow her from the waiting room to her office.

"Welcome, I'm Doctor Robyn Phillips, and I'll be your obstetrician for this pregnancy." The perky blonde smiles at me as my eyes look around the room at all the smiling photos of babies that she has delivered and all her awards. I also give her extra points for not ogling my husband like the receptionist did. She pretty much ignores him within reason.

"Now, today, we want to check the baby's heartbeat and double-check how far along you are." She points to a second room where a bed is situated with an ultrasound machine. "This is exciting, hearing your baby's heartbeat for the first time." She smiles, ushering us into the room. "Please jump up on the bed, pull your top up, and open up your jeans so I can see your belly."

I lay back and unbutton my jeans. Note to self, wear more accessible clothing rather than my favorite skinny jeans, which, if I'm honest, don't really fit me like they used to. "Sorry, this is going to be cold," she says as she squirts some gel onto the machine and places it onto my belly. Instantly, the machine's screen lights up, and the heartbeat can be heard straightaway. She moves the scanner around my belly, looking at different aspects of the baby. "Oh, my," she gasps. Christian and I flinch.

"What is it, Doc?" I can hear the concern in Christian's voice.

"There's a second baby, right behind this one." She points to the two little jelly beans on the screen. Um, what did she just say?

"There's two?" I squeak out.

"Yes, two little babies. Congratulations, you're having twins." Thank God I'm lying down. Otherwise, I think I'd have fainted from the shock.

"Shit, twins," Christian mumbles.

"This is your fault." I kick him from where I'm laying down, and this makes him chuckle.

"I'm a twin." He smiles at the doctor.

"Well, that explains it. Both heartbeats are very strong. It's too early to know what sex they are. You'll have to come back in a month's time. I'd say that you're about eleven weeks, so you will be due in June."

Wow, this all seems so real now. June next year is a long way away. We'll have not only one little baby arriving but two little Taylor babies coming into our lives. After the roller-coaster year I've had, this is just the icing on the top. I clean myself up, and the doctor talks to us about the extra pressures I'll have on my body as I will be carrying twins. She advises me that I probably won't make it to term as they like to deliver twins a little earlier. She prints off the photos of our little jelly beans and hands the photos to us.

CHRISTIAN and I are silent as we walk to the car.

"Fuck," Christian says as he bursts out laughing. "Knowing my luck, it will be twin girls. I'm so fucked." He rakes his hands through his light brown hair.

"I don't care what we have as long as they are healthy. It would be cool if we had a boy and a girl, that way we don't have to have anymore," I add.

"What? You only want two kids?" Christian questions me.

"Well, kind of, yeah."

"I thought we were going to have four."

"Four?" I squeal, settling into the soft leather of Christian's car.

"Two boys and two girls," he says confidently.

I burst out laughing. "Mr. Taylor, you surprise me every day. How about we see how we handle the first two, and then we can negotiate."

"Let me see, let me see." My mum accosts us as we arrive home. We got extra sets of the photos printed for this very reason. I hand them over to Christian's parents.

"Oh my, twins." Christian's mum notices first.

"Twins?" Mum questions.

"Yep, right here, two little jelly beans." His mum shows her.

"You're going to have two babies?" Mum's eyes widen. "We're going to have two grandbabies." She starts to cry.

"Yep, we sure are. Twins." My brain is still trying to work it all out.

"Do we know if they are boys or girls yet?" Mum asks,

"Not until next month, after the wedding in the new year."

"As long as they are healthy, sweetheart, I don't mind." She gives me a teary hug. "I never thought this day would come after everything you have been through." It's been a tough year, being diagnosed with the BRACA gene, having a double mastectomy, thinking I might not have children, and months later, here I am getting everything I never dreamed possible.

"I'm going to stay healthy for my little babies," I promise her.

"Twins," Derrick shouts as we sit around the dinner table at our regular weekly dinner catch-up, this time at my house. Our parents are currently in Texas. Christian's family wanted to show them their home state, so they are visiting them for a week before we have to head to England for the wedding.

"Two little Christians running around. Shit," Axel curses as he sits down with his beer.

"Twice the fun," Christian adds.

"I remember what it was like to be stuck with you, those poor kids," he ribs him.

"Do you know what you're having yet?" Isla asks, staring at the little image of our babies.

"No idea."

"I hope they are girls, just to torture Chris," Oscar announces, and my husband flips him off.

"Yep, I think they will be girls, too," Isla adds.

"As if you're a radiographer, you can't tell from this image," Finn argues with her.

"Whatever, I just have a feeling," she grumbles back.

"I think Sienna and Evan are having a girl," Stacey adds,

"Nah, I think it's a boy, I mean my swimmers are pretty potent," Evan adds. Chris throws a cushion at him.

"Are you saying my swimmers aren't any good? Because I created two kids at once, I'm so potent."

"Jesus, they are arguing about who's stuff is more potent. I don't need to know anything about my brother's swimmers, thank you very much," Charlotte groans.

"So, when do we find out about the sexes of your babies?" Derrick asks.

"Doctor told us next month, so after we get back, they should be able to tell, unless you have a blood test like I did last time and found out," Sienna explains.

"Okay, so we hold off on decorating the nursery, then," Derrick states.

"Hold on, decorating the nursery? Isn't it a little early to be doing that?" Christian grumbles.

"Um... no, there's so much to do, and you now have two, Mr. Taylor, so twice the amount of work."

"And twice the amount of money," Evan adds.

"Hey, Mr. Moneybags, don't you dare grumble about dollars because you loved how awesome Ryder's nursery was," Derrick argues.

"Yes, yes, it was pretty cute, but the bills were not."

"Hey, Kim, how are you?" I pick up the call from Camryn's business partner.

"It's Cammie."

My heart starts pounding. I can't handle it if something has happened to her. "Is she okay? What's happened?" I grip the sofa beside me as Christian's head pops up from where he is in the kitchen. He sees my death grip on the sofa and rushes over to help sit me down.

"Harris is a cheating bastard," Kimberly swears down her phone.

Christian shakes his head in disgust.

"What? No, he appeared so devoted to her."

"Yeah, I thought the same until I saw it with my own eyes."

"You saw him cheating on her?" I'm in utter shock. I never saw this coming.

"Damn right, I did, and poor Cam was right beside me when I did."

"What the..."

"We had a last-minute holiday party to organize last night. They were willing to pay megabucks for it, so we took the job. Big fools we were, the fucking party was Harris' engagement party."

"What the fuck?" Even Christian looks shocked.

"Cammie and I organized his fucking engagement party to someone else."

"That fucker, that fucking fucker. How? Why? I don't understand. How did Cam not know that Harris was with someone else?"

"Apparently, he's quite good at keeping secrets. Why the hell would he do something like this to her? I don't understand. Men can be such fuckers sometimes."

"How is she?"

"She's holed up in her apartment, she is a mess. But you know her, Cammie is going to put on a brave face, but it's a little hard when his engagement is flashed all over Page Six. It's the talk of the town. Their smiling faces are plastered everywhere. She can't escape it."

"I still can't believe him. What the hell kind of game does he think he's playing? Does his new fiancée know about Cam?"

"Probably, from the gossip I have heard, it's definitely not a marriage based on love and commitment," Kimberly says with a sneer.

"Fucking bastard. Do you need me to jump on the next plane and come to New York? I totally can."

"Actually, Olivia called, and Cam's decided to head to England a little earlier and help Olivia get things ready for your wedding."

"I'm in shock, Kim, I want to murder that fucker."

"You and me both."

"I should call her."

"She's on her way to the airport as we speak and has turned off her phone, Harris keeps calling her but give her a call when she lands. I'm sure she'd love to hear from you."

"Okay, will do."

"I better go, work is crazy. Take care and see you soon."

Then she's gone.

"I want to pummel him." Christian flexes his fist.

"Not before me, I can't believe him, and he's engaged. I just..."

Christian wraps his arms around my shoulders, comforting me as the tears start. "I don't get it, Cammie is beautiful, successful, rich in her own right, and she's a fucking catch. Not since Lance has she opened herself up like she did to Harris."

"I know, babe, I know. I don't understand men sometimes."

I give him a snort, "Damn right, men are confusing."

"Yes, but most men don't sneak around with a secret woman while they are publicly dating an awesome one. Also, they don't ask their girlfriend to plan the engagement party."

"I can't believe he fucked her over like this."

Christian rubs his hand along my tiny belly bump. "Babe, please don't stress about it, you're carrying important cargo now." He looks at me with concern in those whiskey-colored eyes. He's right. I don't want to stress out our babies.

"Hey, how are you going, babe?"

"I've been better." Camryn sounds defeated on the phone. I don't blame her.

"Seriously, Cam, I want to downright murder that two-timing bastard." This makes her chuckle.

"You and me both. I feel like a fool. Harris and I definitely didn't hide the fact that we were dating, and now this. Two seconds later, he's engaged to someone else. Was I not good enough?"

"What? No! He is the one who wasn't good enough for you. He's a lying, cheating fuckface," I tell her, feeling my anger bubble to the surface again.

"I should've seen it coming."

"How? How could anyone know that their boyfriend was organizing an engagement party to someone else?"

Camryn lets out a big sigh, "You're right, thank God I have your wedding to keep me occupied. Otherwise, I'd be sitting on the couch at home feeling sorry for myself."

"Camryn Starr never wallows on the couch over some man. She picks herself up and tells him to go fuck himself, then goes back out there and picks up an even hotter man to have some fun with."

This makes her chuckle. "All true, but this time, I don't know, Ness. This time I feel like he has broken me, and I hate him for it."

My stomach sinks. "I know, babe, you thought he might

have been the one, but isn't it better to find out now after only six months together rather than a lifetime?"

She's silent for a couple of moments. "Maybe you're right, at least I have the knowledge that your wedding is going to be filled with hot rock stars to keep me entertained."

"See the silver lining?" We both laugh, but I know it's too soon for her to think about anyone else.

"Ivy is coming up to visit me." Ivy is Camryn's younger sister, who owns her own luxury interior design business in London and decorates the homes of London's elite. She even helped Olivia renovate the castle.

"Oh, that's fantastic. You don't get to see each other much, I'm glad she will be there."

"Yeah, me, too. I better go, I'm shattered from my long flight. Thank you for checking in on me."

"Anytime, I love you, okay."

"I know, love you, too. I'll see you soon."

"Can't wait to squish you."

"Bye, Ness."

"Bye, Cam."

CHRISTIAN

"Welcome to Alnwick Castle," Vanessa's friend, Olivia, greets us at the door of the imposing castle. Ness showed me pictures of it, but it's so much grander than I had ever expected.

"Princess, so good to see you." Derrick gives Olivia a big hug. Then he turns to where Camryn is standing beside her. "Cammie, my Cammie, I'm going to kill that man. I am going to pull his balls off and shove them so far down his throat that he's going to choke on them." Camryn smiles at him weakly. He pulls her to him and gives her a hard, tight hug. When she pulls away, her eyes are glassy.

Then, it's Ness' turn. They hug each other and mumble things to one another.

"Come on inside, Sebastien and Yvette have just arrived," Olivia advises us. We make our way into the imposing castle, a fucking castle. Who would've thought I'd be getting married in one? Olivia explains the history of her family as we enter her home. She tells us how she's now the caretaker of this place while her father's in ill health. This place seems kind of huge for one person to be living in. I'm already lost. I really hope it comes with a map. How does she find the time to look after it? She must have help. How would you clean everything? You would finish one side of the castle and then have to start all over again.

Axel echoes the same sentiment. "You look after this all by yourself? No one else helps you? Don't you have a sister?"

How does Axel know she has a sister?

Olivia's cheeks pink as she responds to Axel's direct question. "It's my duty to help look after this estate as it has been in my family for four hundred years. I don't want to be the one who destroys its legacy. It keeps me very busy. My sister chooses to pursue other opportunities."

Axel and Olivia stare at each other for a fraction longer than is necessary. I notice Axel's nostrils flare, and his eyes turn molten. What's going on there? I know my brother is interested in beautiful women, and Olivia is very attractive. Of course, not my type, but she's most definitely his type physically. Ness told me stories about their time in London, and Olivia seems very proper, not all that wild, so I'd doubt Axel is interested, other than appreciating a good-looking woman.

"Where are all the hot men?" Derrick asks, pulling Olivia's attention away from Axel.

"Maybe some are in the village, but there are generally none around here." She shrugs.

"My poor little princess, now I understand why you needed to let loose in Monaco. You're locked up in the tower waiting for Prince Charming to come and save you, but there are none around for miles." Olivia's face pales, then turns red in embarrassment with Derrick's observations.

"D, now isn't the time," Sienna reprimands him. His eyes widen as he takes in all our families around us.

"Shit, sorry, princess." Derrick, for the first time, looks

embarrassed by the scene he has caused. Olivia quickly waves her hand in the universal sign not to worry and continues on her tour of the large estate.

"Sebastien is currently in the kitchen testing it out, and Yvette is setting up all the dresses in the parlor room. You all must be exhausted from your long journey. Camryn has your room keys and will escort you from here. I just have some business to attend to and will join you again for dinner tonight."

And with that, she's gone, my brother's attention following her until she is no longer in the room. I give him a look, but he just shakes his head. I hope he isn't thinking of doing anything with Olivia, she looks way too innocent for his tastes, and I don't need his antics to mess up my wedding, especially with Mom and Dad here. I narrow my eyes at him, and silent communication settles between us.

"Don't. It's not what you think," are the only words he mumbles to me, which surprises me. I shake my head because, honestly, I don't want to know.

"To the happy couple, here is your key. You have the main bedroom, which is on the top floor, and it's all ready for you." Camryn smiles at us. I may have asked her to do a couple of things in the room before we arrived.

I grab Vanessa and swing her up into my arms, making her squeal.

"Christian," she yells, making everyone laugh.

"No way, wife, I'm whisking you away to your turret, my princess."

"Oh, role play, kinky Christian," Derrick calls out, again making everyone laugh. I shake my head. I'm pretty sure my parents don't need to know I am whisking my wife away to have my wicked way with her. I ignore him and continue up the many flights of stone stairs.

"Babe, there are too many stairs."

"I don't care," I heave. There definitely are too many stairs, but I'm not wimping out. I finally make it to our room, and Vanessa swipes the key to open the door. I continue on through into the room, trying not to hit things.

"Wow, this is, oh my God, there's a fireplace… and… Christian…" She says my name breathlessly as I place her feet back onto the floor. "You…" words seem to fail her at the moment.

Turning her in my arms, I hold her face in my hands. "I wanted to make this perfect, all of it. I wanted to do it right." I take her lips between mine and slowly show her how much I love her. Vanessa's hands grip my sweater as the kiss deepens. I unwillingly break the kiss, and she whimpers, which makes me laugh. "Don't worry, angel, there's more to come, but I want you comfortable first."

I move her toward my romantic setup in front of the fire where a large fur rug has been placed. Around it is a scattering of plush cushions. To the left is a table filled with a platter of chocolate-dipped strawberries and a bottle of sparkling apple juice. She's off the hard stuff now that I have knocked her up. That thought still fills me with pride. Two large glass windows are on either side of the crackling fireplace, and I can already see the snow flurries begin to fall onto the gardens below.

I motion for Vanessa to sit on the rug and move some cushions around to make her comfortable. She snuggles in next to me, watching the snowfall. "This is so beautiful." We lay mesmerized by the flurries of snow.

"Not as beautiful as you." I kiss her temple, making her smile.

"We got pretty lucky, didn't we?" She turns to look up at me with those jade-green eyes that I love so much.

"Yeah, we did." I pause and enjoy the moment we're having before I take it to where I want it to go. "But not as lucky as you're going to be in a moment." I give her a wicked smile.

"Is that so, Mr. Taylor?" she questions, cocking an eyebrow at me.

"Oh, yes, it is, Mrs. Taylor. Now I think you're getting a little hot under the collar sitting here. It might be best if you take something off." I pull off my navy pullover, and Vanessa quickly gets rid of her white one.

"Now what?" she questions me with a bright smile across her beautiful face.

"I think you still seem a little flushed, best we take off these." I help her with her boots. "And these..." I pull her leggings off, but leave her underwear there for the moment, teasing my bride-to-be.

"I think you might be a little overdressed yourself," she says as her hands reach for the buckle of my belt.

"I think you're right, angel, let me quickly fix that for you." I kick off my boots and socks, and quickly pull my jeans off, my heavy dick pushing against the tight briefs. Vanessa's eyes travel to the very spot that's throbbing with need. She licks her lips, and my cock throbs even more under her weighty stare.

"This must go." I pull the long-sleeve T-shirt off over her head, mine joining hers on the floor. I sit back on my knees and take in my gorgeous wife, the glow from the fire illuminating her tanned skin beautifully, those jade eyes sparkling with desire and love. Her body is relaxed pressed against the cushions. I watch as her chest rises and roam my eyes further down her body, over the white cotton underwear she's wearing, and over the new curve of her belly. My hand reaches out and touches it.

"I can't wait until this starts growing." She gives me a yeah, right look. "No, babe, knowing that you're carrying our babies inside of you is the most magical thing I have ever seen. I can't wait to see these babies grow bigger every day. I know that I'm not going through it physically, but seeing it from this side, waiting for the day I can feel them moving around, is the most amazing gift anyone could ever give me."

My emotions bubble to the surface just like every time I think about our babies. It's an overwhelming feeling of pride, nervousness, and awe.

"Me, too, I'm kind of excited to see my belly change, just like it did for Sienna. I loved her belly. I know I am going to complain a lot about it because I'm sure it's going to be uncomfortable, and I have two of them inside me, but still, I think it's kind of amazing."

I gently kiss her belly. "I'm the luckiest man in the world." My kisses start to trail over her body moving from their original destination. Vanessa lets out a small purr of appreciation as I move around her body, over the new curves of her breasts, down her arms giving her goosebumps, over her hip bone, along the edge of her cotton underwear, teasing her, enjoying her squirm beneath my lips. I make my way back up her body, which is warm from the blazing fire, my lips trailing up the sensitive curve of her neck until I reach her perfect lips, ready for me.

My entire body is pressed against her, so I wrap my arms around her and roll onto my back. She lets out a moan. I pull a cushion from my side and place it under my head as my hands move to her hips as she moves our underwear-covered bits against each other. It feels just like high school, fooling around with your underwear on.

Vanessa moves against me, pressing herself harder against my needy dick. Whatever she needs, I'm happy to oblige. Her hands find the band of my boxer briefs and pull them down before she wraps them around my throbbing length. A hiss falls from my lips as she starts stroking me with her perfect rhythm.

"Babe, please," I start to beg because she's too good at stroking me. "I need..." I let out a groan as her mouth wraps around my dick. "I need... to be inside you." I gasp as her mouth works its magic. She just chuckles around my dick, which vibrates through my bones.

"I mean it, Ness, I. Need. To. Be. Inside. Of. You." I push her off my aching cock, and she just gives me a satisfied smirk. I watch as she pulls her white underwear to the side and positions herself over me sinking on my cock. "Yes," we both hiss as I fill her. We both stay still enjoying that first contact of us together before I start moving inside of her. Feeling her wet heat all around me is the best feeling in the world.

I watch as Vanessa's hands travel over her body as she rides me. Her hands trail over her breasts, giving her nipples a couple of quick tweaks, not for herself as she can't feel them since her surgery, but for my visual pleasure. Her teeth sink into her bottom lip as I press myself into her deeper, my fingers digging into her hips as I try to reach the places I know will make her moan. Vanessa matches my rhythm and presses herself into me, her hands falling to my shoulders so she can hang on, those nails digging into my fleshy skin as my rhythm increases.

"Yes, oh fucking yes," she moans as I feel myself hit the spot that gets her going. "There, just there, please..." She begs, chasing her orgasm, the ones that are becoming more intense with her pregnancy. Her nails dig in more, urging me on, urging me to take her over that edge. I'm frantic with need now as I try to give my wife the pleasure she's craving.

And there it is, the silent 'O' that forms on her mouth when I have hit the perfect sensitive spot enough times to get her over. I feel the spasm of her around me, the clenching of her pussy, the perfect sign letting me know I have hit the jackpot, the same one that starts my balls tingling, my dick throbbing even harder until I'm coming myself. My hands grip her harder, my entire body tingling with white heat and floating in pure ecstasy. Vanessa's lifeless body falls against my chest as she nuzzles into my neck.

"I love you, Christian."

"I love you, too, V."

The lull of jet lag makes us both fall asleep, contented and sated against the warmth of the fire.

VANESSA

Sebastien had put on an amazing dinner. I mean, the man is one of the world's best chefs, so I guess we couldn't expect anything less. The boys have retreated to the games room where they are playing pool and drinking whiskey or some boy stuff like that. Our parents have either gone to bed, not used to the jet lag, or are chilling out in the library, and us girls are in the parlor room roasting marshmallows around the fireplace, sipping hot chocolate, and dressed in our pajamas because fuck it, it's snowing outside, and I'm pregnant and want to be comfortable. All the girls and Derrick are huddled on the plush sofas watching the snow fall.

"I still can't believe it," Derrick says to Camryn. It's the first time we have seen her since the bombshell about Harris.

"You and me both." Camryn weakly smiles.

"And he seriously had no idea you were organizing it?" Sienna asks.

Camryn shakes her head.

"His father had set it all up," Kimberly adds. "Camryn has been busy with organizing your wedding and other things, so I took the initial call. If I had known, I'd never have done it." I can see that Kimberly feels awful that she didn't know Harris' family was setting Camryn up. It's a pretty low act.

"At least it was the talk of the town for being the best engagement party of the year." She smiles weakly. "So, I guess it kind of backfired because we're getting so much business off his engagement party."

"Karma," Isla adds.

"I know it might be too soon, but what eligible bachelors are coming to this wedding?" Derrick asks. Of course, he's always matchmaking.

"Derrick..." Camryn rolls her eyes at him.

"I'm sorry, Cammie, but I want to know. It's not all about you," Kimberly butts in as she nudges her friend who makes her laugh a proper laugh.

"We have the Sons of Brooklyn boys," Derrick rattles off.

"Except Blake," Charlotte whispers.

"Yes, yes, sweetie, he's all yours." Derrick smiles. "And we only have Axel left in Dirty Texas, but then again, if the serious fuck-me eyes he was throwing Olivia's way is any indication, then probably not."

Olivia stays quiet, but she's most definitely blushing.

"What about Nate? You know you would be in for a good time with him. I bet he's kinky as fuck," Derrick adds.

"I bet he's a playboy, he looks like one," Sienna adds.

We all nod in agreement. I guess if you own sex clubs around the world, then you're getting sex on tap.

"The California Bros. boys are coming as well," Isla adds.

"So, they will all be free unless Isla is hooking up with Wes on the sly." Derrick looks at Isla, who stays quiet.

"Wait..." Derrick picks up on her non-communication. "You've told us that nothing has happened between Wes and you?"

"You know I'm a hot mess."

"Isla." Derrick's voice lowers. "What's going on?"

"Fine, but I was never going to tell you guys because... well, because of your interrogations."

"But I thought you didn't like Wes like that?" I ask because keeping up with Isla's love life is so damn confusing.

"I don't, but I can still appreciate a hot-as-fuck guy, plus we're friends."

"Friends who obviously fuck," Derrick adds.

Isla rolls her eyes at him. "True, we have just taken our friendship to a different level."

"But why?" Sienna asks, equally invested in this soap opera as the rest of us.

"We got drunk one night, and one thing led to another."

"Issy, you aren't telling us all the juicy stuff," Derrick adds.

"Fine, he had just broken up with this skank he was seeing, who worked in his bar. I told him it was a stupid idea to hook up with his staff, but you know men, they are mesmerized by boobs." We all nod in agreement. "Anyway, he caught her stealing from the till, and he also found out she had a boyfriend who she liked to bang on the bar after hours."

"That sucks," Ivy, Camryn's sister, adds.

"Sure does. He came over and told me all about it, and I decided I'd cheer him up."

"By using your pussy, good idea." Derrick laughs.

"It wasn't like that." Isla makes a face at Derrick. "We just got drunk, and one thing led to another, and we slept together."

"Finn is going to be pissed if he finds out," Stacey tells her.

"Whatever, remember I'm on a Finn detox, so it doesn't matter."

"Seriously, Isla, how the hell do you get yourself into such predicaments?" I ask her.

Her shoulders sag. "I know I am a hot mess. I'm kind of a disaster, and I have no idea why."

We all burst out laughing at her.

"Um... it starts and ends with your feelings for Finn," Stacey tells her.

"Urgh, my feelings. Feelings get in the way and are annoying." She lets out a heavy sigh. "Look, Finn is an idiot, but so am I." She looks at us all, but we stay silent. "I know that the chances of Finn and I being together are slim. I know you all think I'm naïve, but things between us are a little more complicated than what looks like an old teenage crush." She looks defeated. "I now know I'm not enough for Finn," she says sadly. "But, we've had this thing between us going for so long, it's kind of become normal. I've tried to fight it, but we just keep falling back into old patterns. I need it to stop."

"Maybe it's time for a change," Charlotte tells her. "Like moving out of the home you share with Oscar."

"I haven't really lived on my own," Isla responds.

"Maybe a new job as well," Charlotte suggests.

Isla stills. "You mean leave Dirty Texas?" she questions her.

"Yeah, you have worked there your entire adult life. You're with them twenty-four seven. I have known you most of my life, Isla, and don't forget I'm the one who saw the two of you as kids. I know I was young, but I had eyes. Is being the band's assistant always what you wanted to do?"

"I think Charlotte is being Dr. Phil." Derrick smirks.

"I think she is..." Isla pauses, "... but I kind of think she might be right."

"I am?" Charlotte seems shocked.

"Yeah, all my life I have been at the boys' beck and call. Maybe it's time I find myself, find out what I want outside of Dirty Texas."

"Well, we need help," Sienna adds.

"That sounds awesome, but maybe I need to move further away from Finn. You know, instead of next door."

"Sebastien needs an assistant. He's so busy and needs someone who he can trust," Yvette adds.

"Working with Sebastien?" Isla's eyes widen.

"Yeah, you would be based in Europe, so that's pretty far from Finn," Yvette confirms with a smile.

"And you think he'd hire me? I mean I don't know anything about food or chefs or Europe."

Yvette chuckles, "I'm pretty sure working for Dirty Texas for all these years, you're way overqualified for him."

Isla turns to me. "Am I fucking things up for you and Dirty Texas Records if I think about leaving? I mean, you're going to be having a baby soon and..."

"Isla, don't worry about me, I can find a replacement. I just want you to be certain this is the right thing for you to do? Leaving Dirty Texas? Leaving Finn?"

"We know someone who can take over the PR for Dirty Texas," Camryn adds.

"Who?" I question her.

"Harper," she says with a smile. "I don't know why I didn't think of it sooner, but she'd be kind of perfect." Harper Rose runs a super successful PR firm in New York and is best friends with Camryn and Kimberly. She's also heir to the Rose's Hotel chain, a luxury brand throughout the world dealing in boutique hotels. Her older brother, Sam, took over from her father a couple of years ago, and her company runs their PR as well as many other successful brands. Why not add Dirty Texas to it for a while? I'll be at home knee-deep in dirty diapers. "She's coming to the wedding. You could talk to her about it?"

"She could even work from New York. I know the boys are looking at adding an East Coast office to the mix next year." My brain is working out all the logistics. "I think that would work. Depends on what the boys say."

"So, does that mean Isla can go on an adventure with sexy Sebastien?" Derrick adds.

"I can't see why not. I don't think Finn or Oscar are going to like it, but I think Isla deserves a break from all things Dirty

Texas that she has been dealing with over the years. Why not have a change? Maybe then Finn might realize what he has when Isla's not around anymore."

Isla nods. "This is kind of crazy, though?" I can see the wheels turning in her head. She wants to try something new but is scared, probably scared to leave the safe bubble she has created around herself.

"Yes, but you need a new adventure," Stacey adds.

"Forget Finn and start living," Derrick tells her.

"This is your time now, no regrets. This is about you, not them anymore," Charlotte gives her a pep talk.

"Okay, well, if Sebastien is okay with it, then, yeah, I think it's time for a new adventure."

We all cheer with our hot chocolates.

"MERRY CHRISTMAS," everyone sings as we sit down to open our presents. We woke to a full dusting of snow outside, which was pretty amazing to wake up on Christmas Day to a fully white Christmas. Ryder is crawling around like crazy and getting into all the presents. Of course, they are sky high, and he's more interested in pulling the paper off than what lies underneath.

"You have one more present." I hand Christian the oversized white box. Ryder zooms past us, sitting in his miniature Ferrari that Derrick bought him. It's a remote control and being controlled by Evan, who's having entirely too much fun with it. Christian is opening up the huge box, and there's tissue paper everywhere. He digs through it and comes to a red box. He looks up and smirks at me as he opens the next one, then the next one and the next one, until he gets to the last one, which is a pink box.

I didn't want to give anything away, so I had to disguise it. He slowly opens the pink box and sees the note that I wrote addressed to Daddy on it. He opens the pink tissue paper, and that's when I see he realizes what it is. Tears form in those whiskey eyes as his fingers touch the material. He's mumbling to himself, reading what's on it. Everyone is silent as they realize something big is happening. Then Christian pulls out the two baby onesies that say 'Girls Rock' across them. When he looks at me with all that emotion rolling off him, I break down, and tears fall down my cheeks.

"We're having girls?" he questions me. Everyone in the room gasps. All I do is nod my head, unable to speak. "But how?"

"Christian, if you have to ask how, you're doing it wrong," Derrick butts in, making everyone laugh.

I move from my spot and walk over to where he's sitting and join him. "I wanted to give you this for Christmas, so I went back to the doctor's office, they double-checked via ultrasound to see whether they could decipher via that, but they couldn't, so I asked them to go ahead with a blood test to find out." Christian looks shocked.

"We're having two little girls," he whispers.

"Yep, two little girls," I repeat.

"Shit, we're in so much trouble," he whispers to me.

"I know." He leans over and grabs my neck, pulling me into a heated kiss—everyone in the room hollers.

As he breaks the kiss, Christian gently presses his forehead against mine. "This is the best present ever." His smile lights up his face. "Two little girls, I can't believe it... two little girls." I smile at him.

"Two little Taylor princesses."

"Yep, and I have the perfect gift for them." I still, what's he talking about? "I actually have one more present for you," Christian says with a smile. He has already spoiled me rotten with gorgeous jewelry, gift cards to some designer maternity stores, and a gift card for a spa day. What more could there be?

He hands over this beautifully wrapped cubed box with a huge gold bow on top of it.

"Open it," he says excitedly. I slowly pull back the ribbon and open the lid of the box. Inside, sitting in a velvet slip, are keys. I look up at my husband and frown at him. "Wonder what they could be for?" he jokes.

My heart is racing. What on earth could the keys be for?

"Remember how much you loved Big Bear Lake?" he asks me. I nod and wait for him to continue. "Well, while you were away in Paris, the boys and I took a little trip up there to look around..." he pauses. Okay, well, he kept that a secret. "And I thought it might be a great place to bring up our kids." I look at him with curiosity. Is he saying what I think he's saying? "I bought you a house." Shock filters through me. This is what Evan does for Sienna all the time, surprises her with real estate. I was so not expecting Christian to do the same.

"It's beautiful, Ness," Axel tells me. "My brother did well."

Tears are falling down my cheeks. "You bought me a house for us and our little girls?"

"I didn't know we were having two kids when I bought it, but I wanted us to have somewhere we could escape the city. Now we can show them what it's like to ride horses, milk a cow, ride quad bikes, all that cool stuff they can't do in the city."

"I love it, Chris, I love it so much. Thank you, thank you, thank you." I wrap my arms around his neck and smother him in kisses.

CHRISTIAN

"When I see you again, you're going to be walking down that aisle about to become my wife... again." I kiss Vanessa goodbye as I move in with Axel for the night.

"I know we're already married, but I kind of like this tradition. You're going to appreciate me more when you see me," she says, giving me a peck on the cheek.

"Angel, I will one hundred percent appreciate watching you walk toward me down the aisle. Having a night away isn't going to dim that." She rolls her eyes at me.

"Just go have fun with the boys." She pushes me out of our room. "Fine, but one more thing." I step toward her again. "I love you, Mrs. Taylor." I grab her face and kiss the life out of her. "Just want you to remember that." I smile at her.

"Love you, too, Mr. Taylor. Now scat, I have the stuff to do." She pushes me out the door. My shoulders sink as I slowly trudge down toward Axel's room.

"Hey, what's with you?" Axel questions as I plonk down on the extra bed in his room.

"Just don't like being apart from Ness, that's all."

Axel chuckles. "Such a pussy."

I glare at my brother. "Whatever, your time will come, and I can't wait to call you a pussy."

Axel laughs. "That's going to be a long time in hell before that happens."

I raise my brow at him. "Really?" He probably doesn't realize I know a little more about his extracurricular activities with Olivia, thanks to Ness spilling the beans one night while we lazed by the fire.

"If you know something, spit it out." He glares at me.

"What I have heard is you're getting pretty close with one Lady Olivia Pearce. Are you getting ready to become Lord of the Manor?" I tease.

Axel's fists clench as he shoots daggers at me. "She's just a bit of fun, nothing more."

I stare at my twin, he knows he can't hide from me. "You sure?" I test him.

He sits down on the opposite bed. "If you tell anyone, I'll fucking kill you, none of this gossiping shit that we do, okay?" I nod. "Fine, yes, I like Olivia a little more than I should. It's complicated. I'm not sure what the girls have told you about it."

"Nothing much. Ness just said that you and Olivia had hooked up in Monaco, and that was about it."

Axel scrubs his face. "Yeah, it's true." He looks uncomfortable. "They asked me to teach her things."

Yep, I kind of choked on his words. "What do you mean, teach?"

"Sex stuff that she wasn't very experienced in because she's stuck up on a mountain here in the middle of nowhere. Derrick thought I'd be a good candidate for her."

"They'd be right, you have made it clear time and time again that you just want sex, nothing more."

"Yeah..." He trails off.

"But?"

"After you and Ness went home together, which I might add sucked because when it's your own bachelor party, you should be partying."

I give my brother a look.

"Yeah, yeah, I get it. Anyway, Nate took us to The Paradise Club, and the two parties kind of joined together. That's where Derrick approached me. He didn't need to, though, I kind of already had my sights on her."

I knew she'd catch his eye. "And?"

"She's my type in every way." He lets those words sink in.

"But, I thought she was inexperienced?"

"Kind of, I think she's just more cautious around men, except me. I don't know what happened, but it was kind of intense."

"So, have you kept in touch, or was it just a holiday fling?"

He didn't look at me, and that was all the validation I needed. "You've been texting her?"

"Fuck, I wish. She won't talk to me. After that weekend in Monaco, she disappeared, gave me a fake number."

Now I burst out laughing. I don't think Axel has ever been given a fake number in his life. "She must have known she'd see you again, I mean... hello... the wedding."

Axel just shrugs his shoulders. He looks a little lost, which I'm totally taking in because it's a first, and I try not to tease him as much, but it is killing me not to. It's a brother thing. He does generally look confused about it all. "Guess there's a first time for everything, brother. A chick that just isn't into you."

"Asshole, I know you're enjoying this." He glares at me.

"Okay, I'm not going to lie, I am laughing on the inside, but I can see you don't know what to do about her." He nods. It's rare that Axel ever asks me for advice. "Have you tried to talk to her since you arrived?"

"Yes, but she keeps ignoring me, telling me she's busy."

"Well, technically, that's true. She's running this estate by herself, and she is helping Cammie and Kim with the wedding details." Axel nods in agreement. "So, maybe just wait until after the wedding, it's only one more day. Maybe then the stress of hosting it at her home will be gone. We still have New Year's here, don't forget."

"Yeah, maybe you're right," he mumbles.

"I'm sorry, what did you say? I didn't quite hear it."

"I said maybe you're right, asshole." He chuckles.

"Yeah, that's what I thought you said. I just wanted you to repeat it because I think pigs have flown over or something."

"Asshole," he grumbles, flipping me off.

"Yeah, yeah, I know. But can I ask you something?" Axel smiles and nods at me. "Do you like her? I mean, really like her, or are you just pissed because someone turned you down?"

Axel is silent for a moment, thinking it over. "I like her, she's the first girl in forever that I like. Now don't go calling me a pussy, all right because it's not like that, so don't get ahead of yourself. We clicked, especially sexually."

This is kind of shocking.

"I know shocking, the innocent girl clicking with the manwhore rock star." He said it, not me. "I showed her some of the things I'm into and well…"

"Do I really need to hear this?" I ask him.

"No, probably not. But anyway, she shocked me, and in a good way. In a way that I kind of want to keep doing."

"Aww, you've got a crush."

"Yeah, I guess I do, but she wants nothing to do with me. Is this like karma for all the years that I have done this to girls?"

"Probably."

"Well, it sucks."

"Maybe it was just a holiday fling. I mean really, how would you work together? Would you become Lord of the Manor? Would you want to live here away from everything you built in LA?"

"Chris, I just want more sex. We aren't talking about anything more."

I frown at him because that isn't the impression he just gave me.

"I know we'd never work, but..."

"You want to see if it was just a one-off kind of thing between the two of you?"

"Yeah, was it just holiday Olivia?"

"Well, just wait, you still have plenty of time before we have to leave. I mean, you could always extend your stay after we have all gone."

He shrugs. "Come on, let's go catch up with the others. I need a drink."

VANESSA

"You're getting married," Derrick yells, running into my bedroom, waking me.

Sienna stirs beside me. We had a girls' night in my suite while Christian went to his brother's room.

"Come on, are you not excited?" Derrick bounces on the bed, making my stomach turn.

"Stop fucking jumping on the bed where two pregnant women are lying unless you want to be vomited on," Sienna yells at Derrick.

"Shit, sorry." He backs away and grabs the packet of crackers that are beside the bed and hands them to her. She quickly snatches them and eats a couple, then hands them to me. I follow, settling my upset stomach.

There's a knock at the door. "I'll get it," Derrick sings cheerily. "Hey, princess."

"Morning, I thought you might be hungry, so brought up some breakfast." Olivia is holding a tray filled with fresh fruit and juice, bacon, and scrambled eggs and pancakes.

"You're a lifesaver, these girls are starving," Derrick adds.

"Morning, are you ladies up?" Camryn comes strolling in as

Sienna and I come out of the bathroom, damn pregnant belly making me pee. "We have much to do today," she says in full wedding-organizer mode. "Hair and makeup will be here in about forty-five minutes. That will take a while, and they will start with the bridesmaids first and then finish with Vanessa, so she's the freshest. Yvette will come and help you all get dressed, and after that, there are photos before we head downstairs to get you married."

HOURS LATER, everyone's hair and makeup are done, even the parents. Now is the time to try and haul my ass into my dress. I'm nervous now. Yvette helps me and does me up. She's a magician putting in a little extra room for my belly that seems to be ever-expanding. I take a couple of deep breaths as she fastens my veil into my hair, then I take a look at myself in the mirror, and the vision hits me.

"No, no, no, V, don't cry, you'll ruin your makeup." Yvette tries to calm me down, but it's hard because my damn pregnancy hormones are going crazy, and it's my wedding day, and I look beautiful in my wedding dress. Then I start to think about my two little girls in my belly, and that makes me cry even more, and I kind of just want Christian to give me a cuddle.

"Hey, hey, no crying." Camryn rushes in. "Makeup, stat," she calls out, and the makeup artist rushes in, her brush poised and ready to go. "Luckily, they put waterproof makeup on us all. I think we're going to need it." Cammie smiles at me, and I can see the distinct glistening in her eyes.

"Don't you fucking dare start crying on me," I warn her.

"But you look beautiful," she compliments with the biggest smile.

"I know..." And the tears start again.

"I think we might hold off on the makeup. I have a feeling it's about to get worse," Cammie whispers to the makeup artist.

"Here comes the bride," Camryn calls out as I leave the bedroom where Yvette dressed me. I hear everyone's gasp as I take a couple of steps through the room, then complete silence. I look up and see all my family and friends before me, tears in their eyes and smiles on their faces.

Everyone looks beautiful. My mum is dressed in a beautiful burgundy evening dress designed by Yvette, my dad is in a tuxedo, probably for the first time in his life, and he looks so handsome. I look over and see my bridesmaids—Sienna, Camryn, Isla, and Stacey. They look so elegant in their black evening dresses with white orchid bouquets in their hands. And Derrick, bloody hell, that man looks fine as hell in a tux.

Mum is the first to break free from the spell and wraps her arms around me. "You're a vision, sweetheart," she coos, trying to stop herself from falling apart.

"You don't scrub up half bad, kiddo." Dad stands beside Mum, smirking at me.

"You don't scrub up too badly, either." I launch myself into his arms.

"Princess, I'm so bloody proud of you," he tells me as he kisses my forehead. "You found a good one in that boy. He's going to love you and your baby girls something fierce for the rest of your life. You have both been through so much as a young couple, and yet you have come out stronger. I couldn't be happier."

Shit, Dad. I bawl my eyes out and hug him a little tighter.

"Don't wrinkle his suit, Ness," Derrick mumbles, making me laugh as I pull away from my dad.

"You girls look amazing." I move over to where they are standing.

"You look absolutely stunning." Sienna smiles, kissing me.

"Just enjoy today. It's going to go quickly. Take a moment to have some time with Christian," she whispers to me.

"Okay, I think we need to get all our makeup redone again," Camryn announces with a smile.

It's time to marry my man. Charlotte and her photographer friends are walking around taking photos of us as the wedding party makes their way carefully down the grand staircase toward the medieval chapel where the ceremony will be held. Please don't fall, please don't fall. I repeat my mantra as I make my way down the stone stairs.

"Okay, everyone is ready for you," Kimberly says and smiles at me. "The bridesmaids will go first, and then the music will change, and it will be your turn. Are you ready?" she asks, and my wedding party all nod in agreement.

Dad places my hand on his forearm, trying to stop me from shaking. "You're doing good, kiddo."

I nod, not feeling the greatest, my nerves getting the best of me. I'm not sure why I am so bloody nervous when we're already married. I try and center myself, looking down at the gorgeous orchid bouquet resting in my hand. The music starts, and Kimberly is counting the bridesmaids, one by one, as they disappear behind the wooden doors.

Once they have all gone, the doors close again, and the music changes. Kimberly gives me the universal sign to go as she opens up the wooden doors, and I take my first steps down the aisle. My heart is racing a million miles a minute. I can see blurs of faces as I slowly walk down the long aisle. I hear the gasps and well-wishes from the crowd around me, then my eyes meet Christian's, those whiskey-colored eyes looking at me with lust, love, devotion, and pride. I can see the first tear fall down his cheek as he stands at the altar, looking at me in awe.

He looks so handsome in his tuxedo, very James Bond. That thought makes me smile as I think about his request for a James Bond-themed bachelor party. I turn my attention to the rest of the guys standing beside him, looking equally as dapper as my husband. Derrick gives me the biggest smile and two thumbs up, which makes me laugh. We make it to the end, and Dad hands me over to Christian, who can't take his eyes off me.

"You look like an angel," Christian whispers.

"You look like James Bond," I whisper back, making him smile.

We both turn and look at Derrick, who's standing proud, our minister. Yes, Derrick is marrying us, what were we thinking?

"The bride and groom have elected to say their own vows," Derrick announces.

"I, Christian, take you, Vanessa, to be my lawfully wedded wife. I promise to love, honor, and cherish you. I promise not to look at the credit card bills when there's a Louboutin sale on. I promise to cook dinner for you every night. I promise to always leave the toilet seat down and make sure there's enough toilet paper available. I promise to do manly things like chop wood to fulfill your unhealthy lumberjack fantasies. I promise to give you foot massages twice a week."

"Six times," I interrupt.

"Five."

The congregation giggles.

"Four, and that's my final offer."

Christian rolls his eyes. "Fine, I promise to give you foot massages four times a week." This makes me smile. "I promise to love you in sickness and in health. I promise to love you when you're as big as a whale with our babies inside of you. I promise to be a vault when it comes to your secrets and anyone else's."

"Ness, no sharing from the vault," Derrick says, making everyone laugh.

"I promise to take you on regular dates, even when we have kids. I promise to still grab your ass when we're old and gray. But most of all, I promise to be the best husband you'll ever have."

Tears run down my cheeks listening to Christian's vows.

"Oh, and yeah, I promise to love you forever, nearly forgot that. That one is kind of important," he says, making us all laugh. He finishes off by leaning over and kissing my cheek.

"Hey, not yet," Derrick chides him. "Vanessa, it's your turn."

I take a deep breath and hope I can make it through them. "I, Vanessa, take you, Christian, as my lawfully wedded husband. To have and to never let go even when there are manic fans around. They may be little, but they are strong, but I promise no matter what, I won't let you go." This makes him smile. "I promise I'll attempt to cook dinner once a week."

"Four times," Christian adds.

"Two times."

"Sold," Christian agrees, making us laugh.

"I promise to let you watch football in peace and not try and distract you in some kind of way that usually works." I wiggle my eyebrows at him.

"Don't you dare stop doing that, woman," Christian declares.

"I promise that I'll stay healthy for you. I promise that I will believe you when you tell me that man flu is worse than anything else in the world, and I promise to attempt to make you chicken soup just like your mum." Looking over to where his mum is sitting, she gives me a thumbs up. "I promise not to work as much, even though technically, you're the boss and set my hours." This makes him laugh.

"Fine, you're fired," he whispers to me. I give him a stern look. "Fine, but you need to cut back those hours."

"I promise to hide any new purchases from you and pretend that they have always been in my wardrobe. I promise to love, honor, and obey you sometimes. But most of all, I can't wait to spend the rest of my life with you." I wipe the lingering tear from Christian's face.

"I now pronounce you husband and wife," Derrick declares excitedly. "You may kiss the bride."

Christian's face lights up, he takes a step toward me, grabs my face pulling it to his, and the lightest of kisses cover my lips. I can feel him smiling against them. "I love you, Ness," he whispers, before opening his lips for a more passionate kiss, which makes everyone cheer.

"Ladies and Gentlemen, Mr. and Mrs. Christian Taylor," Derrick declares as we start to make our way down the aisle, the smiling faces of our family and friends greet us as we walk. The nerves from early in the day are gone, and new memories of our wedding day linger.

60

CHRISTIAN

"Can I ask for the bride and groom to please come here for the first dance," Derrick calls us to the front of the ballroom. We haven't rehearsed anything, but I'm hoping those lessons Mom made us take when we were younger will pay off. What Ness doesn't know is what's behind the velvet curtain. It's my wedding present to her. She thinks we're dancing to a certain song she picked out, but I have other plans. The first strings of the song she had chosen start as we walk onto the dance floor. Then, it stops. Ness looks around a little annoyed because she thinks someone has ruined our first dance. In one swift move, the curtain falls, and behind it are the Sons of Brooklyn together with Gypsy Sisters.

"What have you planned?" she whispers.

"Just watch and see."

"Congratulations, Christian and Vanessa." Blake congratulates us and continues into the microphone, "Christian wrote a song for you for today, and here it is. It's called 'Angel.'"

The music starts, and I take my shocked bride into my arms, and we dance to the soft sounds of my song dedicated to her. She nuzzles her tear-streaked face into my neck as we lose ourselves to the song, dedicated to the way I feel about her. When it's over, she surprises me with a very public kiss that has the wedding reception hooting and hollering.

"I fucking love you," she mumbles against my lips.

VANESSA IS MY WIFE AGAIN, but this time it's legit. We have said our vows in front of our friends and family. Seeing Vanessa walk down that aisle toward me like a damn angel was more than my little heart could handle. I thought it was going to burst right then and there, I don't think I have ever been so happy. Now she's snuggled up beside me at our table while everyone is up dancing after dinner. "I'm so happy." I kiss her on the cheek.

"Me, too," she agrees, looking out over our friends and family dancing in the ballroom. One of our signed acts, DJ Duo, has been getting everyone up and dancing with their music.

"I think this has been a pretty awesome wedding, don't you?"

"The best."

"This is the start of our lives together, forever," I remind her, which makes her chuckle.

"I'm pretty sure I'm not going anywhere, babe. I have married you twice, I am knocked up with your babies, so this better be forever."

"Okay, okay, I get your point. I wonder what our little girls think about today?" My hand moves and rests on her invisible belly.

"I think they would think it's pretty cool. I mean we got married in a freaking castle. They would most certainly love all the dresses."

I let out a groan. "Are we seriously going to have girly girls who are going to want everything to be pink and shit like that?"

"Yep, sure are. You better get used to it, babe, because these girls are going to rule you."

I groan because it's the truth. Those two little nuggets already have me wrapped around their fingers, and they aren't even born yet. "What are we going to call them?" We haven't had the baby name discussion yet.

"Bloody hell, I have no clue, I don't want to give them weird Hollywood names." I shudder. There's no way in the world do I want to name my kids Apple or Peach. "I honestly haven't really thought about it, but I guess we need to. I was going to deal with baby stuff once we got back from our honeymoon."

I'm whisking Vanessa away to Bora Bora for our honeymoon. I am going to do it right this time, and we're going to have two weeks of nothing but relaxing in the sun and making love on the beach. I know things are going to be crazy when we get back to LA, especially since Isla dropped the bombshell that she's leaving us and going to work for Sebastien in Europe.

I kind of understand what she means by wanting to try something else because she has been working with us since she was eighteen, and she's twenty-eight now, but we're all so used to her being around, so it's going to take a little time getting used to. We thought Oscar would take it hard because that's his little sister, and he has always been overprotective of her, but he surprised her with being one hundred percent supportive of her new adventure.

Finn, on the other hand, not so much. I ran into him at the gym, where he was taking his aggression out on a punching bag the morning after. He confessed that he was pissed that she was leaving, but he understood. I told him to man up if he wanted her, but he said that she needed to go out and see the world, and it wouldn't be fair for him to hold her back like he has been for years. I think Isla leaving for another country might actually force Finn to reveal his feelings, or they might both get over their weird secret infatuation they have for each other. It's totally unhealthy.

Either way, things at Dirty Texas Records are going to be changing next year. With Isla leaving and Ness going on maternity leave, there are going to be lots of new faces on board, and I think that's going to be pretty darn exciting.

61

CHRISTIAN

Six Months Later

"I'm scared, Chris." Vanessa squeezes my hand as we walk into the hospital, well, Vanessa waddles because she's truly the size of a house, but I'd never ever tell her that. I value my life too much. She still looks gorgeous, even with her huge belly and the assortment of limbs that poke out of it. Our girls are very active. She says they get that from their daddy, and she most definitely wasn't saying that with a smile on her face. Usually, that's when she has a foot in her ribs or an elbow on her bladder.

But today is the day I get to meet my two girls, and I'm so excited. We scheduled in a C-section a couple of weeks earlier than full term. Ness's blood pressure was becoming too high, and it was dangerous. She had already been on bed rest for the past month, and you can imagine how happy she was over that—not. Sienna and Evan still have a couple more weeks to go until they get to meet their baby boy. I know, right, another boy, so Dirty Texas 2.0 already has four members—two boys and two girls.

"Right this way, Mr. and Mrs. Taylor," one of the nurses greet us. "Are you ready to meet your babies today?" she asks enthusiastically as I push Vanessa along in her wheelchair.

"Hell, yeah," I answer for a very tongue-tied Ness.

"That's good to hear." We make our way through the labyrinth that is the hospital corridors. "Here we are." She ushers us into our hospital suite. "The midwife and your obstetrician will be here soon." Then she's gone.

"Okay, I'm freaking out now," Vanessa confesses.

Kneeling before her, I soothe her. "You can do this, okay? Just think that today our babies are going to be born, that we're going to get to hold them, and you won't have to be pregnant again." This makes her laugh.

"Are you saying no more kids?" she questions me.

"I'd love more, but if all we have are these two beautiful girls, then I'm fine with that. It has been a really hard pregnancy for you, and I don't want to lose you. I don't need any more chances of that happening. So yeah, what I'm saying is, I am okay with just these two girls."

"Thank you," she smiles weakly at me.

"But we don't have to make any decisions now, let's just concentrate on our babies, okay?" She nods in agreement. "Now, let's do this."

"Congratulations, baby number one." The doctor pulls out of my wife's stomach a bloodied little thing who has a set of lungs on her. As soon as she's placed in my arms, she settles. My God, my heart is exploding, this little pink thing wriggling is mine, I created her with the woman I love.

"Here comes baby number two." She too has a set of lungs on her and is placed on Vanessa's chest. She's looking in awe at our little daughters wriggling around in each of our arms.

"They're here." Vanessa stares in wonderment.

"They certainly are."

"They are loud."

"Yep, I think I might need to buy earplugs now. It seems our girls are going to be really loud."

"Just like their daddy." Vanessa smiles up at me, and seeing her with our baby against her breaks me. I lean down and kiss the ever-loving shit out of her with tears streaming down my face, but I don't care because it's all so overwhelming.

"Thank you for making me the luckiest man in the world." She too is crying.

"Thank you for giving me everything I ever desired," Vanessa whispers back.

Our little family is complete.

"I'M AN UNCLE." Axel stares down at the little baby in his arms, and I can see it hits him, the same love I have for my two little girls has just hit him smack bang like an arrow to the heart. "They are so little." One of the baby's little fingers wraps around onto his. "They are so perfect," he says to no one in particular as he just stares at her.

"Welcome to the club, man." Evan slaps me on the back.

"Not long until you have two to match."

"Not sure how you're going to handle two babies at once, it was hard enough with one."

"It's called helpers." We both laugh.

"So, what did you name them?" Derrick asks as he snuggles with my other daughter.

"Sadie and Ruby," Vanessa states with a huge smile on her face from her hospital bed. Thankfully, she's on the good drugs now. Being cut open couldn't have been nice. I can tell you it wasn't very nice to look at.

"Those names are gorgeous," Sienna coos, rubbing her extremely large belly.

"You better keep those Wyld boys away from my girls," I joke to Evan.

"Um... I think your Taylor girls are going to be trouble. I don't want them corrupting my boys, thank you very much," Evan jokes back.

"I can't believe the two biggest manwhores are married and popping out kids," Finn jokes.

I punch him in the arm. "Watch what you say in front of my daughters, they don't need to know what their stupid daddy did before Mommy."

"Going to be a bit hard when they can look things up on the internet," Oscar adds.

"That's it, no internet for my girls," I say, and everyone in the hospital suite erupts into laughter, startling the babies. Everyone quickly quiets down as the grandparents swoop in and settle the crying babies.

Don't think life can get much better than this.

"THEY WON'T STOP CRYING," I complain as I listen to the piercing screams of my girls.

"Have you changed their nappies?" Vanessa asks.

I stare at her blankly.

"Argh, diapers, I mean diapers," she yells at me. I'm so brain dead I can't understand Australian.

"Yes, and she's been fed, and I played with her. I also took her for a walk. I don't understand why Sadie won't stop crying. It's Sadie, isn't it?" I question, staring at my daughter.

"Check her wrist," Vanessa adds.

We have identical twin girls, so it's hard to work out which one is which. You'd think being their dad, I'd know, but I don't.

So, we decided to leave the hospital band on their wrists to make it a little easier on us.

"Oh my God, Uncle Derrick is here." Derrick strolls into the nursery like a baby whispering superhero, picks Sadie up out of my arms, and cradles her. She stops crying instantly. What the fuck? "What can I say, chicks dig me." He smiles and takes a seat on the pink leather feeding chair. He leans back and starts rocking in it. Slowly, the once-screaming Sadie falls asleep.

"I owe you, man," I say to Derrick when he joins me in the living room on the sofa. Derrick wiggles his eyebrows at me, suggestively. "D, at this point, I'm so exhausted that I'd probably do that to get an ounce of sleep."

"Duly noted, maybe another time. Why don't you and Ness have a sleep? Axel is coming over any minute with your mothers, and we'll be on baby duty for the next couple of hours."

I stand up and grab Derrick's face, and I place a wet kiss on his lips. "I love you, man." Derrick looks shocked as I make my way to the bedroom and crash headfirst onto the covers.

❧

Couple Weeks Later

"Congrats, man." I slap Evan on the back. We're back at the hospital, this time welcoming Evan and Sienna's new baby boy.

"Thanks, you're looking like shit," he says with a smile.

"FU. Babies don't stop screaming."

He chuckles, "Yep, and you have two to feed all at once."

"I'm so glad our mothers stayed. I don't know how we're going to cope when they are gone. I want them to stay until they are potty trained."

Evan bursts out laughing. He understands my pain.

"What did you name your little dude?"

"He is Levi, Levi Wyld."

"Sorry I'm late, my plane just arrived." Isla stands at the door.

The room goes silent, all eyes on Isla. Shit is about to hit the fan.

THE END
Want to know what happens next to
Axel & Olivia
Book 3 - Bound & Dirty

Follow for latest updates via my newsletter
Subscribe here

Come join my Facebook Group here

ABOUT THE AUTHOR

JA Low lives on the Gold Coast in Australia. When she's not writing steamy scenes and admiring hot surfers, she's tending to her husband and two sons and running after her chickens while dreaming up the next epic romance.

Come follow her

Facebook: www.facebook.com/jalowbooks
TikTok: https://geni.us/vrpoMqH
Instagram: www.instagram.com/jalowbooks
Pinterest: www.pinterest.com/jalowbooks
Website: www.jalowbooks.com
Goodreads: https://www.goodreads.com/author/show/14918059.J_A_Low
BookBub: https://www.bookbub.com/authors/ja-low
Amazon Author Page: https://www.amazon.com/stores/JA-Low/author/B01BW9LU0G

Thanks for finishing this book.
Really hope you enjoyed it.
Why not check out my other books.
Have a fantastic day !

Don't forget to leave a review.
xoxo

INTERCONNECTING SERIES

Reading order for interconnected characters.

Dirty Texas Series

Suddenly Dirty

Suddenly Together

Suddenly Bound

Suddenly Trouble

Suddenly Broken

Paradise Club Series

Paradise

International Bad Boys

Hotshot Chef

Playboys of New York

Off Limits

Strictly Forbidden

The Merger

ALSO BY JA LOW

Spin off from Dirty Texas
Under the Spanish Sun Series
Hotshot Chef - Book 1

ALSO BY JA LOW

Spin off Dirty Texas Series

Paradise Club Series
Paradise - Book 1
Lost in Paradise - Book 2
Paradise Found - Book 3
Craving Paradise - Book 4

ALSO BY JA LOW

Connected to The Paradise Club

The Art of Love Series

Arrogant Artist - Book 1

ALSO BY JA LOW

Bratva Jewels

Book 1 - Sapphire

Book 2 - Diamond

Book 3 - Emerald

ALSO BY JA LOW

Connected to The Bratva Jewels

Italian Nights Series

The Sexy Stranger - Book 1

ALSO BY JA LOW

Playboys of New York

Off Limits - Book 1

Strictly Forbidden - Book 2

The Merger - Book 3

Taking Control - Book 4

Without Warning - Book 5

ALSO BY JA LOW

Spin off series to Playboys of New York

The Hartford Brothers Series
Book 1 - Tempting the Billionaire
Book 2 - Playing the Player
Book 3 - Seducing the Doctor

Printed in Great Britain
by Amazon